IMAGE COMICS, INC.

Robert Kirkman - Chief Operating Officer
Erik Larsen - Chief Financial Officer
Todd McFarlane - President
Marc Silvestri - Chief Executive Officer
Jim Valentino - Vice-President
Eric Stephenson - Publisher
Corey Murphy - Director of Sales
Jeff Boison - Director of Publishing Planning & Book Trade Sales
Jeremy Sullivan - Director of Digital Sales
Kat Salazar - Director of PR & Marketing
Branwyn Bigglestone - Controller

Drew Gill - Art Director
Jonathan Chan - Production Manager
Meredith Wallace - Print Manager
Briah Skelly - Publicist
Sasha Head - Sales & Marketing Production Designer
Randy Okamura - Digital Production Designer
David Brothers - Branding Manager
Olivia Ngai - Content Manager
Addison Duke - Production Artist
Vincent Kukua - Production Artist
Tricia Ramos - Production Artist
Jeff Stang - Direct Market Sales Representative
Emilio Bautista - Digital Sales Associate
Leanna Caunter - Accounting Assistant
Chloe Ramos-Peterson - Library Market Sales Representative

IMAGECOMICS.COM

A BYRD OF PARADISE MYSTERY

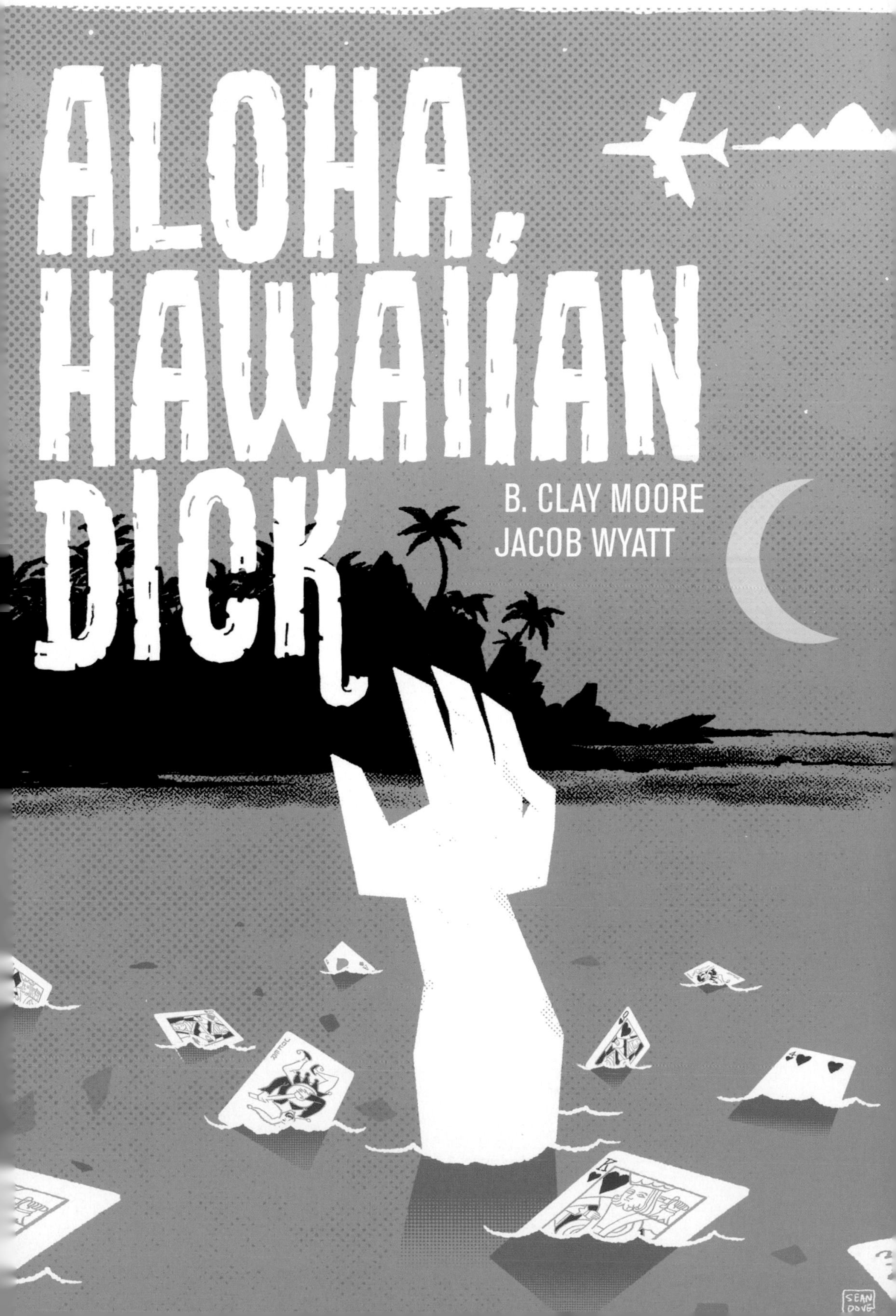
ALOHA, HAWAIIAN DICK
B. CLAY MOORE
JACOB WYATT
SEAN DOVE

Written by
B. CLAY MOORE

Art & Letters by
JACOB WYATT (ISSUES 1-3)
Letters Assist by **KATHRYN WYATT (ISSUE 4)**

Art by
PAUL REINWAND (ISSUE 5)
Layouts by
JACOB WYATT

Issue Covers by **SEAN DOVE**

Trade Cover by **RON SALAS**

Additional Book Design by **VINCENT KUKUA**

Story font created by **STEVEN GRIFFIN**

HAWAIIAN DICK created by
B. CLAY MOORE & STEVEN GRIFFIN

HAWAIIAN DICK, VOL. 4: ALOHA, HAWAIIAN DICK.
NOVEMBER 2016. FIRST PRINTING.

Published by Image Comics, Inc. Office of publication: 2001 Center Street, Sixth Floor, Berkeley, CA 94704. Copyright © 2016 B. Clay Moore and Steven Griffin.
All rights reserved. "Hawaiian Dick," its logo, and the likenesses of all characters herein are trademarks of B. Clay Moore and Steven Griffin, unless otherwise note
Originally published as HAWAIIAN DICK: ALOHA, HAWAIIAN DICK #1-5 in single magazine format. "Image" and the Image Comics logos are registered
trademarks of Image Comics, Inc. No part of this publication may be reproduced or transmitted, in any form or by any means (except for short excerpts for journalis
or review purposes), without the express written permission of Image Comics, Inc. All names, characters, events, and locales in this publication are entirely fictional.
resemblance to actual persons (living or dead), events, or places, without satiric intent, is coincidental. Printed in South Korea.

For international rights, contact: foreignlicensing@imagecomics.com.

ISBN: 978-1-63215-870-3

1954

BYRD IS A FORMER STATESIDE DETECTIVE WHO SHOT HIS YOUNGER BROTHER TO DEATH (FOR AS YET UNKNOWN REASONS), AND WASHED UP IN HONOLULU, WHERE HIS WARTIME BUDDY, DETECTIVE MO KALAMA, HELPS HIM FIND THE OCCASIONAL CASE TO WORK IN ORDER TO MAKE A LITTLE EXTRA CASH. UNFORTUNATELY, THE LIVING EMBODIMENT OF HAWAIIAN MYTHS AND FOLKLORE OFTEN GET IN THE WAY OF SOLVING SAID CASES. KAHAMI IS A FORMER WAITRESS WHO'S TAKEN ON THE TASK OF ASSISTING BYRD IN RUNNING WHAT THERE IS OF HIS BUSINESS, AFTER BYRD HELPED SOLVE THE MURDER OF HER SISTER, BY (THE NOW DEAD) BISHOP MASAKI.

CHRIS DUQUE IS AN FBI AGENT WHO'S RECENTLY SERVED BYRD WITH A SUBPOENA FROM THE HOUSE UN-AMERICAN ACTIVITIES COMMITTEE. ANTHONY ANTONIO ("THE THINKER") IS A FORMER MOB CONSIGLIERE WHO NOW RUNS A GIFT SHOP IN HONOLULU, AND MAY OR MAY NOT BE INVOLVED IN RUNNING THE CRIME RACKETS LEFT BEHIND IN THE WAKE OF MASAKI'S DEATH.

NATURALLY, WE OPEN IN SUBURBAN KANSAS CITY.

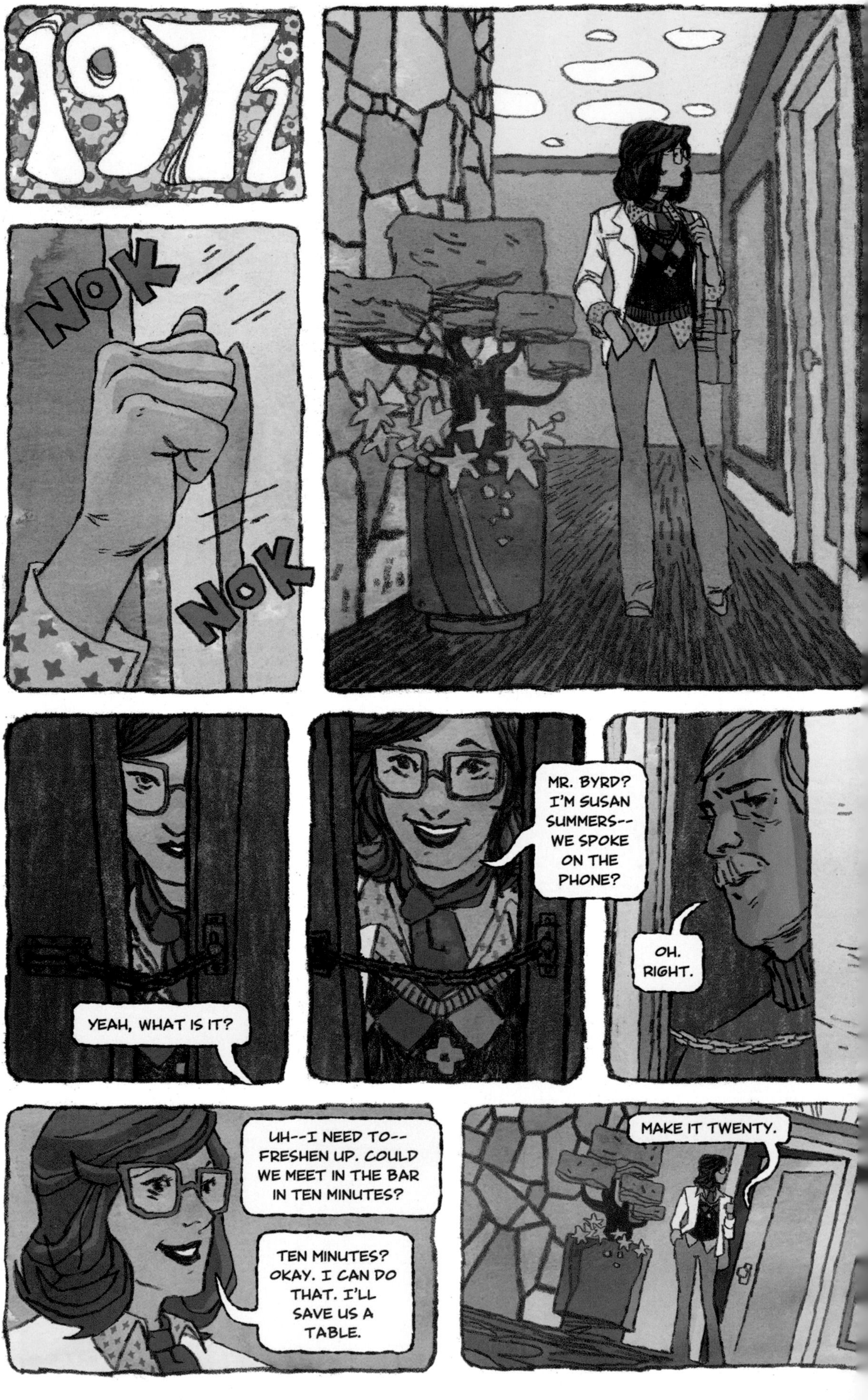
1972
NOK
NOK
YEAH, WHAT IS IT?
MR. BYRD? I'M SUSAN SUMMERS--WE SPOKE ON THE PHONE?
OH. RIGHT.
UH--I NEED TO--FRESHEN UP. COULD WE MEET IN THE BAR IN TEN MINUTES?
TEN MINUTES? OKAY. I CAN DO THAT. I'LL SAVE US A TABLE.
MAKE IT TWENTY.

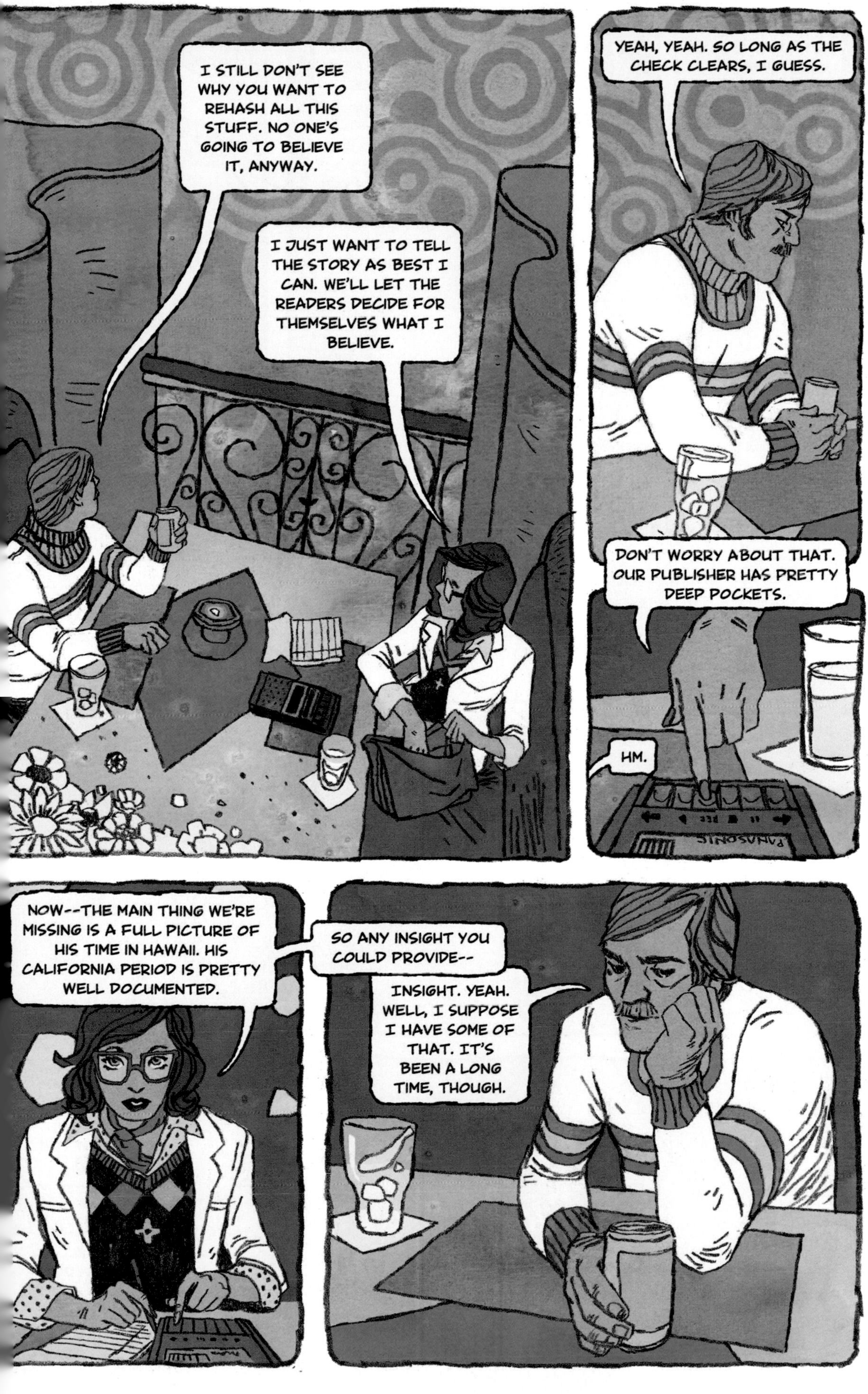
I STILL DON'T SEE WHY YOU WANT TO REHASH ALL THIS STUFF. NO ONE'S GOING TO BELIEVE IT, ANYWAY.
I JUST WANT TO TELL THE STORY AS BEST I CAN. WE'LL LET THE READERS DECIDE FOR THEMSELVES WHAT I BELIEVE.
YEAH, YEAH. SO LONG AS THE CHECK CLEARS, I GUESS.
DON'T WORRY ABOUT THAT. OUR PUBLISHER HAS PRETTY DEEP POCKETS.
HM.
PANASONIC
NOW--THE MAIN THING WE'RE MISSING IS A FULL PICTURE OF HIS TIME IN HAWAII. HIS CALIFORNIA PERIOD IS PRETTY WELL DOCUMENTED.
SO ANY INSIGHT YOU COULD PROVIDE--
INSIGHT. YEAH. WELL, I SUPPOSE I HAVE SOME OF THAT. IT'S BEEN A LONG TIME, THOUGH.

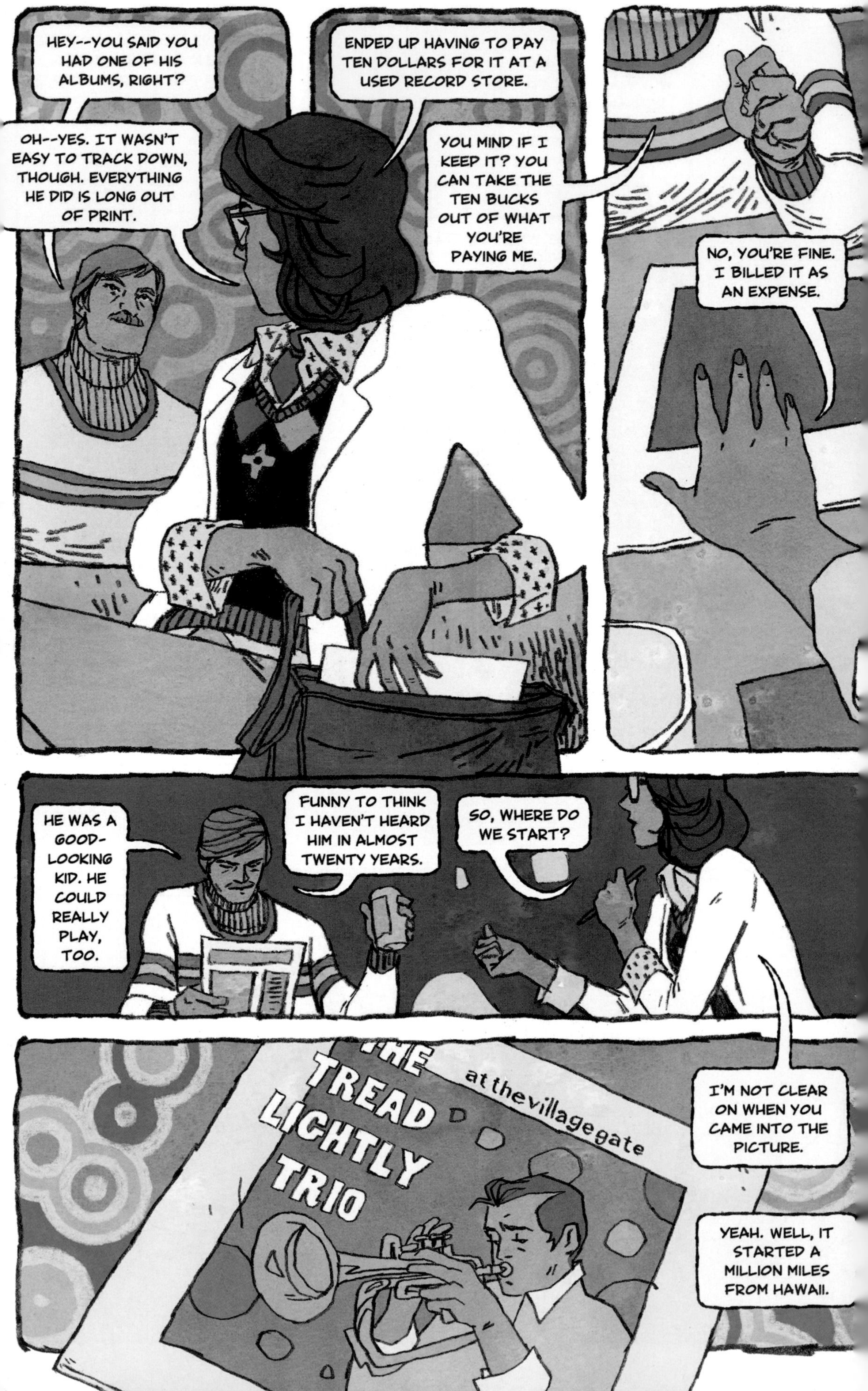

HEY--YOU SAID YOU HAD ONE OF HIS ALBUMS, RIGHT?
OH--YES. IT WASN'T EASY TO TRACK DOWN, THOUGH. EVERYTHING HE DID IS LONG OUT OF PRINT.
ENDED UP HAVING TO PAY TEN DOLLARS FOR IT AT A USED RECORD STORE.
YOU MIND IF I KEEP IT? YOU CAN TAKE THE TEN BUCKS OUT OF WHAT YOU'RE PAYING ME.
NO, YOU'RE FINE. I BILLED IT AS AN EXPENSE.
HE WAS A GOOD-LOOKING KID. HE COULD REALLY PLAY, TOO.
FUNNY TO THINK I HAVEN'T HEARD HIM IN ALMOST TWENTY YEARS.
SO, WHERE DO WE START?
THE TREAD LIGHTLY TRIO
at the village gate
I'M NOT CLEAR ON WHEN YOU CAME INTO THE PICTURE.
YEAH. WELL, IT STARTED A MILLION MILES FROM HAWAII.

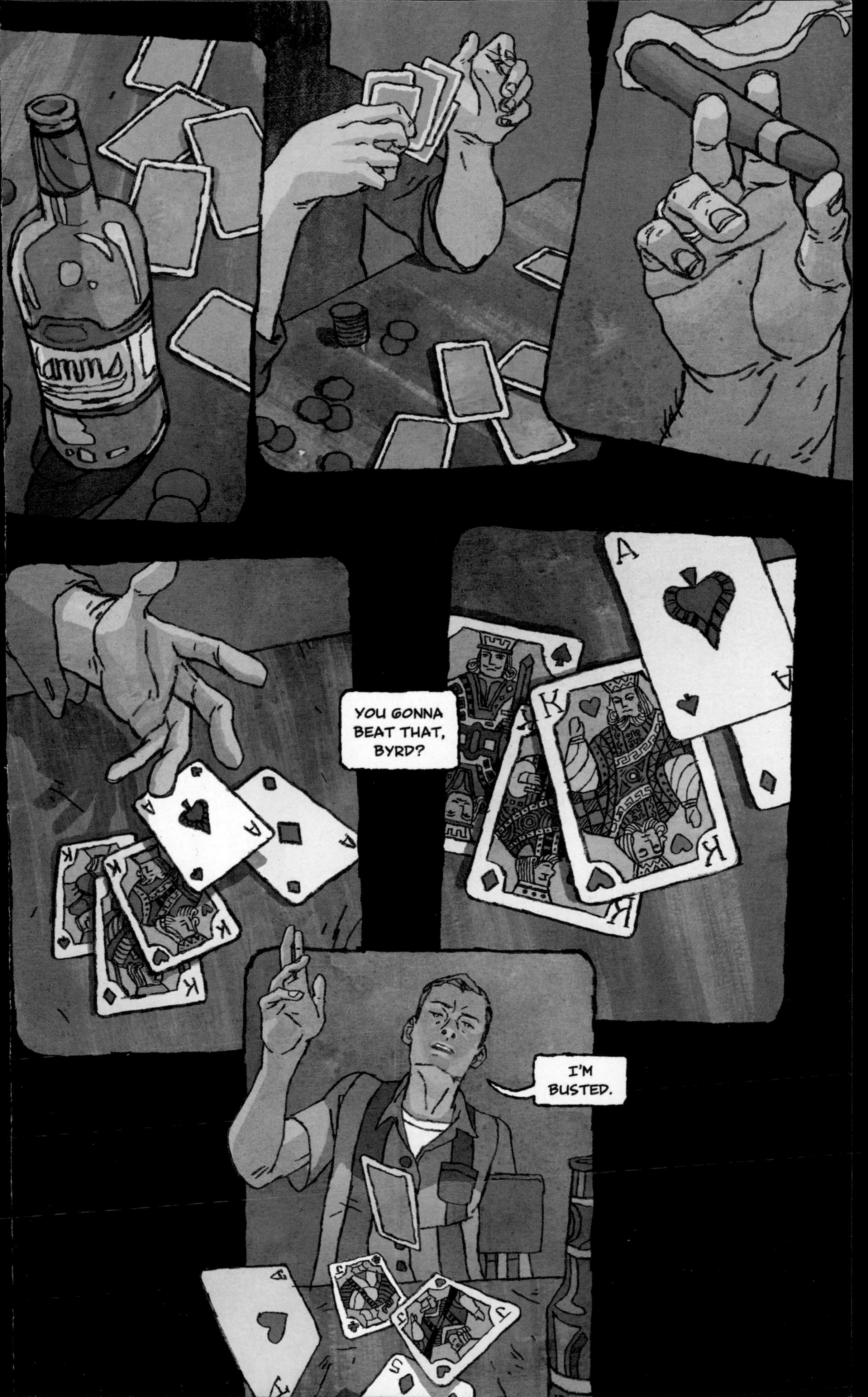
YOU GONNA BEAT THAT, BYRD?
I'M BUSTED.

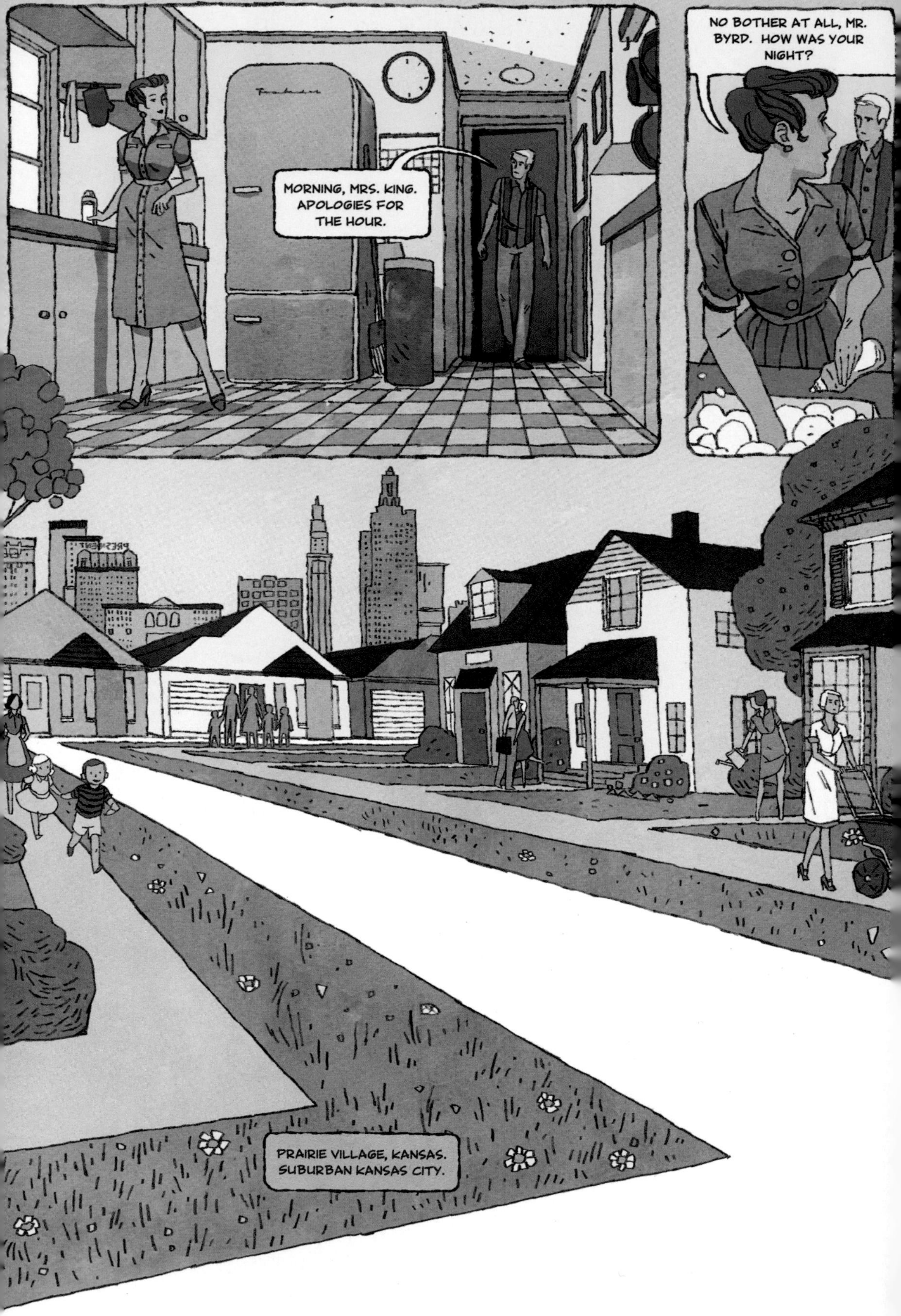
MORNING, MRS. KING. APOLOGIES FOR THE HOUR.
NO BOTHER AT ALL, MR. BYRD. HOW WAS YOUR NIGHT?
PRAIRIE VILLAGE, KANSAS. SUBURBAN KANSAS CITY.

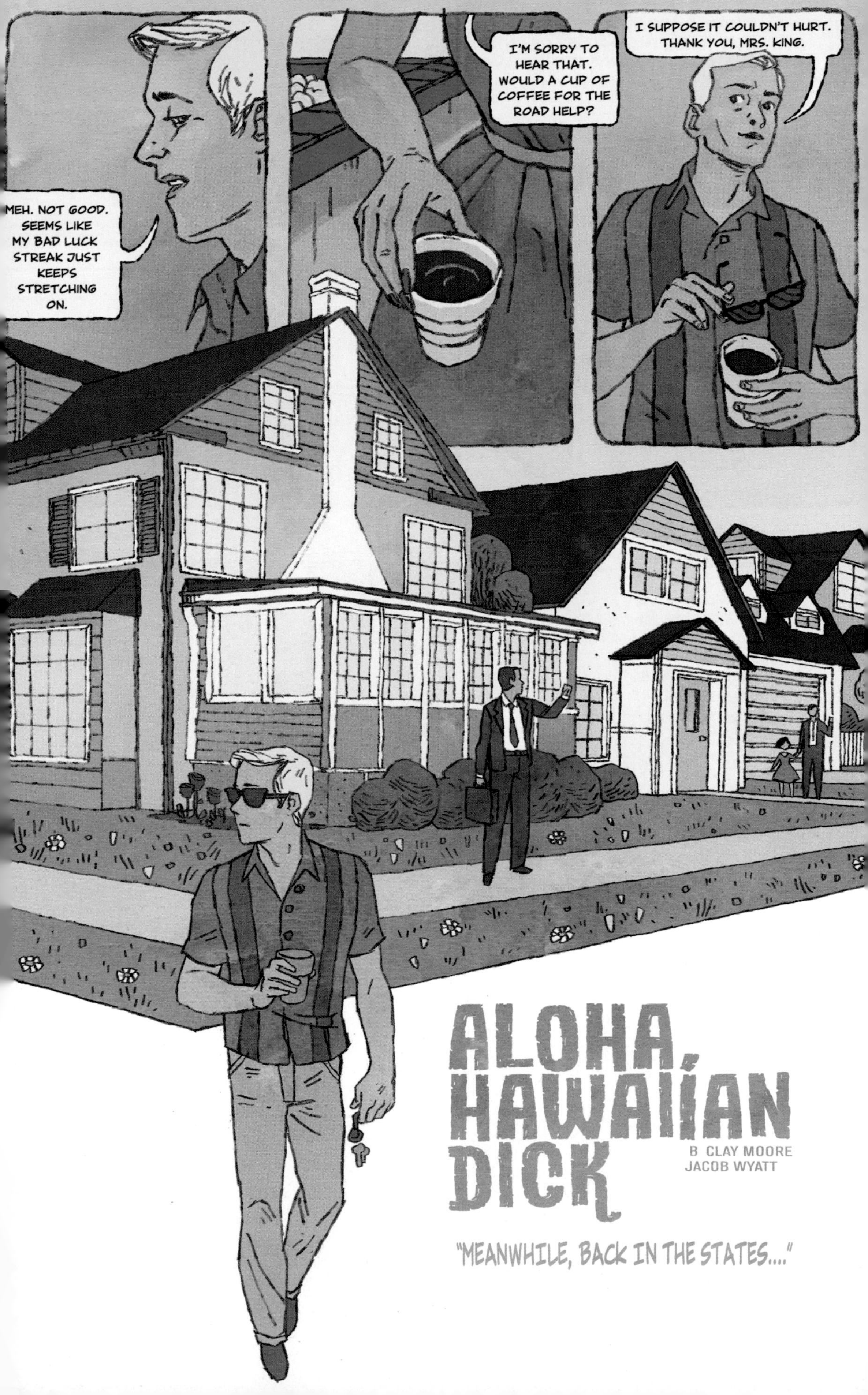

MEH. NOT GOOD. SEEMS LIKE MY BAD LUCK STREAK JUST KEEPS STRETCHING ON.
I'M SORRY TO HEAR THAT. WOULD A CUP OF COFFEE FOR THE ROAD HELP?
I SUPPOSE IT COULDN'T HURT. THANK YOU, MRS. KING.
ALOHA, HAWAIIAN DICK
B CLAY MOORE
JACOB WYATT
"MEANWHILE, BACK IN THE STATES...."

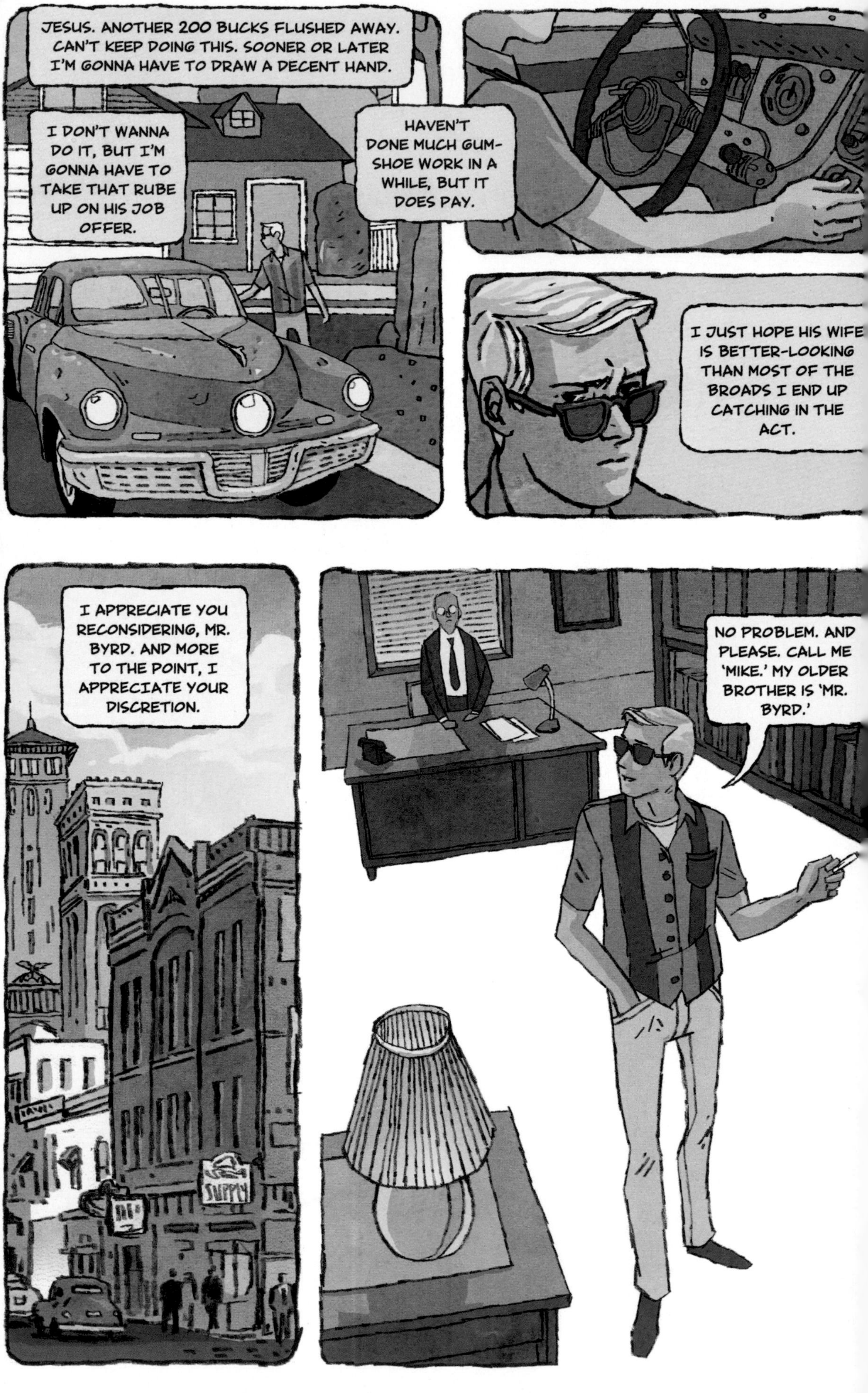
JESUS. ANOTHER 200 BUCKS FLUSHED AWAY. CAN'T KEEP DOING THIS. SOONER OR LATER I'M GONNA HAVE TO DRAW A DECENT HAND.
I DON'T WANNA DO IT, BUT I'M GONNA HAVE TO TAKE THAT RUBE UP ON HIS JOB OFFER.
HAVEN'T DONE MUCH GUM-SHOE WORK IN A WHILE, BUT IT DOES PAY.
I JUST HOPE HIS WIFE IS BETTER-LOOKING THAN MOST OF THE BROADS I END UP CATCHING IN THE ACT.
I APPRECIATE YOU RECONSIDERING, MR. BYRD. AND MORE TO THE POINT, I APPRECIATE YOUR DISCRETION.
NO PROBLEM. AND PLEASE. CALL ME 'MIKE.' MY OLDER BROTHER IS 'MR. BYRD.'
SUPPLY

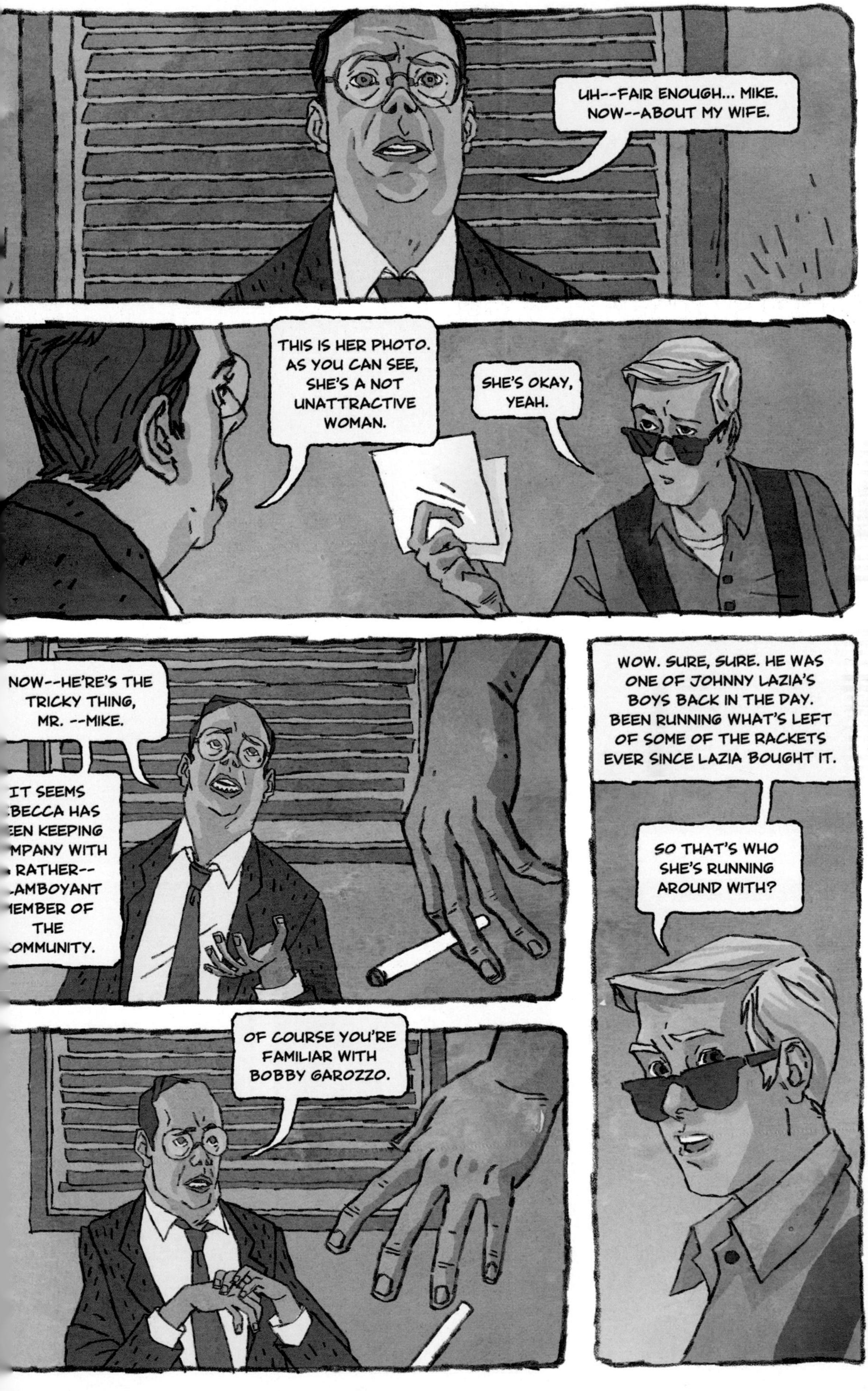
UH--FAIR ENOUGH... MIKE. NOW--ABOUT MY WIFE.
THIS IS HER PHOTO. AS YOU CAN SEE, SHE'S A NOT UNATTRACTIVE WOMAN.
SHE'S OKAY, YEAH.
NOW--HE'RE'S THE TRICKY THING, MR. --MIKE.
IT SEEMS BECCA HAS EEN KEEPING MPANY WITH RATHER-- AMBOYANT MEMBER OF THE OMMUNITY.
OF COURSE YOU'RE FAMILIAR WITH BOBBY GAROZZO.
WOW. SURE, SURE. HE WAS ONE OF JOHNNY LAZIA'S BOYS BACK IN THE DAY. BEEN RUNNING WHAT'S LEFT OF SOME OF THE RACKETS EVER SINCE LAZIA BOUGHT IT.
SO THAT'S WHO SHE'S RUNNING AROUND WITH?

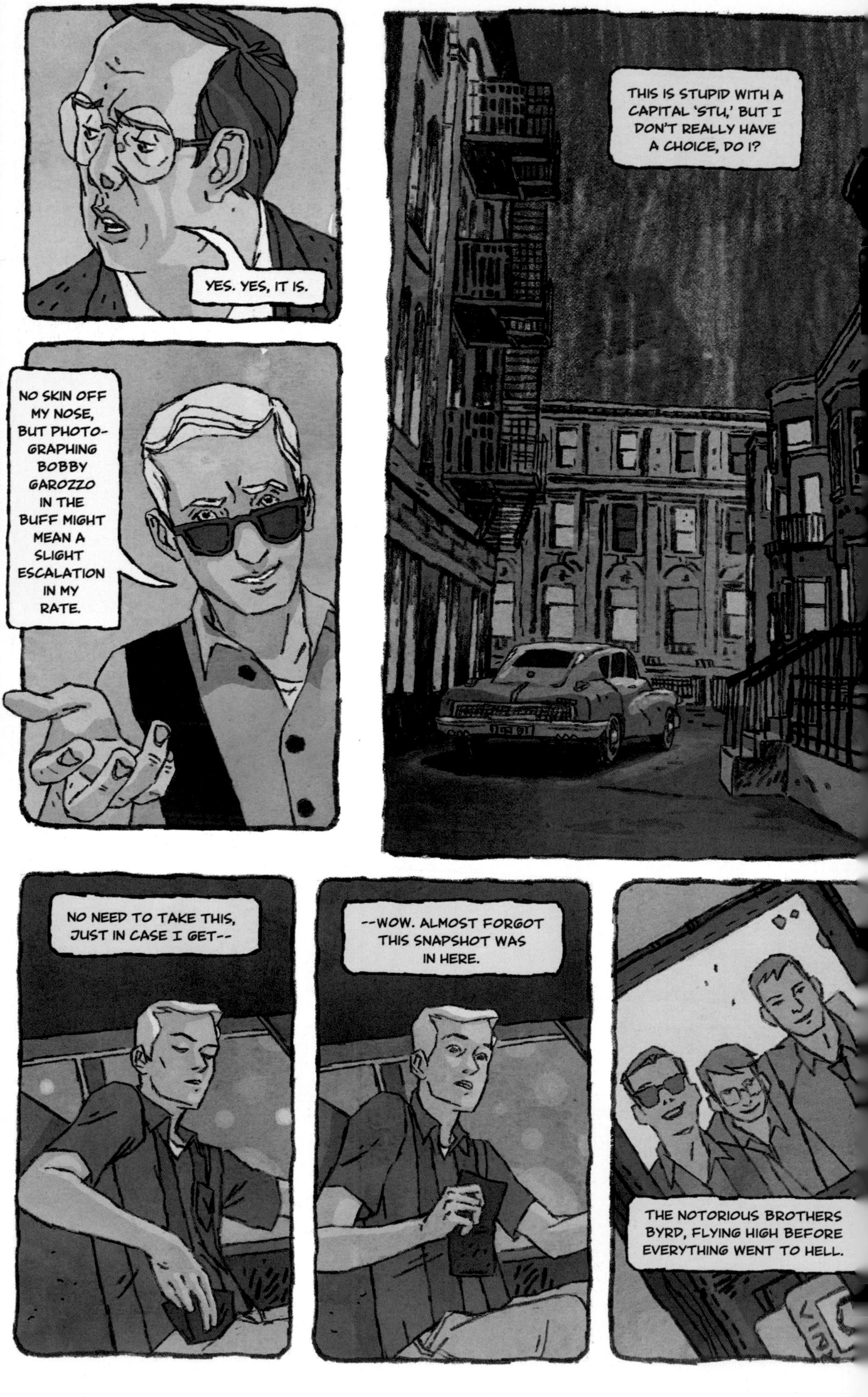
YES. YES, IT IS.
NO SKIN OFF MY NOSE, BUT PHOTOGRAPHING BOBBY GAROZZO IN THE BUFF MIGHT MEAN A SLIGHT ESCALATION IN MY RATE.
THIS IS STUPID WITH A CAPITAL 'STU,' BUT I DON'T REALLY HAVE A CHOICE, DO I?
NO NEED TO TAKE THIS, JUST IN CASE I GET--
--WOW. ALMOST FORGOT THIS SNAPSHOT WAS IN HERE.
THE NOTORIOUS BROTHERS BYRD, FLYING HIGH BEFORE EVERYTHING WENT TO HELL.

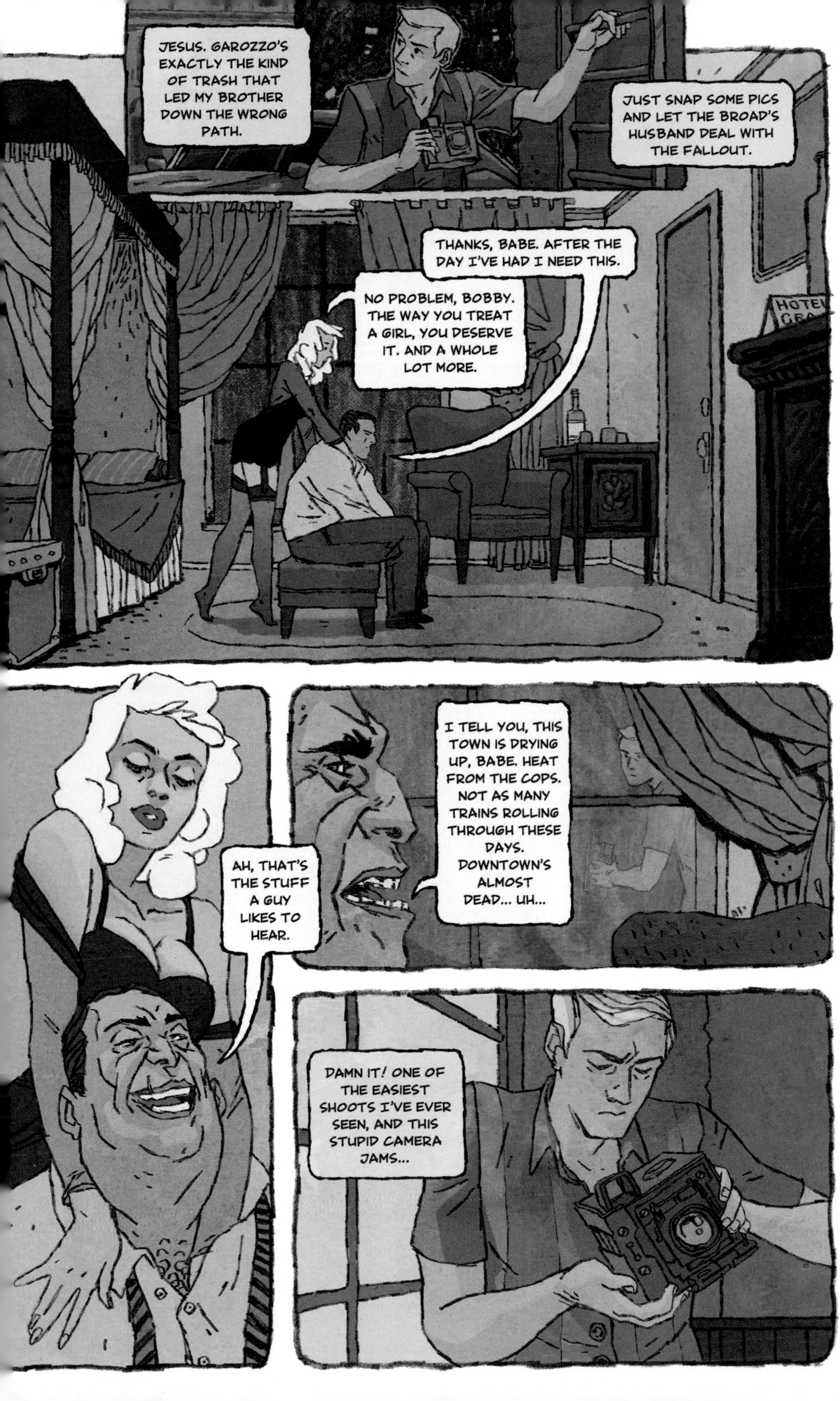
JESUS. GAROZZO'S EXACTLY THE KIND OF TRASH THAT LED MY BROTHER DOWN THE WRONG PATH.
JUST SNAP SOME PICS AND LET THE BROAD'S HUSBAND DEAL WITH THE FALLOUT.
THANKS, BABE. AFTER THE DAY I'VE HAD I NEED THIS.
NO PROBLEM, BOBBY. THE WAY YOU TREAT A GIRL, YOU DESERVE IT. AND A WHOLE LOT MORE.
I TELL YOU, THIS TOWN IS DRYING UP, BABE. HEAT FROM THE COPS. NOT AS MANY TRAINS ROLLING THROUGH THESE DAYS. DOWNTOWN'S ALMOST DEAD... UH...
AH, THAT'S THE STUFF A GUY LIKES TO HEAR.
DAMN IT! ONE OF THE EASIEST SHOOTS I'VE EVER SEEN, AND THIS STUPID CAMERA JAMS...

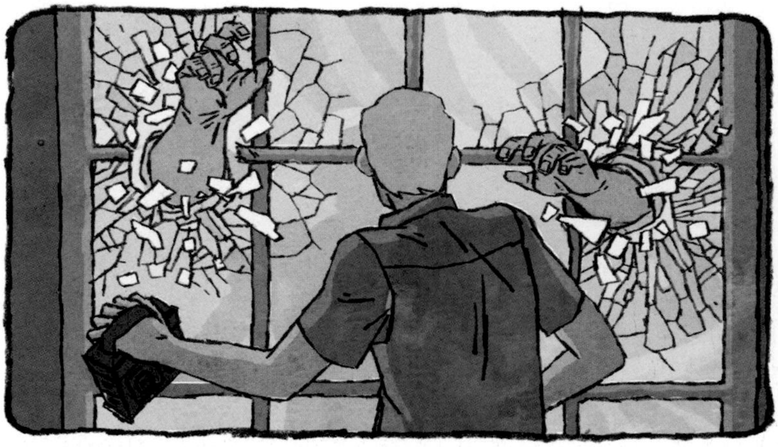

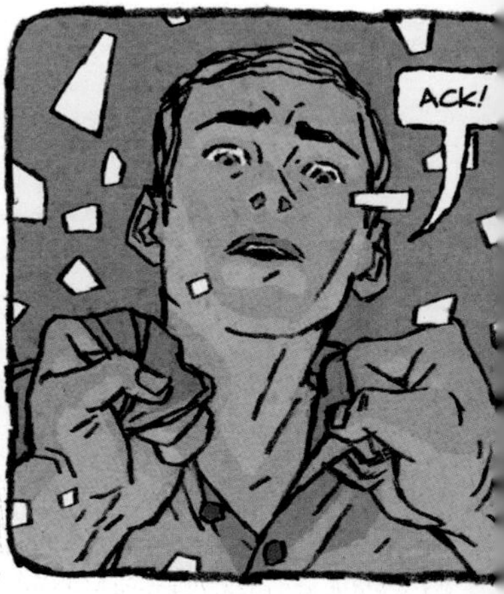
ACK!

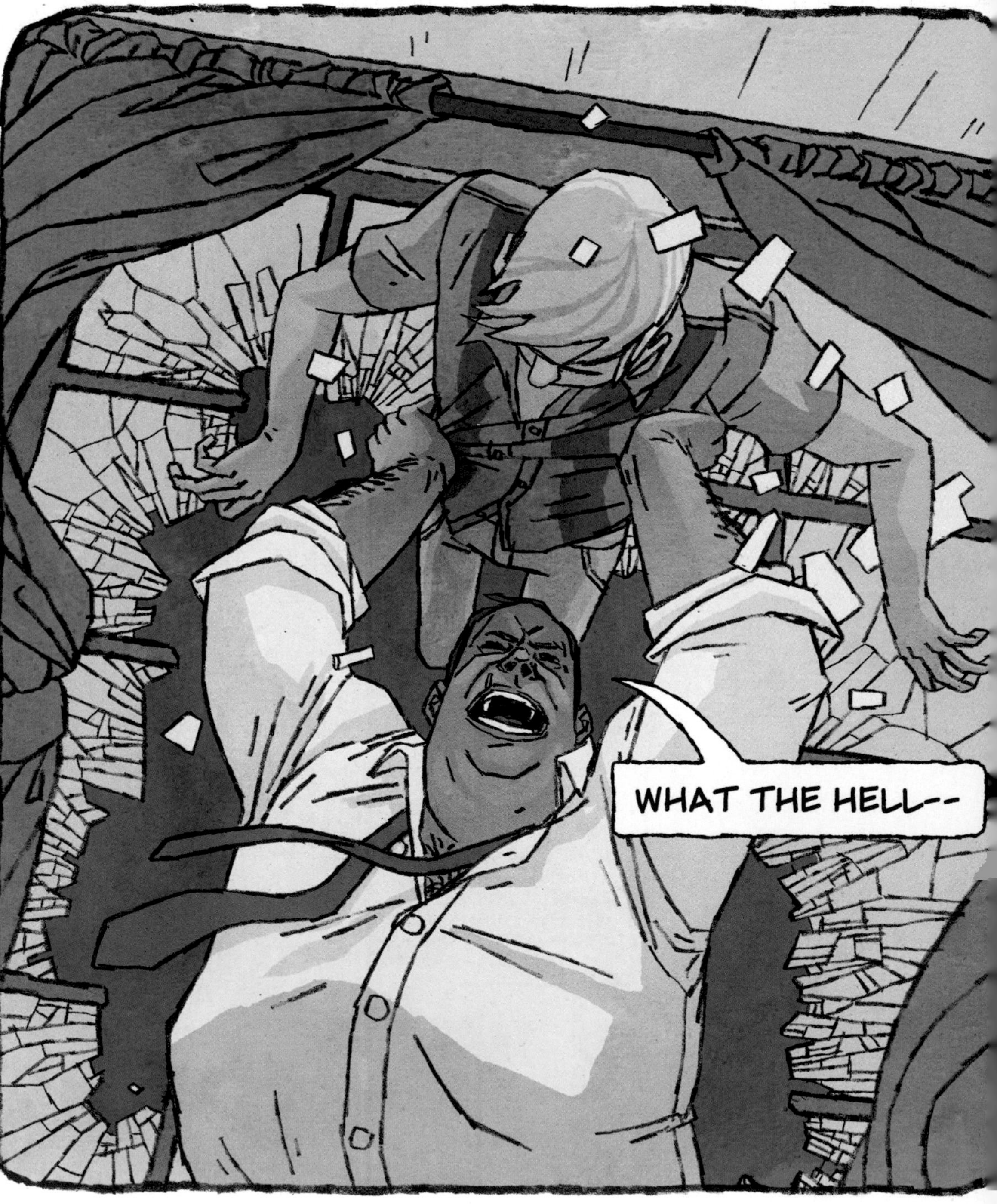
WHAT THE HELL--

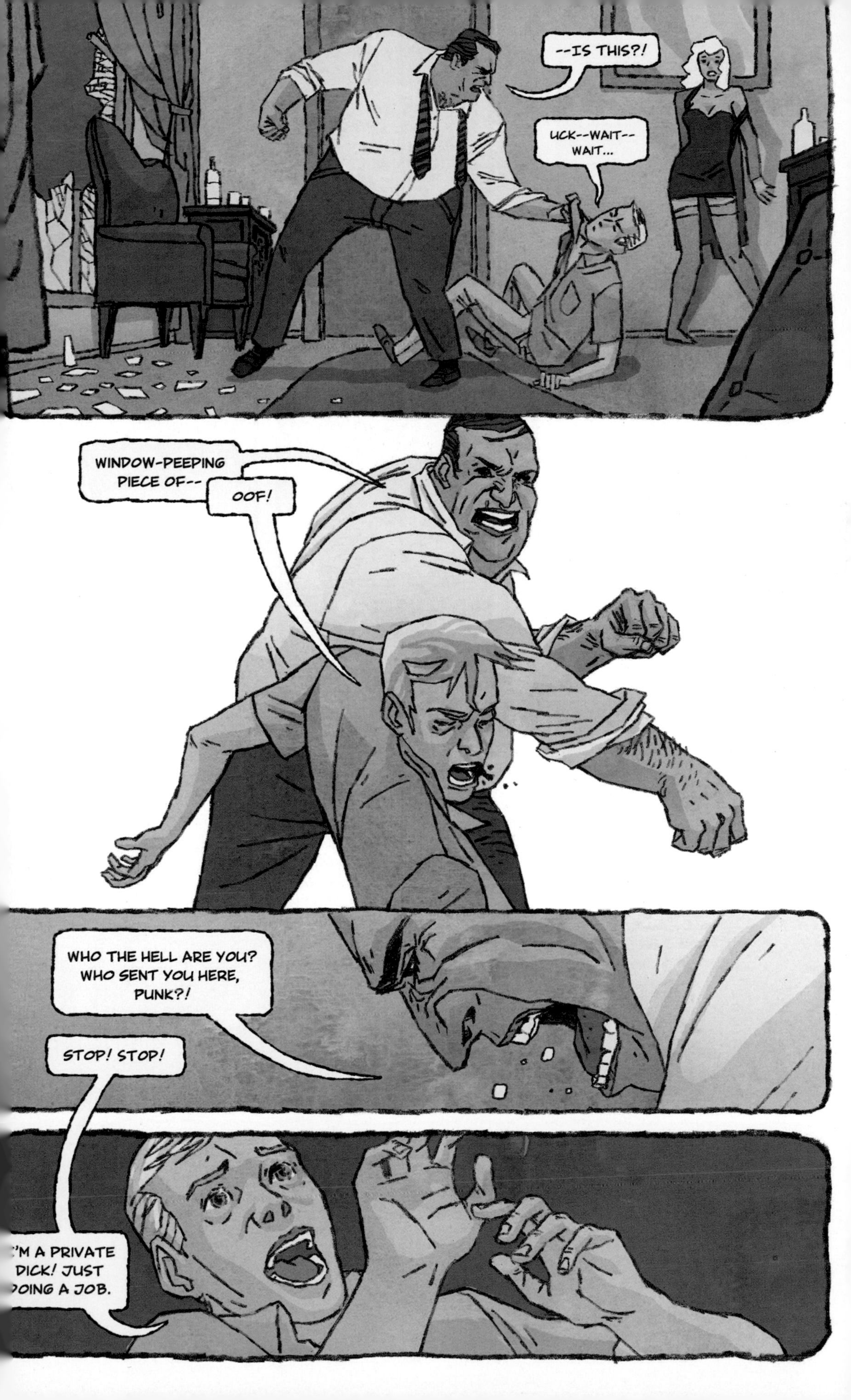
--IS THIS?!
UCK--WAIT--
WAIT...
WINDOW-PEEPING
PIECE OF--
OOF!
WHO THE HELL ARE YOU?
WHO SENT YOU HERE,
PUNK?!
STOP! STOP!
'M A PRIVATE
DICK! JUST
OING A JOB.

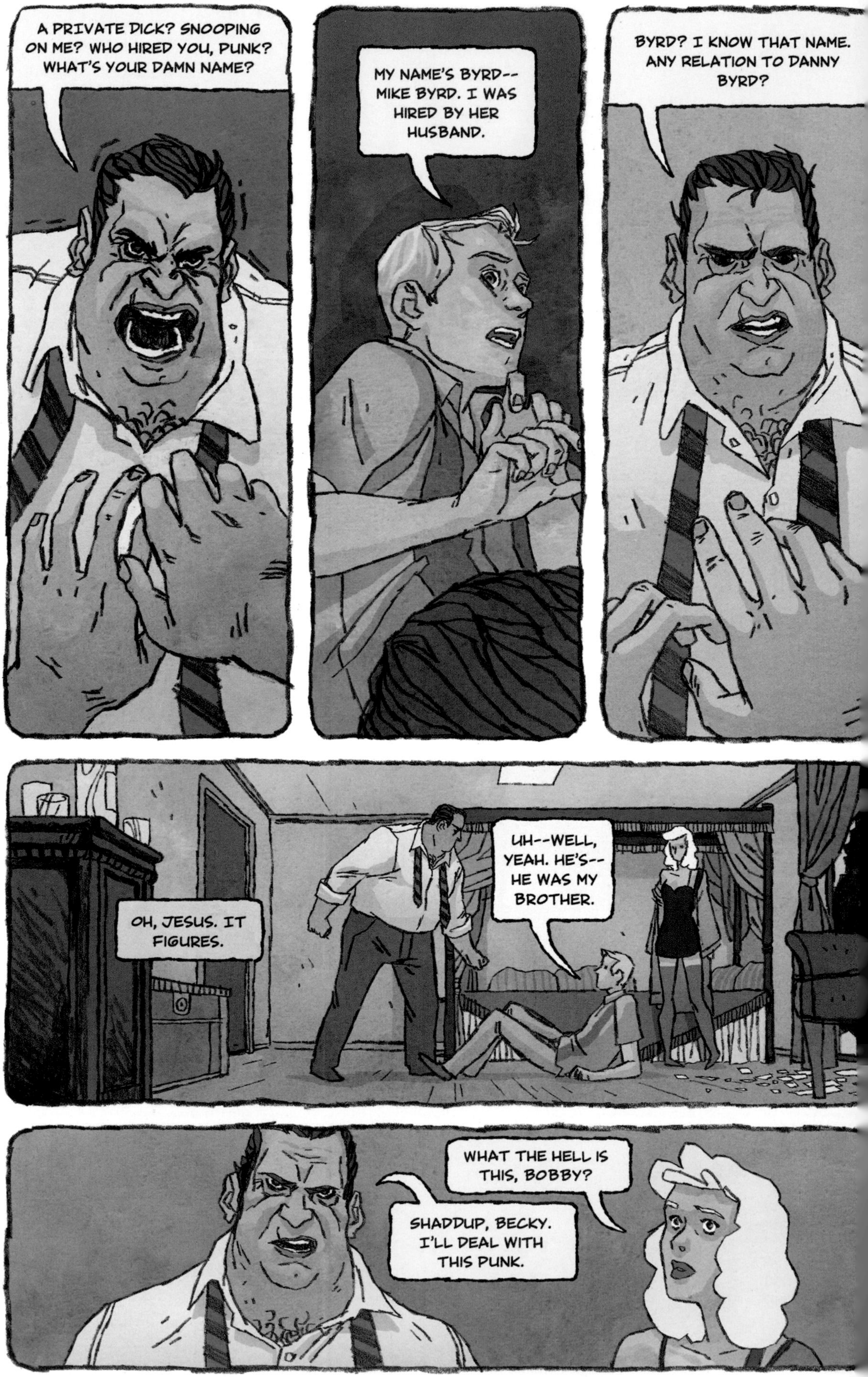
A PRIVATE DICK? SNOOPING ON ME? WHO HIRED YOU, PUNK? WHAT'S YOUR DAMN NAME?
MY NAME'S BYRD-- MIKE BYRD. I WAS HIRED BY HER HUSBAND.
BYRD? I KNOW THAT NAME. ANY RELATION TO DANNY BYRD?
UH--WELL, YEAH. HE'S-- HE WAS MY BROTHER.
OH, JESUS. IT FIGURES.
WHAT THE HELL IS THIS, BOBBY?
SHADDUP, BECKY. I'LL DEAL WITH THIS PUNK.

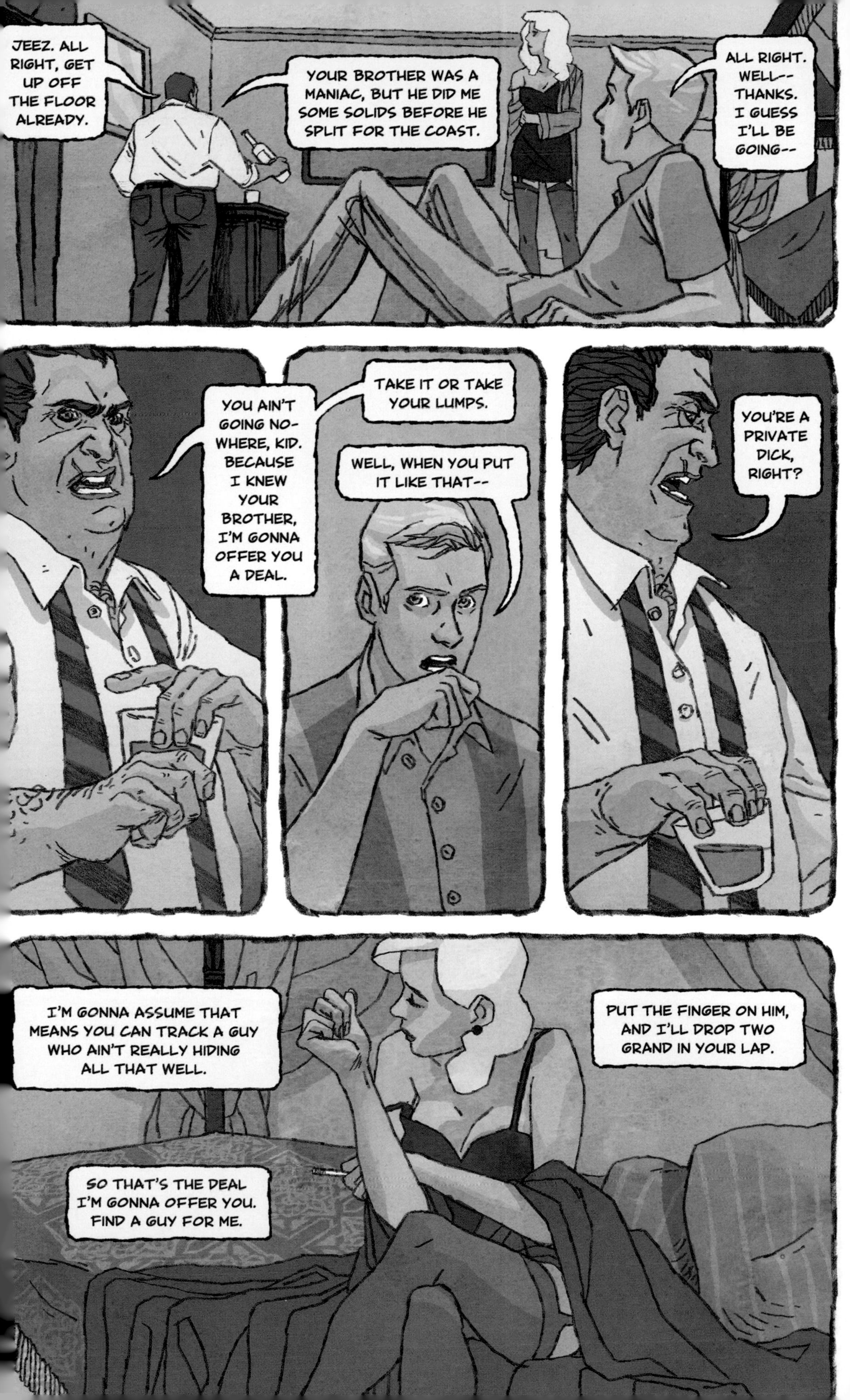
JEEZ. ALL RIGHT, GET UP OFF THE FLOOR ALREADY.
YOUR BROTHER WAS A MANIAC, BUT HE DID ME SOME SOLIDS BEFORE HE SPLIT FOR THE COAST.
ALL RIGHT. WELL-- THANKS. I GUESS I'LL BE GOING--
YOU AIN'T GOING NO-WHERE, KID. BECAUSE I KNEW YOUR BROTHER, I'M GONNA OFFER YOU A DEAL.
TAKE IT OR TAKE YOUR LUMPS.
WELL, WHEN YOU PUT IT LIKE THAT--
YOU'RE A PRIVATE DICK, RIGHT?
I'M GONNA ASSUME THAT MEANS YOU CAN TRACK A GUY WHO AIN'T REALLY HIDING ALL THAT WELL.
PUT THE FINGER ON HIM, AND I'LL DROP TWO GRAND IN YOUR LAP.
SO THAT'S THE DEAL I'M GONNA OFFER YOU. FIND A GUY FOR ME.

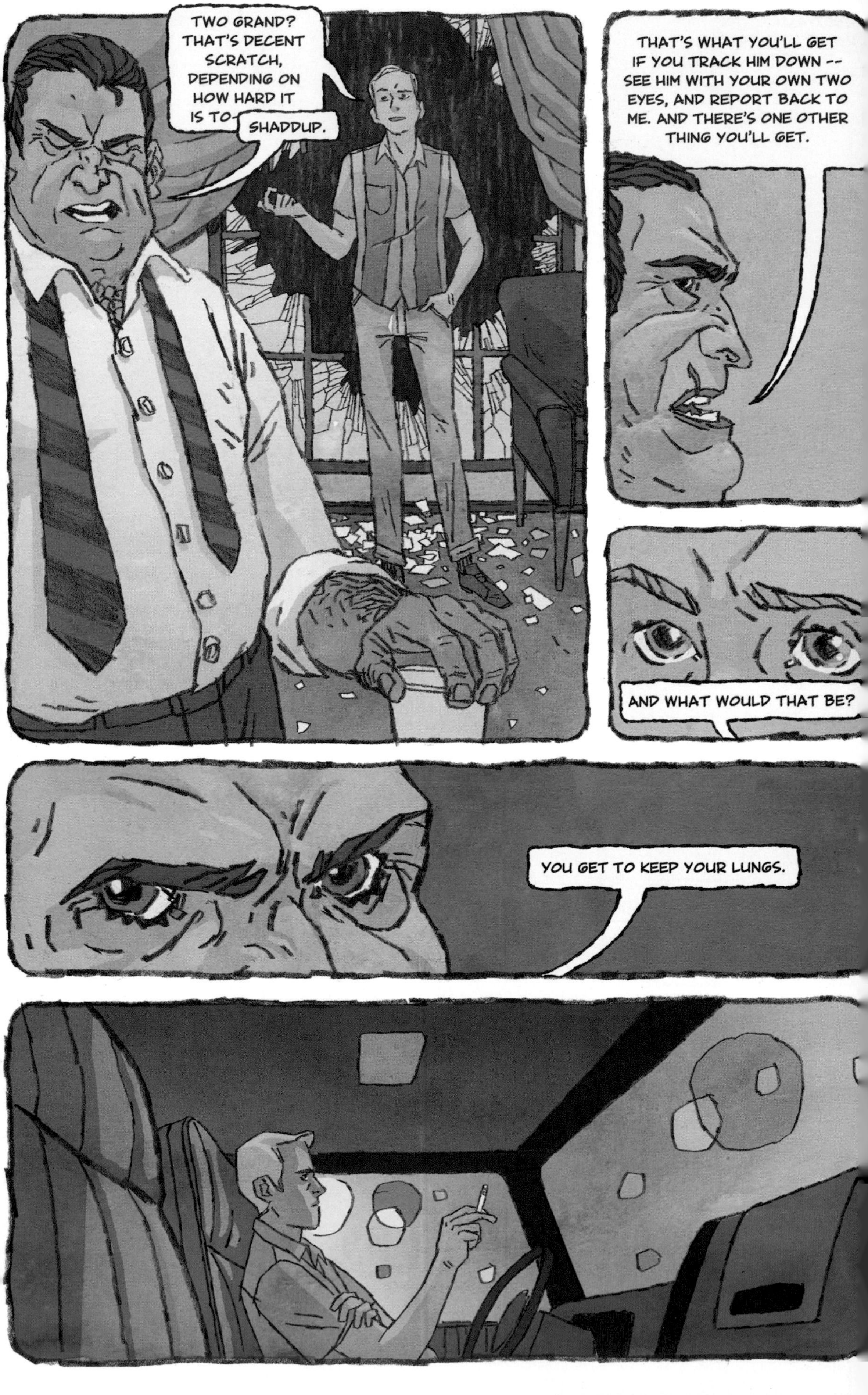
TWO GRAND? THAT'S DECENT SCRATCH, DEPENDING ON HOW HARD IT IS TO-
SHADDUP.
THAT'S WHAT YOU'LL GET IF YOU TRACK HIM DOWN -- SEE HIM WITH YOUR OWN TWO EYES, AND REPORT BACK TO ME. AND THERE'S ONE OTHER THING YOU'LL GET.
AND WHAT WOULD THAT BE?
YOU GET TO KEEP YOUR LUNGS.

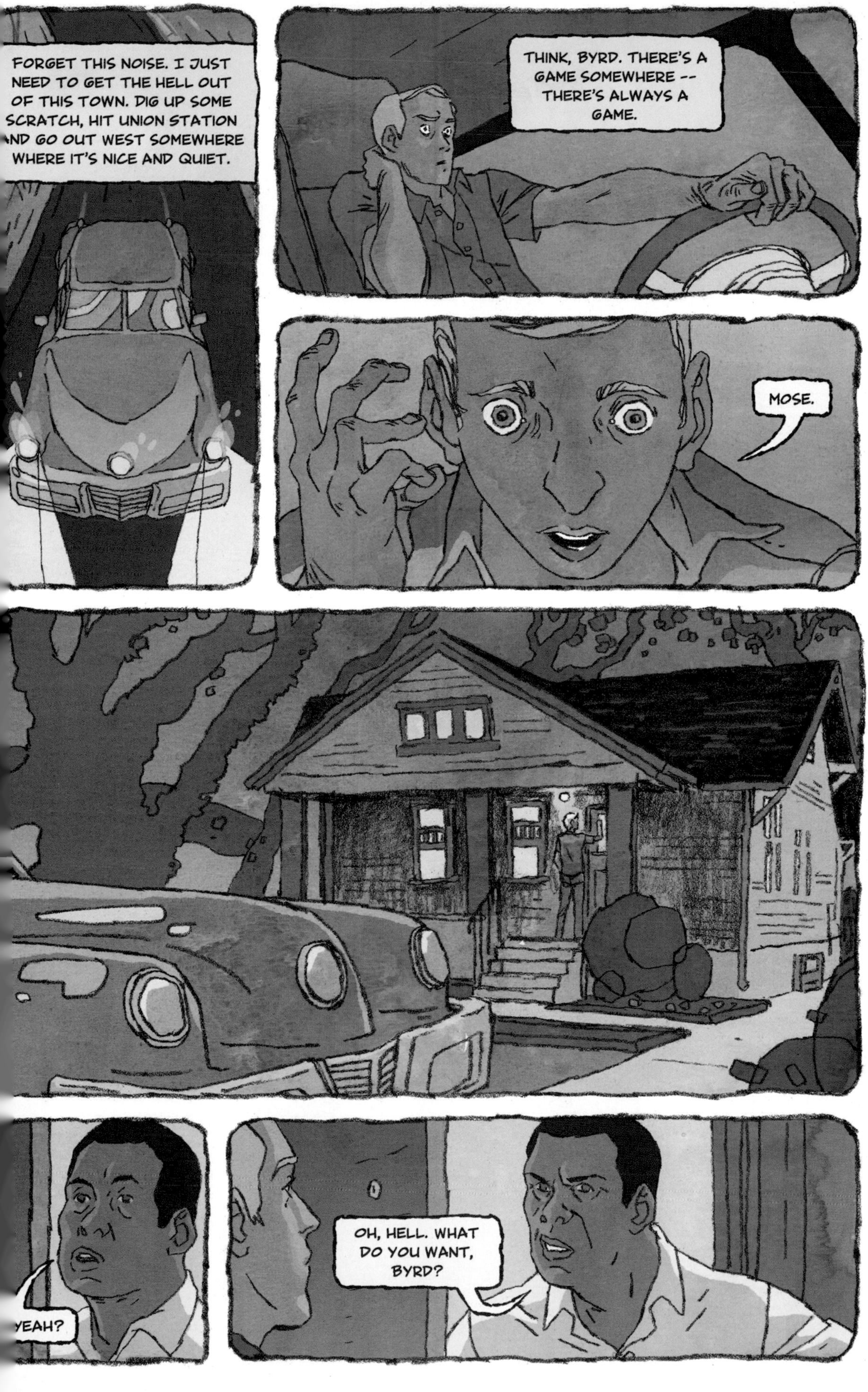
FORGET THIS NOISE. I JUST NEED TO GET THE HELL OUT OF THIS TOWN. DIG UP SOME SCRATCH, HIT UNION STATION AND GO OUT WEST SOMEWHERE WHERE IT'S NICE AND QUIET.
THINK, BYRD. THERE'S A GAME SOMEWHERE -- THERE'S ALWAYS A GAME.
MOSE.
YEAH?
OH, HELL. WHAT DO YOU WANT, BYRD?

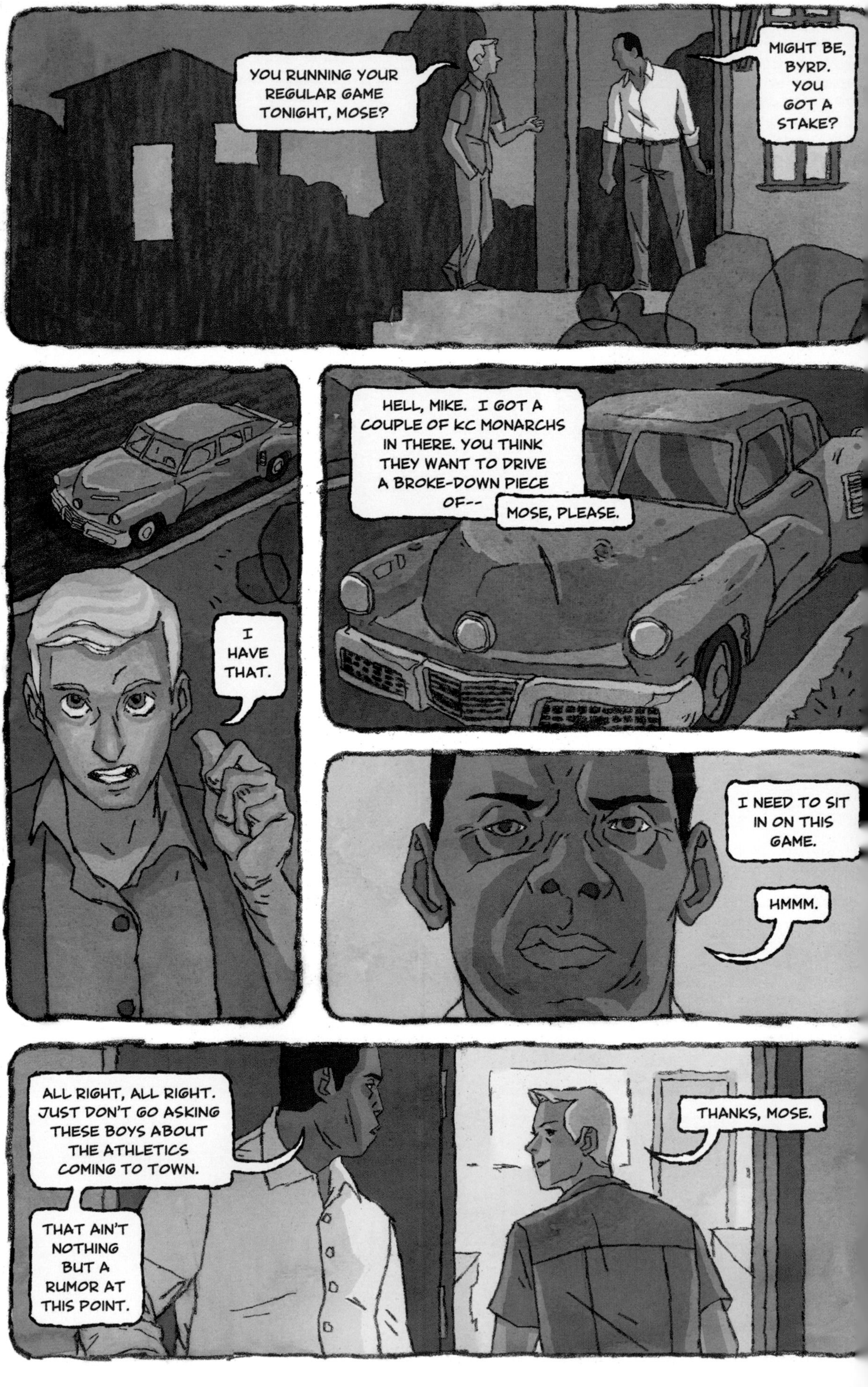
YOU RUNNING YOUR REGULAR GAME TONIGHT, MOSE?
MIGHT BE, BYRD. YOU GOT A STAKE?
I HAVE THAT.
HELL, MIKE. I GOT A COUPLE OF KC MONARCHS IN THERE. YOU THINK THEY WANT TO DRIVE A BROKE-DOWN PIECE OF--
MOSE, PLEASE.
I NEED TO SIT IN ON THIS GAME.
HMMM.
ALL RIGHT, ALL RIGHT. JUST DON'T GO ASKING THESE BOYS ABOUT THE ATHLETICS COMING TO TOWN.
THAT AIN'T NOTHING BUT A RUMOR AT THIS POINT.
THANKS, MOSE.

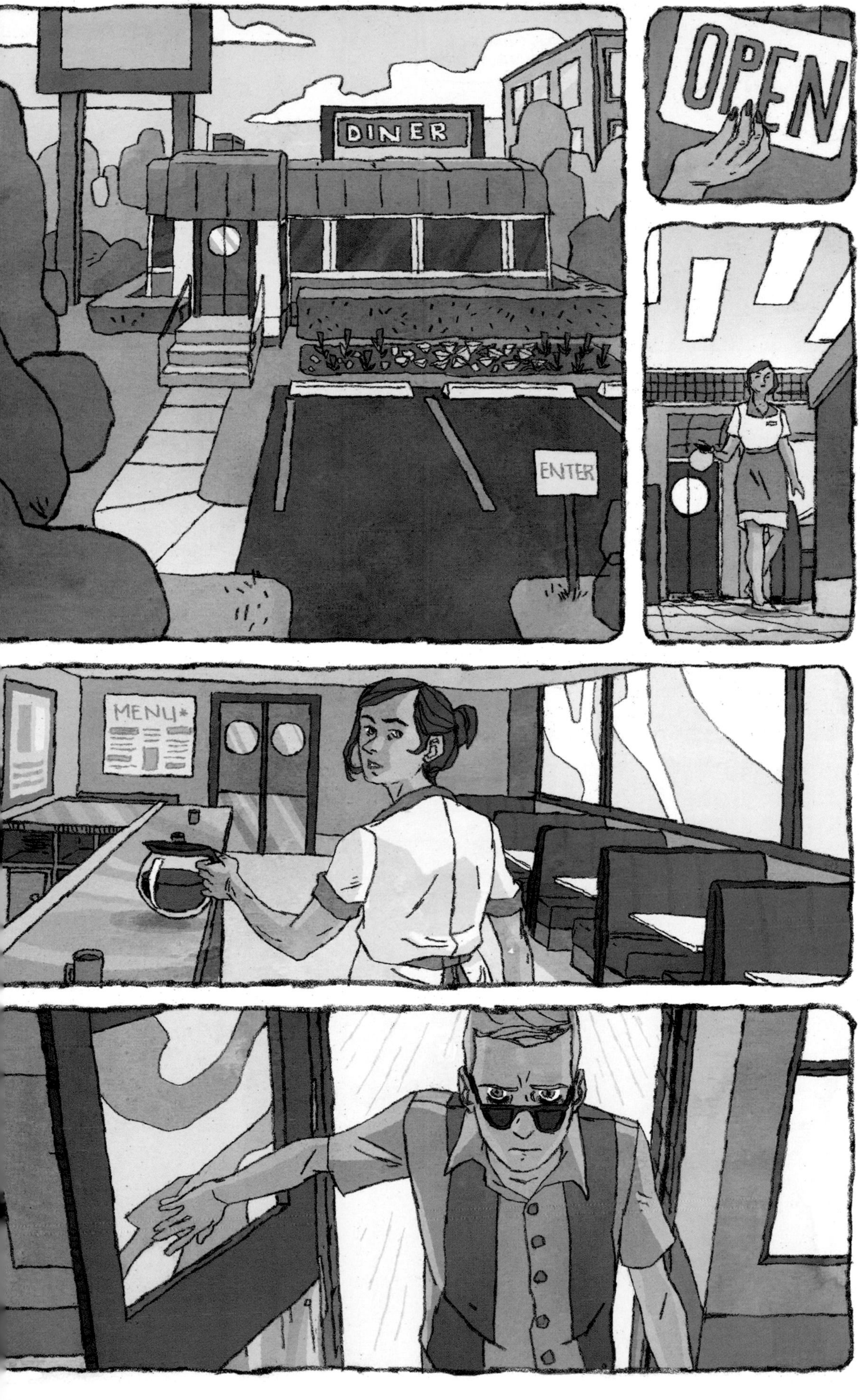
DINER
ENTER
OPEN
MENU*

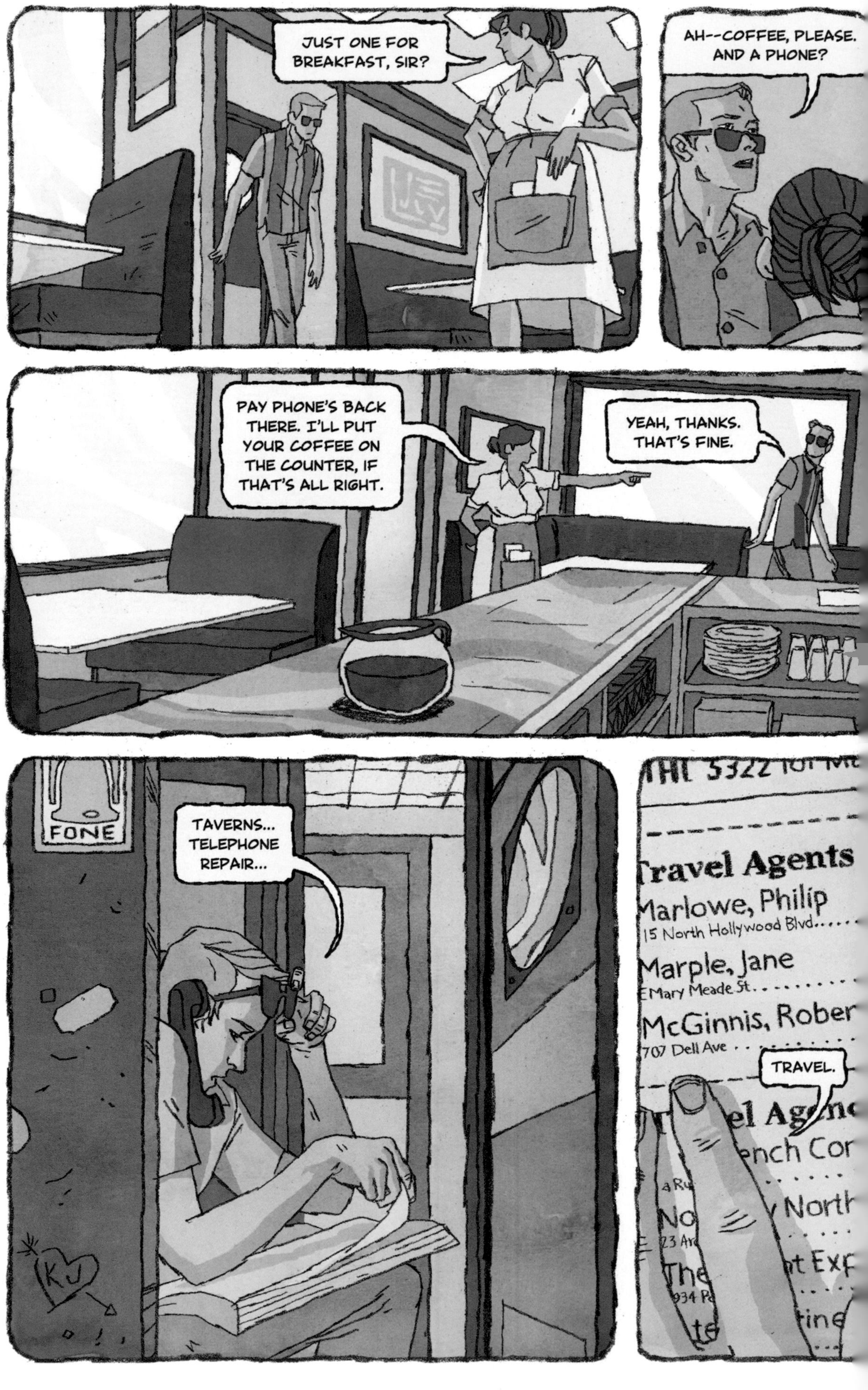
JUST ONE FOR BREAKFAST, SIR?
AH--COFFEE, PLEASE. AND A PHONE?
PAY PHONE'S BACK THERE. I'LL PUT YOUR COFFEE ON THE COUNTER, IF THAT'S ALL RIGHT.
YEAH, THANKS. THAT'S FINE.
FONE
TAVERNS... TELEPHONE REPAIR...
Travel Agents
Marlowe, Philip
15 North Hollywood Blvd
Marple, Jane
Mary Meade St
McGinnis, Rober
707 Dell Ave
TRAVEL.

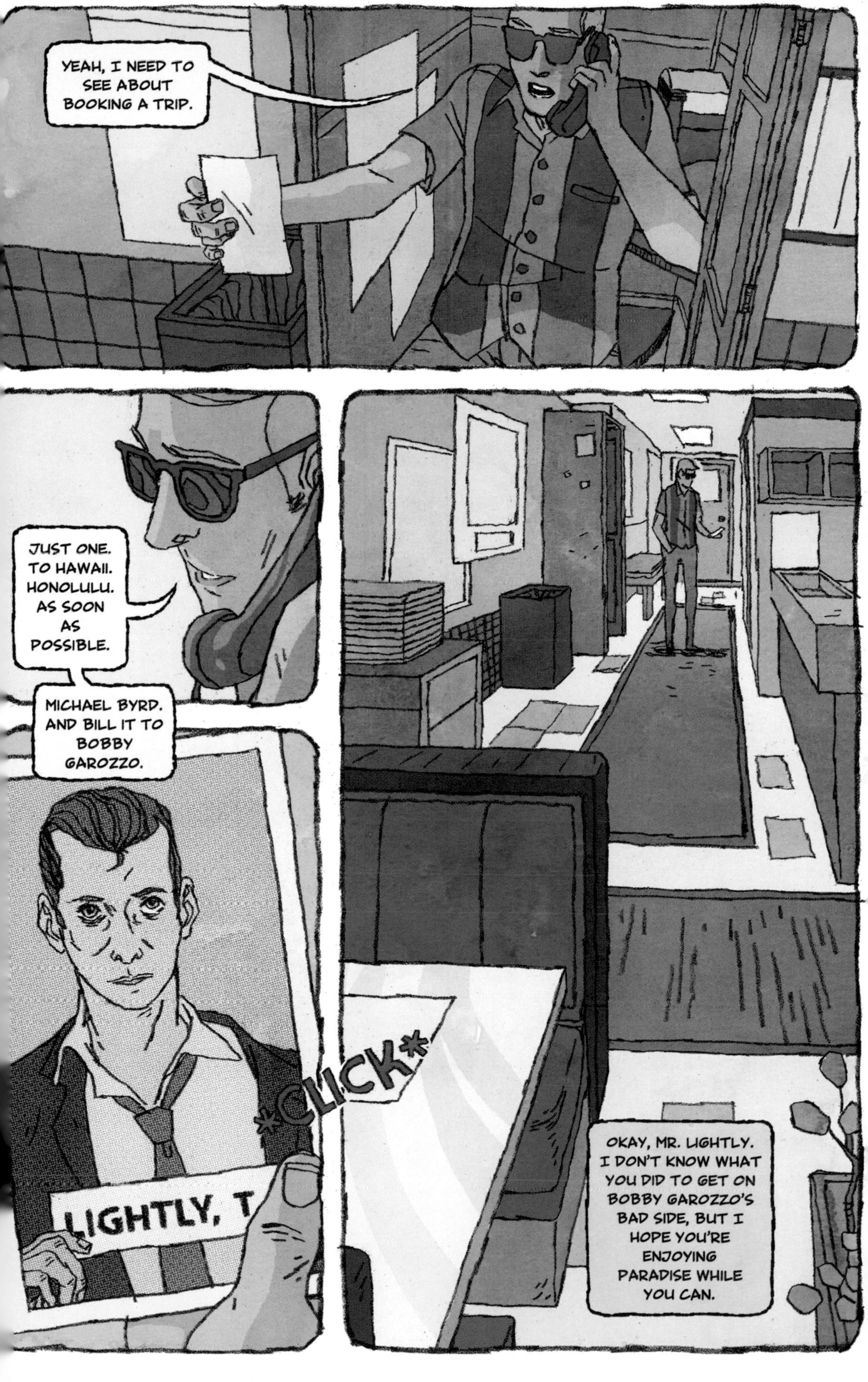
YEAH, I NEED TO SEE ABOUT BOOKING A TRIP.
JUST ONE. TO HAWAII. HONOLULU. AS SOON AS POSSIBLE.
MICHAEL BYRD. AND BILL IT TO BOBBY GAROZZO.
LIGHTLY, T
CLICK
OKAY, MR. LIGHTLY. I DON'T KNOW WHAT YOU DID TO GET ON BOBBY GAROZZO'S BAD SIDE, BUT I HOPE YOU'RE ENJOYING PARADISE WHILE YOU CAN.

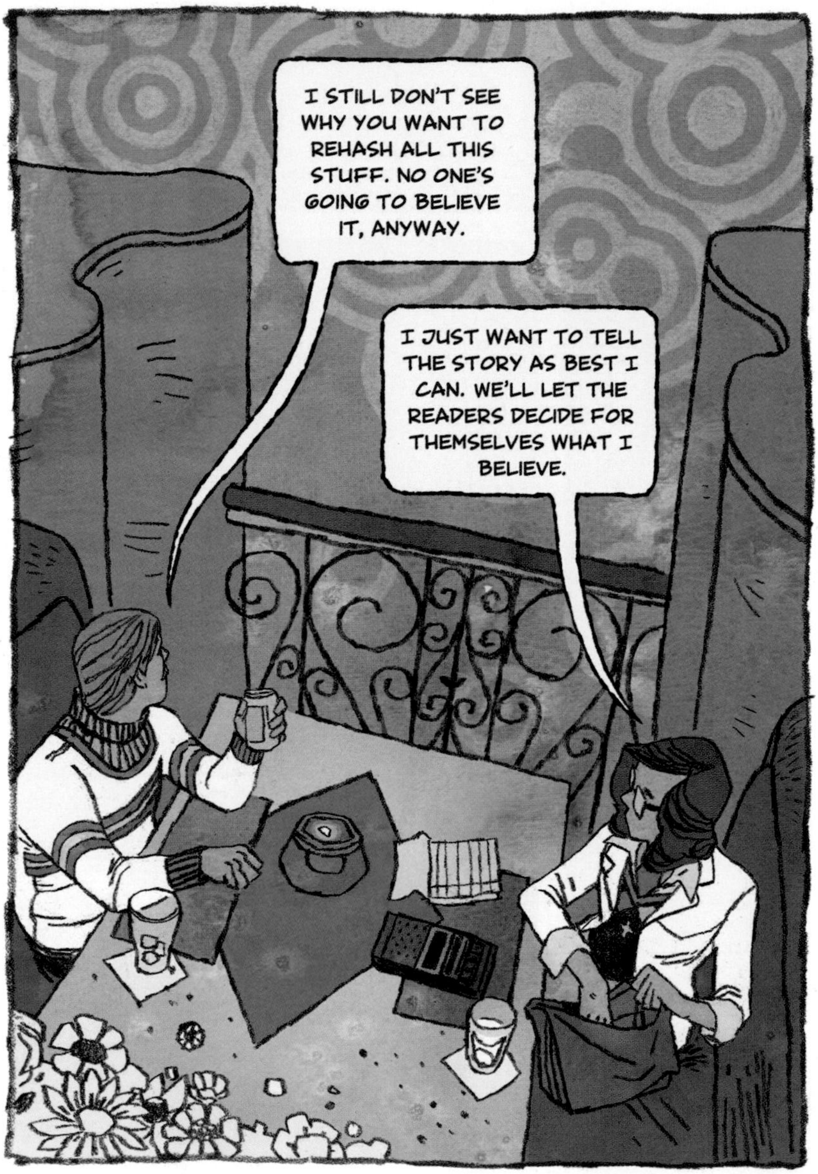
I STILL DON'T SEE WHY YOU WANT TO REHASH ALL THIS STUFF. NO ONE'S GOING TO BELIEVE IT, ANYWAY.
I JUST WANT TO TELL THE STORY AS BEST I CAN. WE'LL LET THE READERS DECIDE FOR THEMSELVES WHAT I BELIEVE.

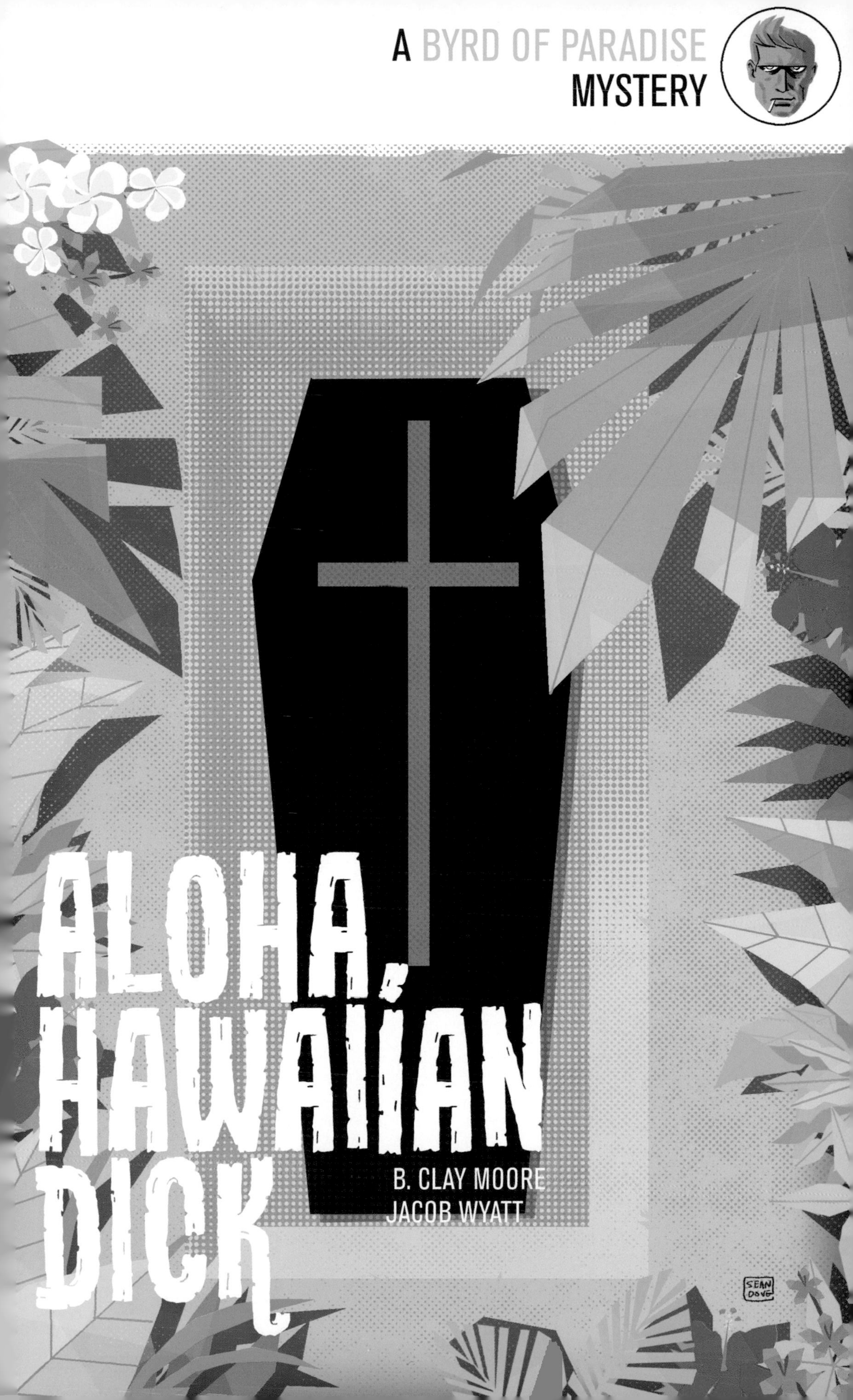
A BYRD OF PARADISE MYSTERY
ALOHA, HAWAIIAN DICK
B. CLAY MOORE
JACOB WYATT
SEAN DOVE

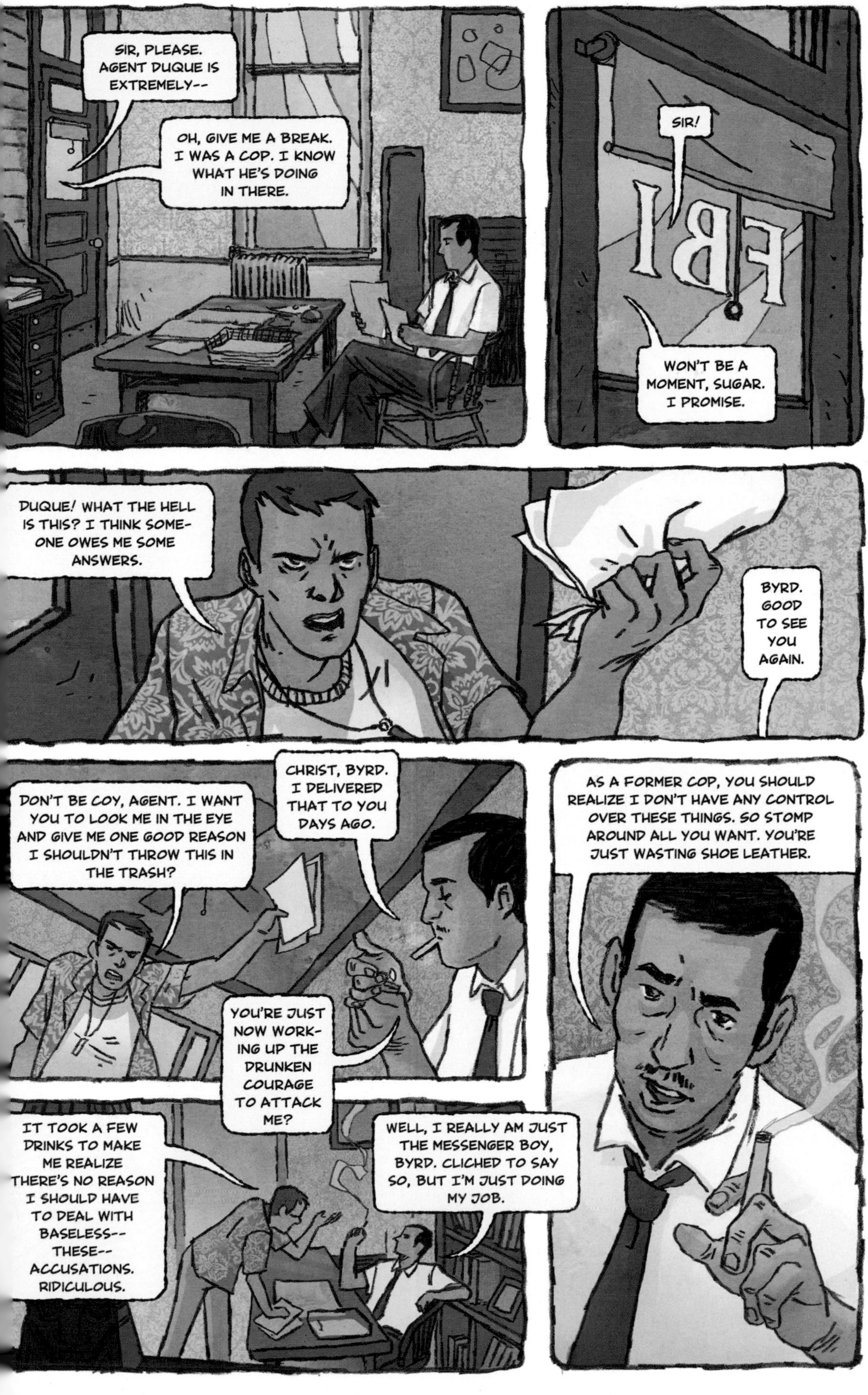
SIR, PLEASE. AGENT DUQUE IS EXTREMELY--
OH, GIVE ME A BREAK. I WAS A COP. I KNOW WHAT HE'S DOING IN THERE.
SIR!
FBI
WON'T BE A MOMENT, SUGAR. I PROMISE.
DUQUE! WHAT THE HELL IS THIS? I THINK SOME-ONE OWES ME SOME ANSWERS.
BYRD. GOOD TO SEE YOU AGAIN.
DON'T BE COY, AGENT. I WANT YOU TO LOOK ME IN THE EYE AND GIVE ME ONE GOOD REASON I SHOULDN'T THROW THIS IN THE TRASH?
CHRIST, BYRD. I DELIVERED THAT TO YOU DAYS AGO.
YOU'RE JUST NOW WORK-ING UP THE DRUNKEN COURAGE TO ATTACK ME?
IT TOOK A FEW DRINKS TO MAKE ME REALIZE THERE'S NO REASON I SHOULD HAVE TO DEAL WITH BASELESS-- THESE-- ACCUSATIONS. RIDICULOUS.
WELL, I REALLY AM JUST THE MESSENGER BOY, BYRD. CLICHED TO SAY SO, BUT I'M JUST DOING MY JOB.
AS A FORMER COP, YOU SHOULD REALIZE I DON'T HAVE ANY CONTROL OVER THESE THINGS. SO STOMP AROUND ALL YOU WANT. YOU'RE JUST WASTING SHOE LEATHER.

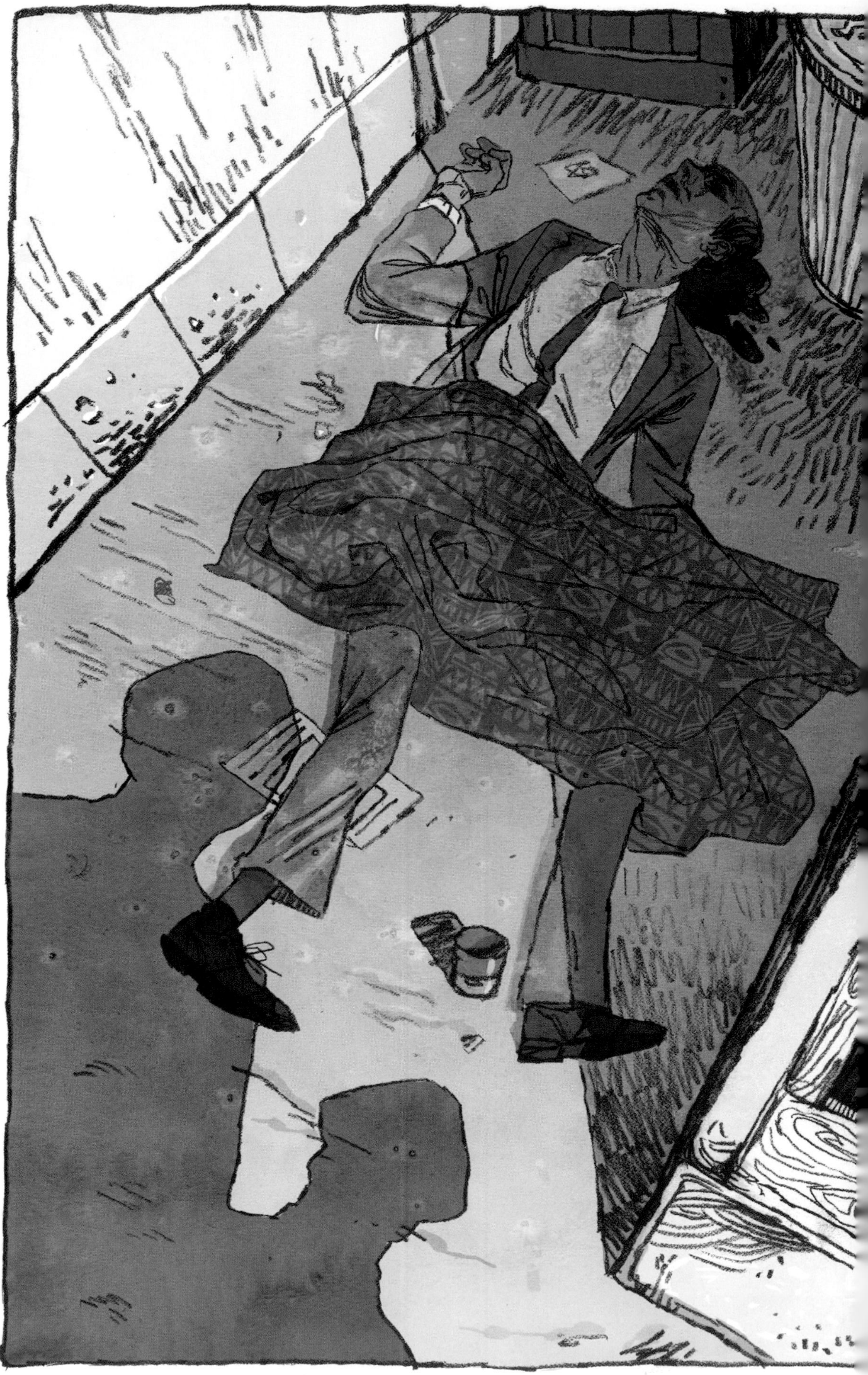

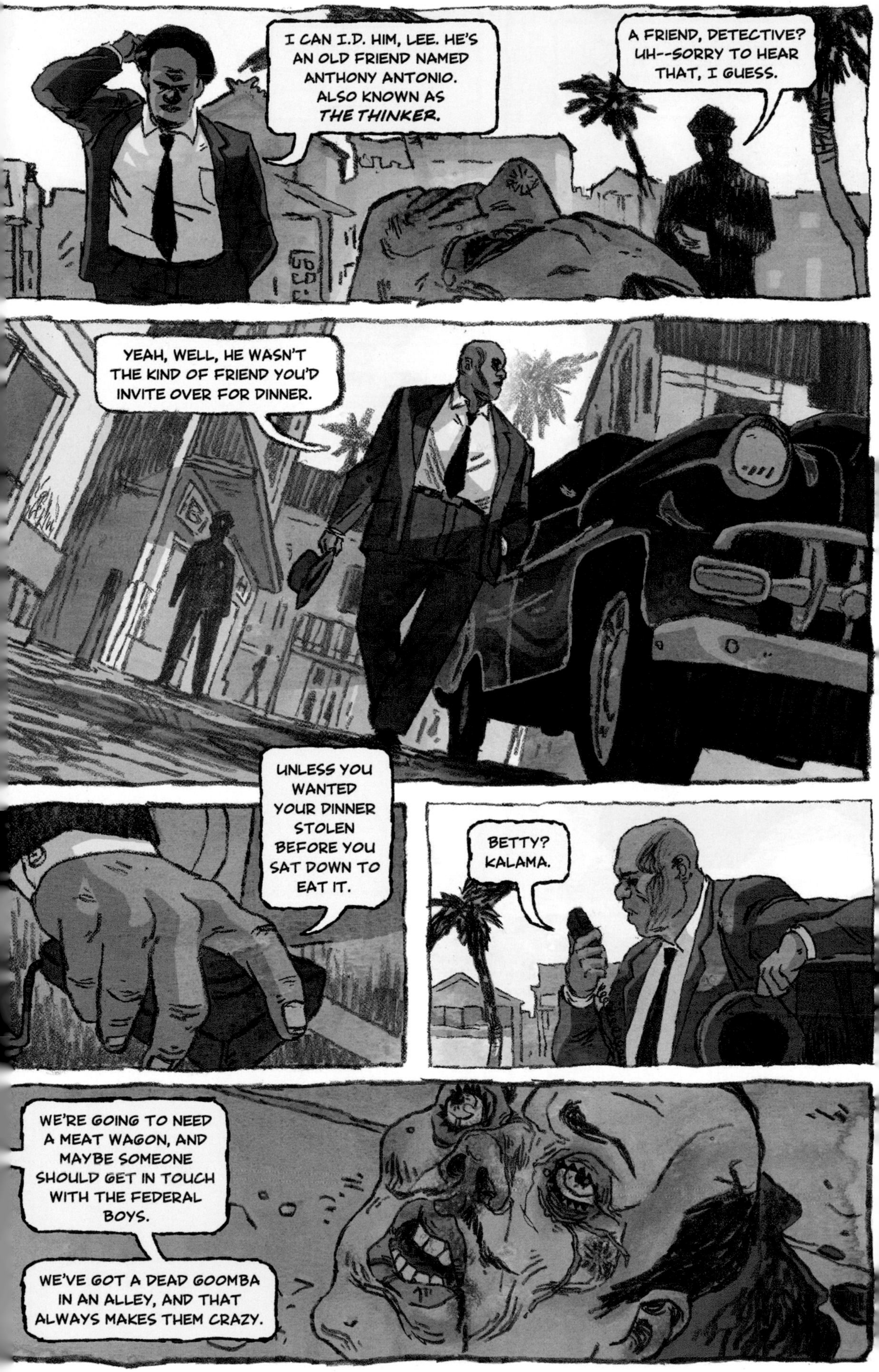
I CAN I.D. HIM, LEE. HE'S AN OLD FRIEND NAMED ANTHONY ANTONIO. ALSO KNOWN AS *THE THINKER.*
A FRIEND, DETECTIVE? UH--SORRY TO HEAR THAT, I GUESS.
YEAH, WELL, HE WASN'T THE KIND OF FRIEND YOU'D INVITE OVER FOR DINNER.
UNLESS YOU WANTED YOUR DINNER STOLEN BEFORE YOU SAT DOWN TO EAT IT.
BETTY? KALAMA.
WE'RE GOING TO NEED A MEAT WAGON, AND MAYBE SOMEONE SHOULD GET IN TOUCH WITH THE FEDERAL BOYS.
WE'VE GOT A DEAD GOOMBA IN AN ALLEY, AND THAT ALWAYS MAKES THEM CRAZY.

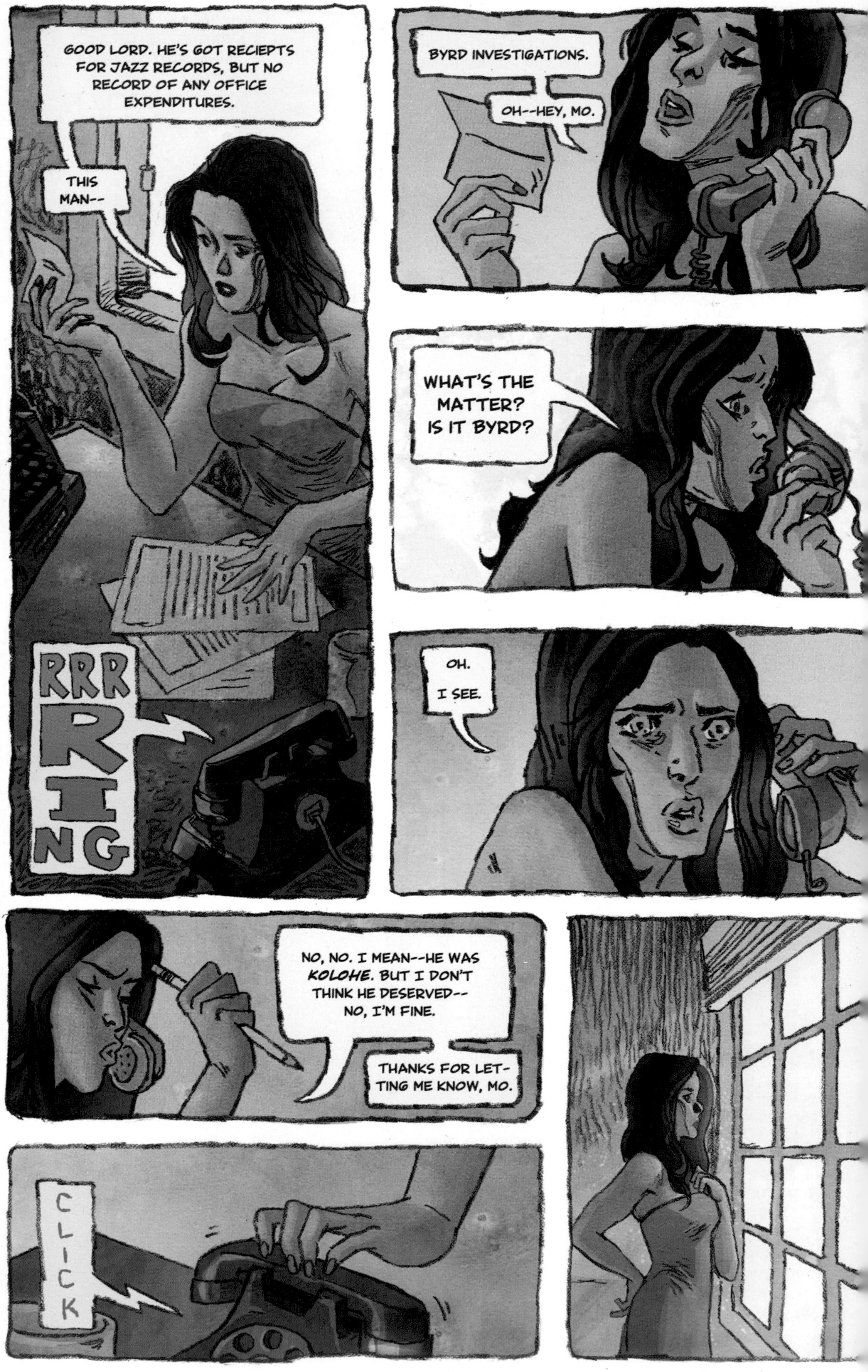
GOOD LORD. HE'S GOT RECIEPTS FOR JAZZ RECORDS, BUT NO RECORD OF ANY OFFICE EXPENDITURES.
THIS MAN--
RRRRING
BYRD INVESTIGATIONS.
OH--HEY, MO.
WHAT'S THE MATTER? IS IT BYRD?
OH.
I SEE.
NO, NO. I MEAN--HE WAS *KOLOHE*. BUT I DON'T THINK HE DESERVED-- NO, I'M FINE.
THANKS FOR LETTING ME KNOW, MO.
CLICK

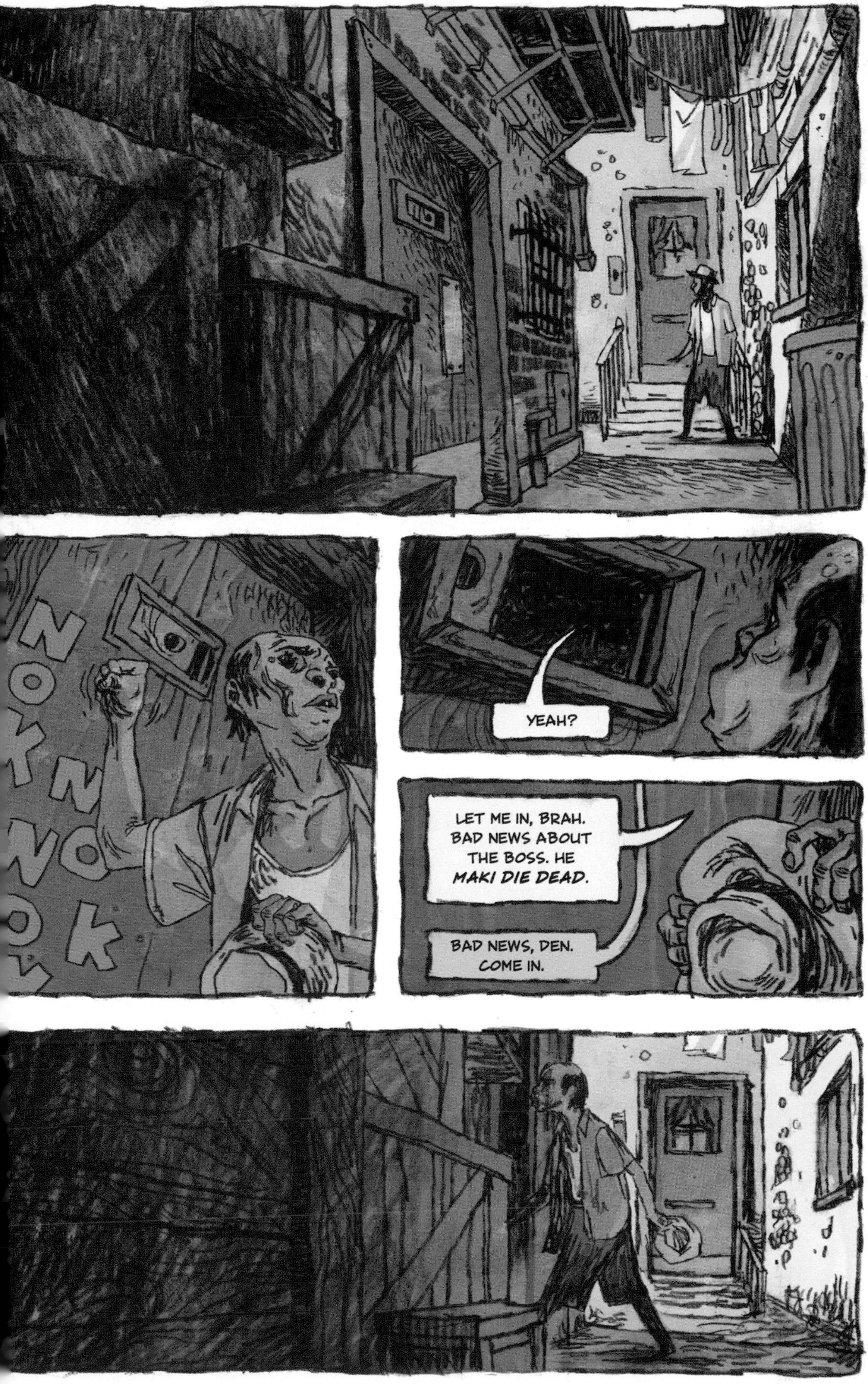
KNOCK KNOCK
YEAH?
LET ME IN, BRAH. BAD NEWS ABOUT THE BOSS. HE *MAKI DIE DEAD*.
BAD NEWS, DEN. COME IN.

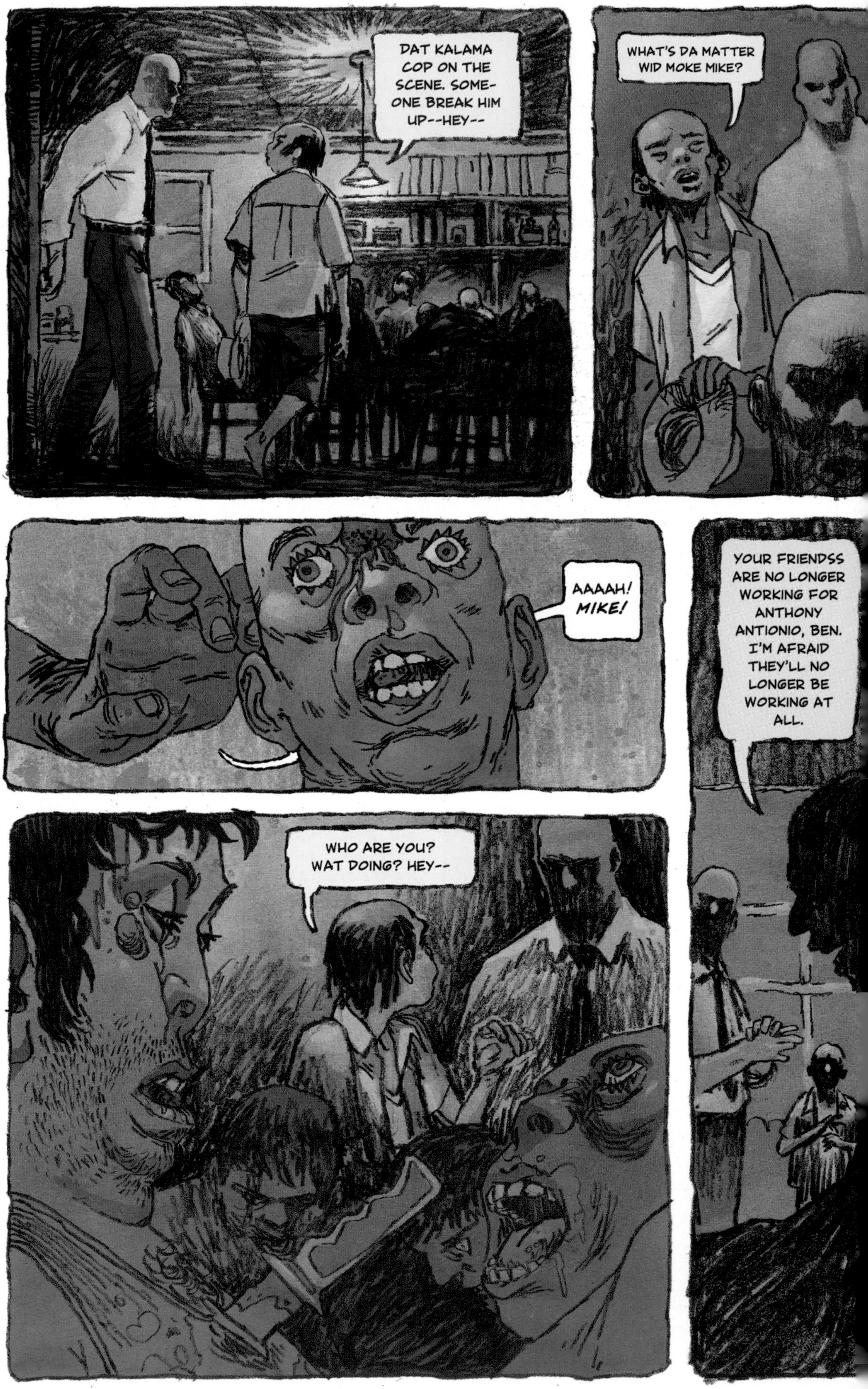
DAT KALAMA COP ON THE SCENE. SOME-ONE BREAK HIM UP--HEY--
WHAT'S DA MATTER WID MOKE MIKE?
AAAAH! MIKE!
YOUR FRIENDSS ARE NO LONGER WORKING FOR ANTHONY ANTIONIO, BEN. I'M AFRAID THEY'LL NO LONGER BE WORKING AT ALL.
WHO ARE YOU? WAT DOING? HEY--

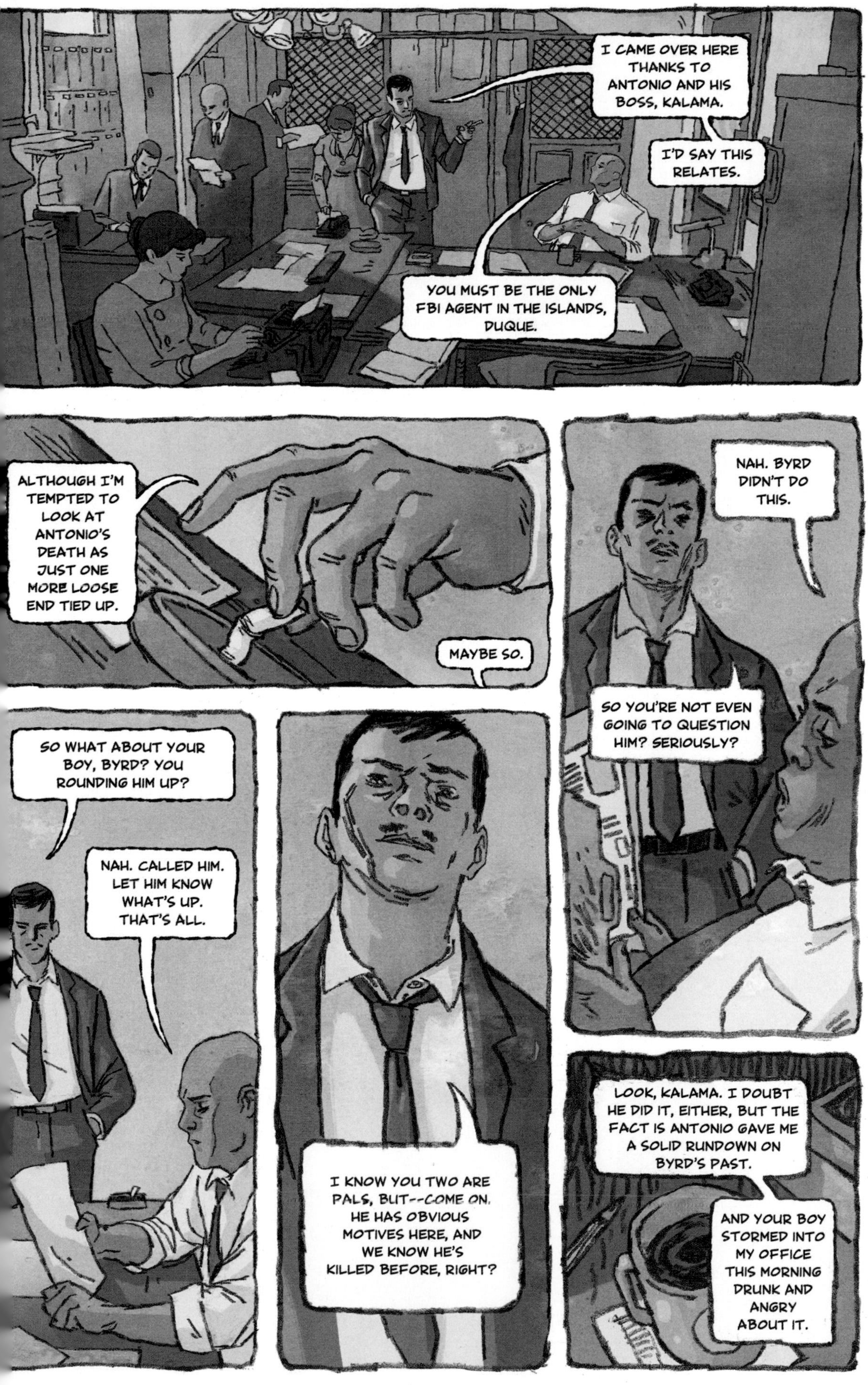
I CAME OVER HERE THANKS TO ANTONIO AND HIS BOSS, KALAMA.
I'D SAY THIS RELATES.
YOU MUST BE THE ONLY FBI AGENT IN THE ISLANDS, DUQUE.
ALTHOUGH I'M TEMPTED TO LOOK AT ANTONIO'S DEATH AS JUST ONE MORE LOOSE END TIED UP.
MAYBE SO.
NAH. BYRD DIDN'T DO THIS.
SO YOU'RE NOT EVEN GOING TO QUESTION HIM? SERIOUSLY?
SO WHAT ABOUT YOUR BOY, BYRD? YOU ROUNDING HIM UP?
NAH. CALLED HIM. LET HIM KNOW WHAT'S UP. THAT'S ALL.
I KNOW YOU TWO ARE PALS, BUT--COME ON. HE HAS OBVIOUS MOTIVES HERE, AND WE KNOW HE'S KILLED BEFORE, RIGHT?
LOOK, KALAMA. I DOUBT HE DID IT, EITHER, BUT THE FACT IS ANTONIO GAVE ME A SOLID RUNDOWN ON BYRD'S PAST.
AND YOUR BOY STORMED INTO MY OFFICE THIS MORNING DRUNK AND ANGRY ABOUT IT.

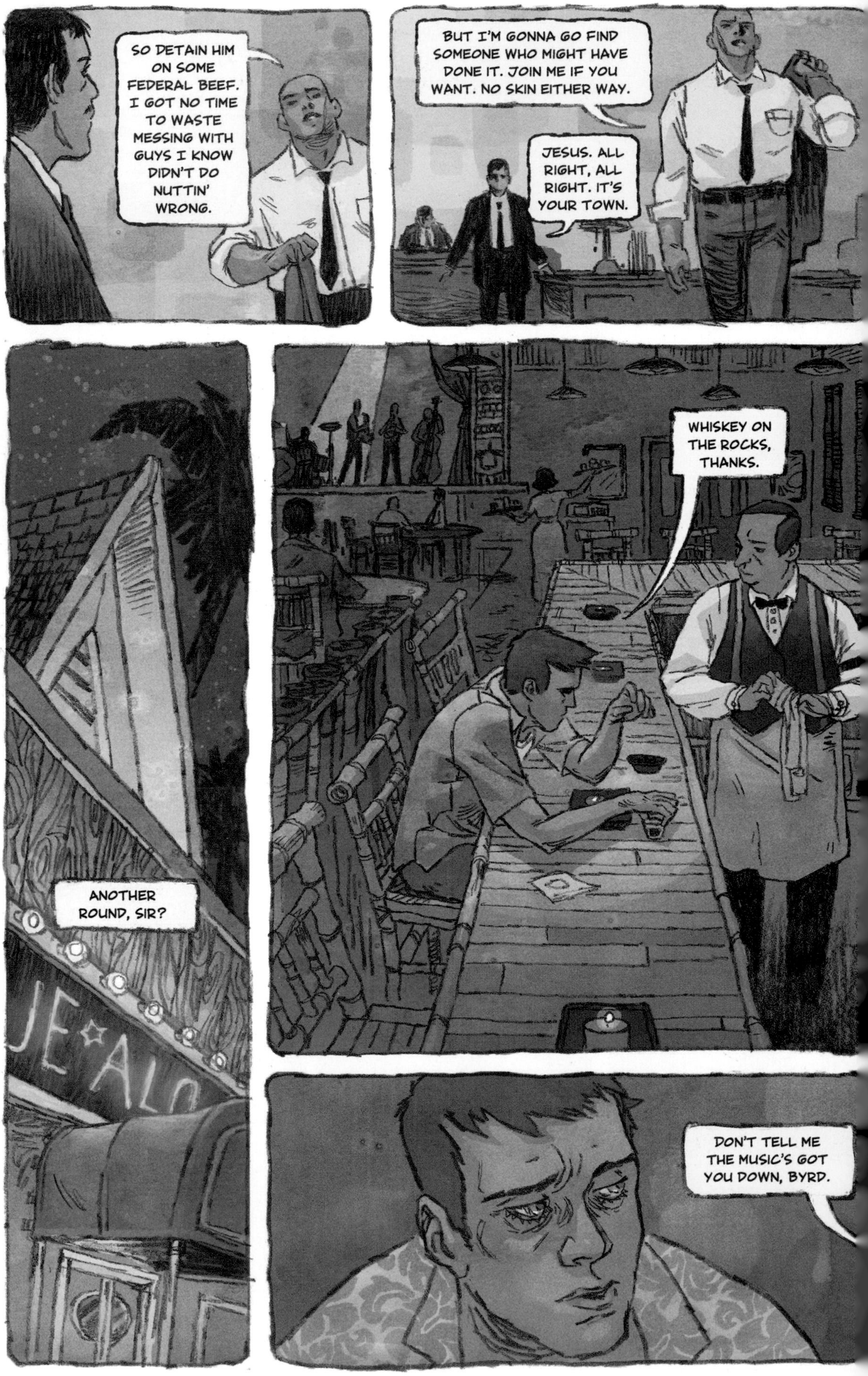
SO DETAIN HIM ON SOME FEDERAL BEEF. I GOT NO TIME TO WASTE MESSING WITH GUYS I KNOW DIDN'T DO NUTTIN' WRONG.
BUT I'M GONNA GO FIND SOMEONE WHO MIGHT HAVE DONE IT. JOIN ME IF YOU WANT. NO SKIN EITHER WAY.
JESUS. ALL RIGHT, ALL RIGHT. IT'S YOUR TOWN.
JE★ALO
ANOTHER ROUND, SIR?
WHISKEY ON THE ROCKS, THANKS.
DON'T TELL ME THE MUSIC'S GOT YOU DOWN, BYRD.

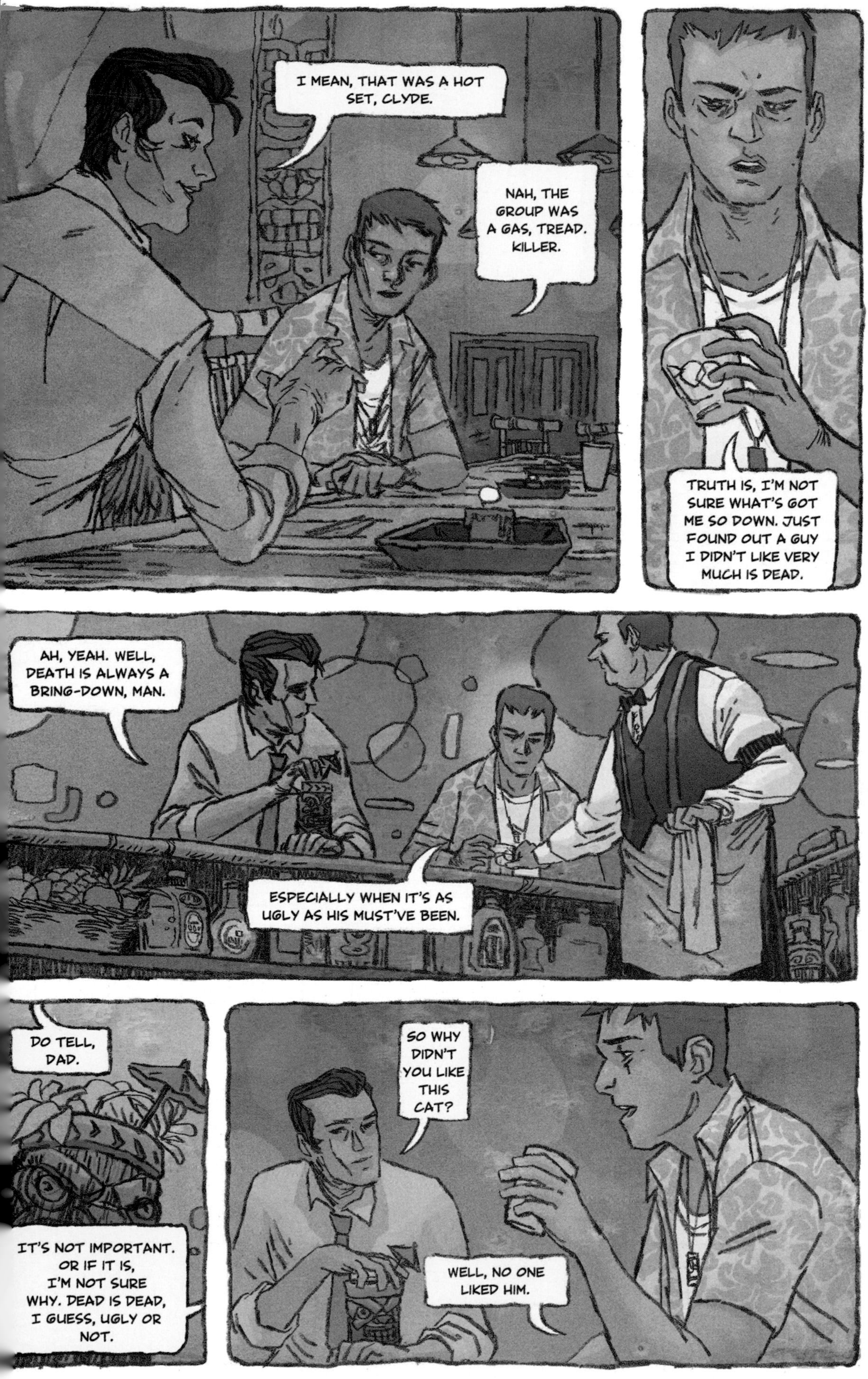
I MEAN, THAT WAS A HOT SET, CLYDE.
NAH, THE GROUP WAS A GAS, TREAD. KILLER.
TRUTH IS, I'M NOT SURE WHAT'S GOT ME SO DOWN. JUST FOUND OUT A GUY I DIDN'T LIKE VERY MUCH IS DEAD.
AH, YEAH. WELL, DEATH IS ALWAYS A BRING-DOWN, MAN.
ESPECIALLY WHEN IT'S AS UGLY AS HIS MUST'VE BEEN.
DO TELL, DAD.
IT'S NOT IMPORTANT. OR IF IT IS, I'M NOT SURE WHY. DEAD IS DEAD, I GUESS, UGLY OR NOT.
SO WHY DIDN'T YOU LIKE THIS CAT?
WELL, NO ONE LIKED HIM.

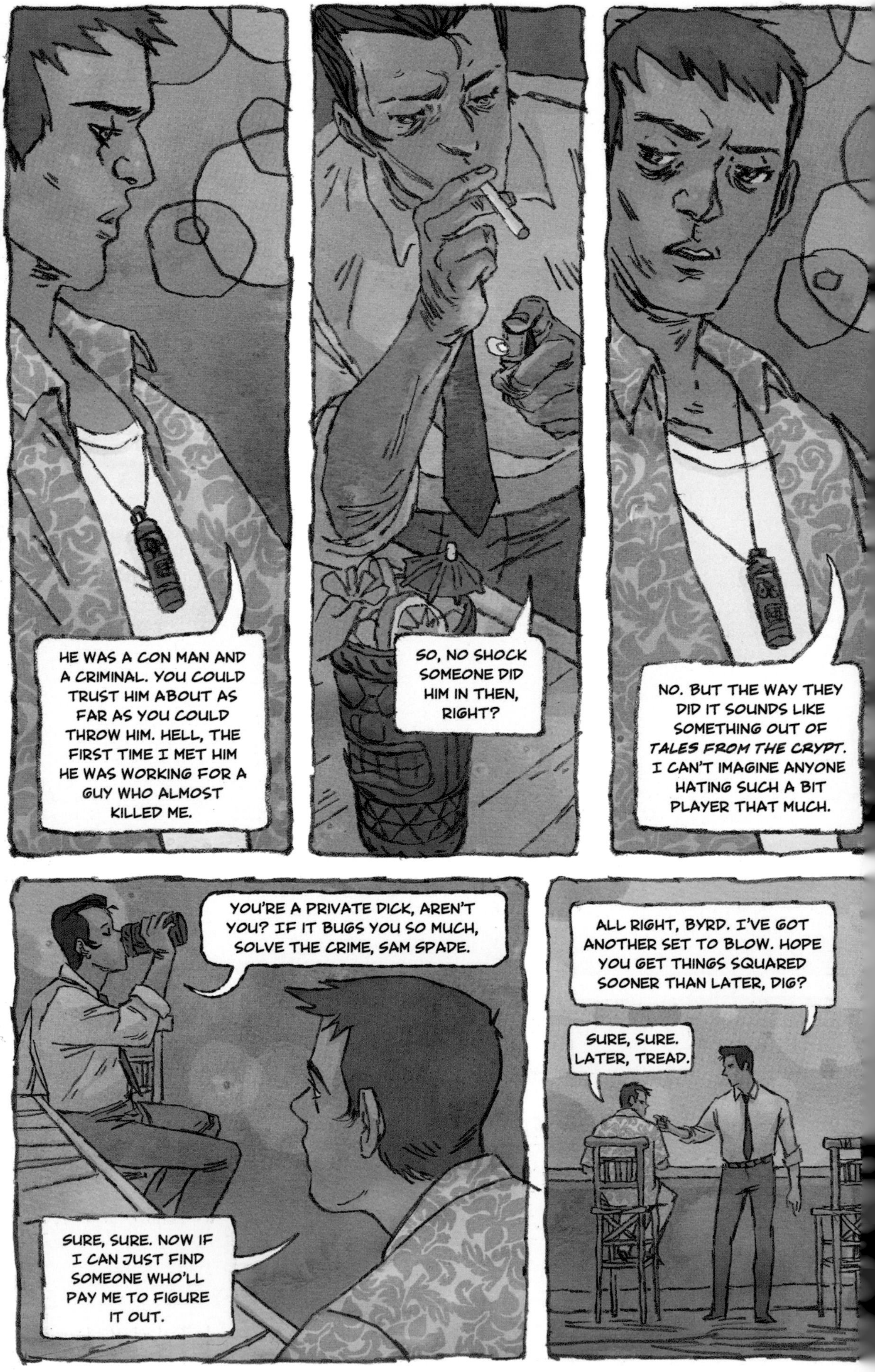
HE WAS A CON MAN AND A CRIMINAL. YOU COULD TRUST HIM ABOUT AS FAR AS YOU COULD THROW HIM. HELL, THE FIRST TIME I MET HIM HE WAS WORKING FOR A GUY WHO ALMOST KILLED ME.
SO, NO SHOCK SOMEONE DID HIM IN THEN, RIGHT?
NO. BUT THE WAY THEY DID IT SOUNDS LIKE SOMETHING OUT OF *TALES FROM THE CRYPT*. I CAN'T IMAGINE ANYONE HATING SUCH A BIT PLAYER THAT MUCH.
YOU'RE A PRIVATE DICK, AREN'T YOU? IF IT BUGS YOU SO MUCH, SOLVE THE CRIME, SAM SPADE.
SURE, SURE. NOW IF I CAN JUST FIND SOMEONE WHO'LL PAY ME TO FIGURE IT OUT.
ALL RIGHT, BYRD. I'VE GOT ANOTHER SET TO BLOW. HOPE YOU GET THINGS SQUARED SOONER THAN LATER, DIG?
SURE, SURE. LATER, TREAD.

WHEN WAS THE LAST TIME YOU WORE THIS SHIRT?

...OT SINCE I ...AS ON THE ...ORCE BACK HOME.

...AREFUL, ...OU'RE ...NCHING ME.

ISLAND LIFE HASN'T DONE MUCH FOR YOUR NECKLINE.

YOU CLEAN UP PRETTY WELL, *HAOLE*.

I'M NOT EVEN SURE WHY WE'RE DOING THIS. YOU THINK THAT GUY WOULD HAVE BLINKED IF I'D BEEN SHOT BACK AT THE SANDS?

SHUSH, BYRD. HAVE SOME RESPECT FOR THE DEAD, KAY? HE DID ME A FAVOR ONCE, AND THE THOUGHT OF HIM BEING BURIED ALONE MAKES ME SAD.

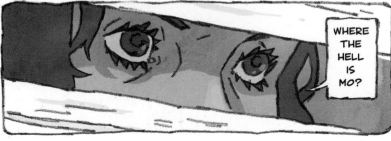

WHERE THE HELL IS MO?

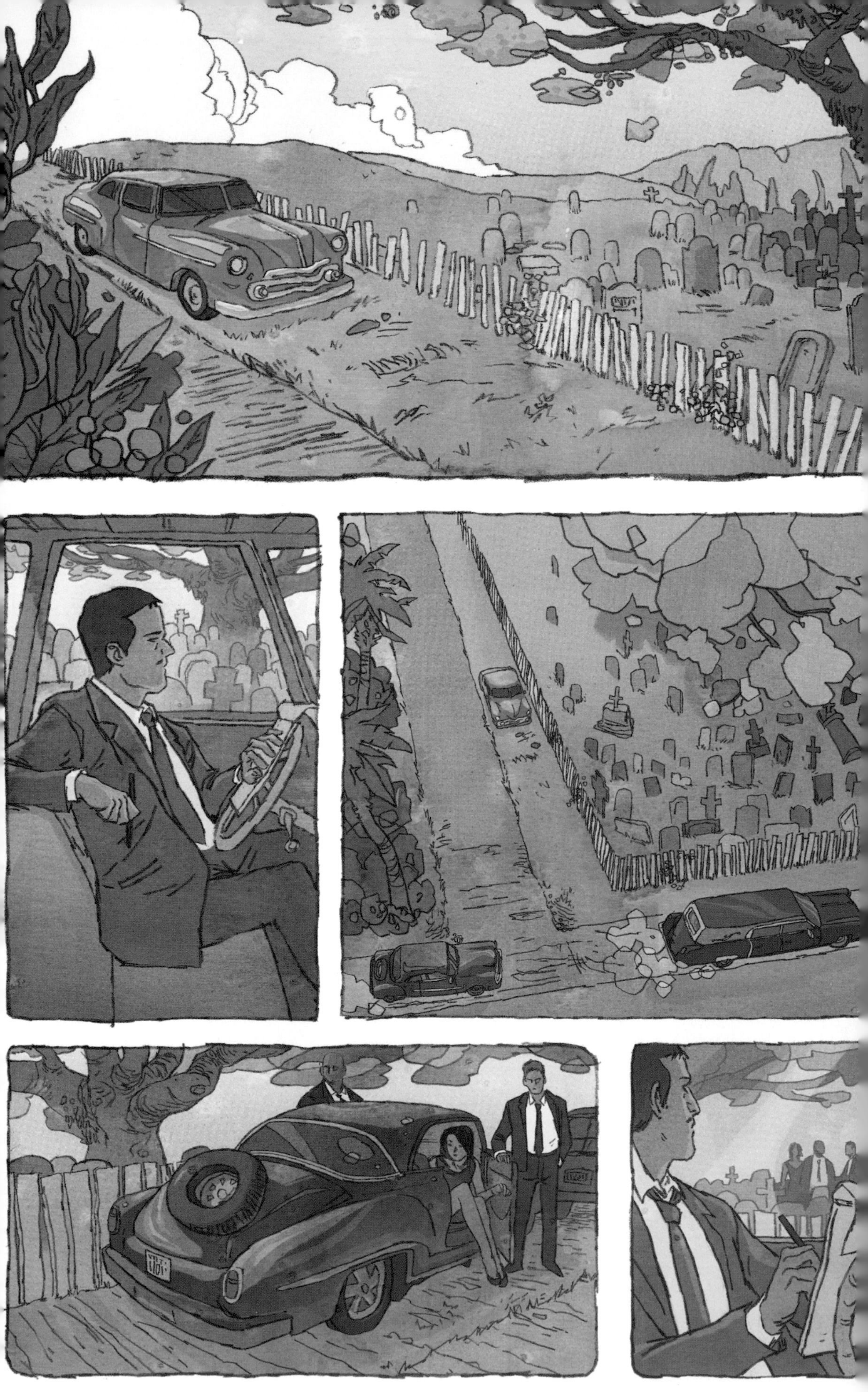

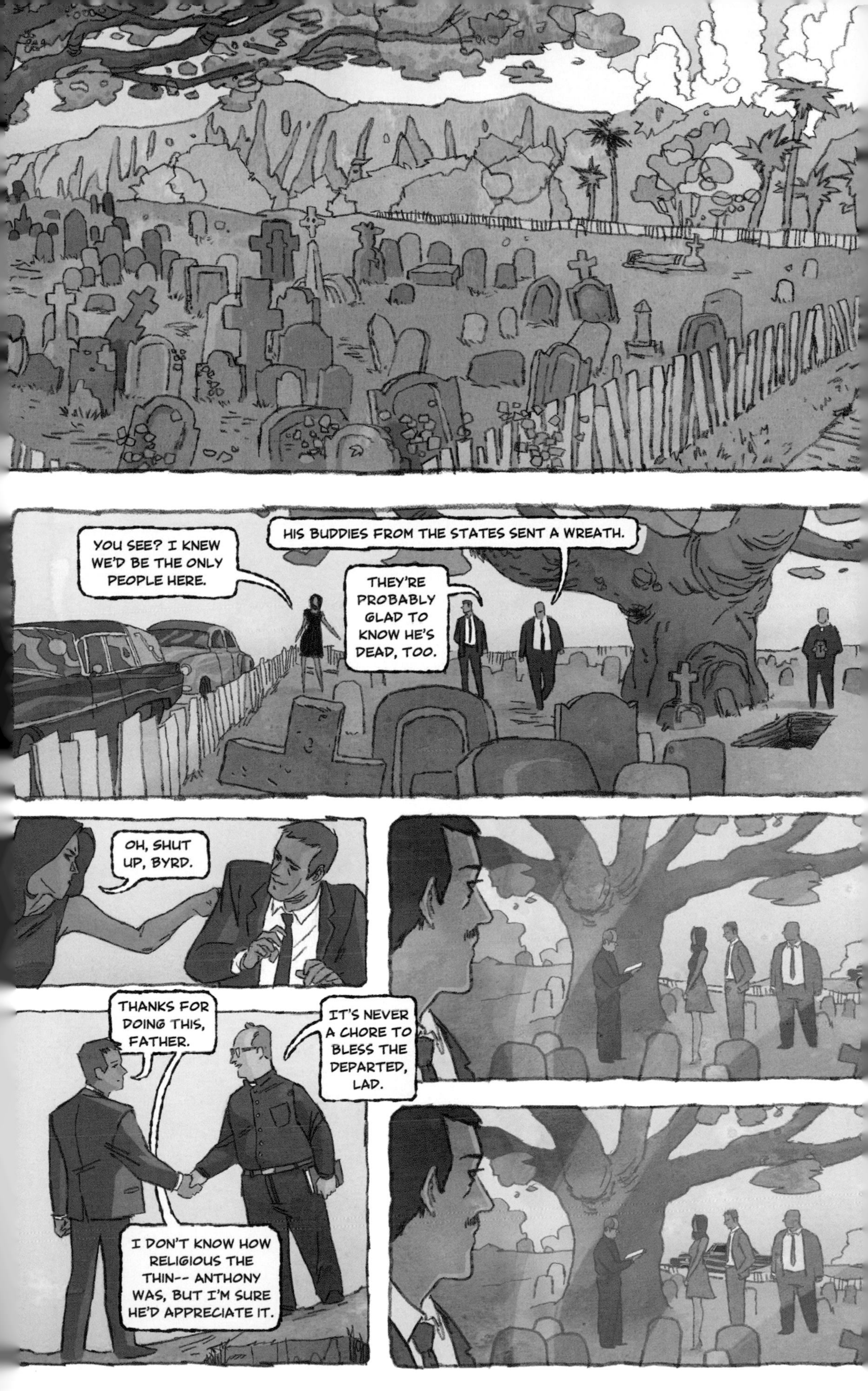
YOU SEE? I KNEW WE'D BE THE ONLY PEOPLE HERE.
HIS BUDDIES FROM THE STATES SENT A WREATH.
THEY'RE PROBABLY GLAD TO KNOW HE'S DEAD, TOO.
OH, SHUT UP, BYRD.
THANKS FOR DOING THIS, FATHER.
I DON'T KNOW HOW RELIGIOUS THE THIN-- ANTHONY WAS, BUT I'M SURE HE'D APPRECIATE IT.
IT'S NEVER A CHORE TO BLESS THE DEPARTED, LAD.

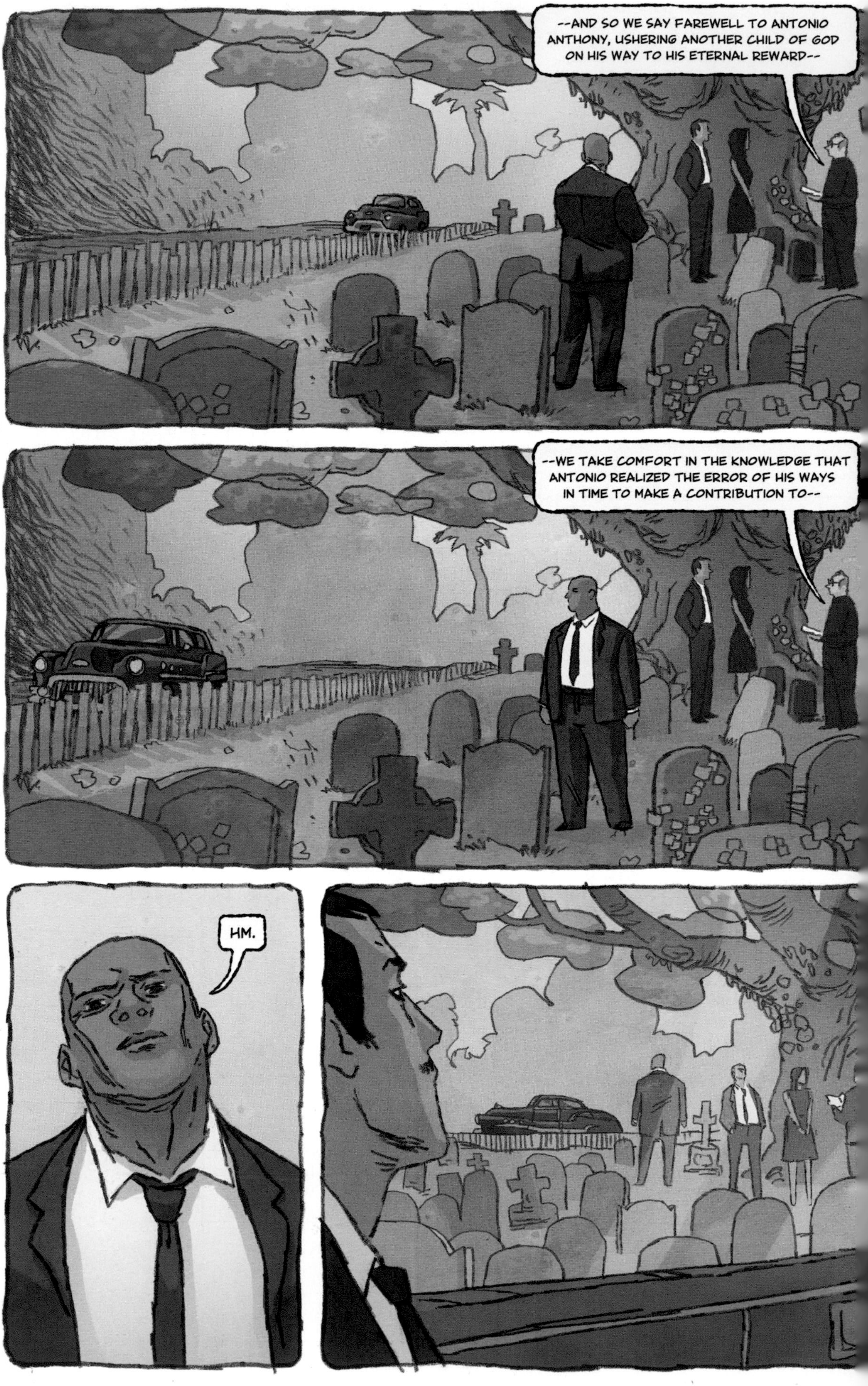
--AND SO WE SAY FAREWELL TO ANTONIO ANTHONY, USHERING ANOTHER CHILD OF GOD ON HIS WAY TO HIS ETERNAL REWARD--
--WE TAKE COMFORT IN THE KNOWLEDGE THAT ANTONIO REALIZED THE ERROR OF HIS WAYS IN TIME TO MAKE A CONTRIBUTION TO--
HM.

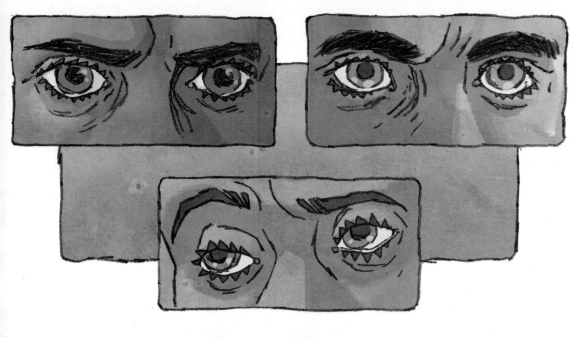

DIDN'T LIKE THE WAY THAT BIG COP WAS LOOKING AT US, BOSS. THOUGHT IT WAS KIND OF RISKY SHOWING UP HERE.

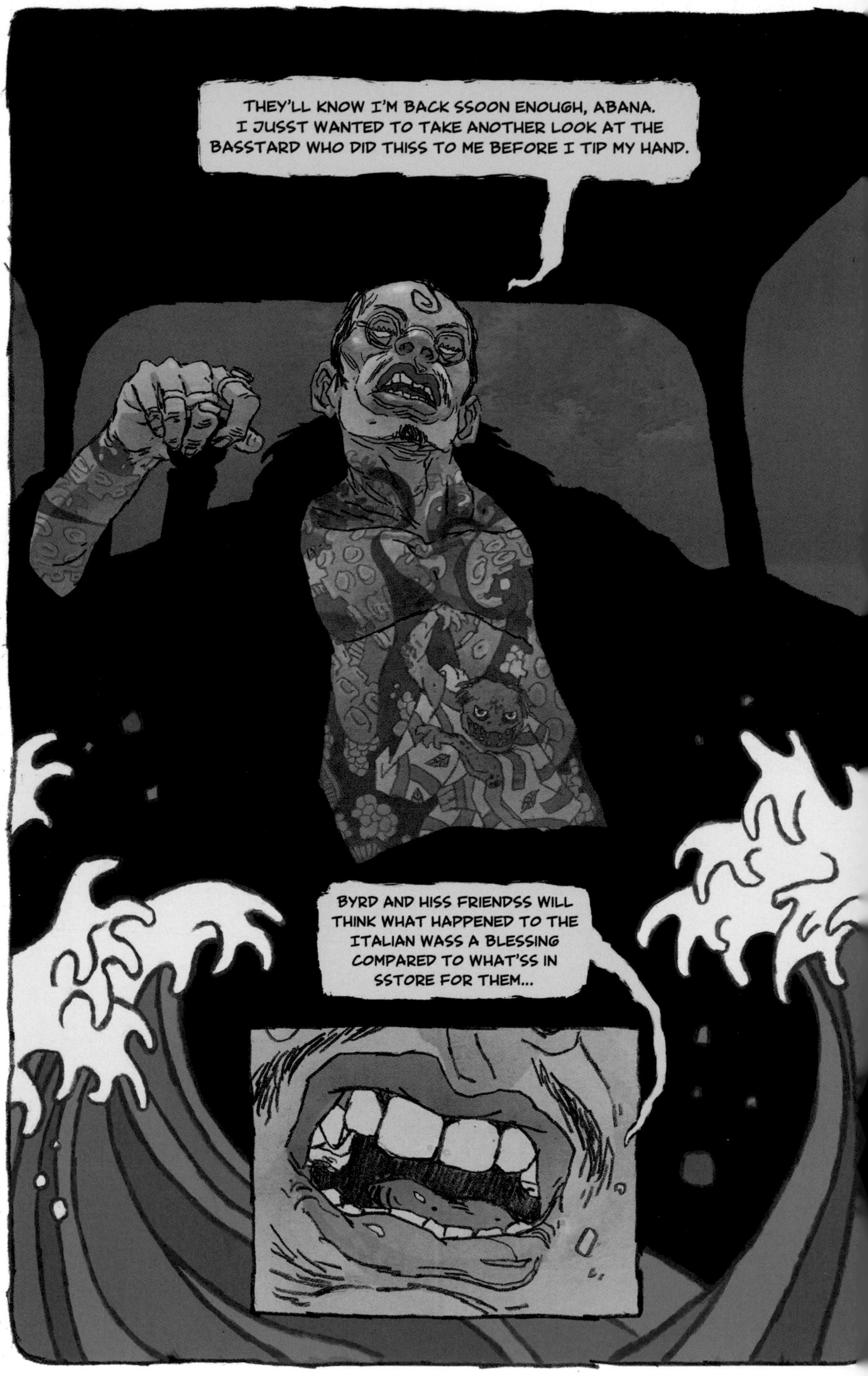
THEY'LL KNOW I'M BACK SSOON ENOUGH, ABANA. I JUSST WANTED TO TAKE ANOTHER LOOK AT THE BASSTARD WHO DID THISS TO ME BEFORE I TIP MY HAND.
BYRD AND HISS FRIENDSS WILL THINK WHAT HAPPENED TO THE ITALIAN WASS A BLESSING COMPARED TO WHAT'SS IN SSTORE FOR THEM...

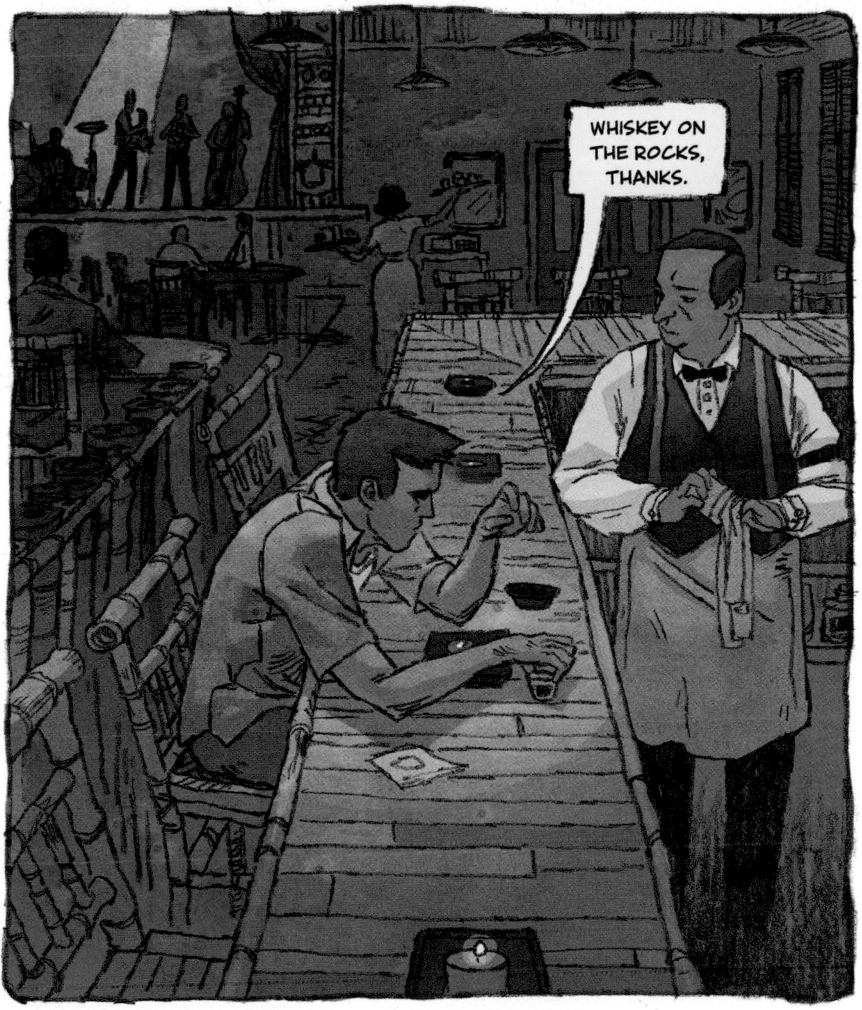
WHISKEY ON THE ROCKS, THANKS.

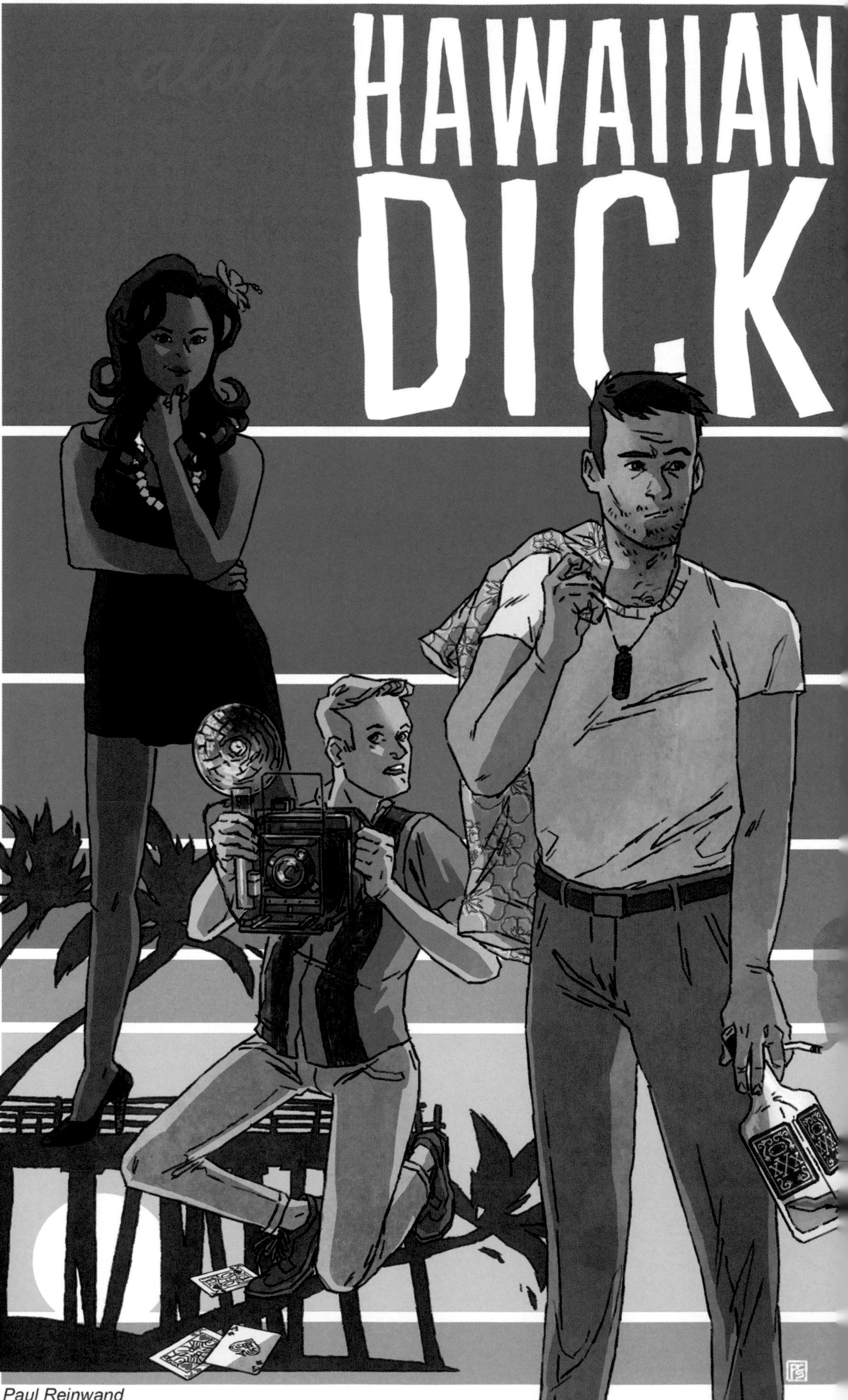
HAWAIIAN
DICK
Paul Reinwand

A BYRD OF PARADISE
MYSTERY

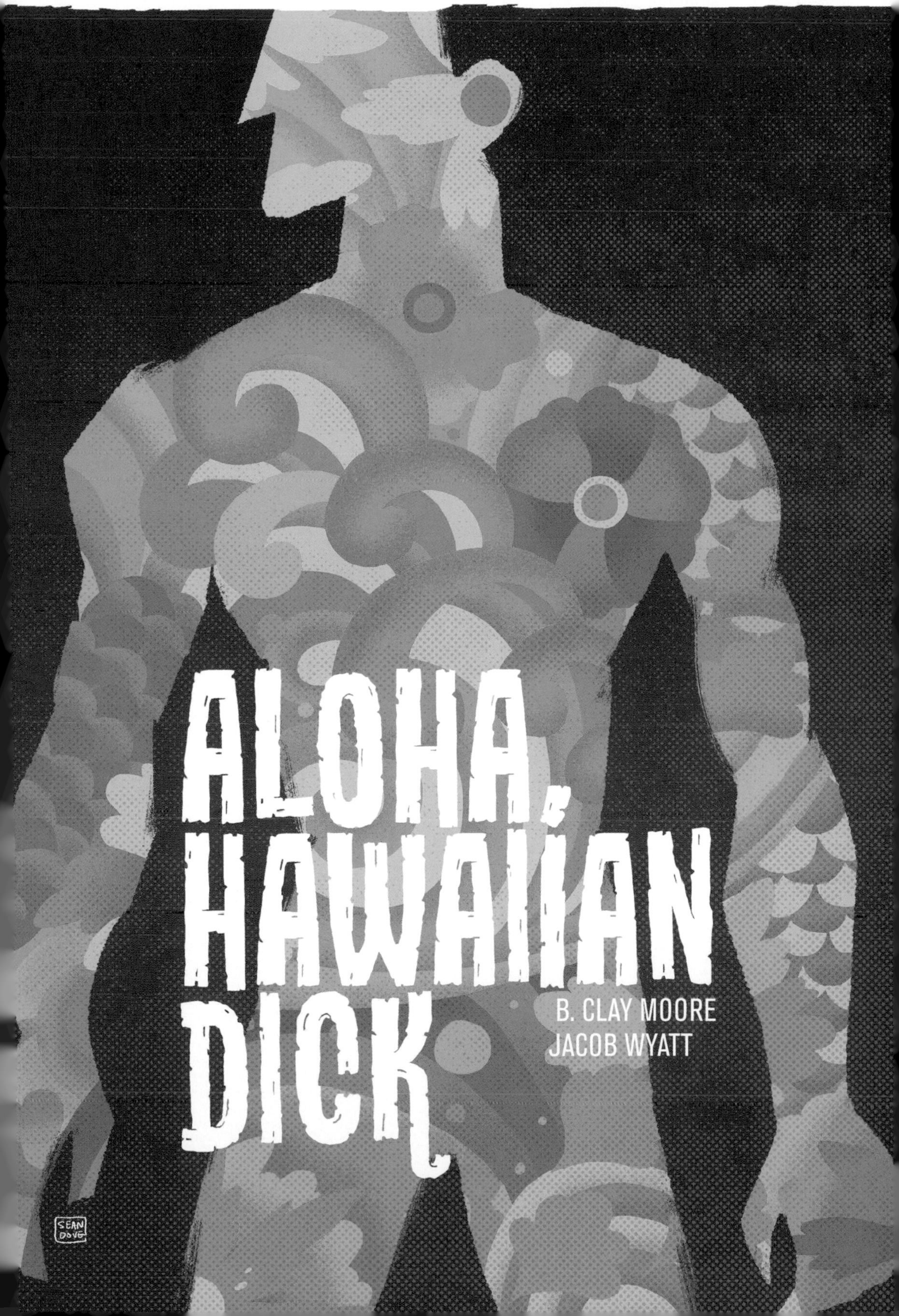
ALOHA,
HAWAIIAN
DICK
B. CLAY MOORE
JACOB WYATT
SEAN DOVE

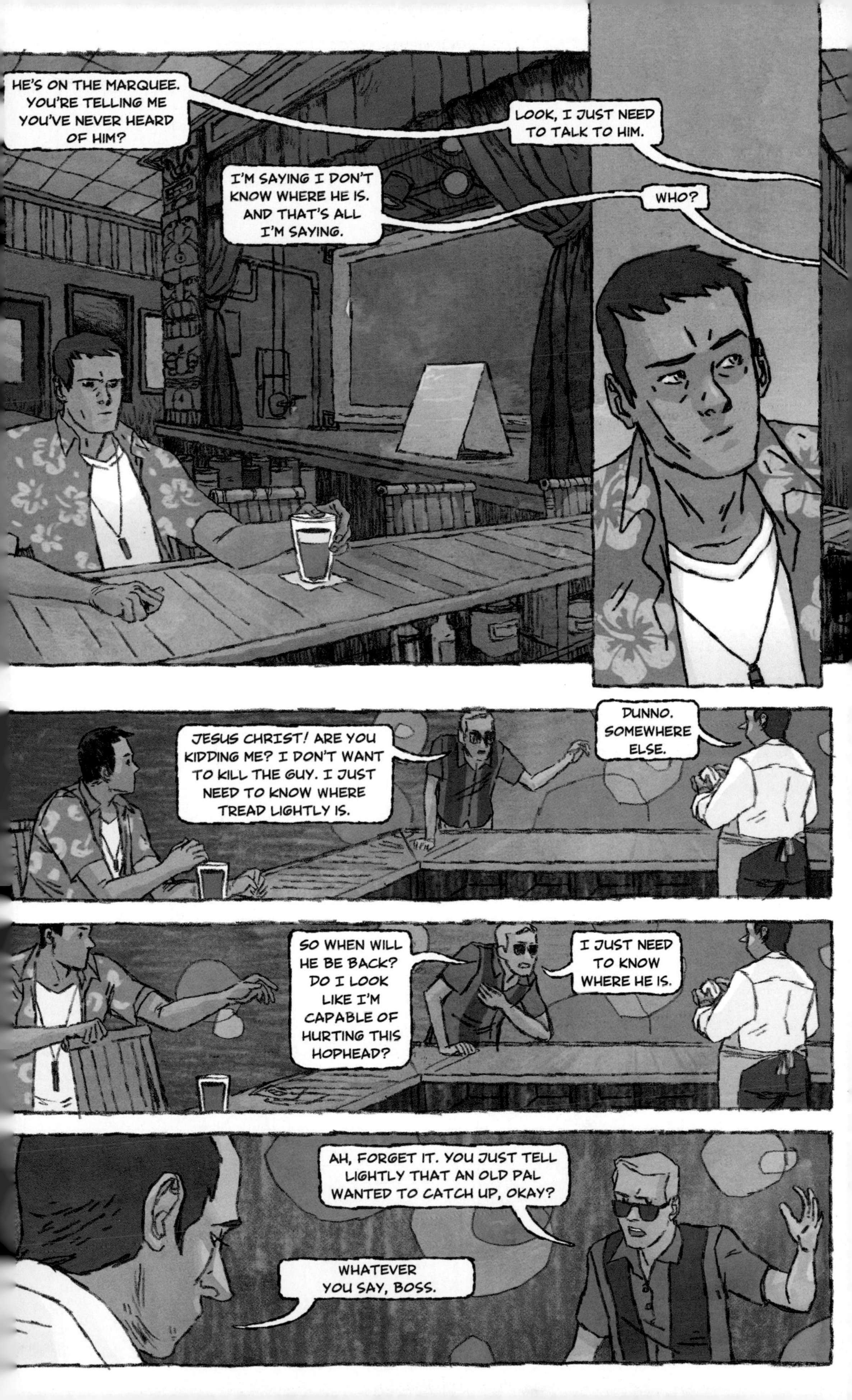
HE'S ON THE MARQUEE. YOU'RE TELLING ME YOU'VE NEVER HEARD OF HIM?
LOOK, I JUST NEED TO TALK TO HIM.
I'M SAYING I DON'T KNOW WHERE HE IS. AND THAT'S ALL I'M SAYING.
WHO?
JESUS CHRIST! ARE YOU KIDDING ME? I DON'T WANT TO KILL THE GUY. I JUST NEED TO KNOW WHERE TREAD LIGHTLY IS.
DUNNO. SOMEWHERE ELSE.
SO WHEN WILL HE BE BACK? DO I LOOK LIKE I'M CAPABLE OF HURTING THIS HOPHEAD?
I JUST NEED TO KNOW WHERE HE IS.
AH, FORGET IT. YOU JUST TELL LIGHTLY THAT AN OLD PAL WANTED TO CATCH UP, OKAY?
WHATEVER YOU SAY, BOSS.

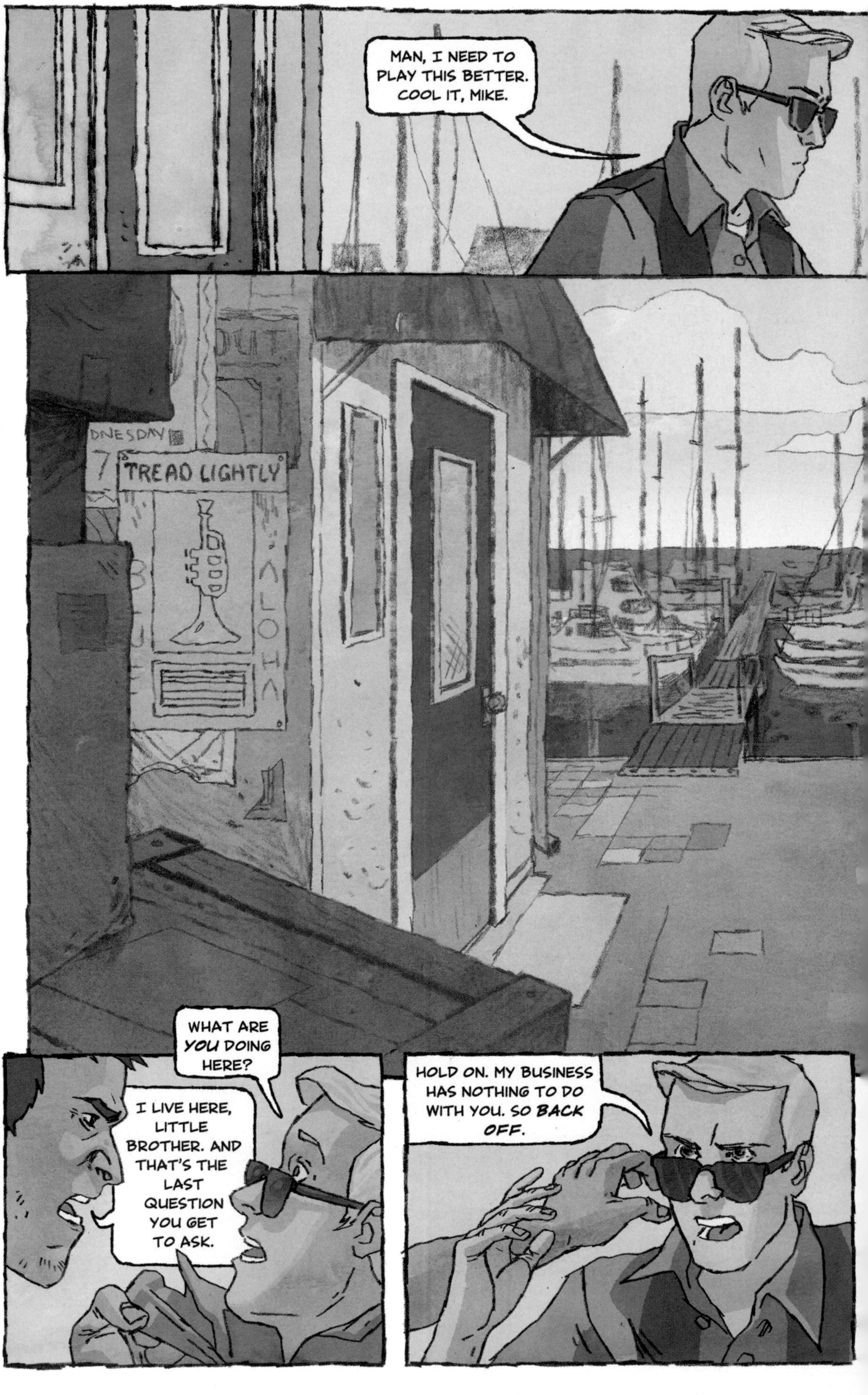
MAN, I NEED TO PLAY THIS BETTER. COOL IT, MIKE.
DNESDAY
7
TREAD LIGHTLY
ALOHA
WHAT ARE *YOU* DOING HERE?
I LIVE HERE, LITTLE BROTHER. AND THAT'S THE LAST QUESTION YOU GET TO ASK.
HOLD ON. MY BUSINESS HAS NOTHING TO DO WITH YOU. SO ***BACK OFF***.

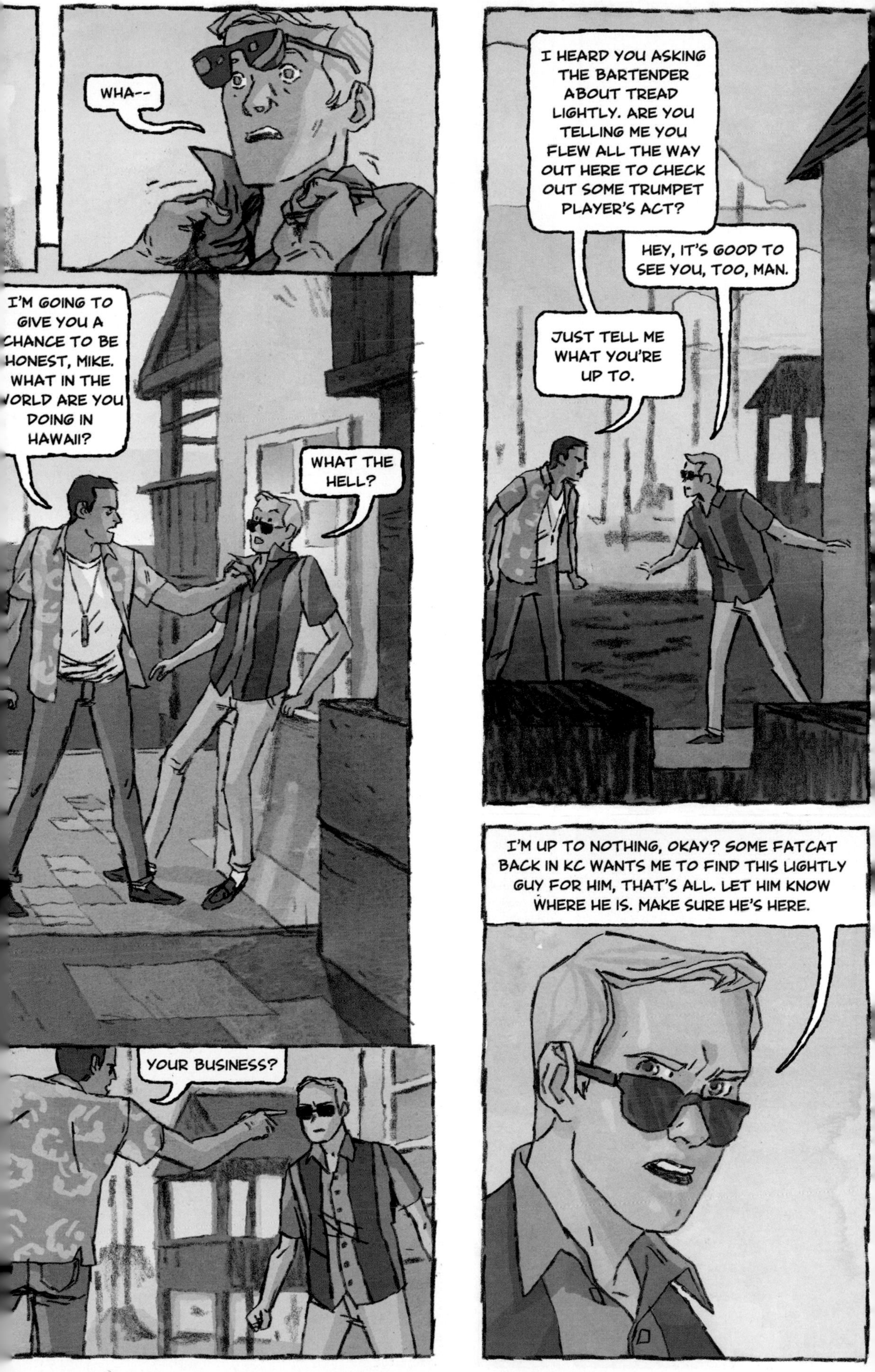
WHA--
I'M GOING TO GIVE YOU A CHANCE TO BE HONEST, MIKE. WHAT IN THE WORLD ARE YOU DOING IN HAWAII?
WHAT THE HELL?
YOUR BUSINESS?
I HEARD YOU ASKING THE BARTENDER ABOUT TREAD LIGHTLY. ARE YOU TELLING ME YOU FLEW ALL THE WAY OUT HERE TO CHECK OUT SOME TRUMPET PLAYER'S ACT?
HEY, IT'S GOOD TO SEE YOU, TOO, MAN.
JUST TELL ME WHAT YOU'RE UP TO.
I'M UP TO NOTHING, OKAY? SOME FATCAT BACK IN KC WANTS ME TO FIND THIS LIGHTLY GUY FOR HIM, THAT'S ALL. LET HIM KNOW WHERE HE IS. MAKE SURE HE'S HERE.

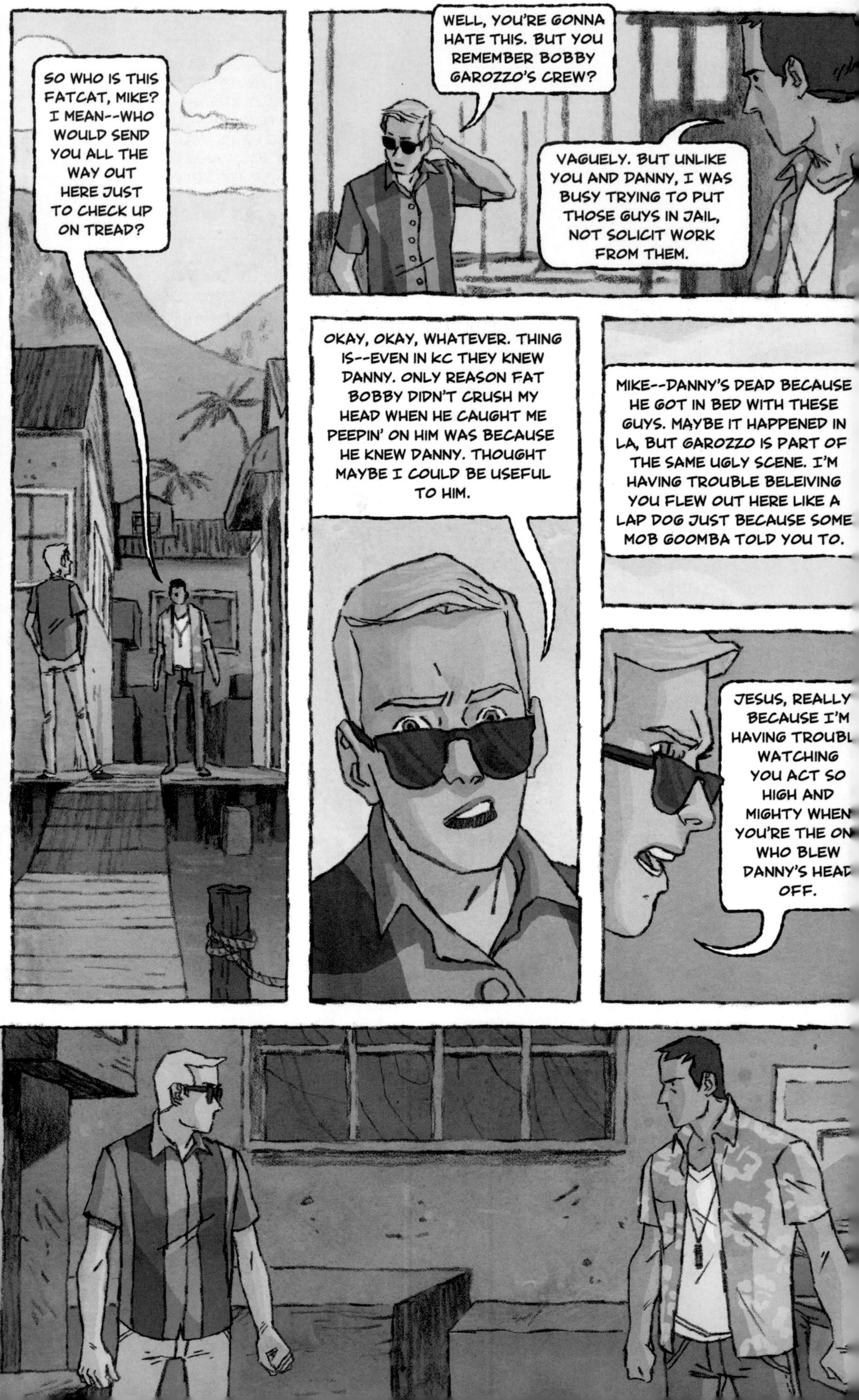
SO WHO IS THIS FATCAT, MIKE? I MEAN--WHO WOULD SEND YOU ALL THE WAY OUT HERE JUST TO CHECK UP ON TREAD?
WELL, YOU'RE GONNA HATE THIS. BUT YOU REMEMBER BOBBY GAROZZO'S CREW?
VAGUELY. BUT UNLIKE YOU AND DANNY, I WAS BUSY TRYING TO PUT THOSE GUYS IN JAIL, NOT SOLICIT WORK FROM THEM.
OKAY, OKAY, WHATEVER. THING IS--EVEN IN KC THEY KNEW DANNY. ONLY REASON FAT BOBBY DIDN'T CRUSH MY HEAD WHEN HE CAUGHT ME PEEPIN' ON HIM WAS BECAUSE HE KNEW DANNY. THOUGHT MAYBE I COULD BE USEFUL TO HIM.
MIKE--DANNY'S DEAD BECAUSE HE GOT IN BED WITH THESE GUYS. MAYBE IT HAPPENED IN LA, BUT GAROZZO IS PART OF THE SAME UGLY SCENE. I'M HAVING TROUBLE BELEIVING YOU FLEW OUT HERE LIKE A LAP DOG JUST BECAUSE SOME MOB GOOMBA TOLD YOU TO.
JESUS, REALLY BECAUSE I'M HAVING TROUBL WATCHING YOU ACT SO HIGH AND MIGHTY WHEN YOU'RE THE ON WHO BLEW DANNY'S HEAD OFF.

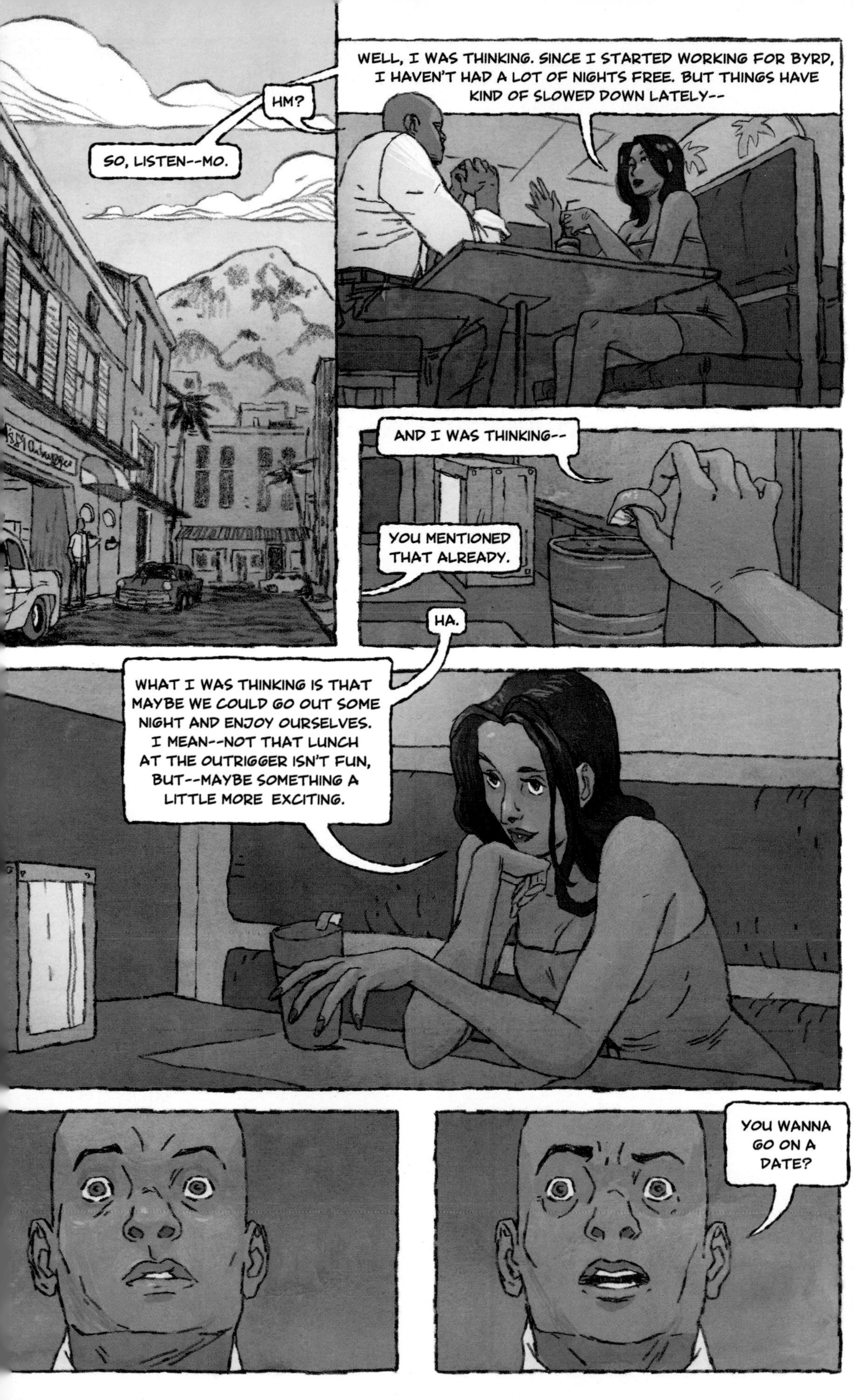
SO, LISTEN--MO.
HM?
WELL, I WAS THINKING. SINCE I STARTED WORKING FOR BYRD, I HAVEN'T HAD A LOT OF NIGHTS FREE. BUT THINGS HAVE KIND OF SLOWED DOWN LATELY--
AND I WAS THINKING--
YOU MENTIONED THAT ALREADY.
HA.
WHAT I WAS THINKING IS THAT MAYBE WE COULD GO OUT SOME NIGHT AND ENJOY OURSELVES. I MEAN--NOT THAT LUNCH AT THE OUTRIGGER ISN'T FUN, BUT--MAYBE SOMETHING A LITTLE MORE EXCITING.
YOU WANNA GO ON A DATE?

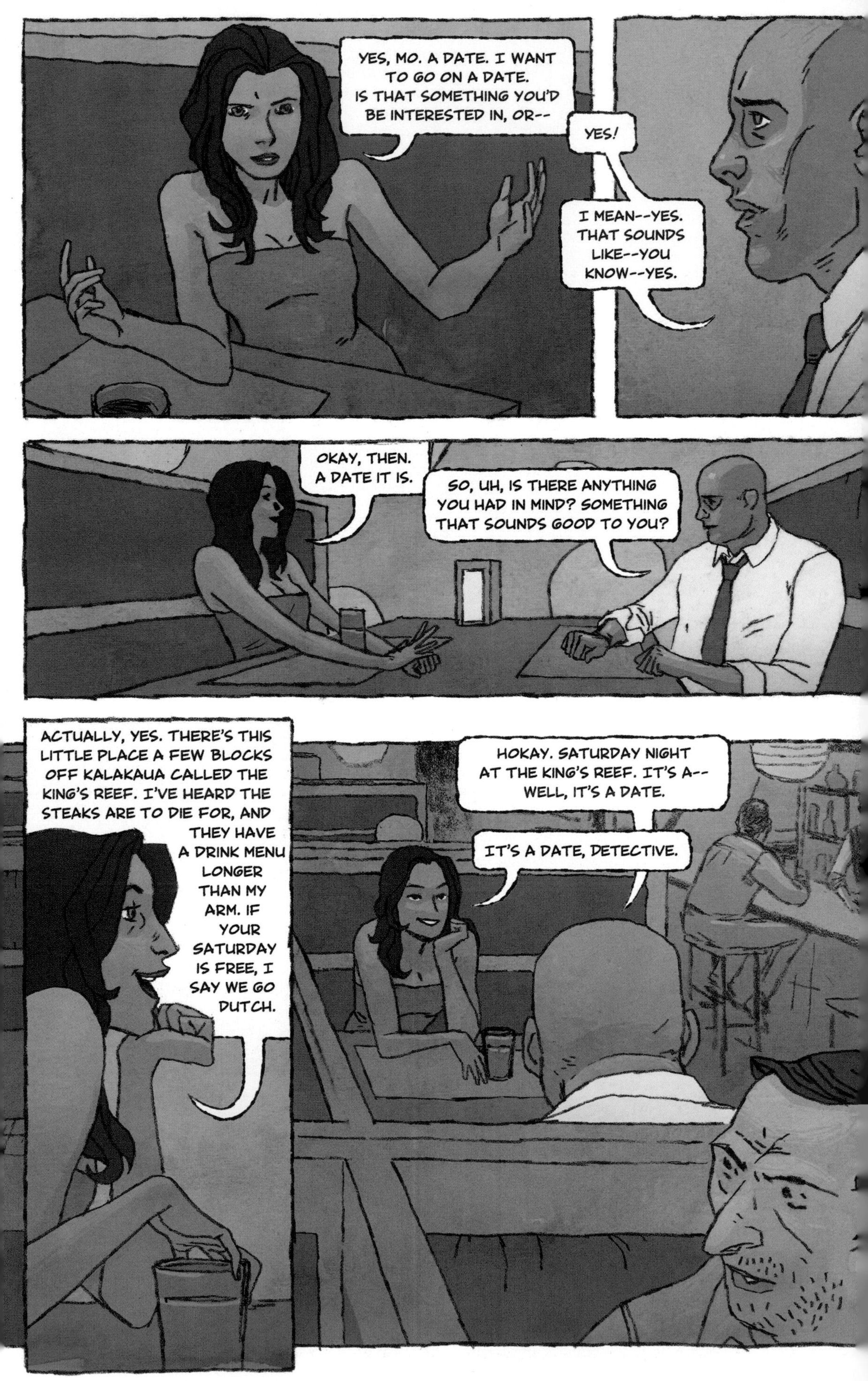
YES, MO. A DATE. I WANT TO GO ON A DATE. IS THAT SOMETHING YOU'D BE INTERESTED IN, OR--
YES!
I MEAN--YES. THAT SOUNDS LIKE--YOU KNOW--YES.
OKAY, THEN. A DATE IT IS.
SO, UH, IS THERE ANYTHING YOU HAD IN MIND? SOMETHING THAT SOUNDS GOOD TO YOU?
ACTUALLY, YES. THERE'S THIS LITTLE PLACE A FEW BLOCKS OFF KALAKAUA CALLED THE KING'S REEF. I'VE HEARD THE STEAKS ARE TO DIE FOR, AND THEY HAVE A DRINK MENU LONGER THAN MY ARM. IF YOUR SATURDAY IS FREE, I SAY WE GO DUTCH.
HOKAY. SATURDAY NIGHT AT THE KING'S REEF. IT'S A--WELL, IT'S A DATE.
IT'S A DATE, DETECTIVE.

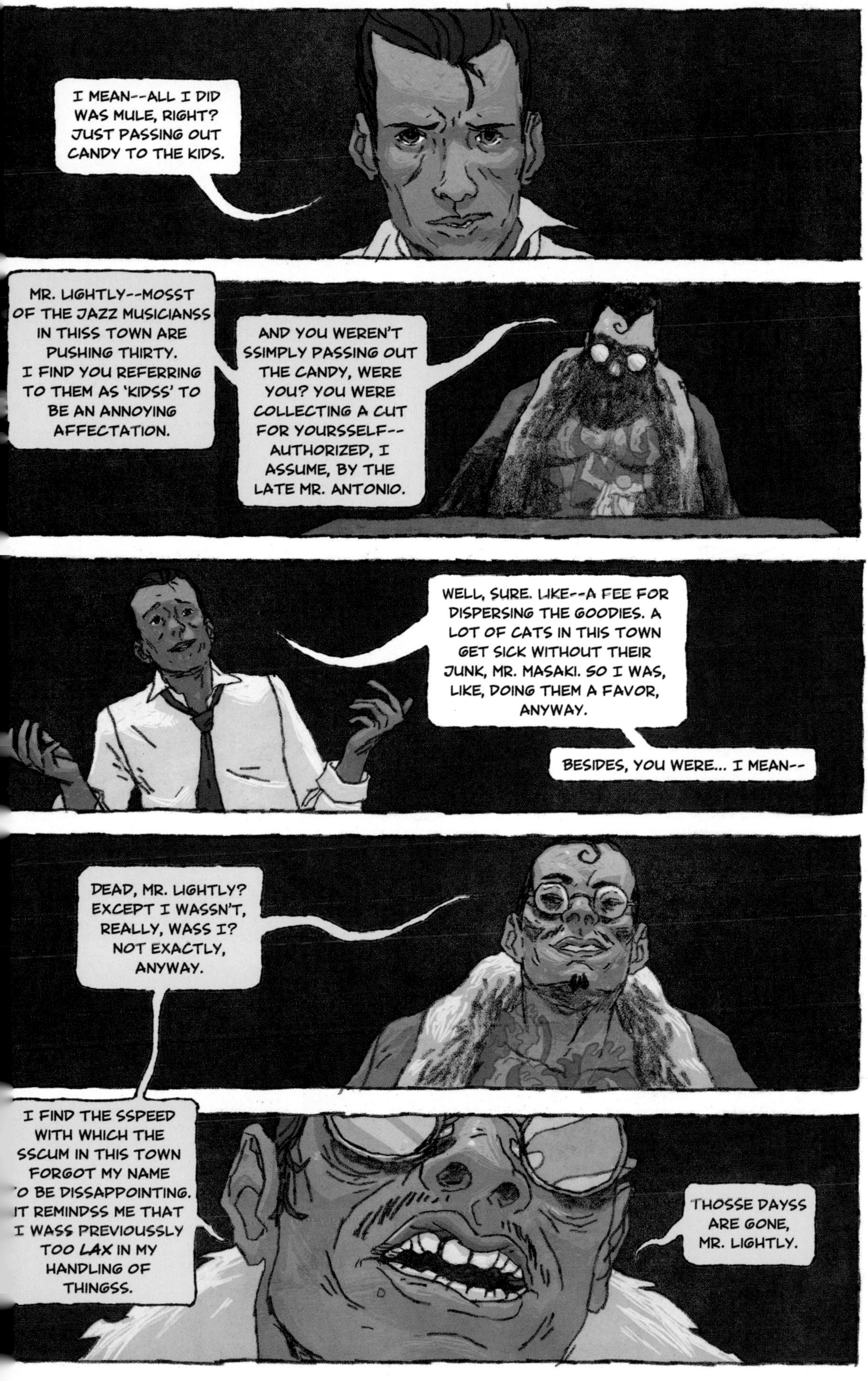
I MEAN--ALL I DID WAS MULE, RIGHT? JUST PASSING OUT CANDY TO THE KIDS.
MR. LIGHTLY--MOSST OF THE JAZZ MUSICIANSS IN THISS TOWN ARE PUSHING THIRTY. I FIND YOU REFERRING TO THEM AS 'KIDSS' TO BE AN ANNOYING AFFECTATION.
AND YOU WEREN'T SSIMPLY PASSING OUT THE CANDY, WERE YOU? YOU WERE COLLECTING A CUT FOR YOURSSELF--AUTHORIZED, I ASSUME, BY THE LATE MR. ANTONIO.
WELL, SURE. LIKE--A FEE FOR DISPERSING THE GOODIES. A LOT OF CATS IN THIS TOWN GET SICK WITHOUT THEIR JUNK, MR. MASAKI. SO I WAS, LIKE, DOING THEM A FAVOR, ANYWAY.
BESIDES, YOU WERE... I MEAN--
DEAD, MR. LIGHTLY? EXCEPT I WASSN'T, REALLY, WASS I? NOT EXACTLY, ANYWAY.
I FIND THE SSPEED WITH WHICH THE SSCUM IN THIS TOWN FORGOT MY NAME TO BE DISSAPPOINTING. IT REMINDSS ME THAT I WASS PREVIOUSSLY TOO *LAX* IN MY HANDLING OF THINGSS.
THOSSE DAYSS ARE GONE, MR. LIGHTLY.

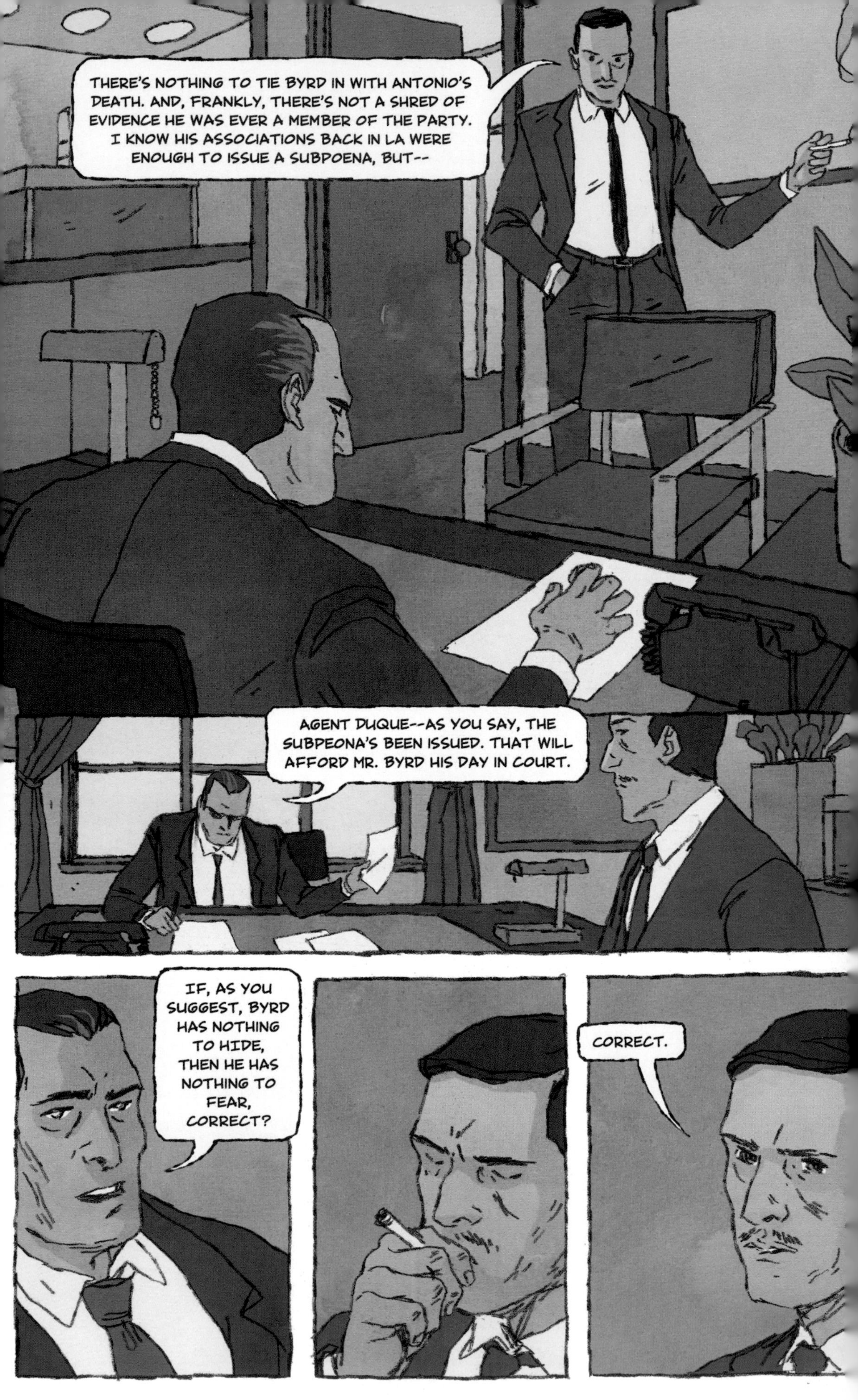
THERE'S NOTHING TO TIE BYRD IN WITH ANTONIO'S DEATH. AND, FRANKLY, THERE'S NOT A SHRED OF EVIDENCE HE WAS EVER A MEMBER OF THE PARTY. I KNOW HIS ASSOCIATIONS BACK IN LA WERE ENOUGH TO ISSUE A SUBPOENA, BUT--
AGENT DUQUE--AS YOU SAY, THE SUBPEONA'S BEEN ISSUED. THAT WILL AFFORD MR. BYRD HIS DAY IN COURT.
IF, AS YOU SUGGEST, BYRD HAS NOTHING TO HIDE, THEN HE HAS NOTHING TO FEAR, CORRECT?
CORRECT.

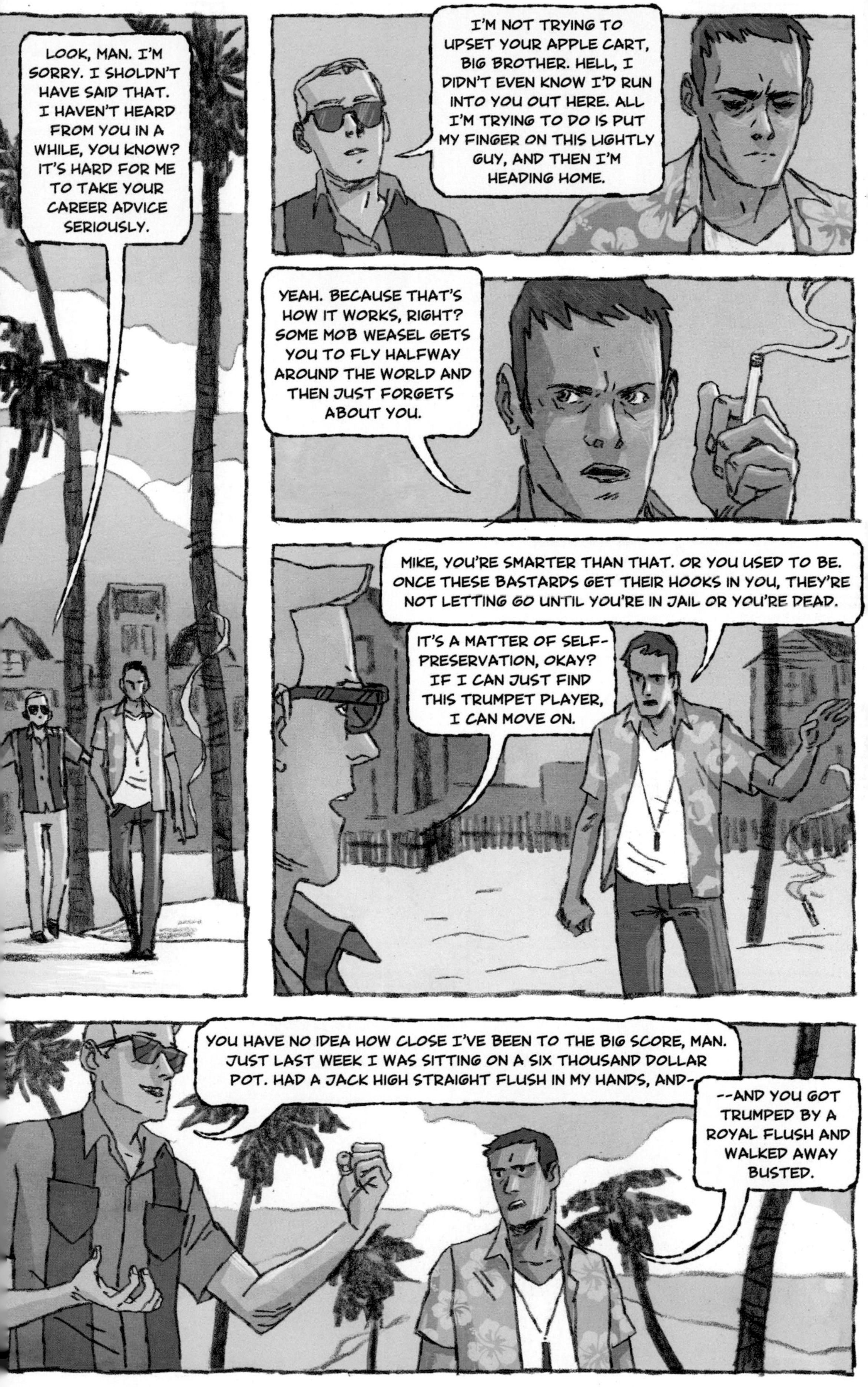
LOOK, MAN. I'M SORRY. I SHOLDN'T HAVE SAID THAT. I HAVEN'T HEARD FROM YOU IN A WHILE, YOU KNOW? IT'S HARD FOR ME TO TAKE YOUR CAREER ADVICE SERIOUSLY.
I'M NOT TRYING TO UPSET YOUR APPLE CART, BIG BROTHER. HELL, I DIDN'T EVEN KNOW I'D RUN INTO YOU OUT HERE. ALL I'M TRYING TO DO IS PUT MY FINGER ON THIS LIGHTLY GUY, AND THEN I'M HEADING HOME.
YEAH. BECAUSE THAT'S HOW IT WORKS, RIGHT? SOME MOB WEASEL GETS YOU TO FLY HALFWAY AROUND THE WORLD AND THEN JUST FORGETS ABOUT YOU.
MIKE, YOU'RE SMARTER THAN THAT. OR YOU USED TO BE. ONCE THESE BASTARDS GET THEIR HOOKS IN YOU, THEY'RE NOT LETTING GO UNTIL YOU'RE IN JAIL OR YOU'RE DEAD.
IT'S A MATTER OF SELF-PRESERVATION, OKAY? IF I CAN JUST FIND THIS TRUMPET PLAYER, I CAN MOVE ON.
YOU HAVE NO IDEA HOW CLOSE I'VE BEEN TO THE BIG SCORE, MAN. JUST LAST WEEK I WAS SITTING ON A SIX THOUSAND DOLLAR POT. HAD A JACK HIGH STRAIGHT FLUSH IN MY HANDS, AND--
--AND YOU GOT TRUMPED BY A ROYAL FLUSH AND WALKED AWAY BUSTED.

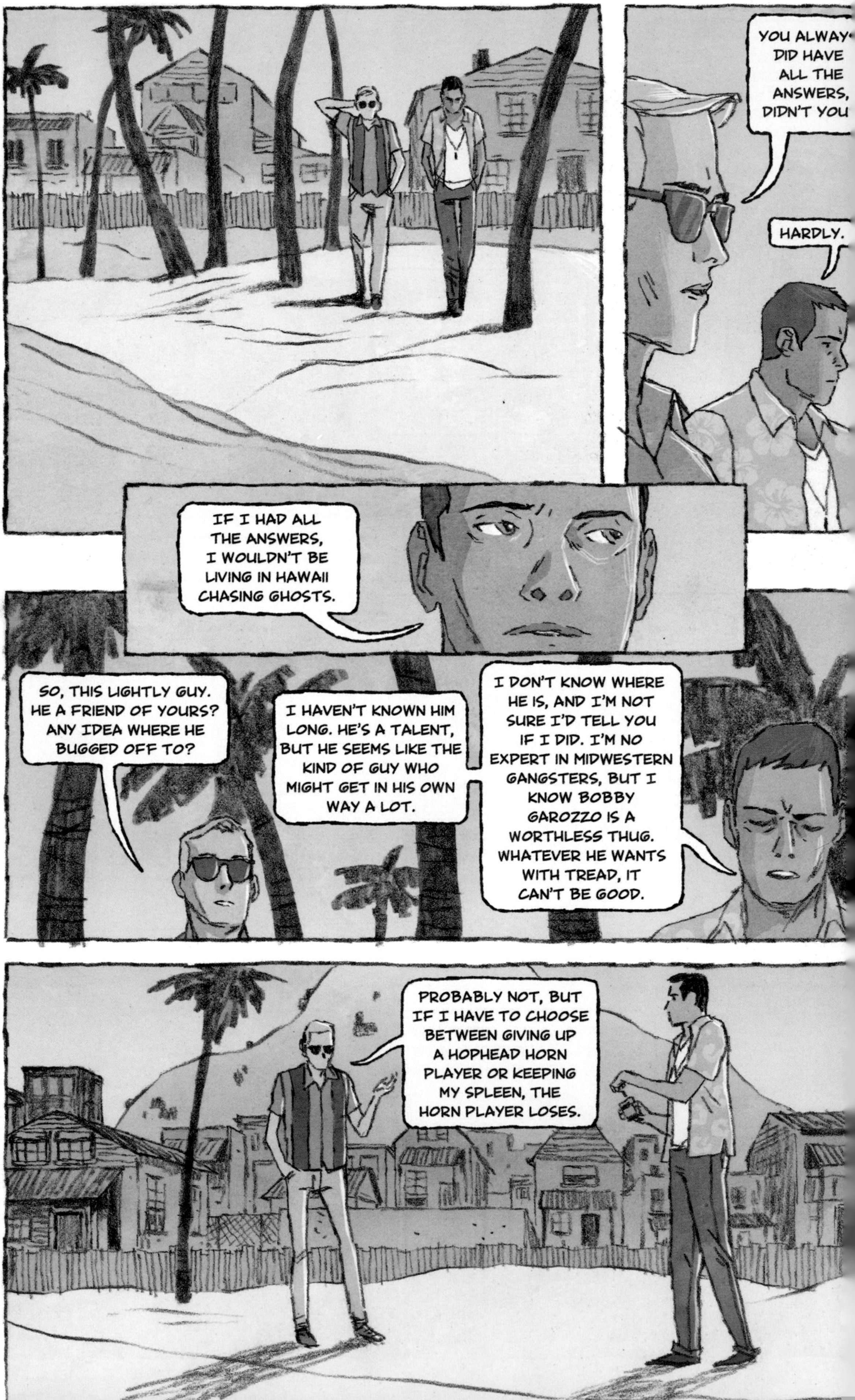
YOU ALWAYS DID HAVE ALL THE ANSWERS, DIDN'T YOU
HARDLY.
IF I HAD ALL THE ANSWERS, I WOULDN'T BE LIVING IN HAWAII CHASING GHOSTS.
SO, THIS LIGHTLY GUY. HE A FRIEND OF YOURS? ANY IDEA WHERE HE BUGGED OFF TO?
I HAVEN'T KNOWN HIM LONG. HE'S A TALENT, BUT HE SEEMS LIKE THE KIND OF GUY WHO MIGHT GET IN HIS OWN WAY A LOT.
I DON'T KNOW WHERE HE IS, AND I'M NOT SURE I'D TELL YOU IF I DID. I'M NO EXPERT IN MIDWESTERN GANGSTERS, BUT I KNOW BOBBY GAROZZO IS A WORTHLESS THUG. WHATEVER HE WANTS WITH TREAD, IT CAN'T BE GOOD.
PROBABLY NOT, BUT IF I HAVE TO CHOOSE BETWEEN GIVING UP A HOPHEAD HORN PLAYER OR KEEPING MY SPLEEN, THE HORN PLAYER LOSES.

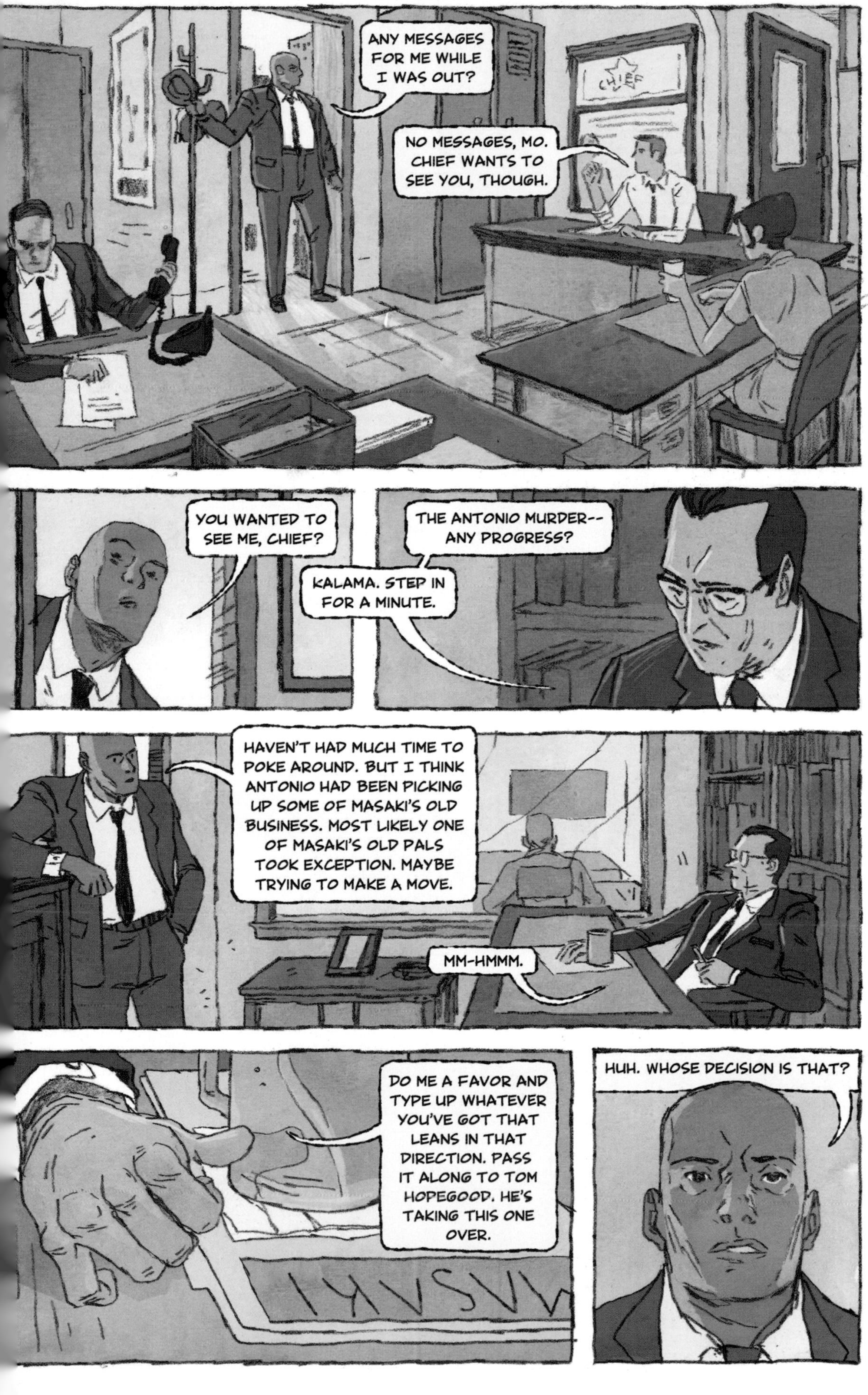
ANY MESSAGES FOR ME WHILE I WAS OUT?
CHIEF
NO MESSAGES, MO. CHIEF WANTS TO SEE YOU, THOUGH.
YOU WANTED TO SEE ME, CHIEF?
THE ANTONIO MURDER-- ANY PROGRESS?
KALAMA. STEP IN FOR A MINUTE.
HAVEN'T HAD MUCH TIME TO POKE AROUND. BUT I THINK ANTONIO HAD BEEN PICKING UP SOME OF MASAKI'S OLD BUSINESS. MOST LIKELY ONE OF MASAKI'S OLD PALS TOOK EXCEPTION. MAYBE TRYING TO MAKE A MOVE.
MM-HMMM.
DO ME A FAVOR AND TYPE UP WHATEVER YOU'VE GOT THAT LEANS IN THAT DIRECTION. PASS IT ALONG TO TOM HOPEGOOD. HE'S TAKING THIS ONE OVER.
HUH. WHOSE DECISION IS THAT?

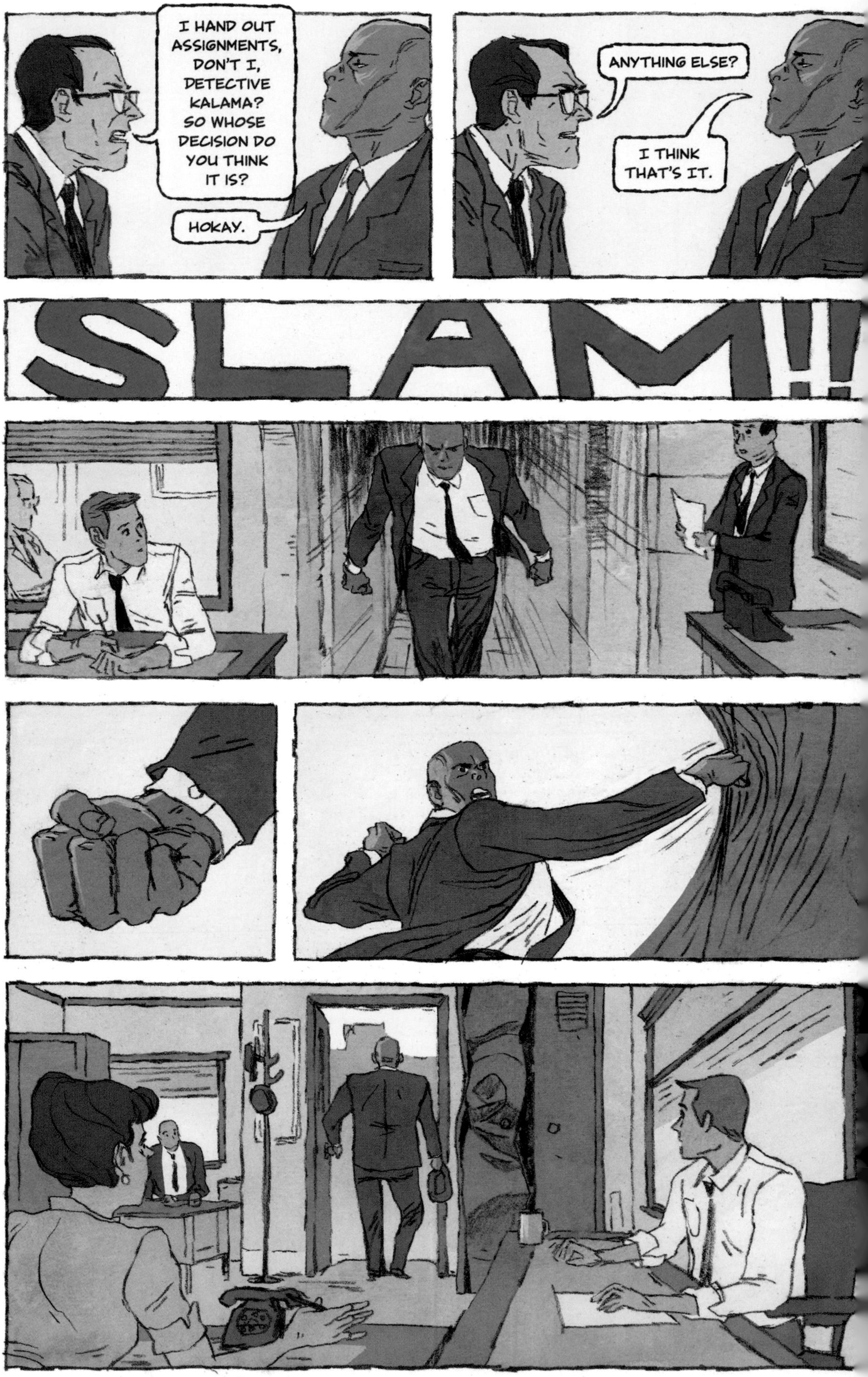
I HAND OUT ASSIGNMENTS, DON'T I, DETECTIVE KALAMA? SO WHOSE DECISION DO YOU THINK IT IS?
HOKAY.
ANYTHING ELSE?
I THINK THAT'S IT.
SLAM!!

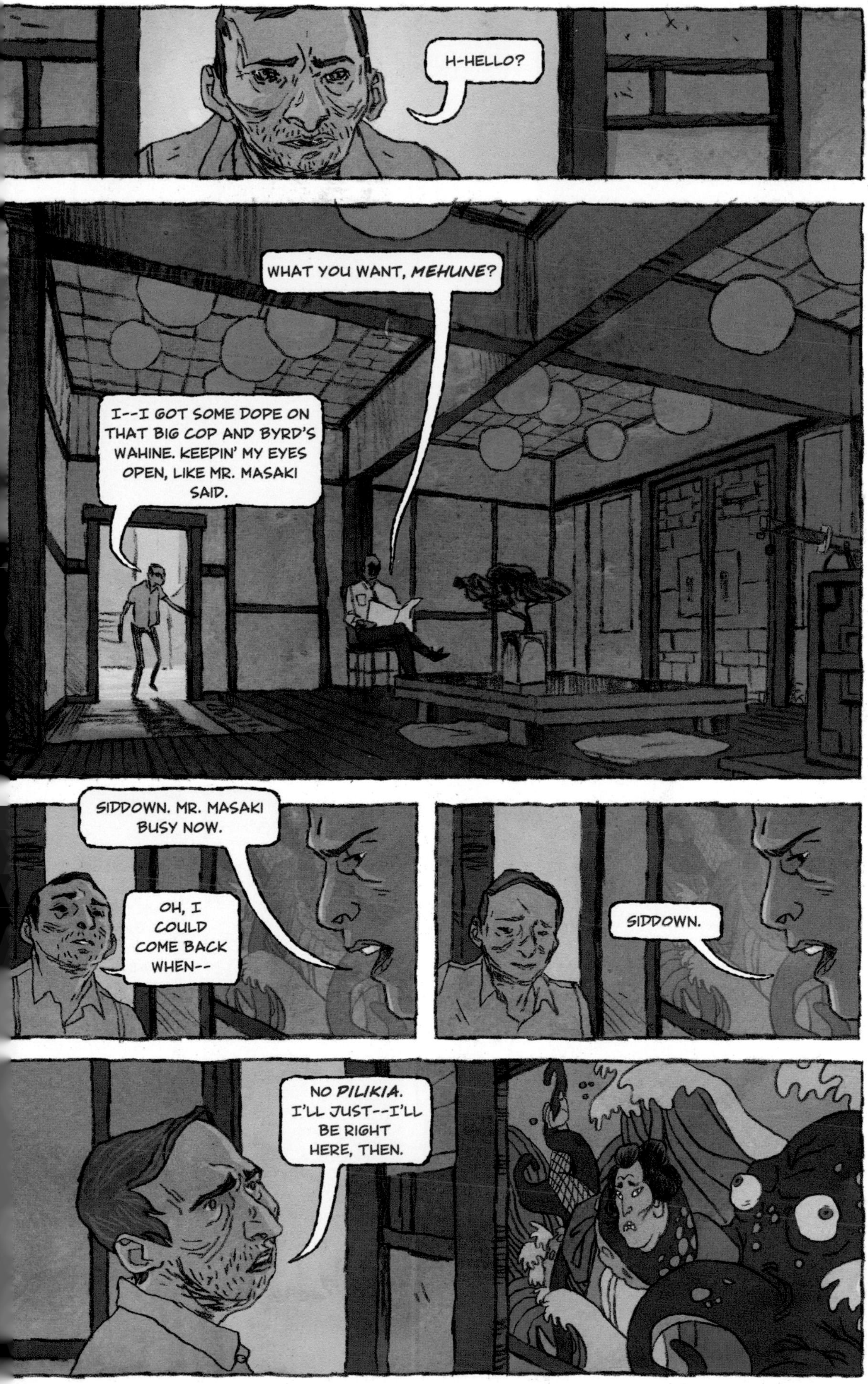
H-HELLO?
WHAT YOU WANT, *MEHUNE*?
I--I GOT SOME DOPE ON THAT BIG COP AND BYRD'S WAHINE. KEEPIN' MY EYES OPEN, LIKE MR. MASAKI SAID.
SIDDOWN. MR. MASAKI BUSY NOW.
OH, I COULD COME BACK WHEN--
SIDDOWN.
NO *PILIKIA*. I'LL JUST--I'LL BE RIGHT HERE, THEN.

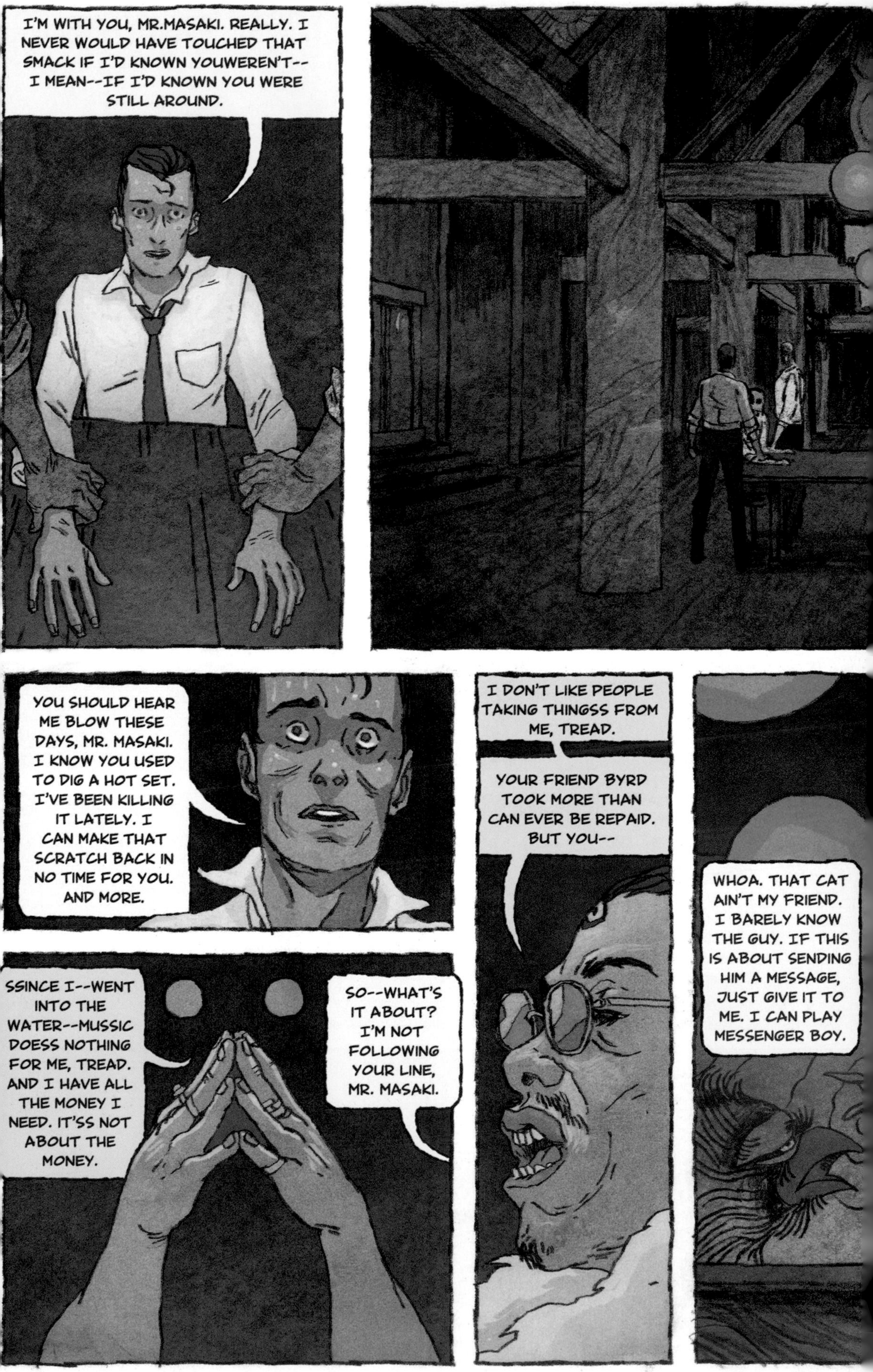
I'M WITH YOU, MR.MASAKI. REALLY. I NEVER WOULD HAVE TOUCHED THAT SMACK IF I'D KNOWN YOUWEREN'T-- I MEAN--IF I'D KNOWN YOU WERE STILL AROUND.
YOU SHOULD HEAR ME BLOW THESE DAYS, MR. MASAKI. I KNOW YOU USED TO DIG A HOT SET. I'VE BEEN KILLING IT LATELY. I CAN MAKE THAT SCRATCH BACK IN NO TIME FOR YOU. AND MORE.
SSINCE I--WENT INTO THE WATER--MUSSIC DOESS NOTHING FOR ME, TREAD. AND I HAVE ALL THE MONEY I NEED. IT'SS NOT ABOUT THE MONEY.
SO--WHAT'S IT ABOUT? I'M NOT FOLLOWING YOUR LINE, MR. MASAKI.
I DON'T LIKE PEOPLE TAKING THINGSS FROM ME, TREAD.
YOUR FRIEND BYRD TOOK MORE THAN CAN EVER BE REPAID. BUT YOU--
WHOA. THAT CAT AIN'T MY FRIEND. I BARELY KNOW THE GUY. IF THIS IS ABOUT SENDING HIM A MESSAGE, JUST GIVE IT TO ME. I CAN PLAY MESSENGER BOY.

I BELIEVE YOU, TREAD.

SSO TELL ME HOW YOU'RE GOING TO RECTIFY THE SSITUATION.

I DON'T--RECTIFY IT? LIKE, SHARE MY CUT? YEAH, MAN. IT'S ALL YOURS. YOU KNOW--ONCE I SCROUNGE UP ENOUGH GREEN TO PAY YOU BACK. I'LL DOUBLE UP AT THE BLUE ALOHA AND SEE ABOUT PICKING UP A GIG OR TWO DOWNTOWN.

BUT YOU--YOUR TRANSGRESSIONSS ARE EASIER TO BALANCE.

MAN, IT AIN'T HAPPENING AGAIN. IF YOU NEED IT DONE, I'M YOUR MAN. I PROMISE, MR. MASAKI.

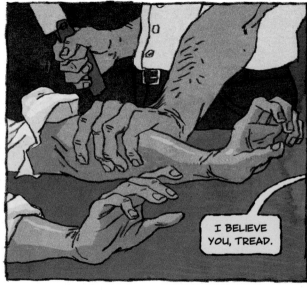

I BELIEVE YOU, TREAD.

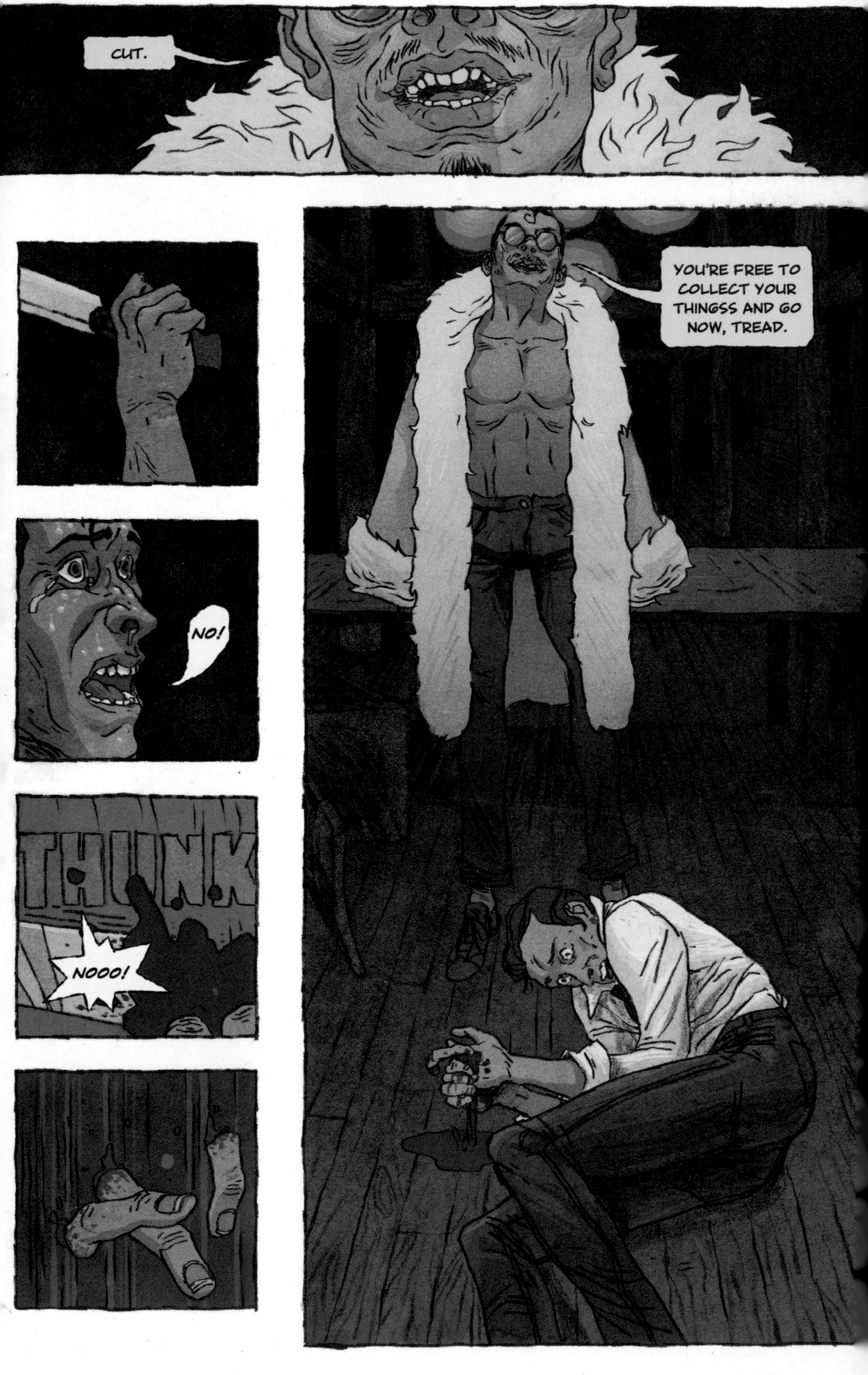
CUT.
NO!
THUNK
NOOO!
YOU'RE FREE TO COLLECT YOUR THINGSS AND GO NOW, TREAD.

I'M UP TO NOTHING, OKAY? SOME FATCAT BACK IN KC WANTS ME TO FIND THIS LIGHTLY GUY FOR HIM, THAT'S ALL. LET HIM KNOW WHERE HE IS. MAKE SURE HE'S HERE.

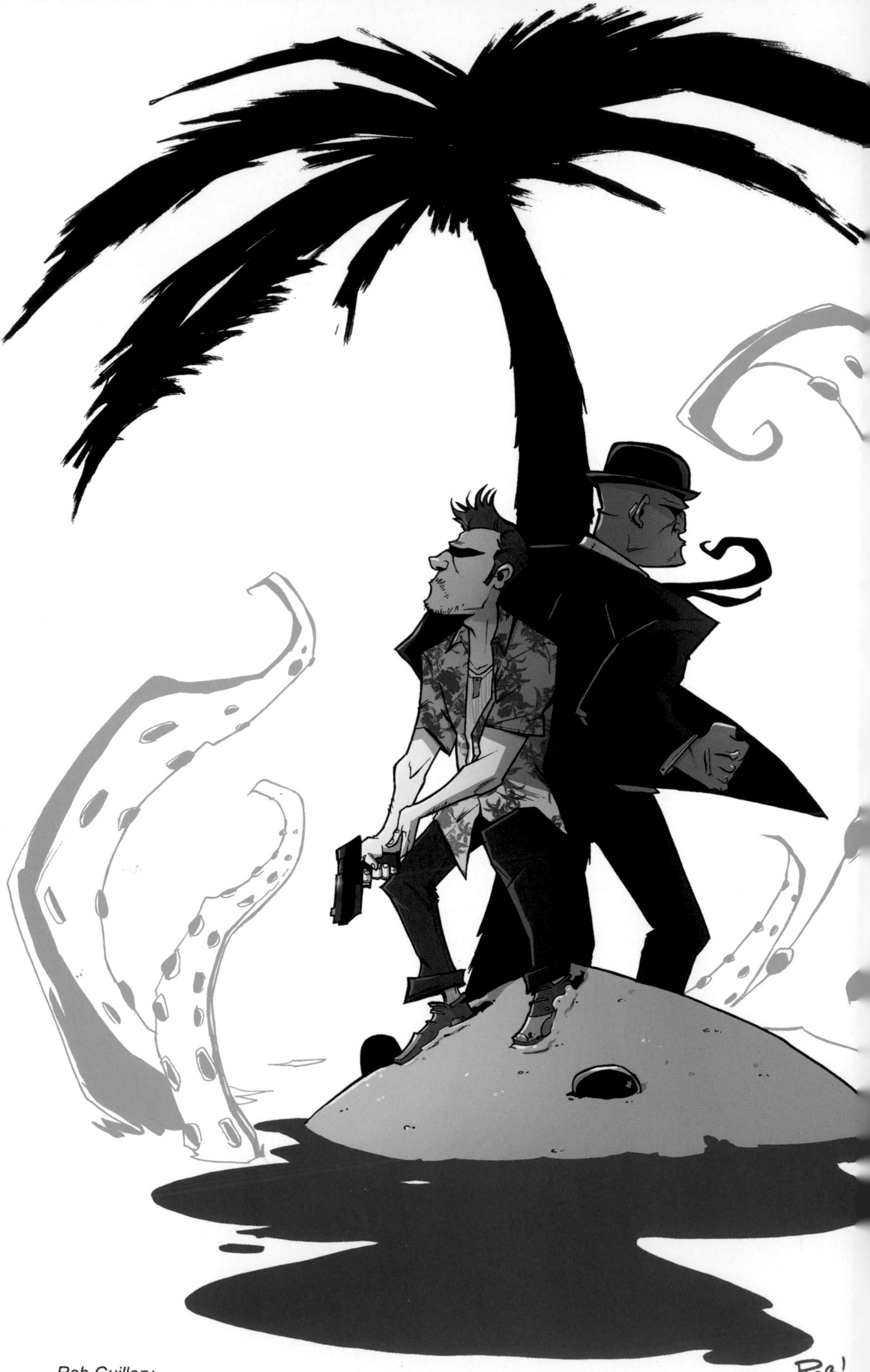

Rob Guillory

A BYRD OF PARADISE MYSTERY

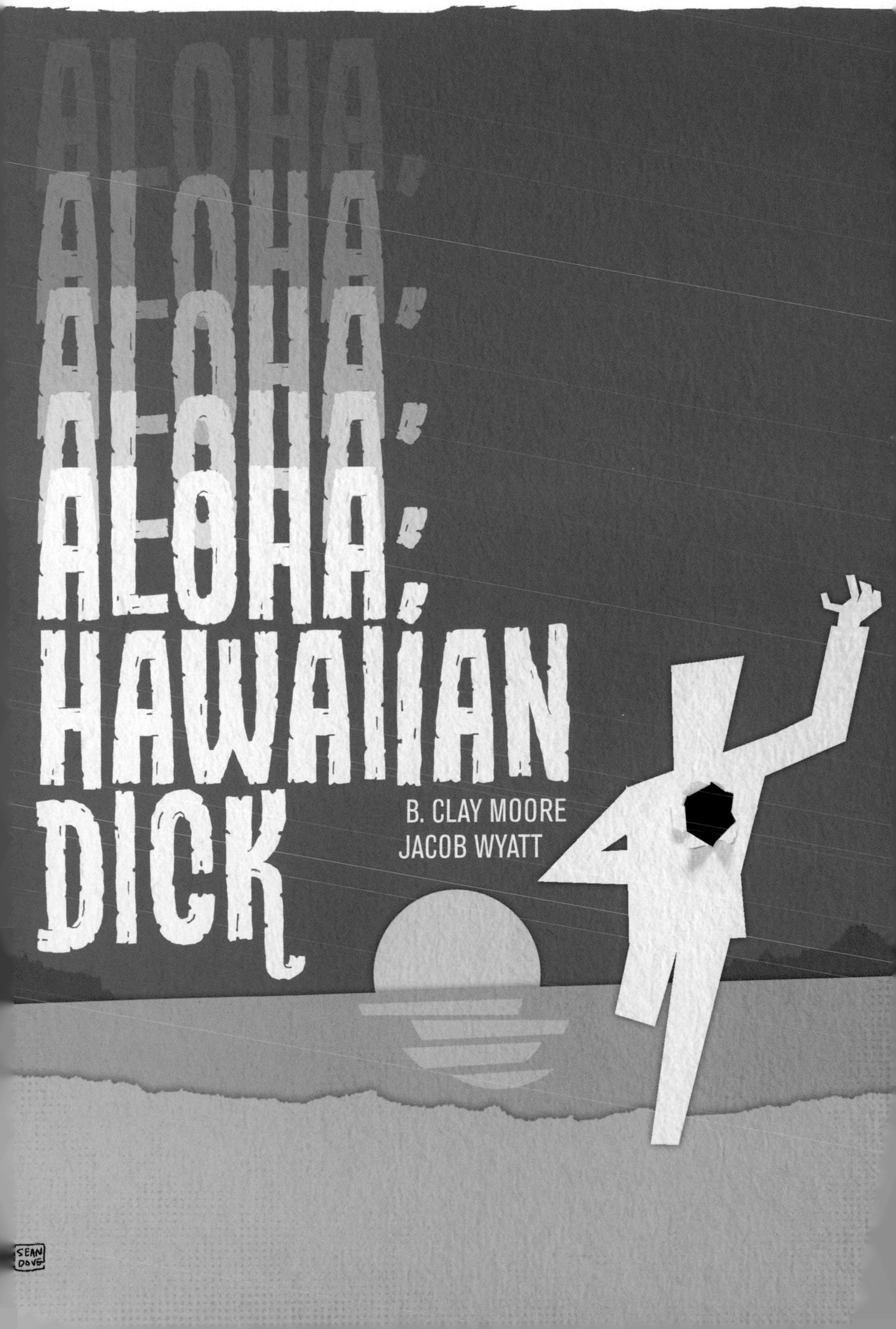
ALOHA, ALOHA, ALOHA, ALOHA, ALOHA,
HAWAIIAN DICK
B. CLAY MOORE
JACOB WYATT
SEAN DOVE

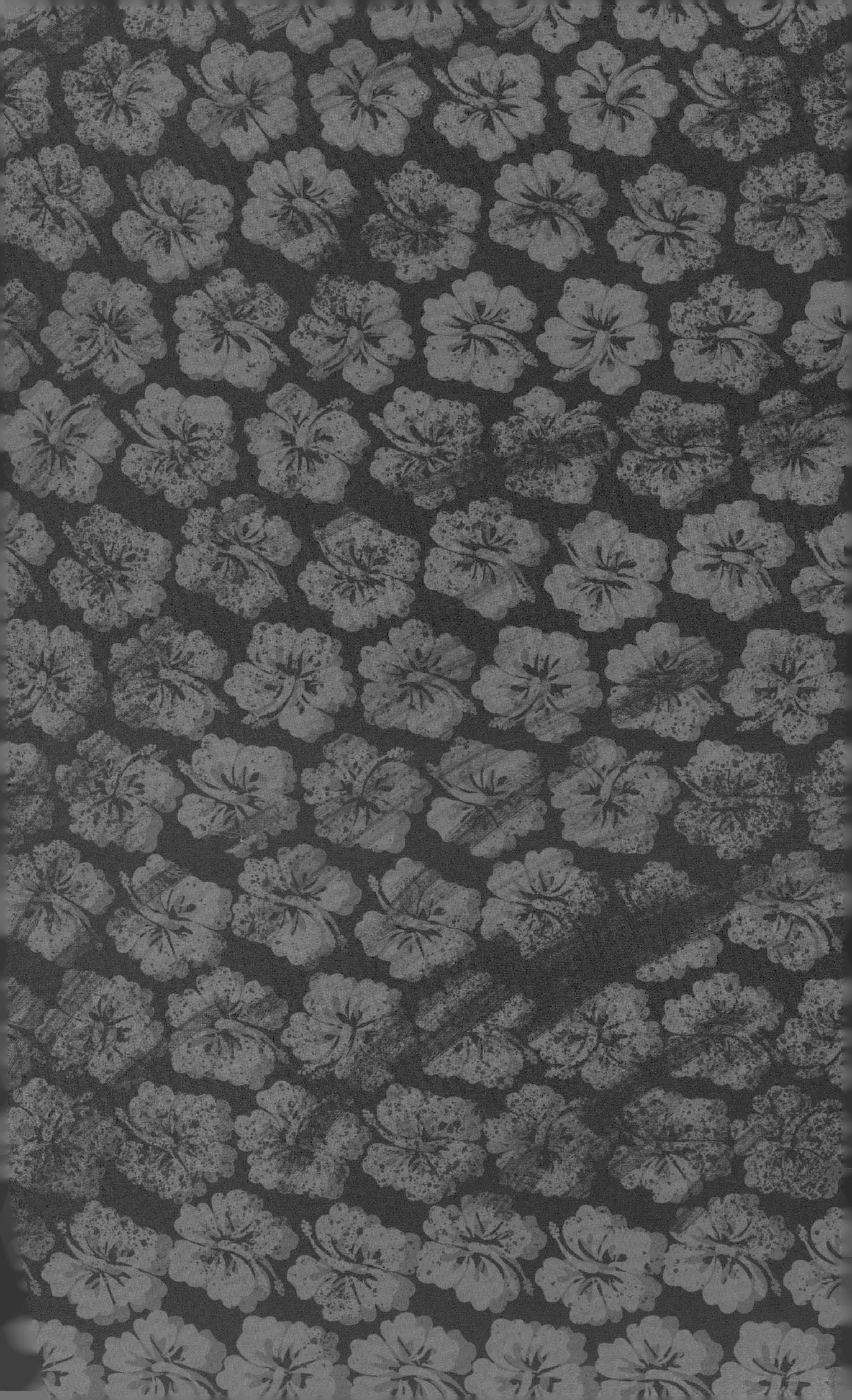

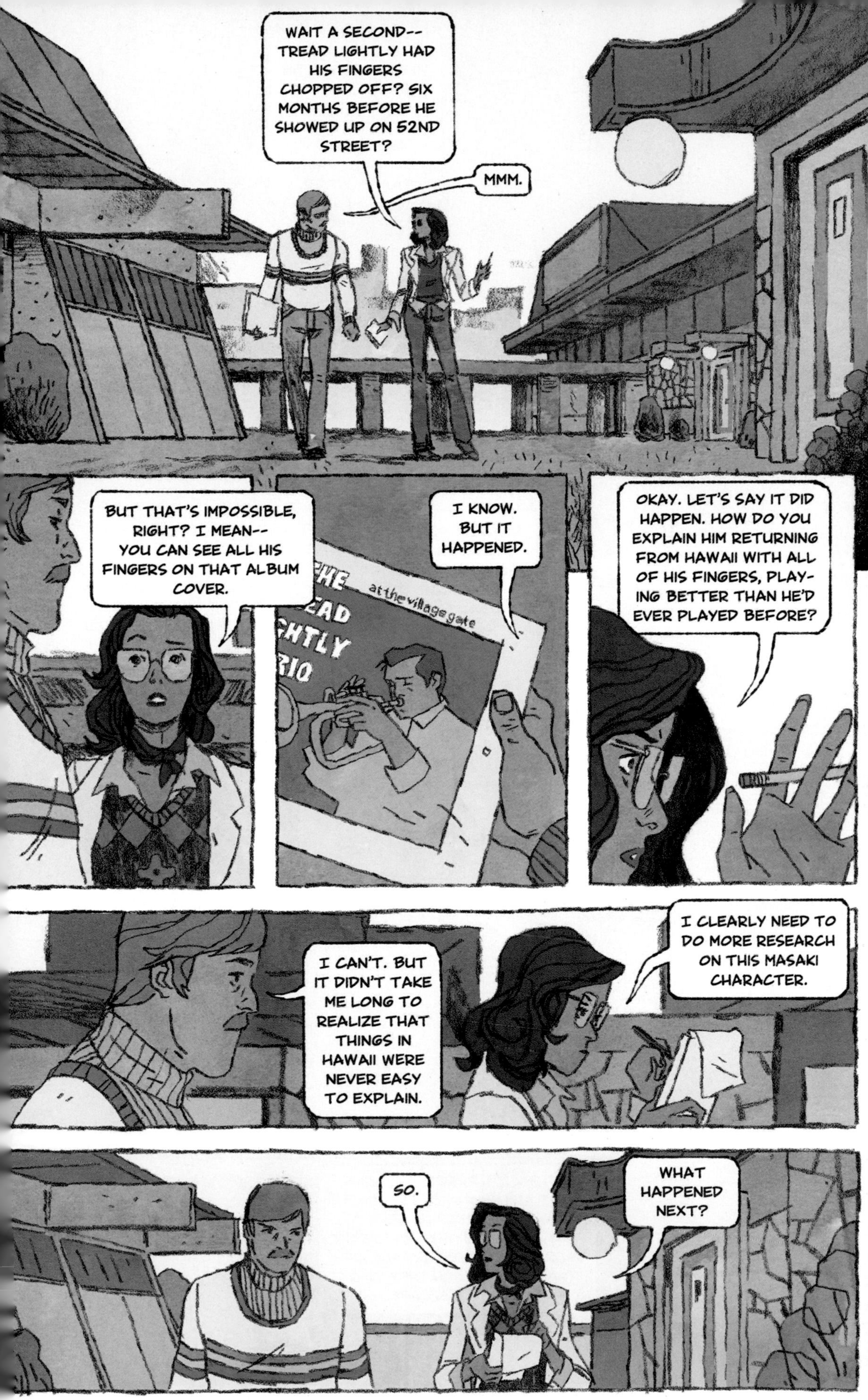
WAIT A SECOND-- TREAD LIGHTLY HAD HIS FINGERS CHOPPED OFF? SIX MONTHS BEFORE HE SHOWED UP ON 52ND STREET?
MMM.
BUT THAT'S IMPOSSIBLE, RIGHT? I MEAN-- YOU CAN SEE ALL HIS FINGERS ON THAT ALBUM COVER.
I KNOW. BUT IT HAPPENED.
at the village gate
OKAY. LET'S SAY IT DID HAPPEN. HOW DO YOU EXPLAIN HIM RETURNING FROM HAWAII WITH ALL OF HIS FINGERS, PLAYING BETTER THAN HE'D EVER PLAYED BEFORE?
I CAN'T. BUT IT DIDN'T TAKE ME LONG TO REALIZE THAT THINGS IN HAWAII WERE NEVER EASY TO EXPLAIN.
I CLEARLY NEED TO DO MORE RESEARCH ON THIS MASAKI CHARACTER.
SO.
WHAT HAPPENED NEXT?

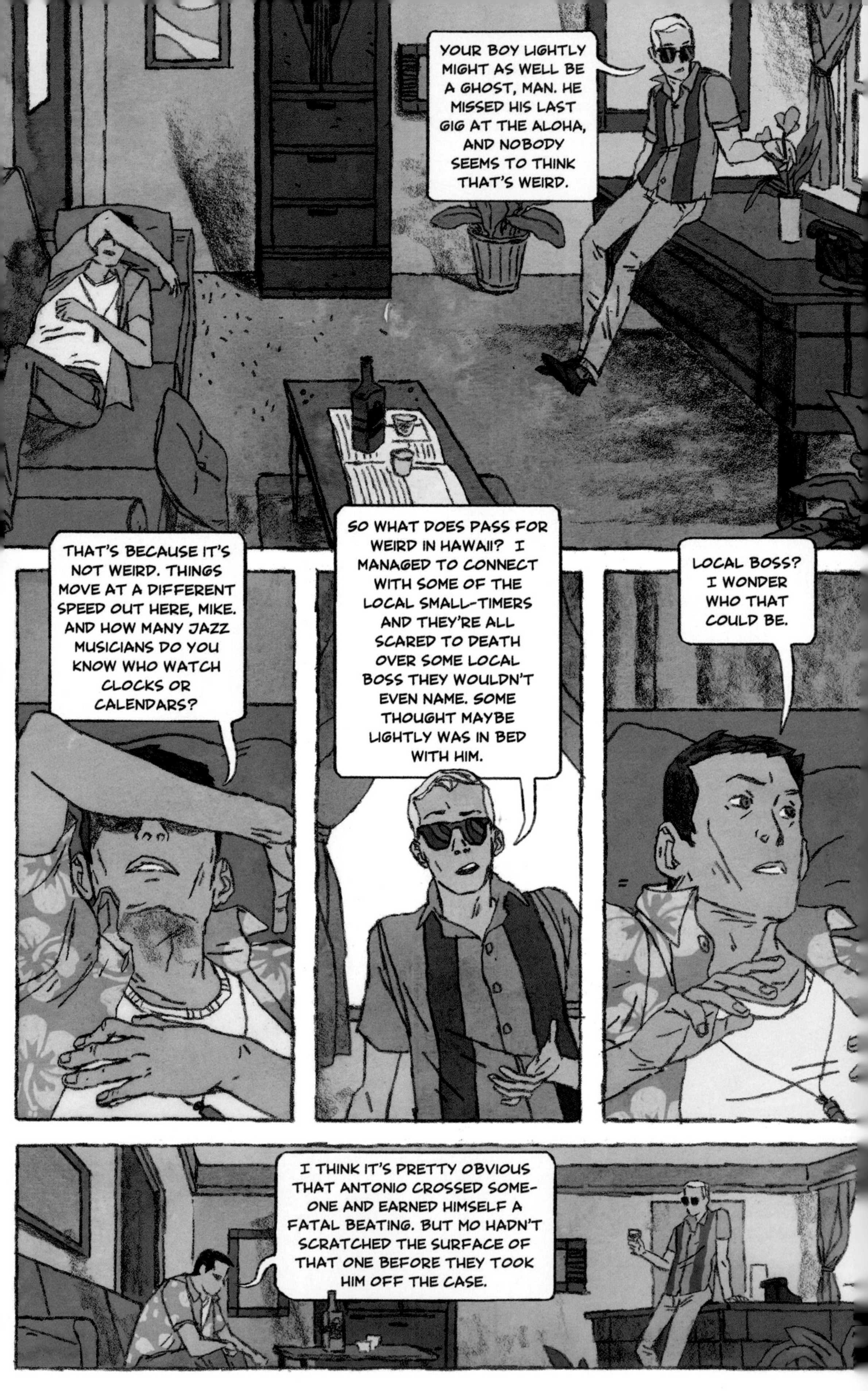
YOUR BOY LIGHTLY MIGHT AS WELL BE A GHOST, MAN. HE MISSED HIS LAST GIG AT THE ALOHA, AND NOBODY SEEMS TO THINK THAT'S WEIRD.
THAT'S BECAUSE IT'S NOT WEIRD. THINGS MOVE AT A DIFFERENT SPEED OUT HERE, MIKE. AND HOW MANY JAZZ MUSICIANS DO YOU KNOW WHO WATCH CLOCKS OR CALENDARS?
SO WHAT DOES PASS FOR WEIRD IN HAWAII? I MANAGED TO CONNECT WITH SOME OF THE LOCAL SMALL-TIMERS AND THEY'RE ALL SCARED TO DEATH OVER SOME LOCAL BOSS THEY WOULDN'T EVEN NAME. SOME THOUGHT MAYBE LIGHTLY WAS IN BED WITH HIM.
LOCAL BOSS? I WONDER WHO THAT COULD BE.
I THINK IT'S PRETTY OBVIOUS THAT ANTONIO CROSSED SOME-ONE AND EARNED HIMSELF A FATAL BEATING. BUT MO HADN'T SCRATCHED THE SURFACE OF THAT ONE BEFORE THEY TOOK HIM OFF THE CASE.

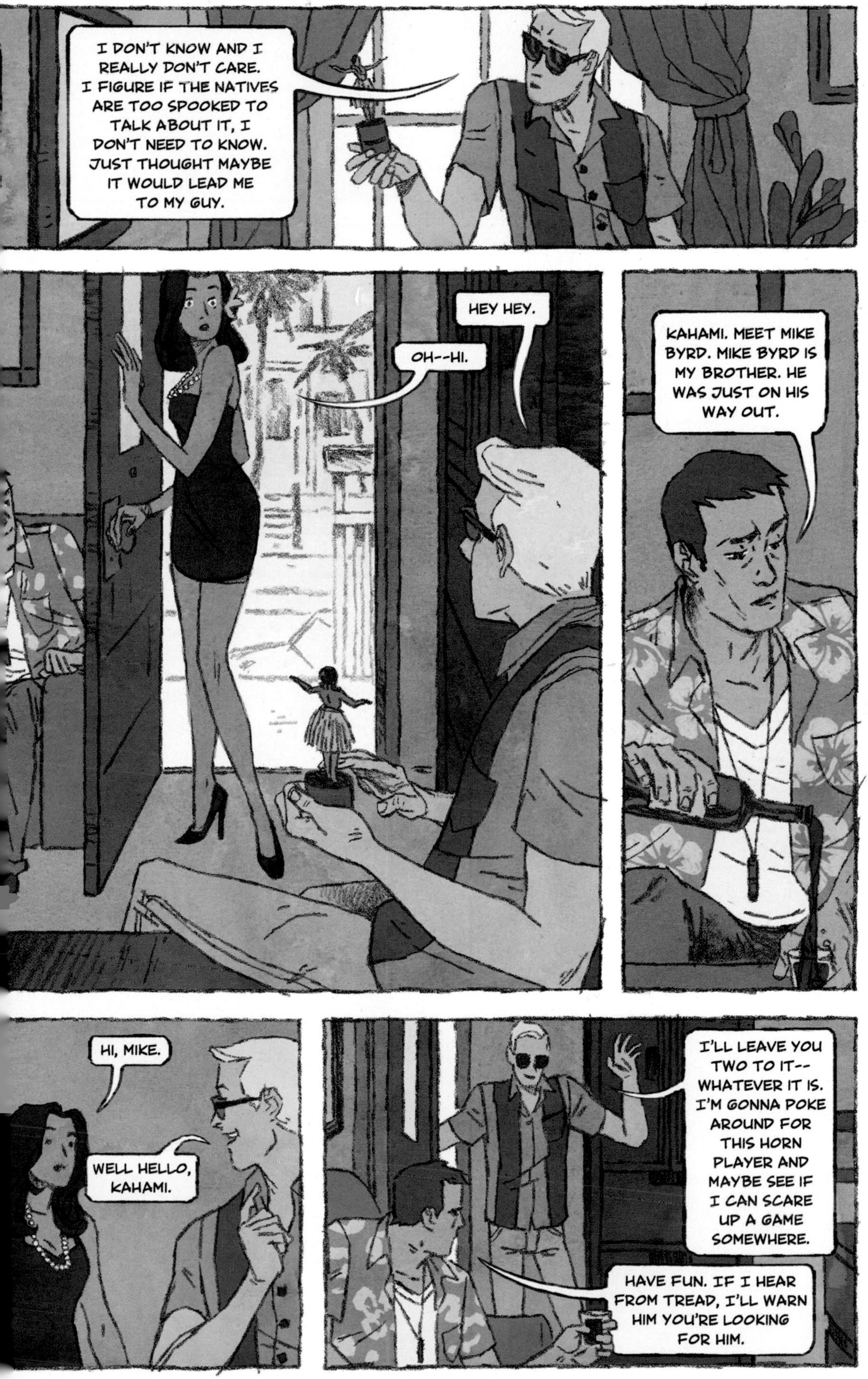
I DON'T KNOW AND I REALLY DON'T CARE. I FIGURE IF THE NATIVES ARE TOO SPOOKED TO TALK ABOUT IT, I DON'T NEED TO KNOW. JUST THOUGHT MAYBE IT WOULD LEAD ME TO MY GUY.
HEY HEY.
OH--HI.
KAHAMI. MEET MIKE BYRD. MIKE BYRD IS MY BROTHER. HE WAS JUST ON HIS WAY OUT.
HI, MIKE.
WELL HELLO, KAHAMI.
I'LL LEAVE YOU TWO TO IT--WHATEVER IT IS. I'M GONNA POKE AROUND FOR THIS HORN PLAYER AND MAYBE SEE IF I CAN SCARE UP A GAME SOMEWHERE.
HAVE FUN. IF I HEAR FROM TREAD, I'LL WARN HIM YOU'RE LOOKING FOR HIM.

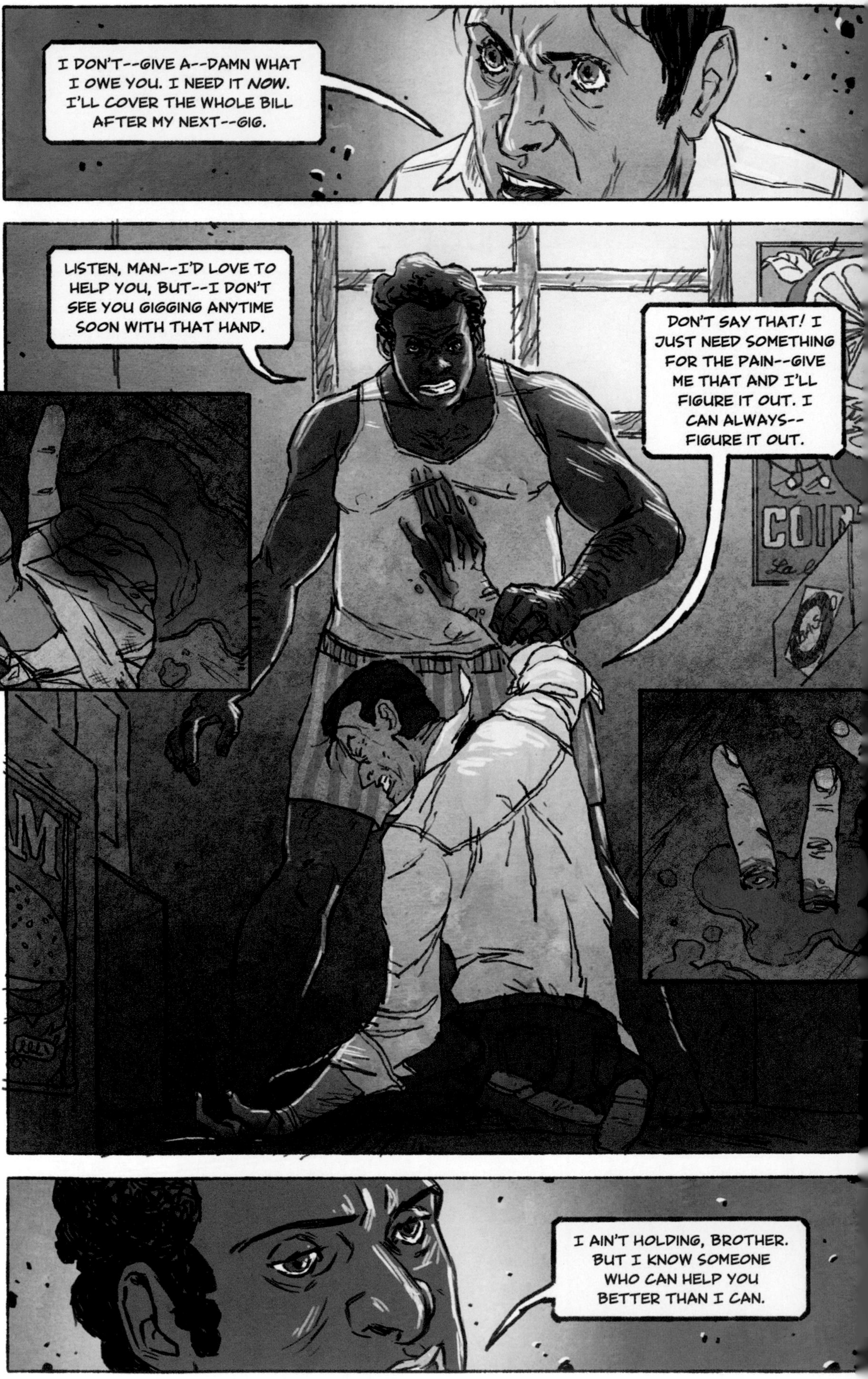
I DON'T--GIVE A--DAMN WHAT I OWE YOU. I NEED IT *NOW*. I'LL COVER THE WHOLE BILL AFTER MY NEXT--GIG.
LISTEN, MAN--I'D LOVE TO HELP YOU, BUT--I DON'T SEE YOU GIGGING ANYTIME SOON WITH THAT HAND.
DON'T SAY THAT! I JUST NEED SOMETHING FOR THE PAIN--GIVE ME THAT AND I'LL FIGURE IT OUT. I CAN ALWAYS--FIGURE IT OUT.
I AIN'T HOLDING, BROTHER. BUT I KNOW SOMEONE WHO CAN HELP YOU BETTER THAN I CAN.

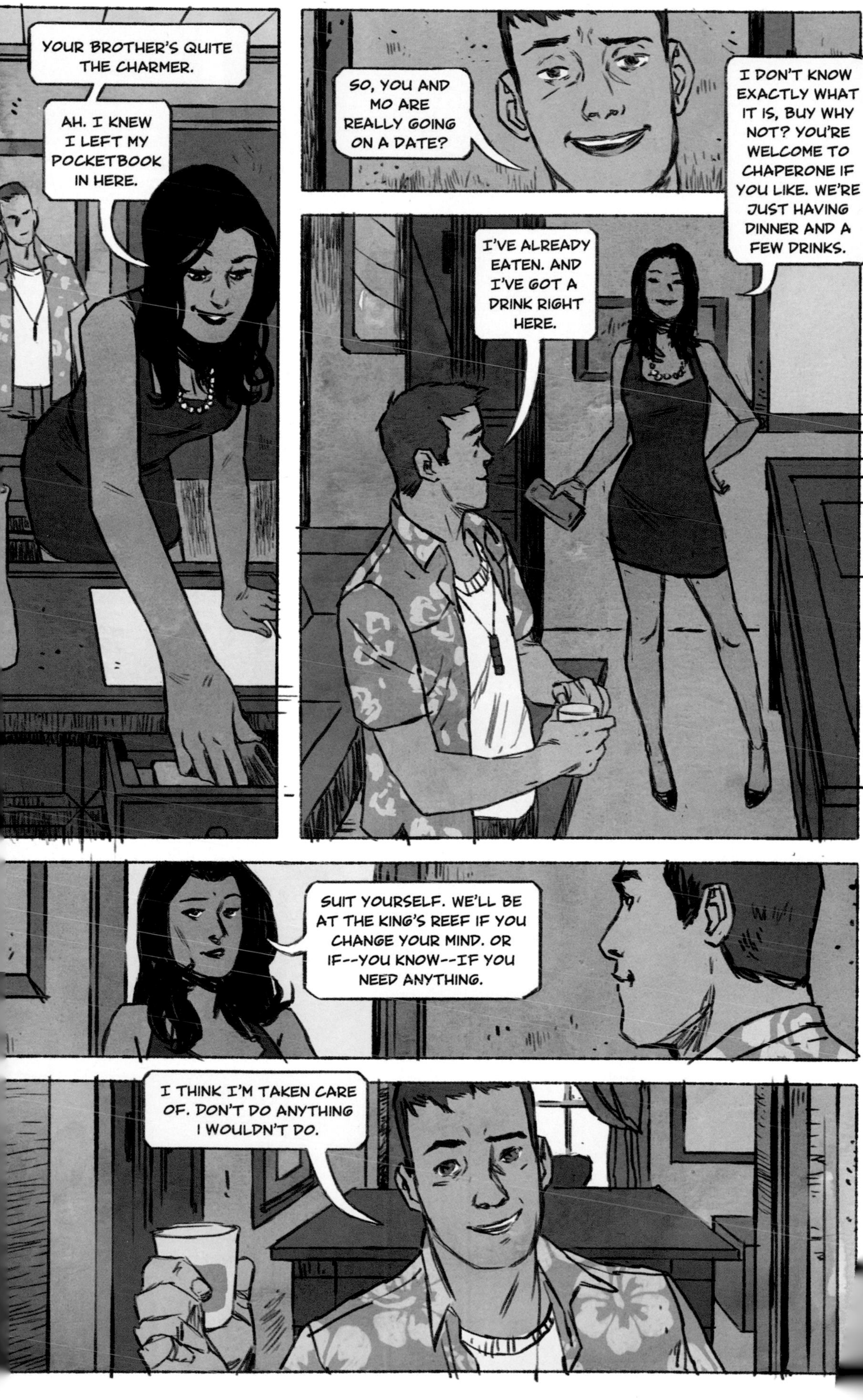
YOUR BROTHER'S QUITE THE CHARMER.
AH. I KNEW I LEFT MY POCKETBOOK IN HERE.
SO, YOU AND MO ARE REALLY GOING ON A DATE?
I DON'T KNOW EXACTLY WHAT IT IS, BUY WHY NOT? YOU'RE WELCOME TO CHAPERONE IF YOU LIKE. WE'RE JUST HAVING DINNER AND A FEW DRINKS.
I'VE ALREADY EATEN. AND I'VE GOT A DRINK RIGHT HERE.
SUIT YOURSELF. WE'LL BE AT THE KING'S REEF IF YOU CHANGE YOUR MIND. OR IF--YOU KNOW--IF YOU NEED ANYTHING.
I THINK I'M TAKEN CARE OF. DON'T DO ANYTHING I WOULDN'T DO.

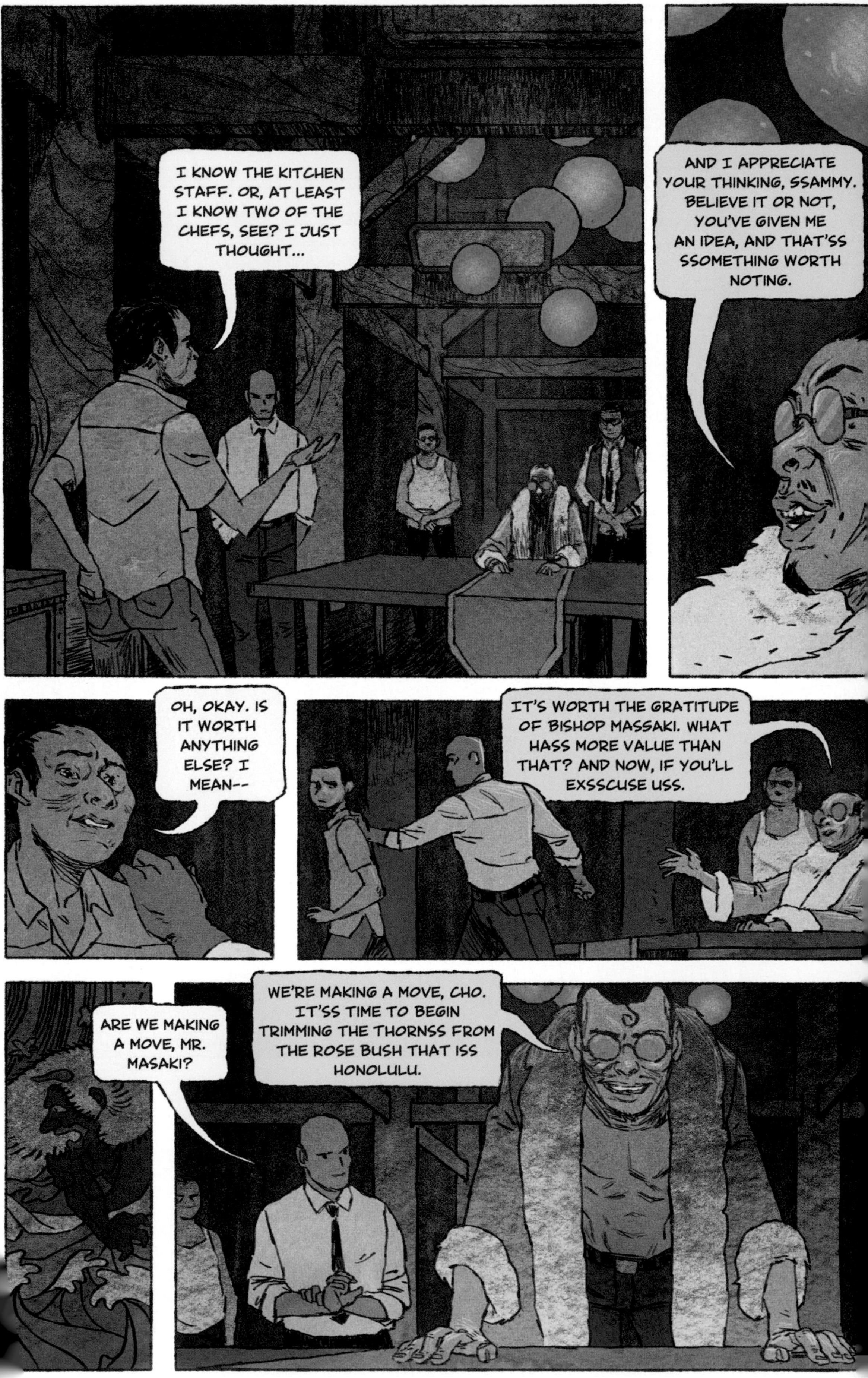
I KNOW THE KITCHEN STAFF. OR, AT LEAST I KNOW TWO OF THE CHEFS, SEE? I JUST THOUGHT...
AND I APPRECIATE YOUR THINKING, SSAMMY. BELIEVE IT OR NOT, YOU'VE GIVEN ME AN IDEA, AND THAT'SS SSOMETHING WORTH NOTING.
OH, OKAY. IS IT WORTH ANYTHING ELSE? I MEAN--
IT'S WORTH THE GRATITUDE OF BISHOP MASSAKI. WHAT HASS MORE VALUE THAN THAT? AND NOW, IF YOU'LL EXSSCUSE USS.
ARE WE MAKING A MOVE, MR. MASAKI?
WE'RE MAKING A MOVE, CHO. IT'SS TIME TO BEGIN TRIMMING THE THORNSS FROM THE ROSE BUSH THAT ISS HONOLULU.

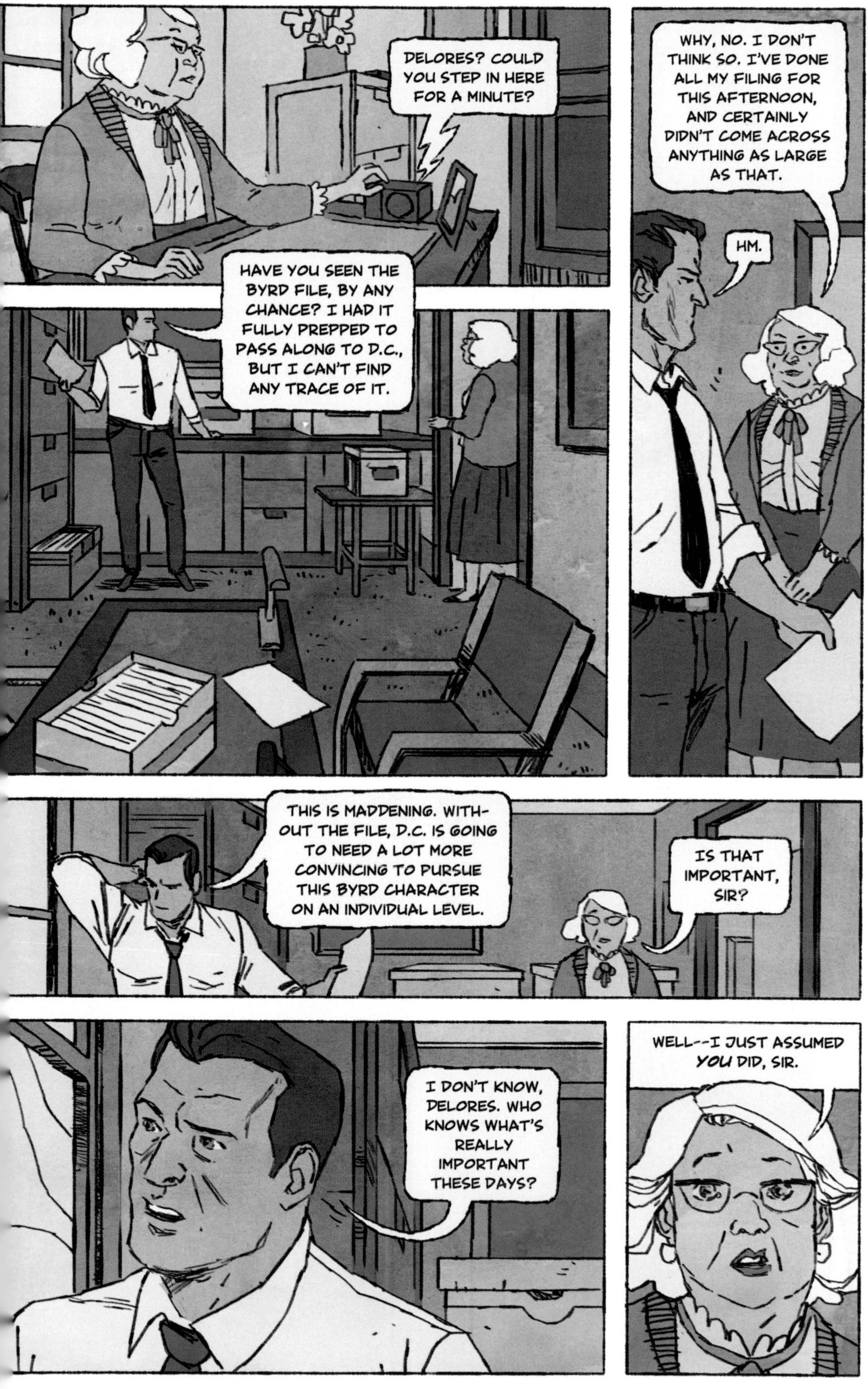
DELORES? COULD YOU STEP IN HERE FOR A MINUTE?
HAVE YOU SEEN THE BYRD FILE, BY ANY CHANCE? I HAD IT FULLY PREPPED TO PASS ALONG TO D.C., BUT I CAN'T FIND ANY TRACE OF IT.
WHY, NO. I DON'T THINK SO. I'VE DONE ALL MY FILING FOR THIS AFTERNOON, AND CERTAINLY DIDN'T COME ACROSS ANYTHING AS LARGE AS THAT.
HM.
THIS IS MADDENING. WITHOUT THE FILE, D.C. IS GOING TO NEED A LOT MORE CONVINCING TO PURSUE THIS BYRD CHARACTER ON AN INDIVIDUAL LEVEL.
IS THAT IMPORTANT, SIR?
I DON'T KNOW, DELORES. WHO KNOWS WHAT'S REALLY IMPORTANT THESE DAYS?
WELL--I JUST ASSUMED YOU DID, SIR.

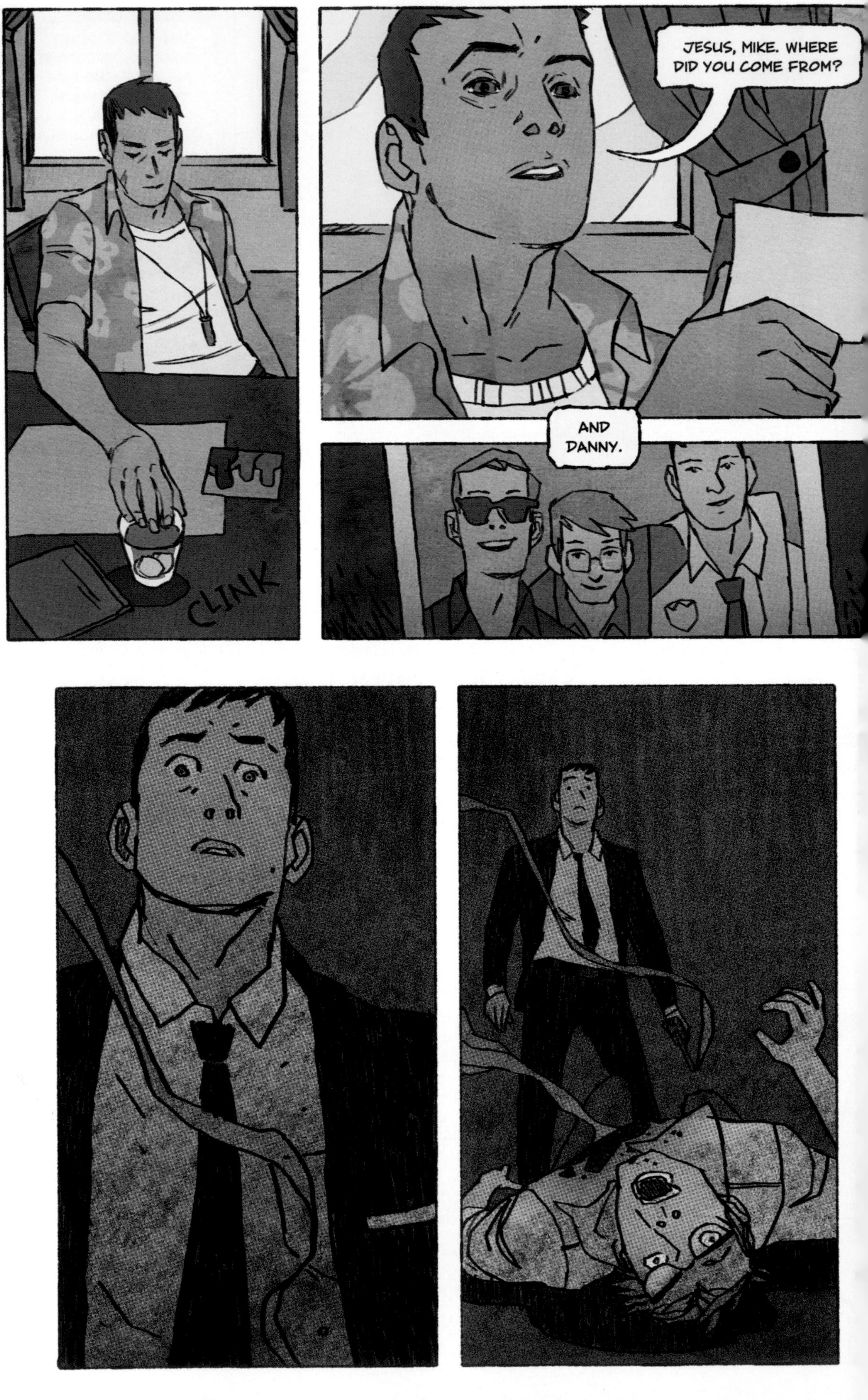
CLINK
JESUS, MIKE. WHERE DID YOU COME FROM?
AND DANNY.

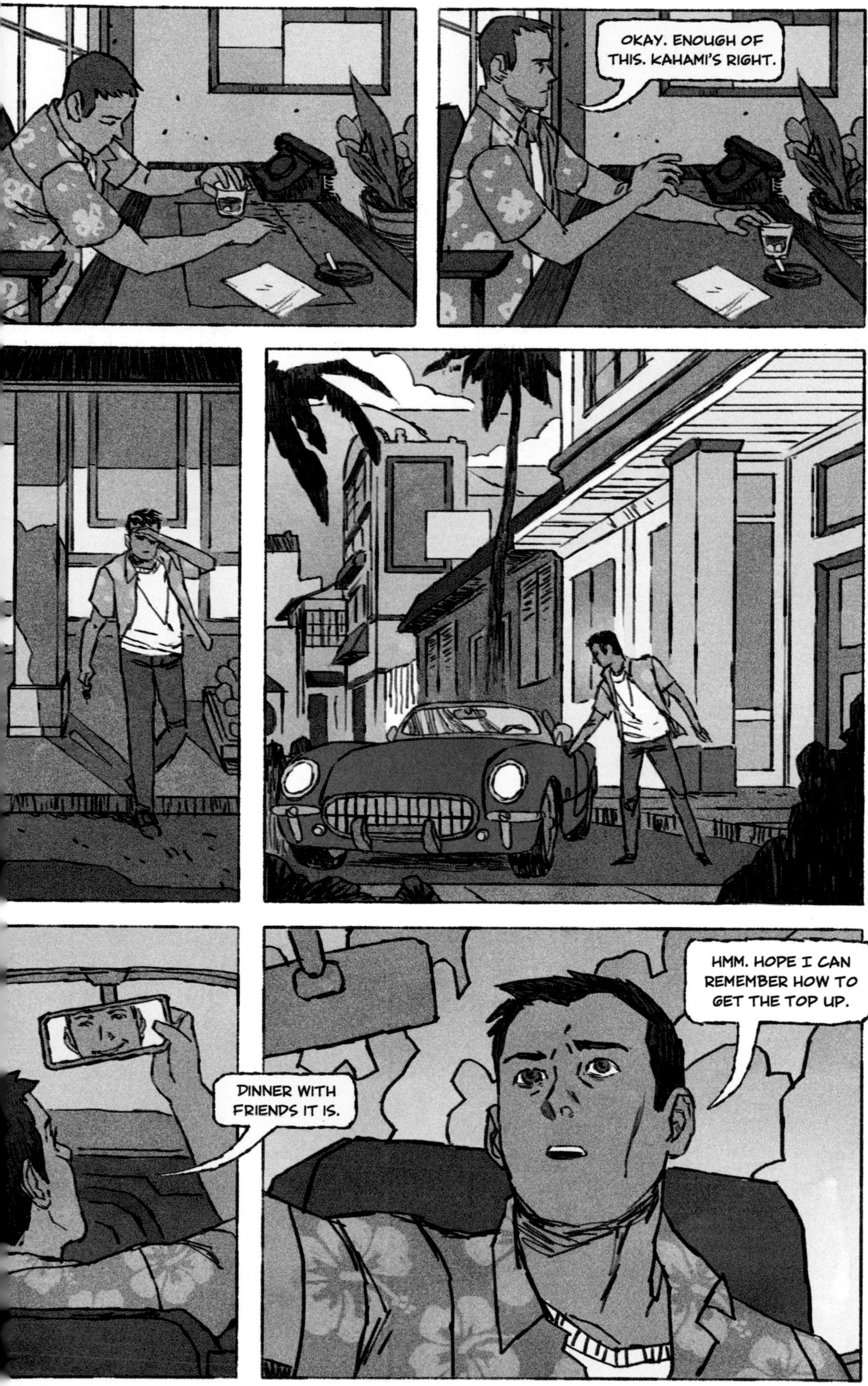
OKAY. ENOUGH OF THIS. KAHAMI'S RIGHT.
DINNER WITH FRIENDS IT IS.
HMM. HOPE I CAN REMEMBER HOW TO GET THE TOP UP.

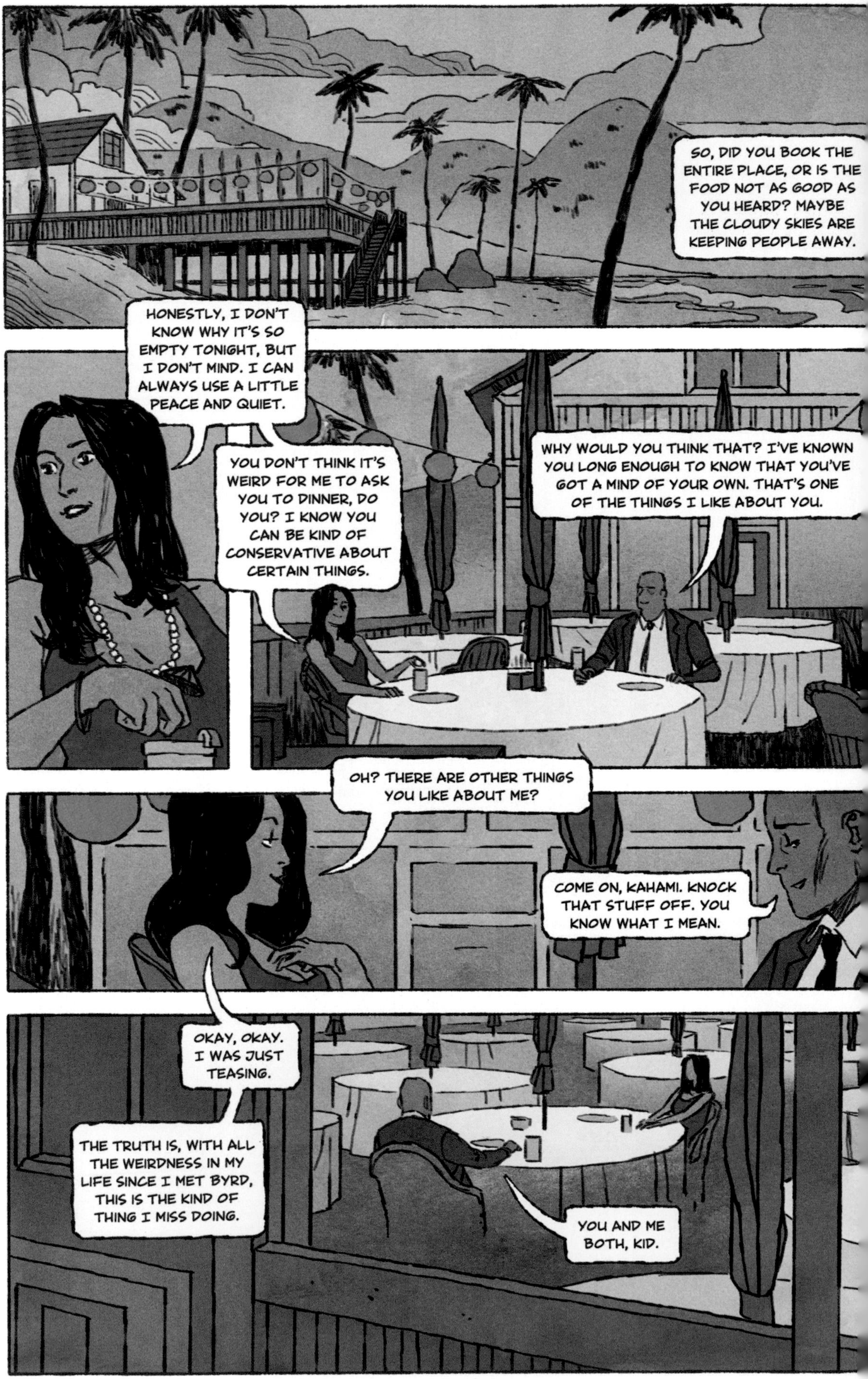
SO, DID YOU BOOK THE ENTIRE PLACE, OR IS THE FOOD NOT AS GOOD AS YOU HEARD? MAYBE THE CLOUDY SKIES ARE KEEPING PEOPLE AWAY.
HONESTLY, I DON'T KNOW WHY IT'S SO EMPTY TONIGHT, BUT I DON'T MIND. I CAN ALWAYS USE A LITTLE PEACE AND QUIET.
YOU DON'T THINK IT'S WEIRD FOR ME TO ASK YOU TO DINNER, DO YOU? I KNOW YOU CAN BE KIND OF CONSERVATIVE ABOUT CERTAIN THINGS.
WHY WOULD YOU THINK THAT? I'VE KNOWN YOU LONG ENOUGH TO KNOW THAT YOU'VE GOT A MIND OF YOUR OWN. THAT'S ONE OF THE THINGS I LIKE ABOUT YOU.
OH? THERE ARE OTHER THINGS YOU LIKE ABOUT ME?
COME ON, KAHAMI. KNOCK THAT STUFF OFF. YOU KNOW WHAT I MEAN.
OKAY, OKAY. I WAS JUST TEASING.
THE TRUTH IS, WITH ALL THE WEIRDNESS IN MY LIFE SINCE I MET BYRD, THIS IS THE KIND OF THING I MISS DOING.
YOU AND ME BOTH, KID.

I'M SSURE THIS RUSE SSEEMSS ELABORATE TO YOU GENTLEMEN. AND I SSUPPOSE IT IS.

BUT THISS ISS ABOUT MORE THAN SSOME PETTY REVENGE. THERE ARE THOSE ON THE ISLAND WHO BELIEVE THAT DETECTIVE KALAMA AND HISS *HAOLE* FRIEND SSOMEHOW GOT THE BETTER OF ME.

I'M HUMBLE ENOUGH TO ADMIT THAT THERE MAY BE A KERNEL OF TRUTH IN THAT SSENTIMENT. MY CURRENT-- CONDITION--ISS PROOF ENOUGH OF THAT, WOULDN'T YOU SSAY?

I DUNNO, BOSS. WE NEVER LOST FAITH.

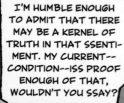

AND THAT ISS WHY YOU ARE HERE, CHO. AND WHY SSO MANY OTHERSS ARE NO LONGER WITH USS.

SSO, YESS. THISS ISS ABOUT SSENDING A MESSAGE. COMMUNI- CATING INTENT.

AND DEMON- SSTRATING THAT THERE ARE NO LIMITSS TO WHAT WE CAN DO IN THISS TOWN.

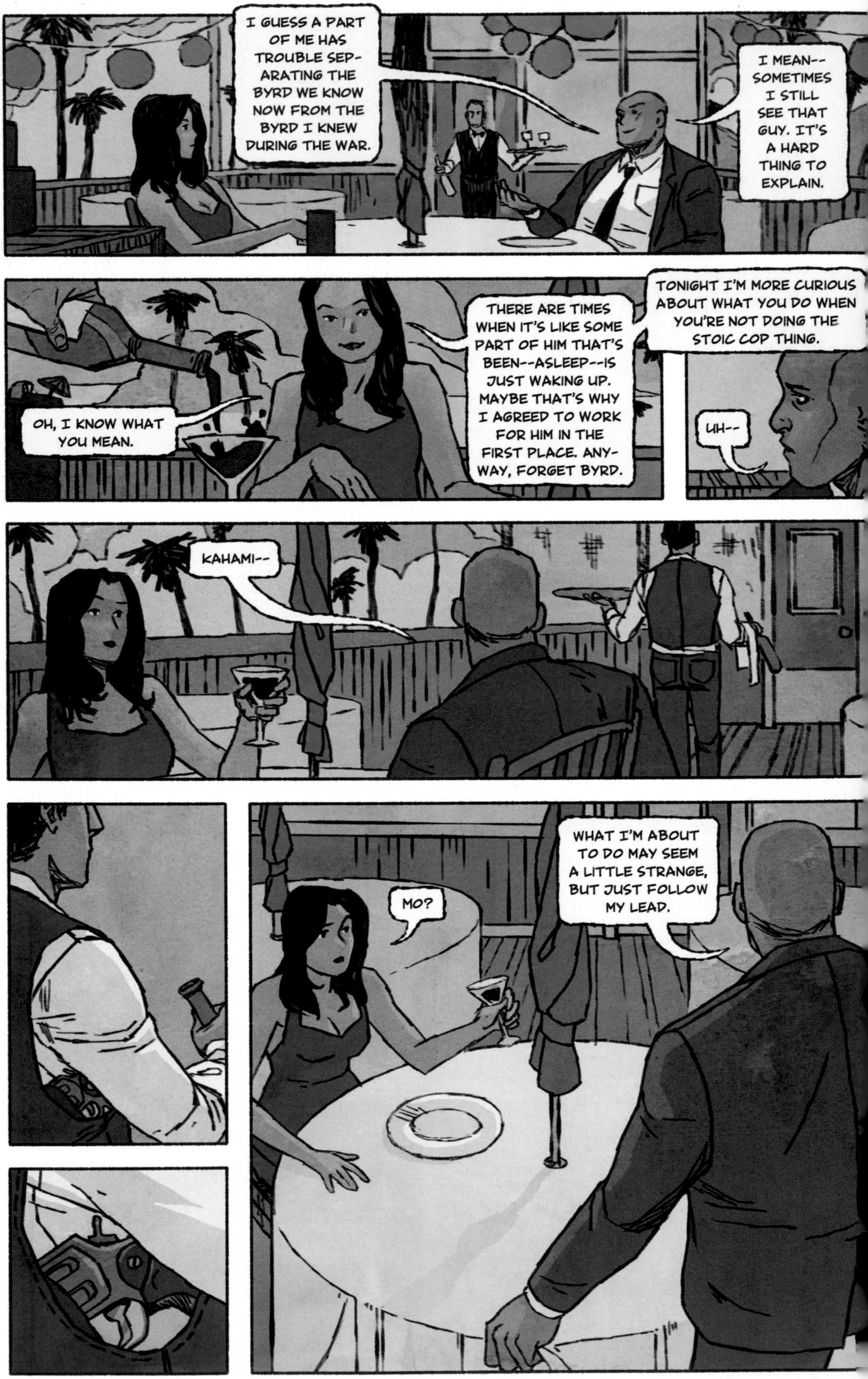
I GUESS A PART OF ME HAS TROUBLE SEP-ARATING THE BYRD WE KNOW NOW FROM THE BYRD I KNEW DURING THE WAR.
I MEAN-- SOMETIMES I STILL SEE THAT GUY. IT'S A HARD THING TO EXPLAIN.
OH, I KNOW WHAT YOU MEAN.
THERE ARE TIMES WHEN IT'S LIKE SOME PART OF HIM THAT'S BEEN--ASLEEP--IS JUST WAKING UP. MAYBE THAT'S WHY I AGREED TO WORK FOR HIM IN THE FIRST PLACE. ANY-WAY, FORGET BYRD.
TONIGHT I'M MORE CURIOUS ABOUT WHAT YOU DO WHEN YOU'RE NOT DOING THE STOIC COP THING.
UH--
KAHAMI--
MO?
WHAT I'M ABOUT TO DO MAY SEEM A LITTLE STRANGE, BUT JUST FOLLOW MY LEAD.

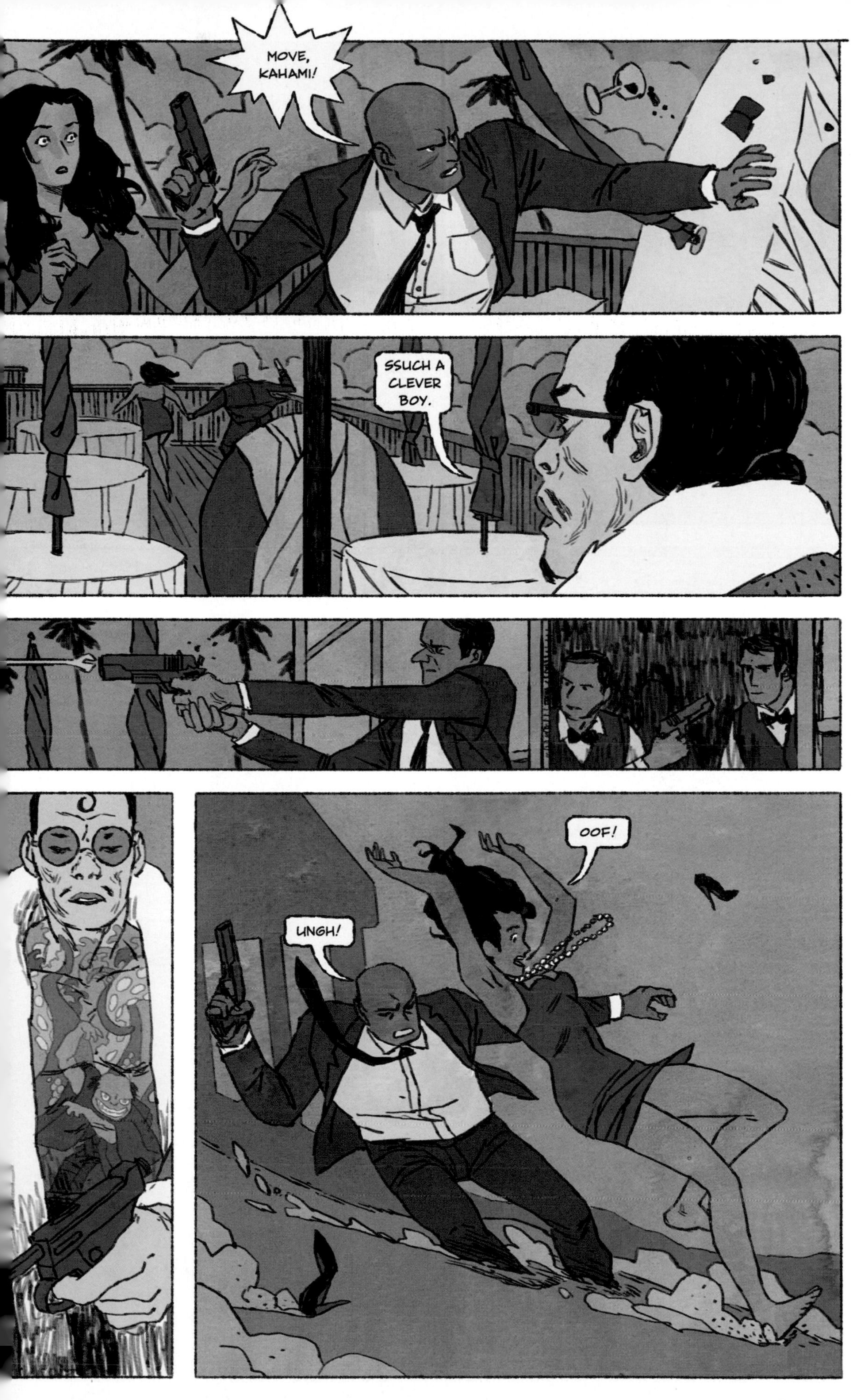
MOVE, KAHAMI!
SSUCH A CLEVER BOY.
OOF!
UNGH!

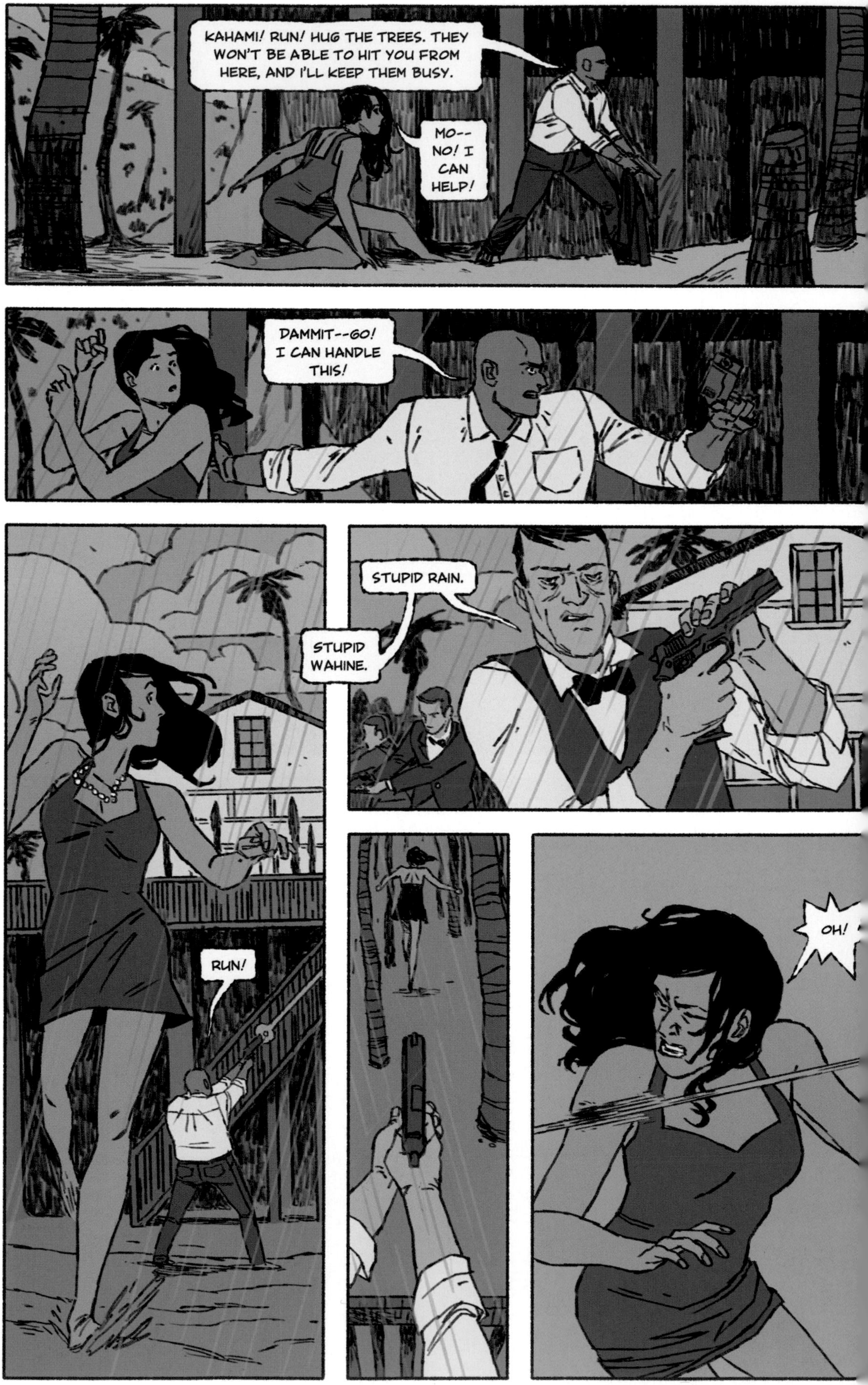
KAHAMI! RUN! HUG THE TREES. THEY WON'T BE ABLE TO HIT YOU FROM HERE, AND I'LL KEEP THEM BUSY.
MO-- NO! I CAN HELP!
DAMMIT--GO! I CAN HANDLE THIS!
STUPID RAIN.
STUPID WAHINE.
RUN!
OH!

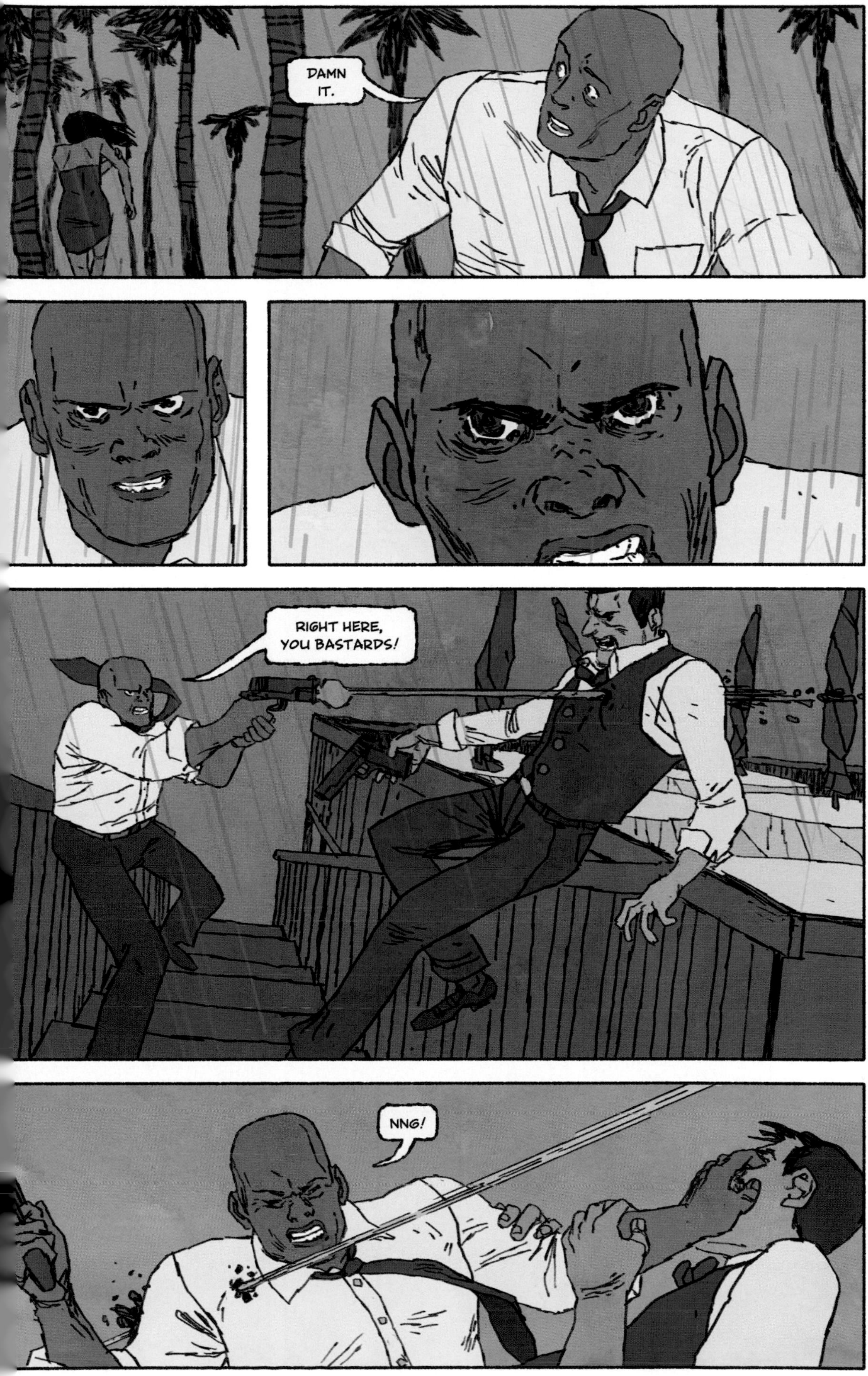
DAMN IT.
RIGHT HERE, YOU BASTARDS!
NNG!

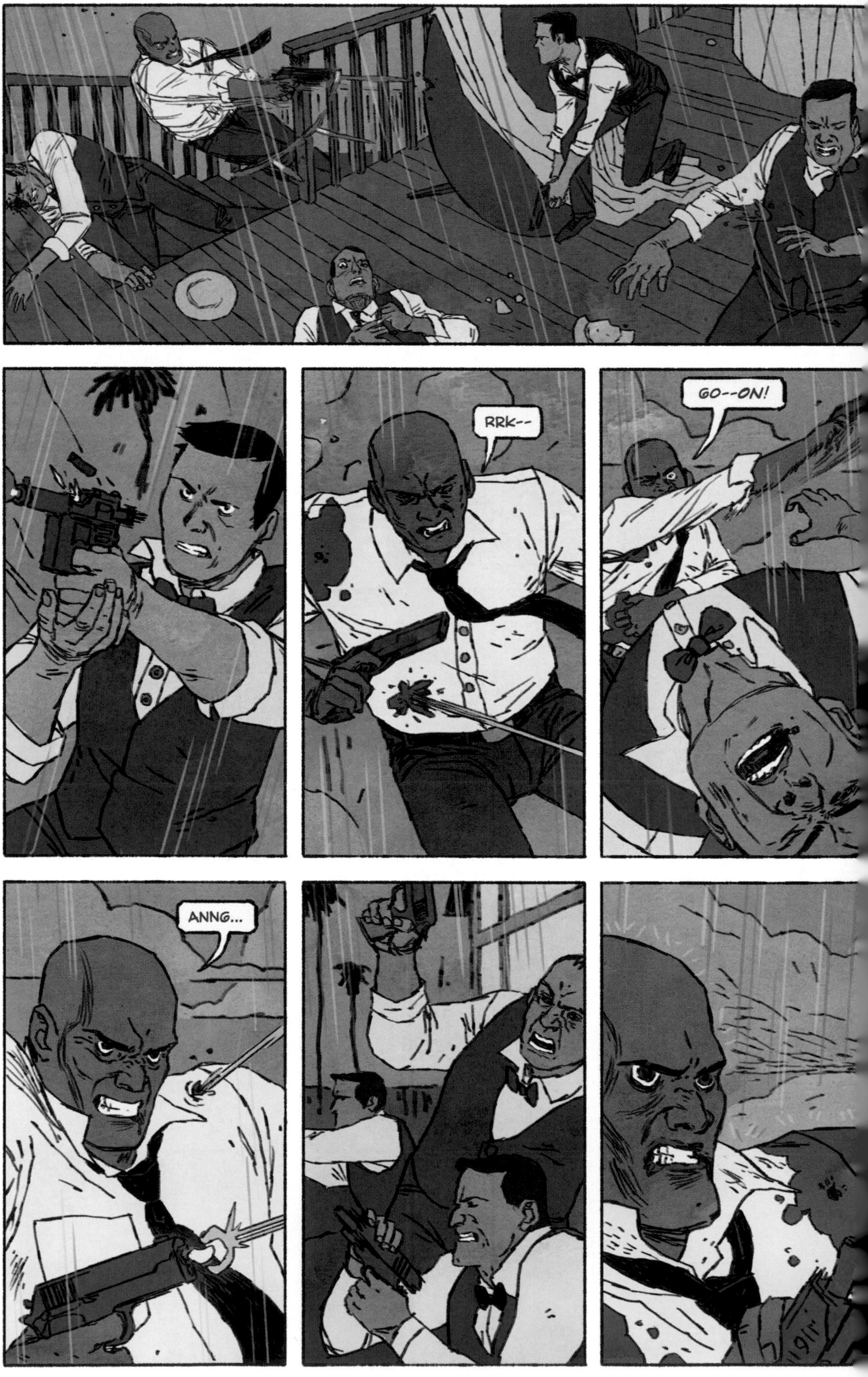
RRK--
GO--ON!
ANNG...

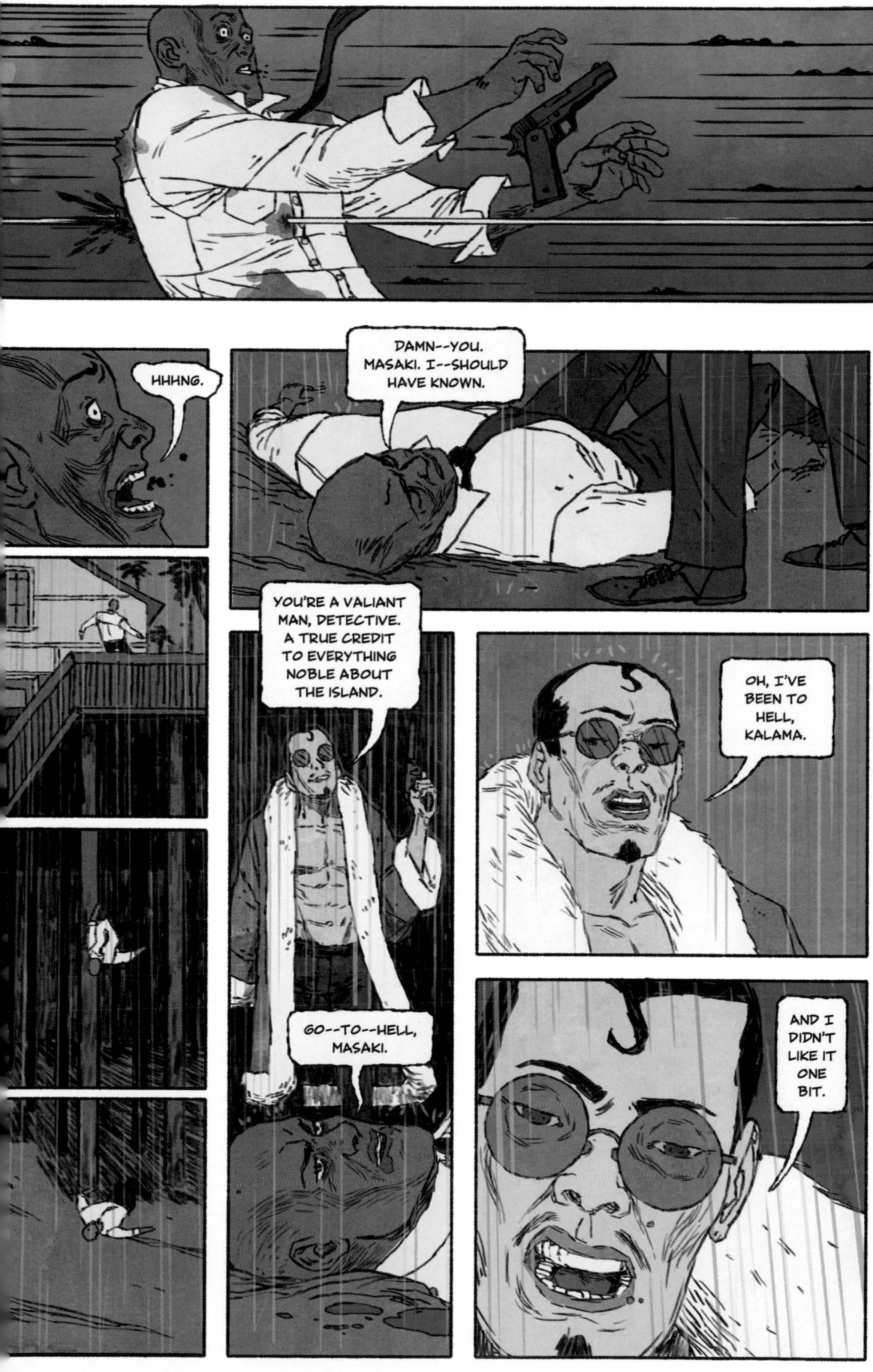
HHHNG.
DAMN--YOU. MASAKI. I--SHOULD HAVE KNOWN.
YOU'RE A VALIANT MAN, DETECTIVE. A TRUE CREDIT TO EVERYTHING NOBLE ABOUT THE ISLAND.
GO--TO--HELL, MASAKI.
OH, I'VE BEEN TO HELL, KALAMA.
AND I DIDN'T LIKE IT ONE BIT.

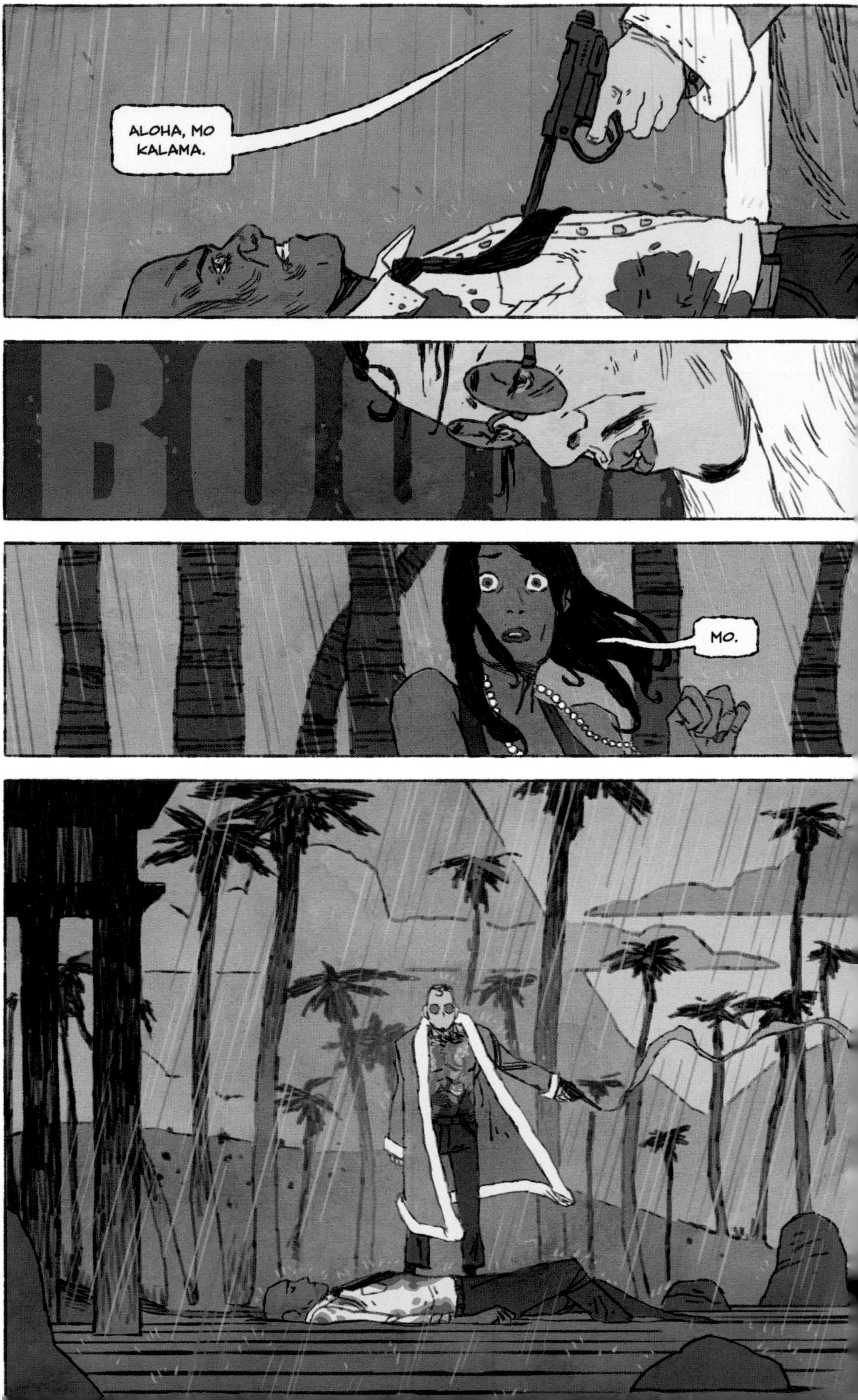
ALOHA, MO KALAMA.
BO
MO.

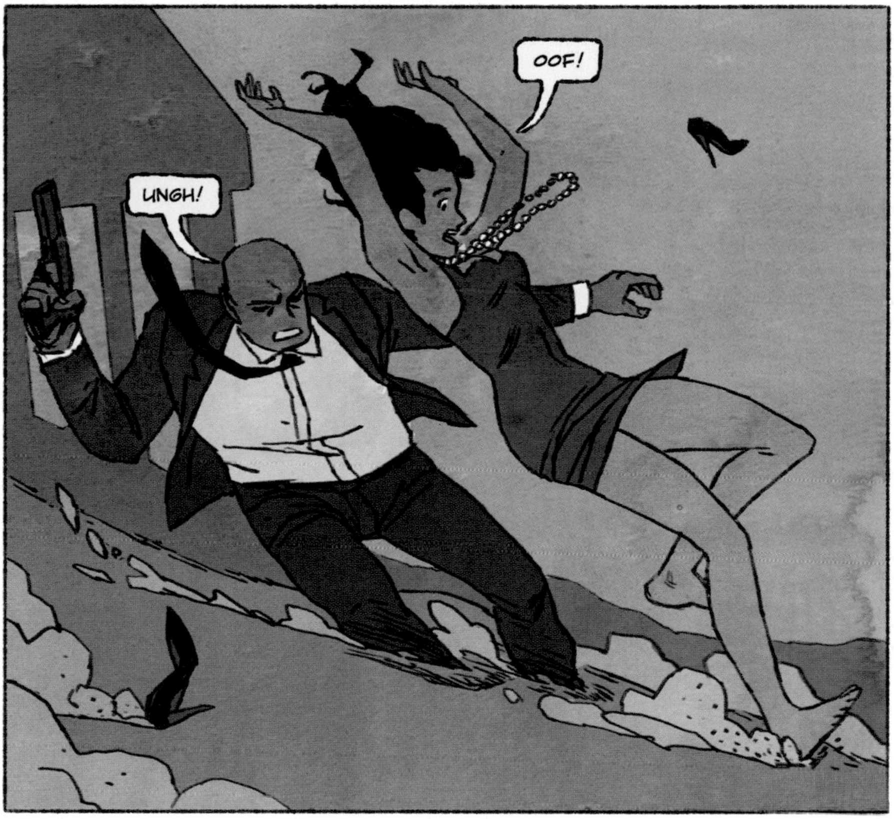
UNGH!
OOF!

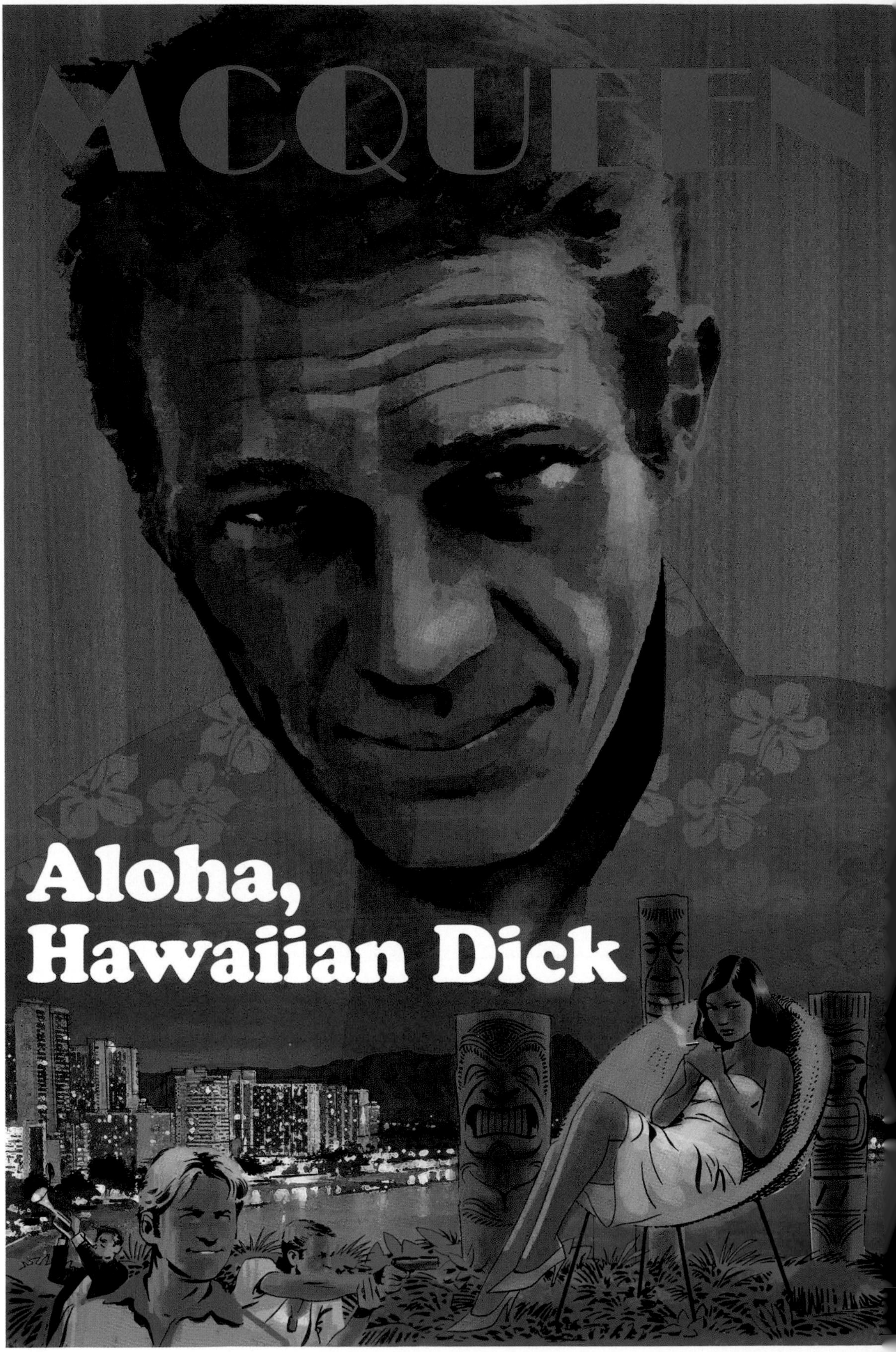
McQUEEN
Aloha,
Hawaiian Dick

STEVE McQUEEN/NANCY KWAN IN **"ALOHA, HAWAIIAN DICK"** A CLAYMORE PRESENTATION•CO-STARRING **JEFF BRIDGES•TOSHIRO MIF**
FEATURING **CHET BAKER** AS "TREAD LIGHTLY"•SCREENPLAY BY WALTER HILL• FROM THE GRAPHIC NOVEL BY B. CLAY MOORE AND JAKE W
MUSIC BY QUINCY JONES•A SOLAR PRODUCTION•PRODUCED BY JENNINGS LANG AND SYDNEY POLLACK•DIRECTED BY JOHN FRANKENHEI
FILMED IN TODD-AO 35•TECHNICOLOR®•A NATIONAL GENERAL PICTURES RELEASE

A BYRD OF PARADISE MYSTERY

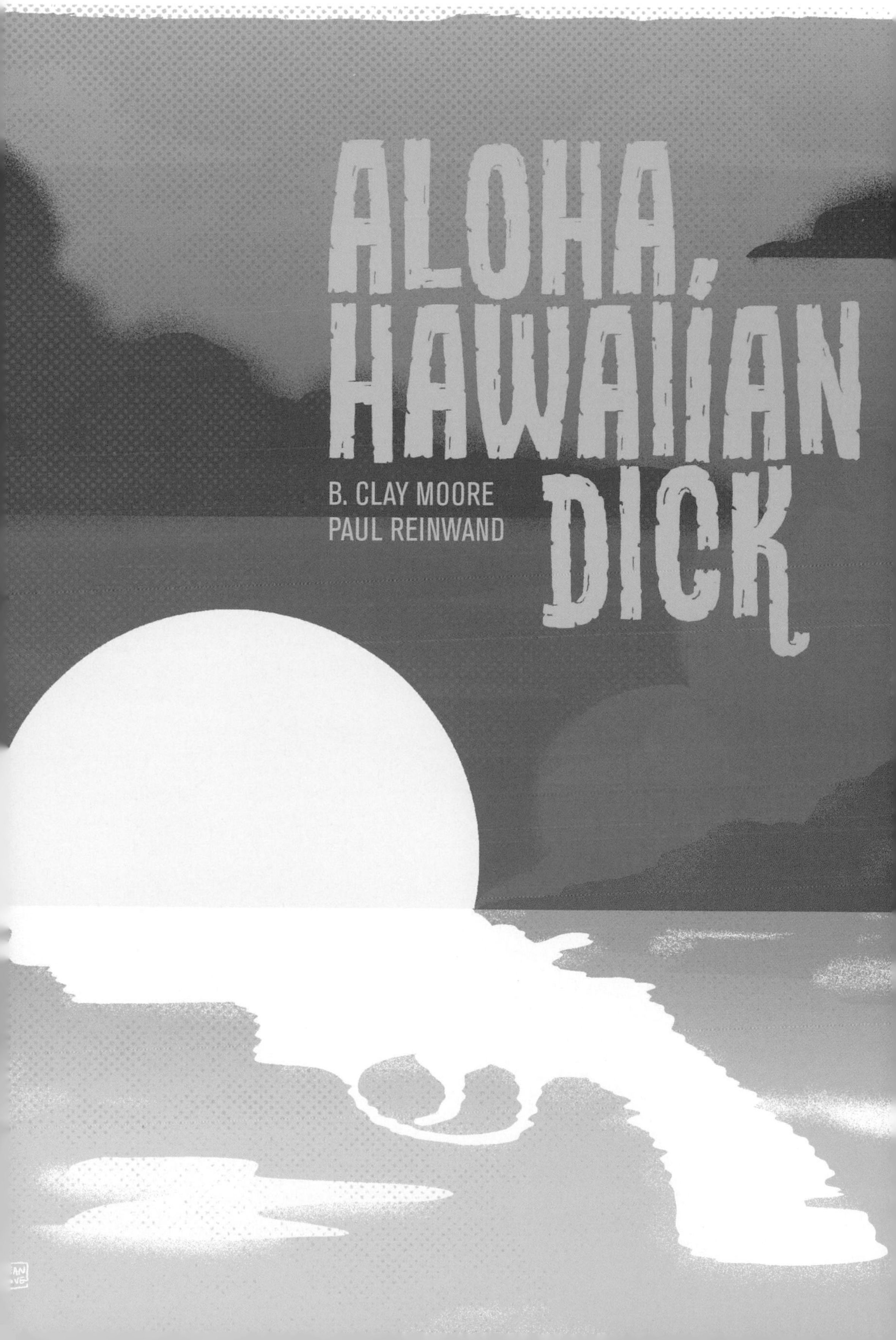

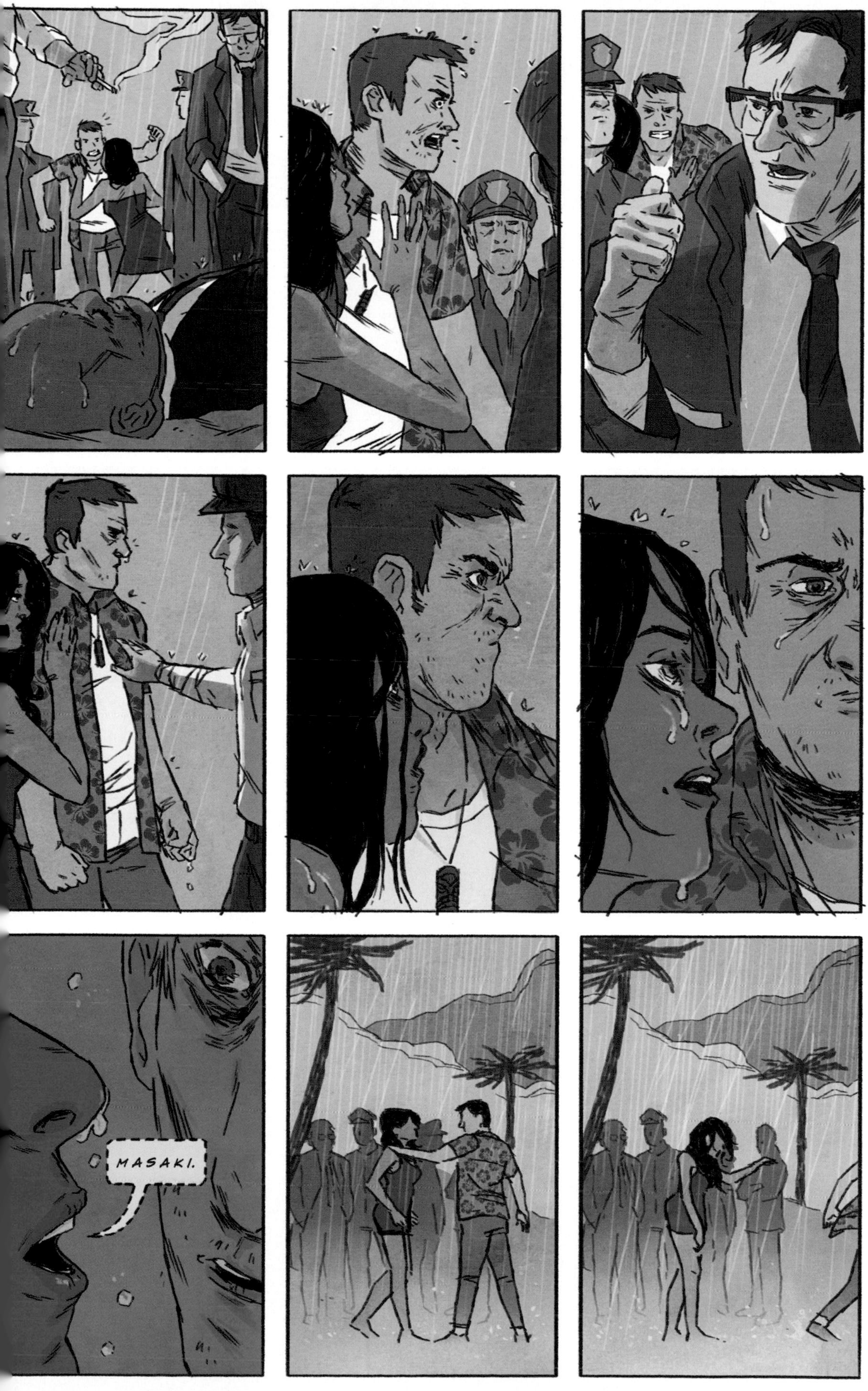
MASAKI.

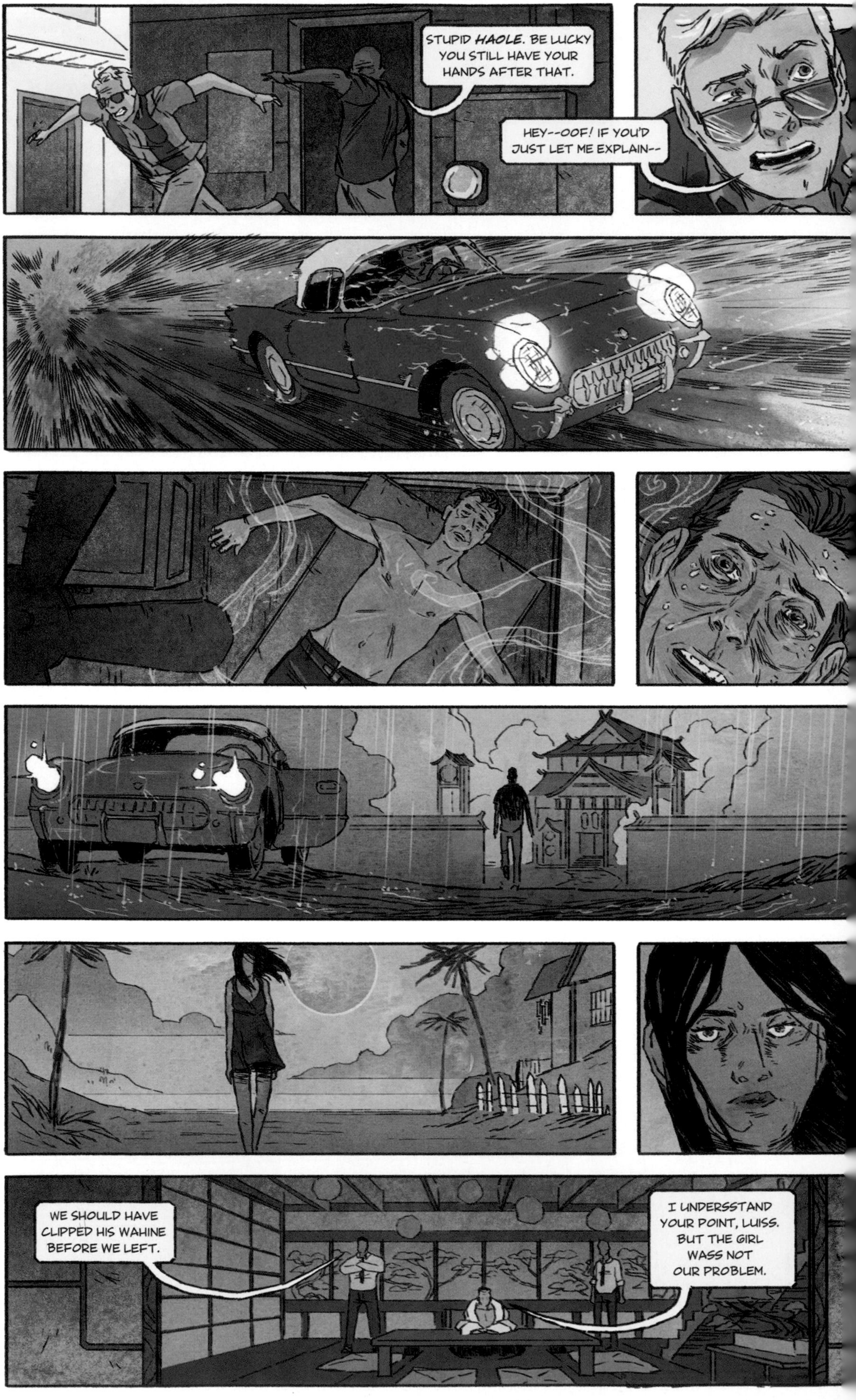
STUPID *HAOLE*. BE LUCKY YOU STILL HAVE YOUR HANDS AFTER THAT.
HEY--OOF! IF YOU'D JUST LET ME EXPLAIN--
WE SHOULD HAVE CLIPPED HIS WAHINE BEFORE WE LEFT.
I UNDERSSTAND YOUR POINT, LUISS. BUT THE GIRL WASS NOT OUR PROBLEM.

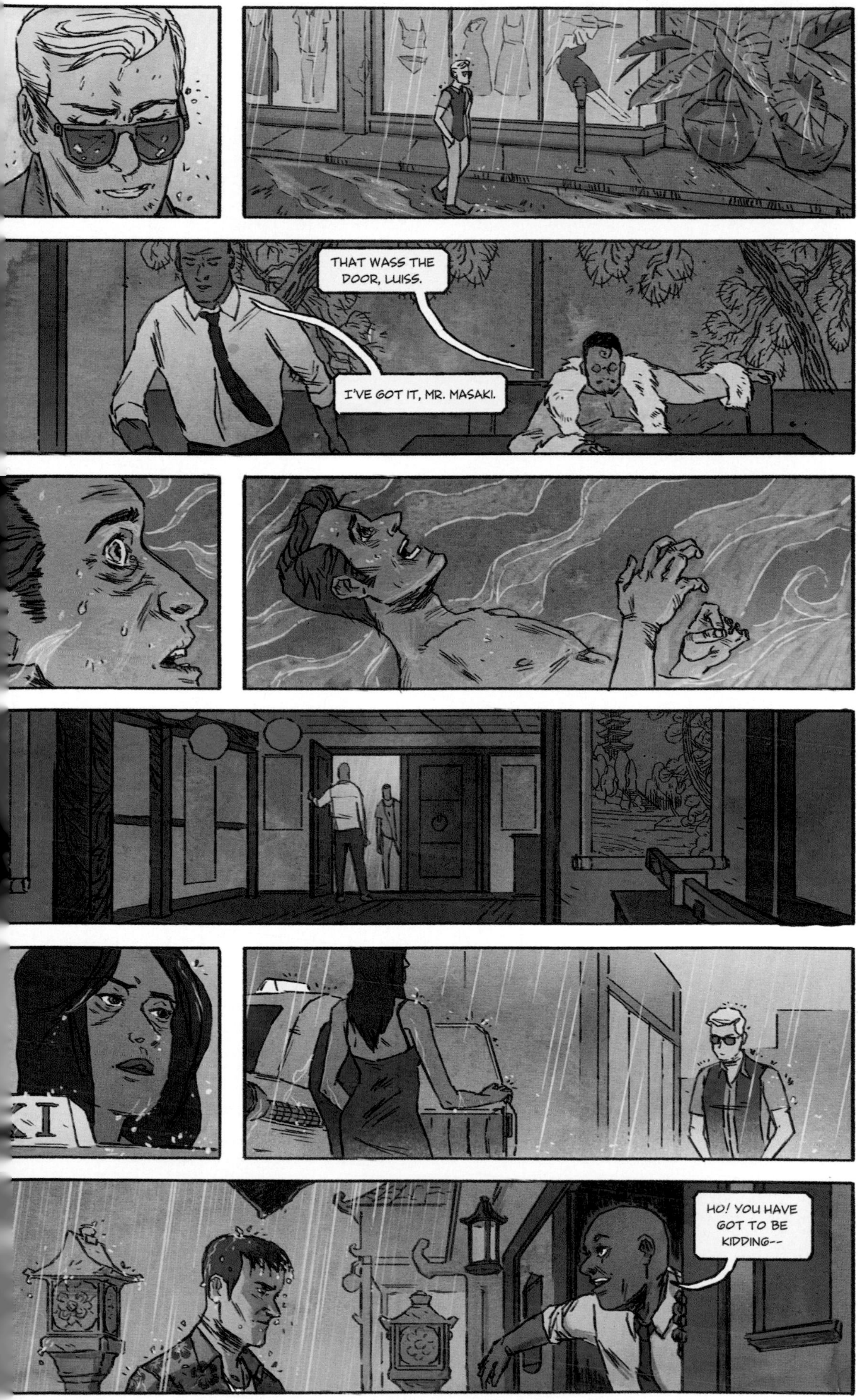
THAT WASS THE DOOR, LUISS.
I'VE GOT IT, MR. MASAKI.
HO! YOU HAVE GOT TO BE KIDDING--

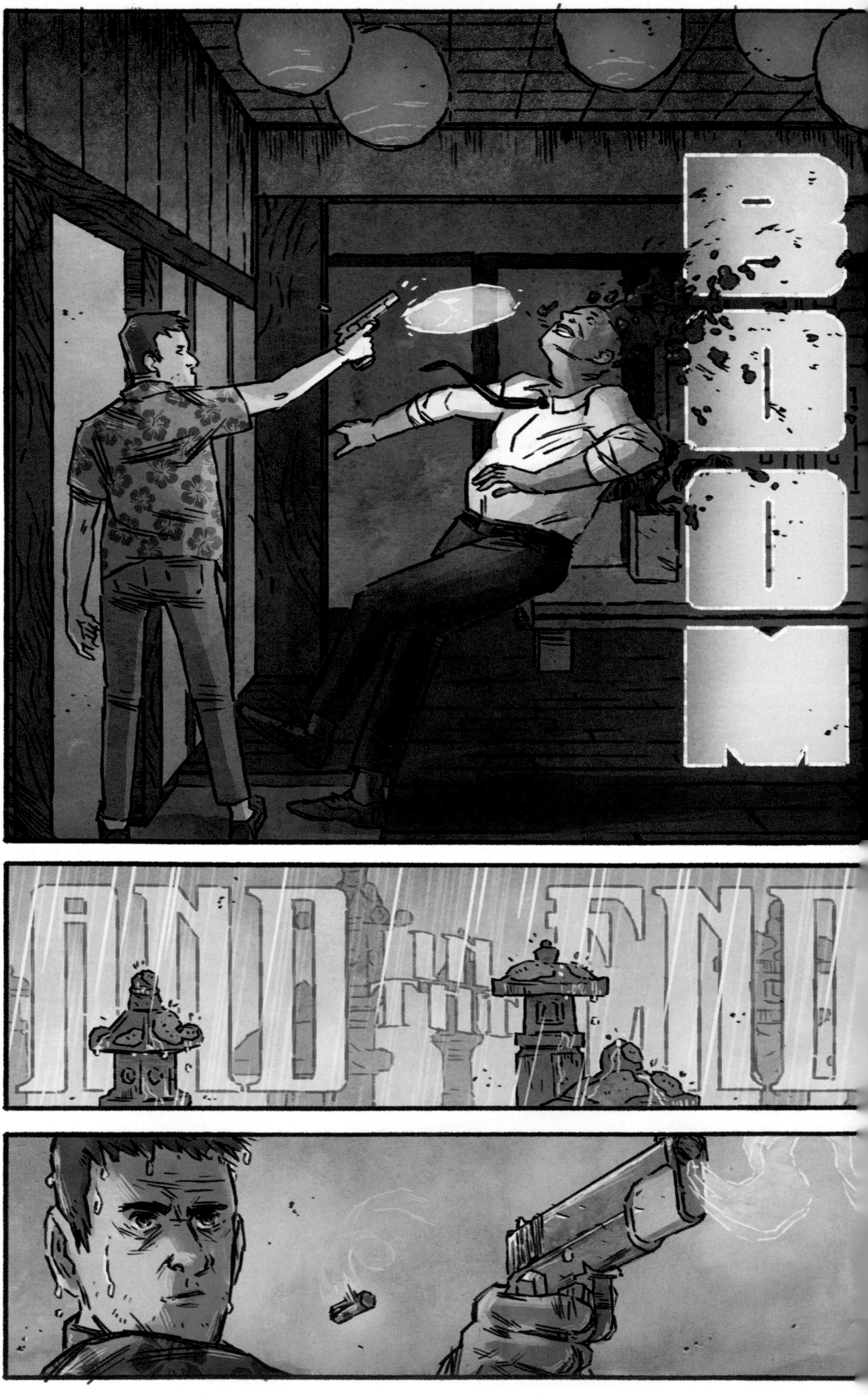
BOOM

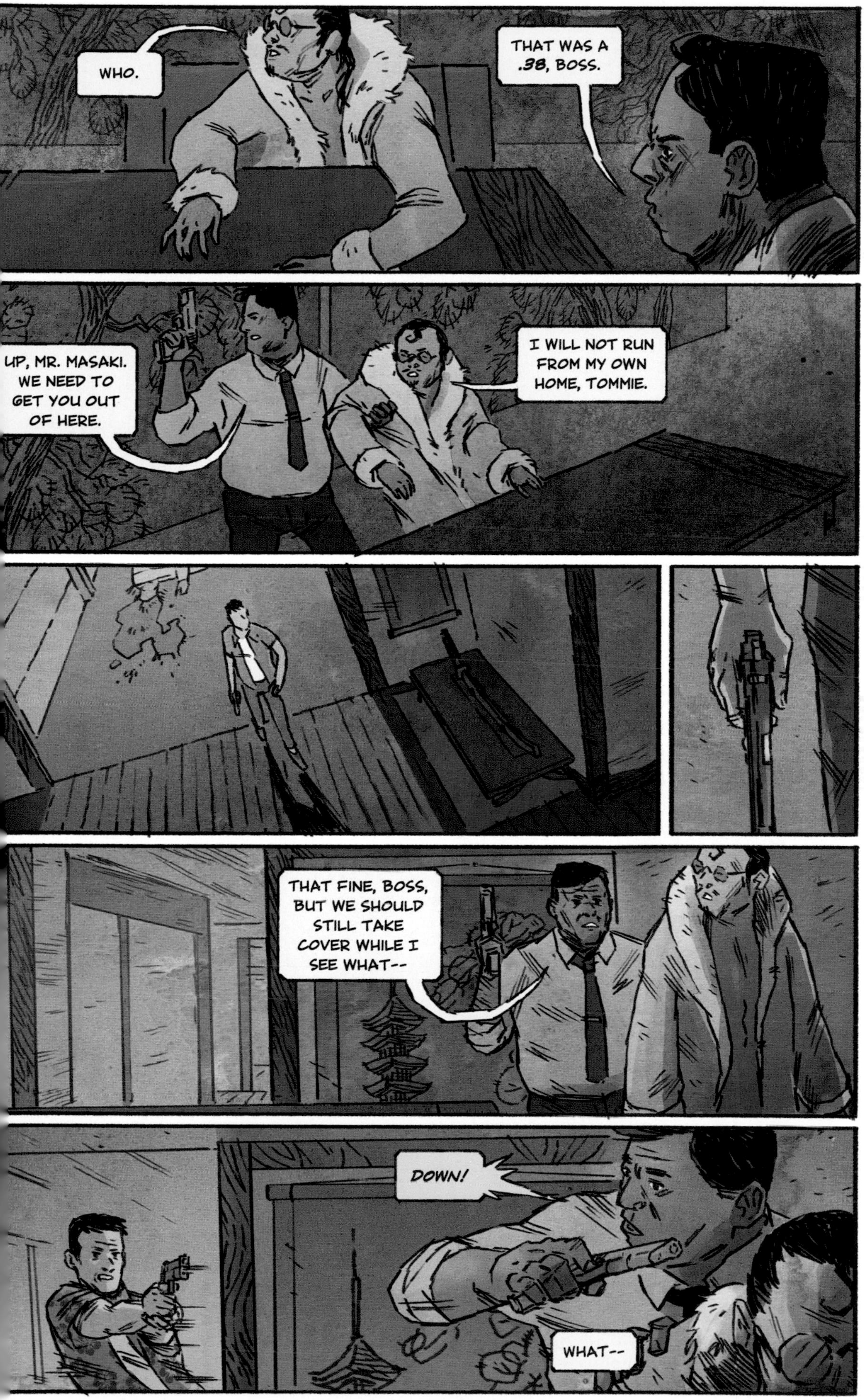
WHO.
THAT WAS A .38, BOSS.
UP, MR. MASAKI. WE NEED TO GET YOU OUT OF HERE.
I WILL NOT RUN FROM MY OWN HOME, TOMMIE.
THAT FINE, BOSS, BUT WE SHOULD STILL TAKE COVER WHILE I SEE WHAT--
DOWN!
WHAT--

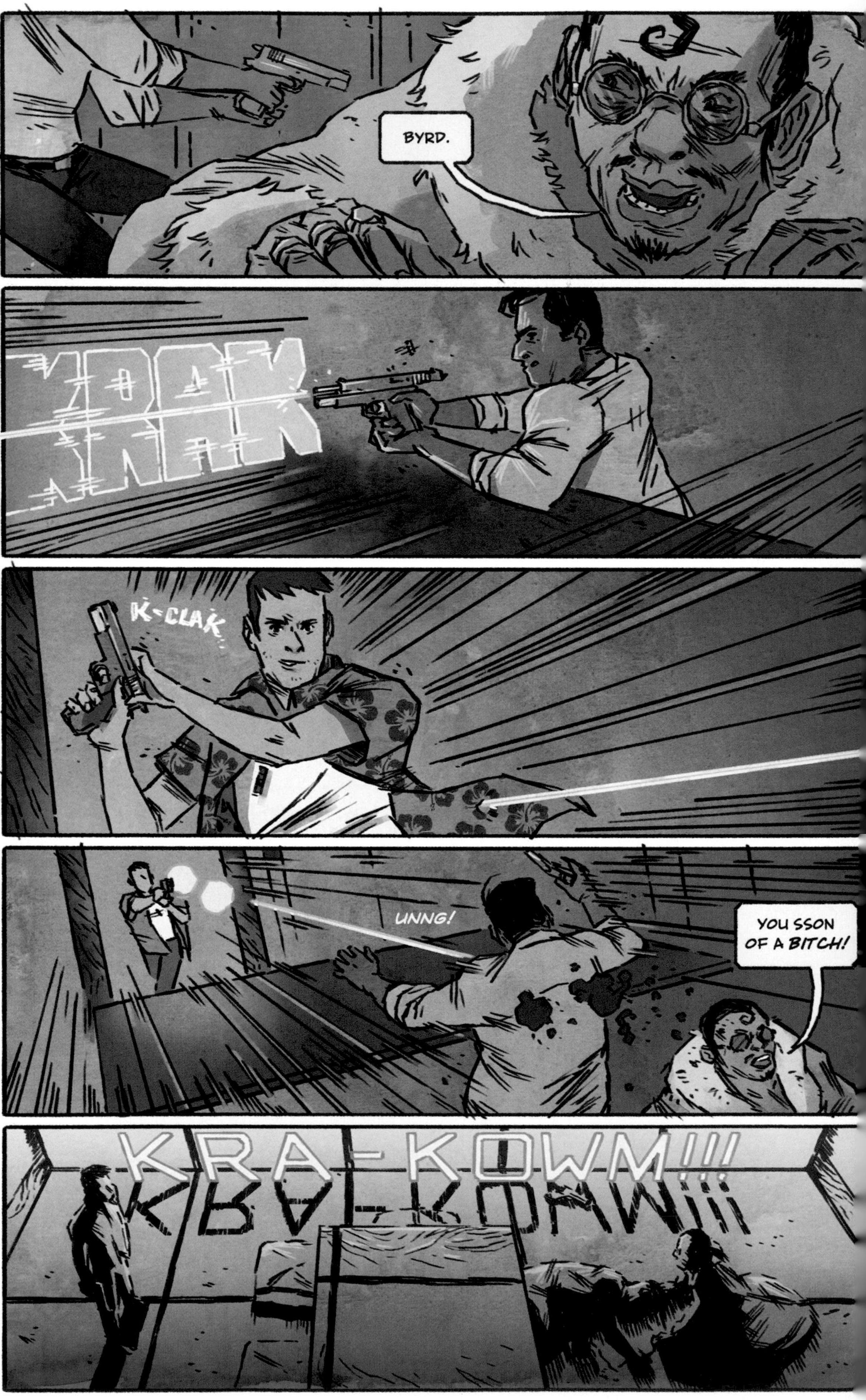
BYRD.
KRAK
K-CLAK
UNNG!
YOU SSON OF A BITCH!
KRA-KOWM!!!

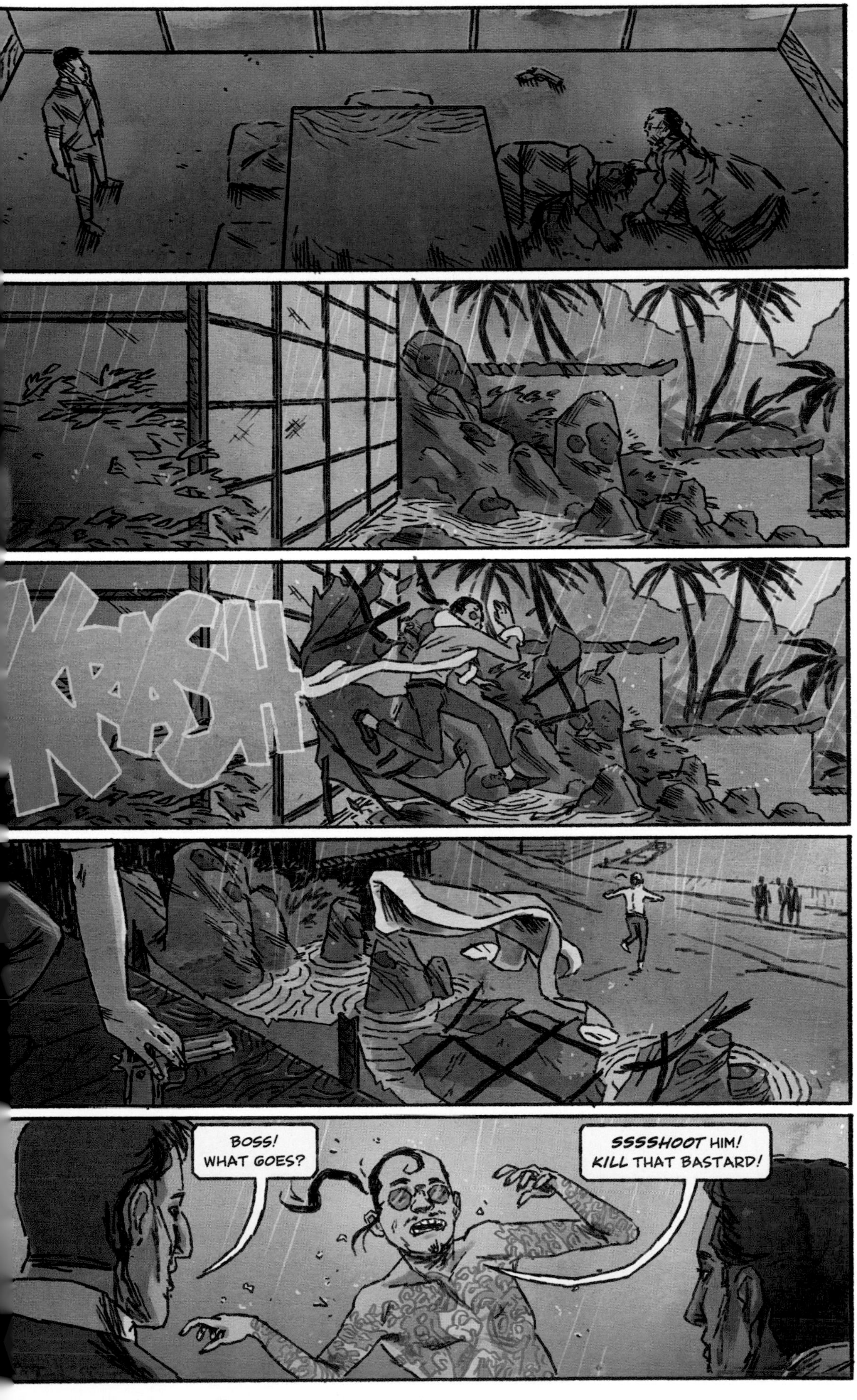
KRASH
BOSS! WHAT GOES?
SSSSHOOT HIM! KILL THAT BASTARD!

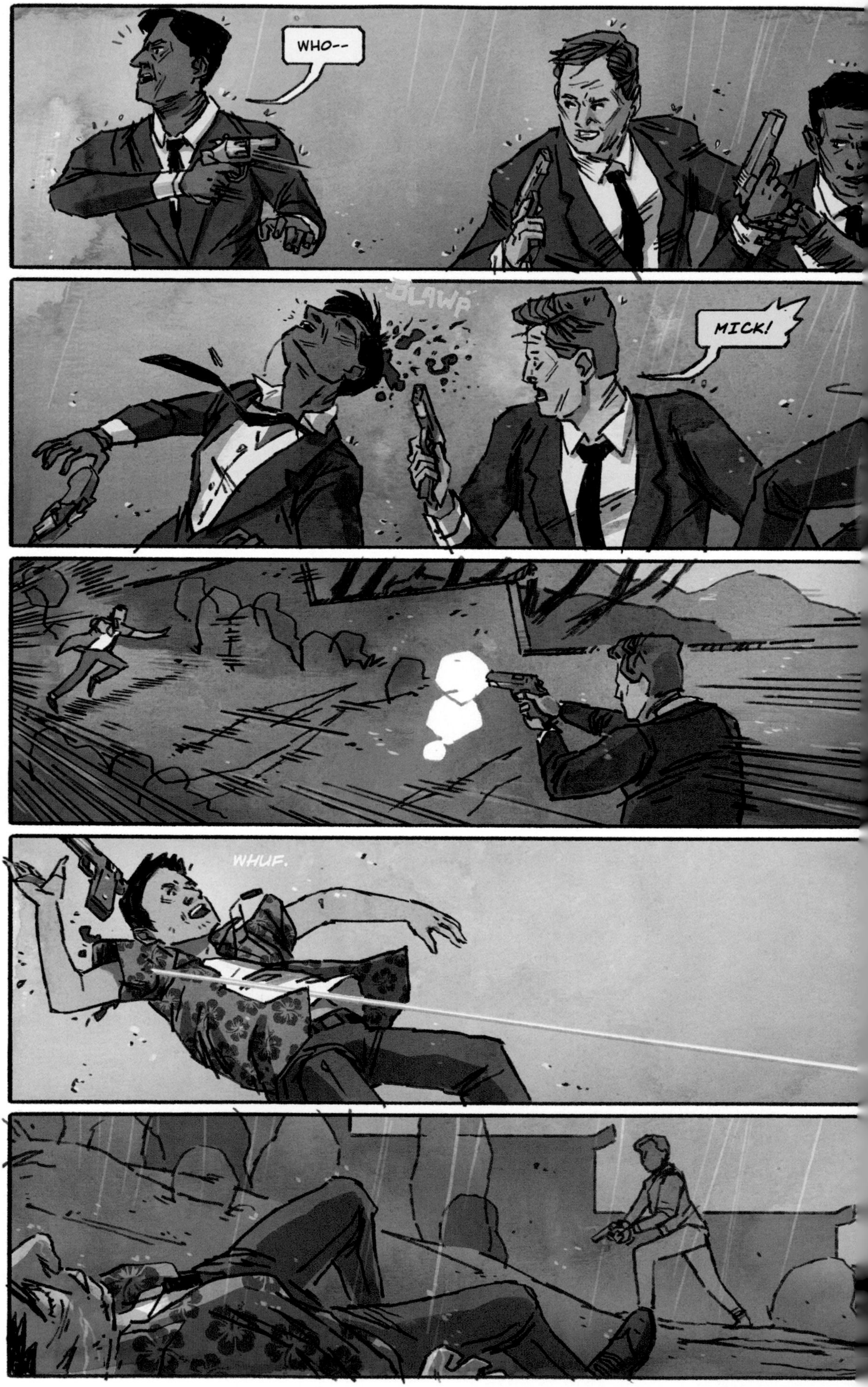
WHO--
BLAWP
MICK!
WHUF.

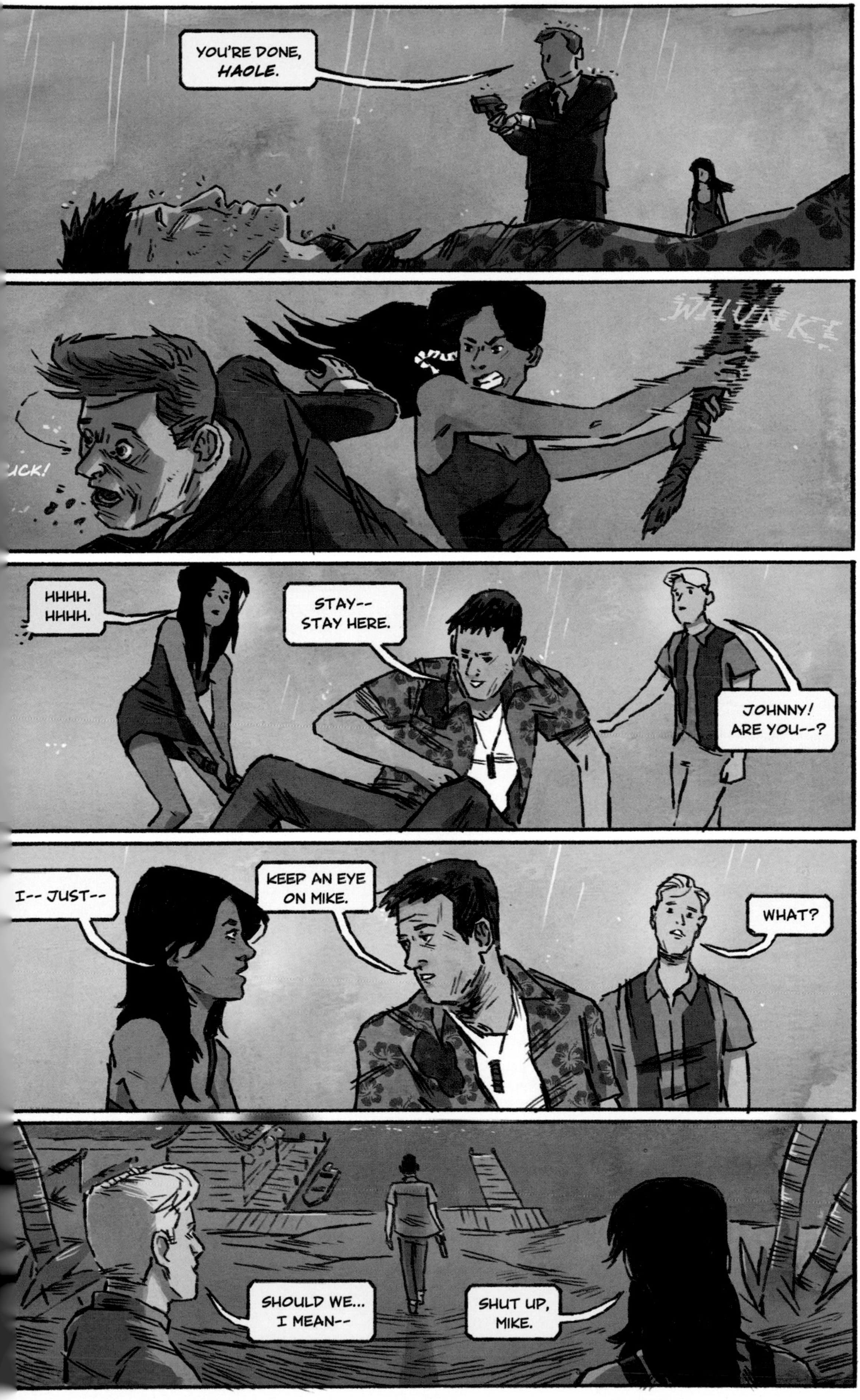
YOU'RE DONE, HAOLE.
WHUNK!
UCK!
HHHH. HHHH.
STAY-- STAY HERE.
JOHNNY! ARE YOU--?
I-- JUST--
KEEP AN EYE ON MIKE.
WHAT?
SHOULD WE... I MEAN--
SHUT UP, MIKE.

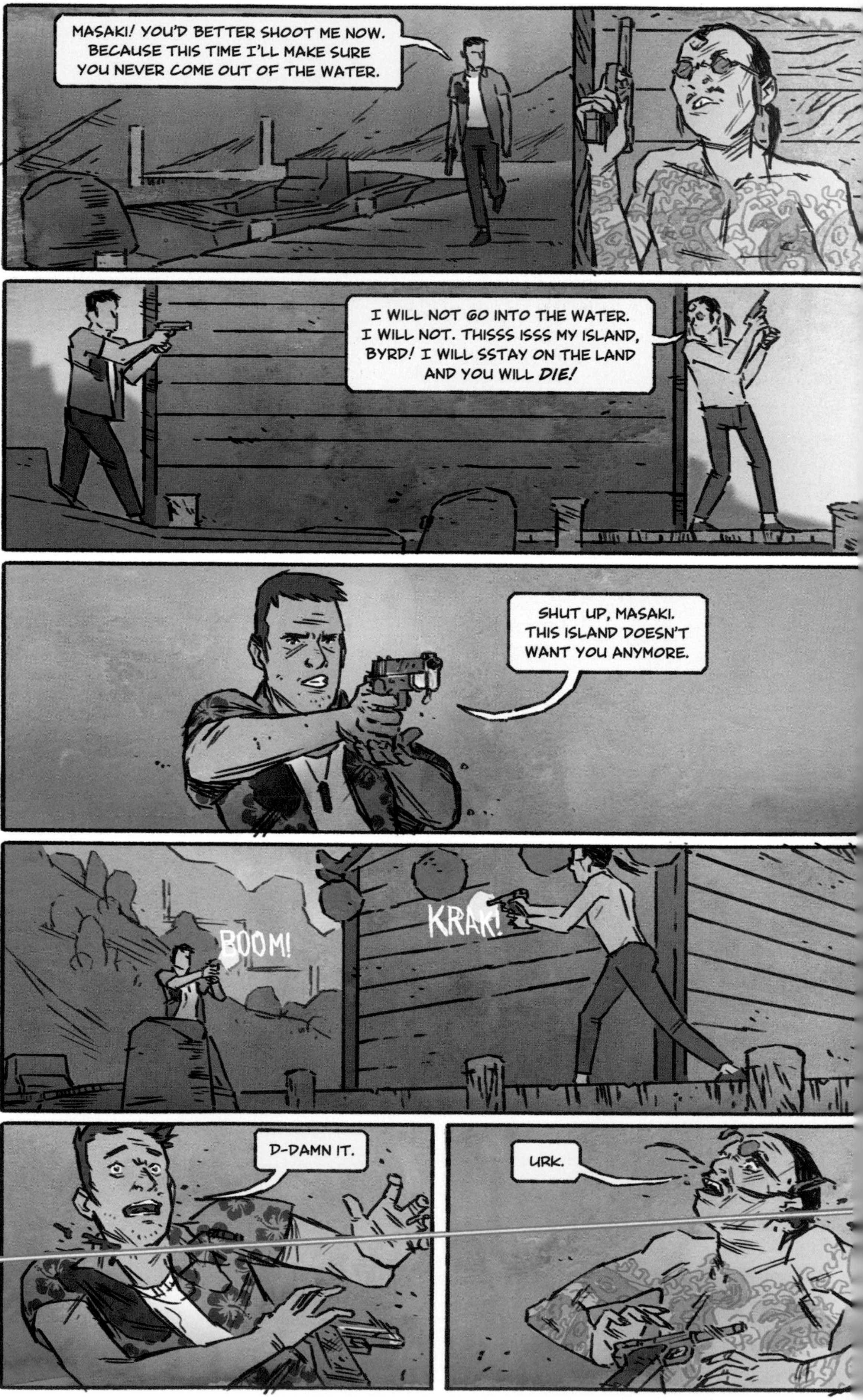
MASAKI! YOU'D BETTER SHOOT ME NOW. BECAUSE THIS TIME I'LL MAKE SURE YOU NEVER COME OUT OF THE WATER.
I WILL NOT GO INTO THE WATER. I WILL NOT. THISSS ISSS MY ISLAND, BYRD! I WILL SSTAY ON THE LAND AND YOU WILL *DIE!*
SHUT UP, MASAKI. THIS ISLAND DOESN'T WANT YOU ANYMORE.
BOOM!
KRAK!
D-DAMN IT.
URK.

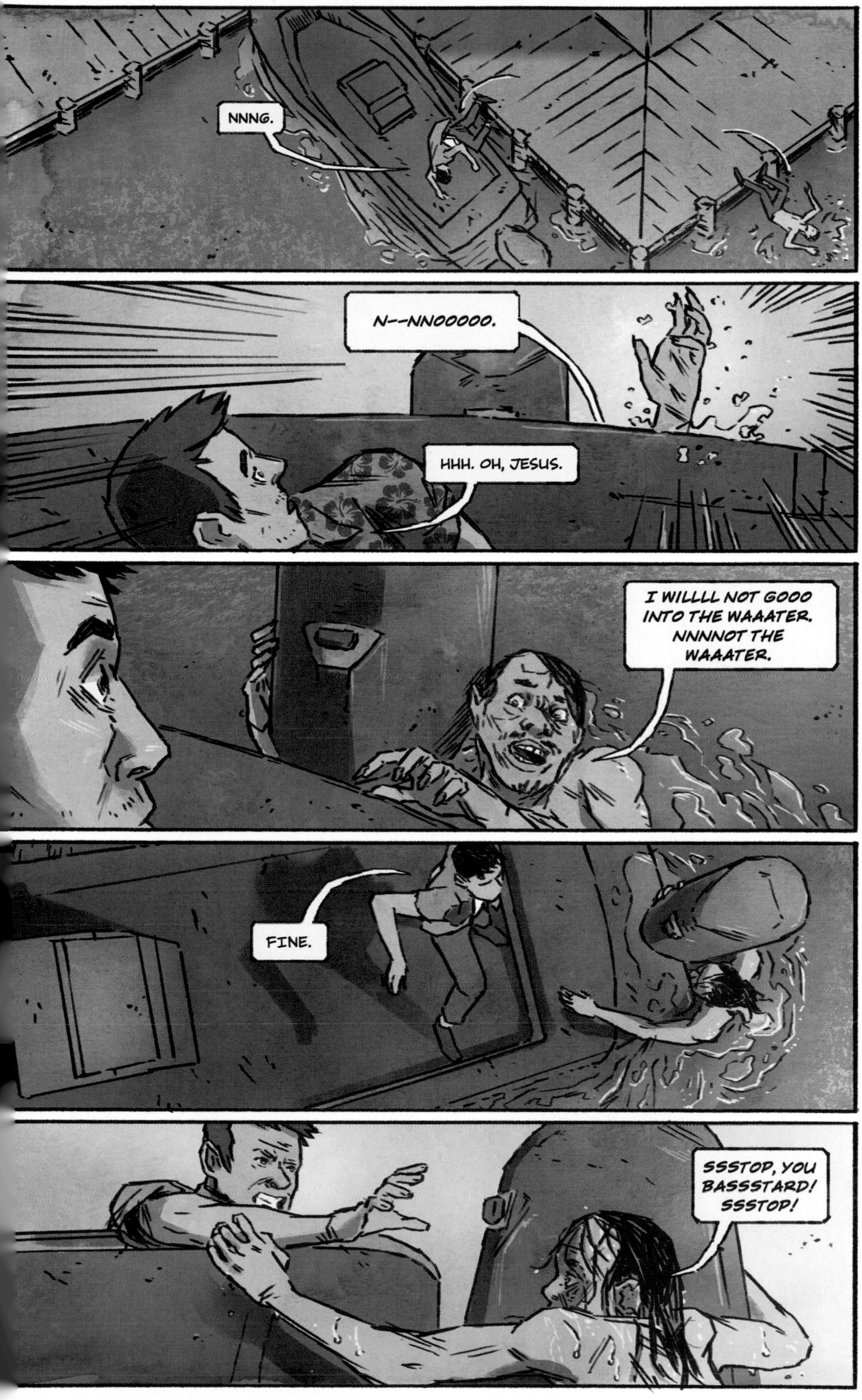
NNNG.
N--NNOOOOO.
HHH. OH, JESUS.
I WILLLL NOT GOOO INTO THE WAAATER. NNNNOT THE WAAATER.
FINE.
SSSTOP, YOU BASSSTARD! SSSTOP!

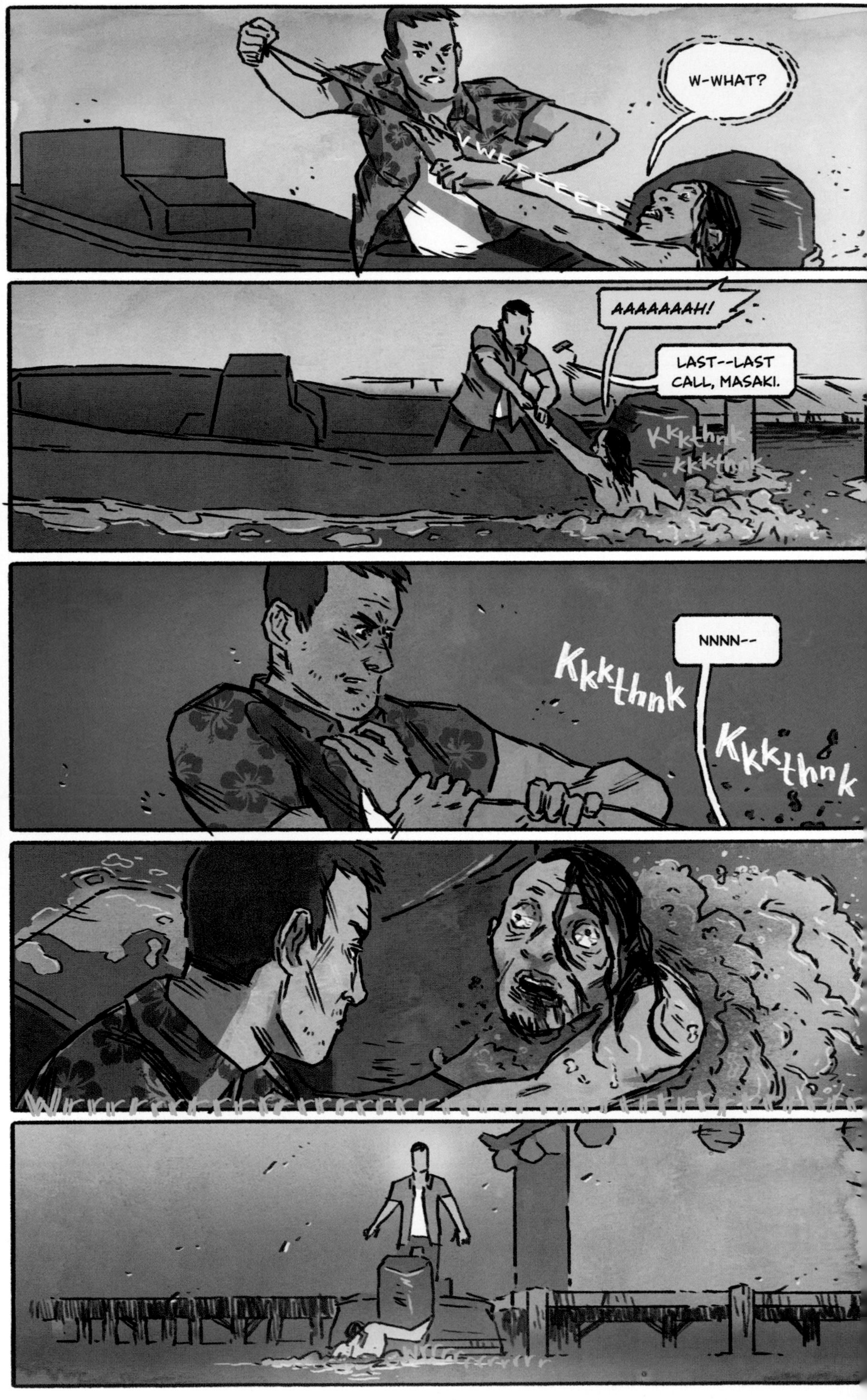
W-WHAT?
VWEEEEEEP
AAAAAAAH!
LAST--LAST CALL, MASAKI.
Kkkthnk
kkkthnk
NNNN--
Kkkthnk
Kkkthnk
Wrrrrrrrrrrrrrrrrrrrrrrrrrrrrrrrr

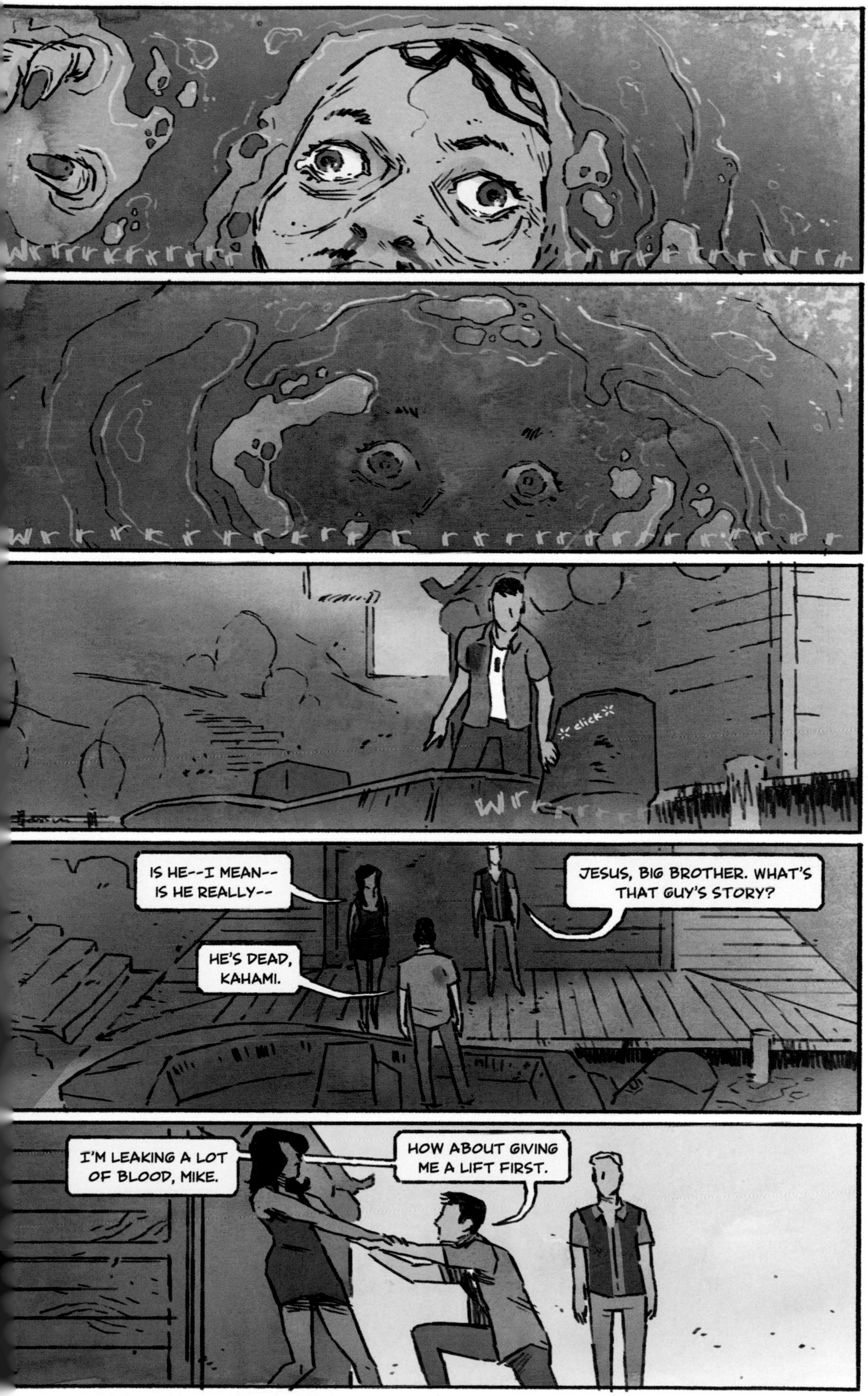

Wrrrrrrrrrrr
rrrrrrrrrrrr
Wrrrrrrrrrrrrrrrrrrrrrrrrrrrr
click
Wrrrrrr
IS HE--I MEAN--
IS HE REALLY--
JESUS, BIG BROTHER. WHAT'S
THAT GUY'S STORY?
HE'S DEAD,
KAHAMI.
I'M LEAKING A LOT
OF BLOOD, MIKE.
HOW ABOUT GIVING
ME A LIFT FIRST.

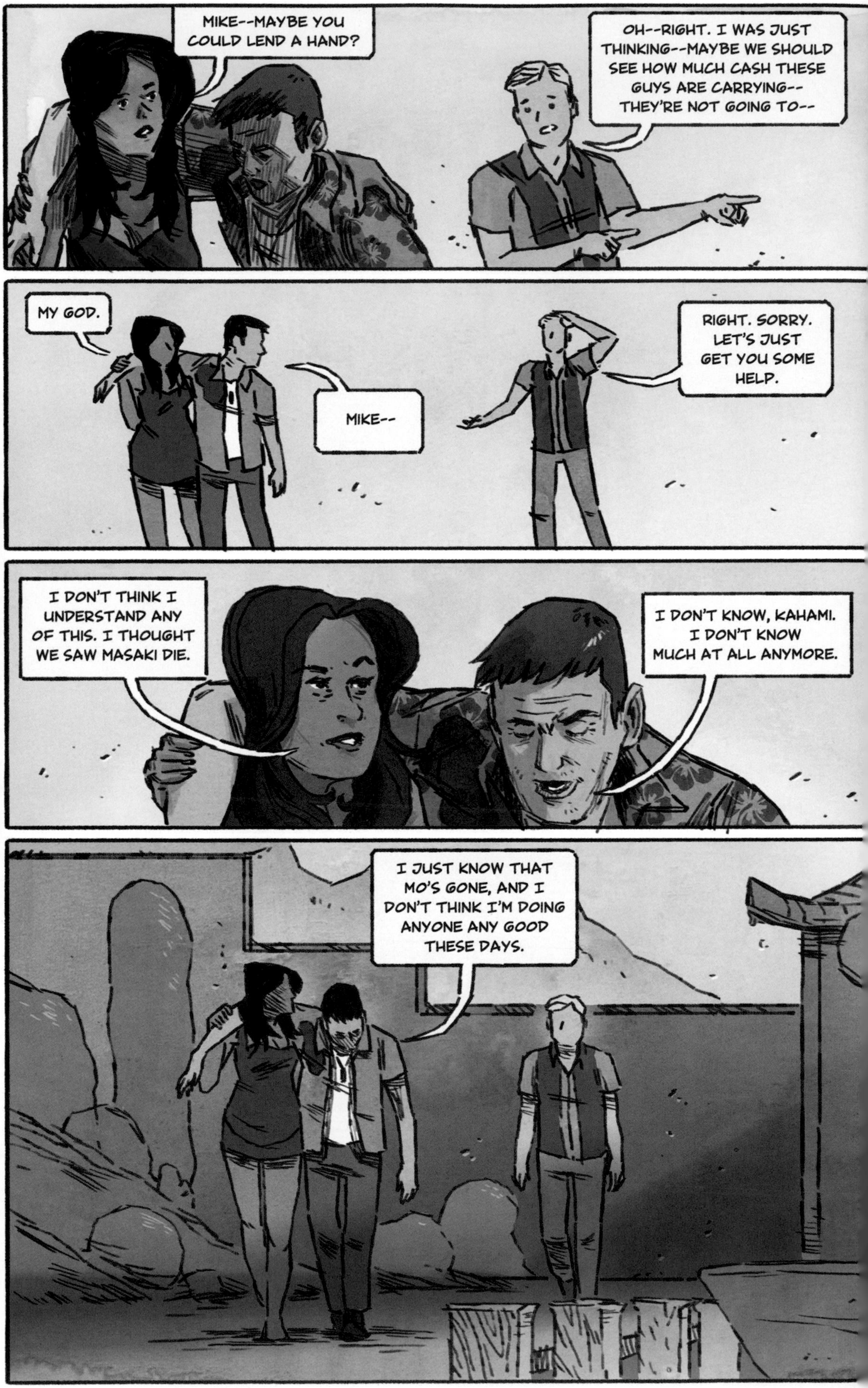
MIKE--MAYBE YOU COULD LEND A HAND?
OH--RIGHT. I WAS JUST THINKING--MAYBE WE SHOULD SEE HOW MUCH CASH THESE GUYS ARE CARRYING--THEY'RE NOT GOING TO--
MY GOD.
MIKE--
RIGHT. SORRY. LET'S JUST GET YOU SOME HELP.
I DON'T THINK I UNDERSTAND ANY OF THIS. I THOUGHT WE SAW MASAKI DIE.
I DON'T KNOW, KAHAMI. I DON'T KNOW MUCH AT ALL ANYMORE.
I JUST KNOW THAT MO'S GONE, AND I DON'T THINK I'M DOING ANYONE ANY GOOD THESE DAYS.

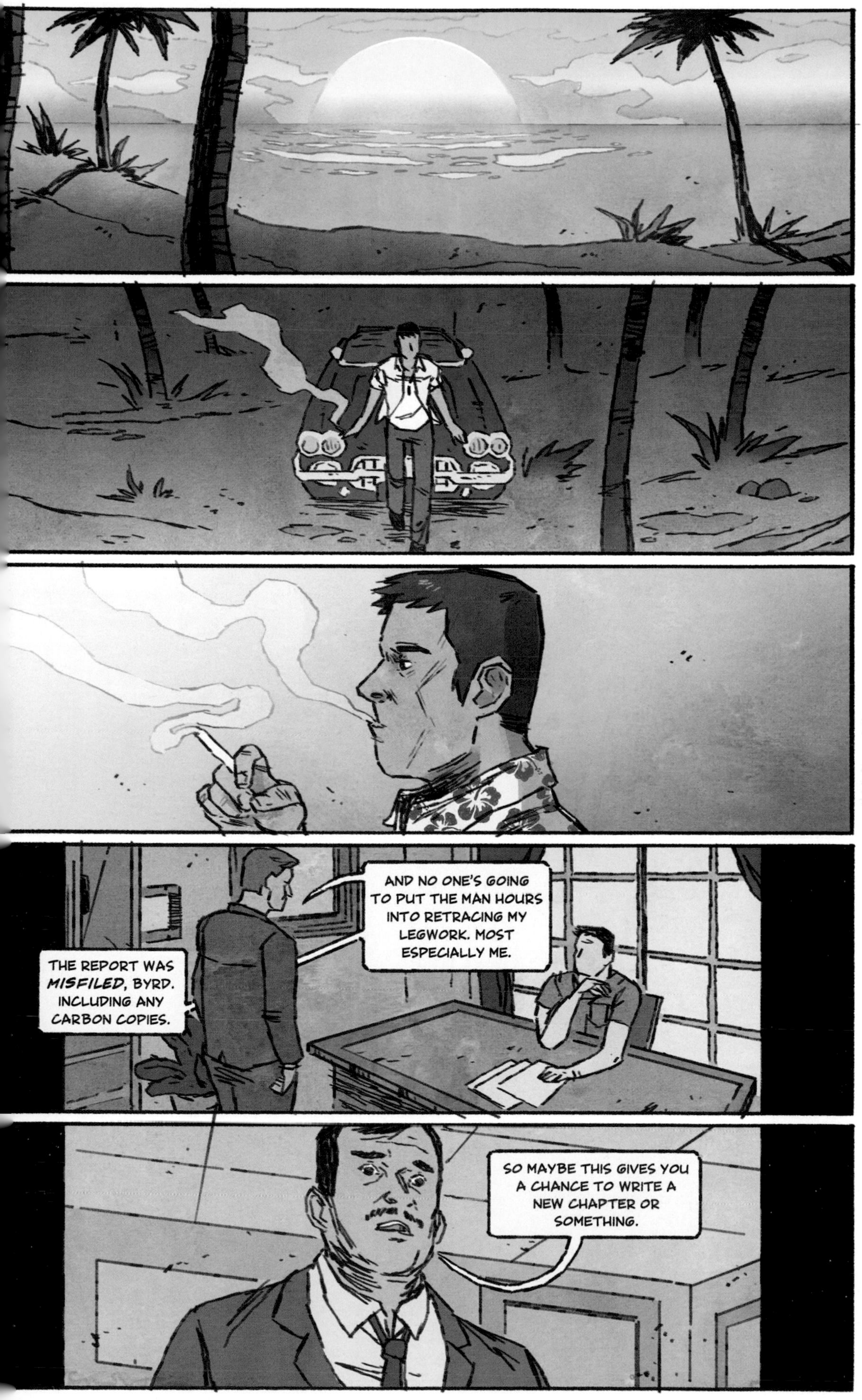

AND NO ONE'S GOING TO PUT THE MAN HOURS INTO RETRACING MY LEGWORK. MOST ESPECIALLY ME.
THE REPORT WAS *MISFILED*, BYRD. INCLUDING ANY CARBON COPIES.
SO MAYBE THIS GIVES YOU A CHANCE TO WRITE A NEW CHAPTER OR SOMETHING.

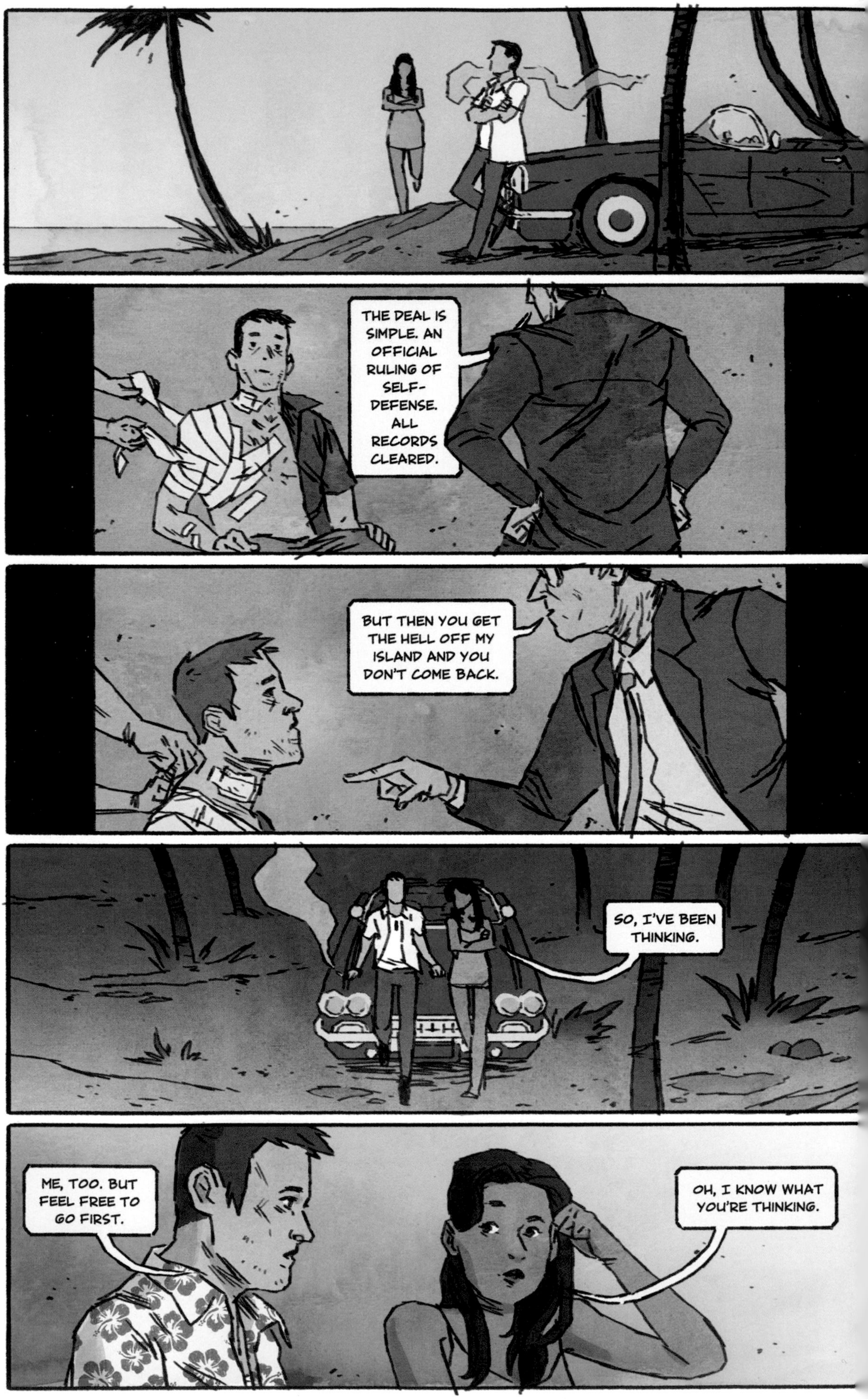
THE DEAL IS SIMPLE. AN OFFICIAL RULING OF SELF-DEFENSE. ALL RECORDS CLEARED.
BUT THEN YOU GET THE HELL OFF MY ISLAND AND YOU DON'T COME BACK.
SO, I'VE BEEN THINKING.
ME, TOO. BUT FEEL FREE TO GO FIRST.
OH, I KNOW WHAT YOU'RE THINKING.

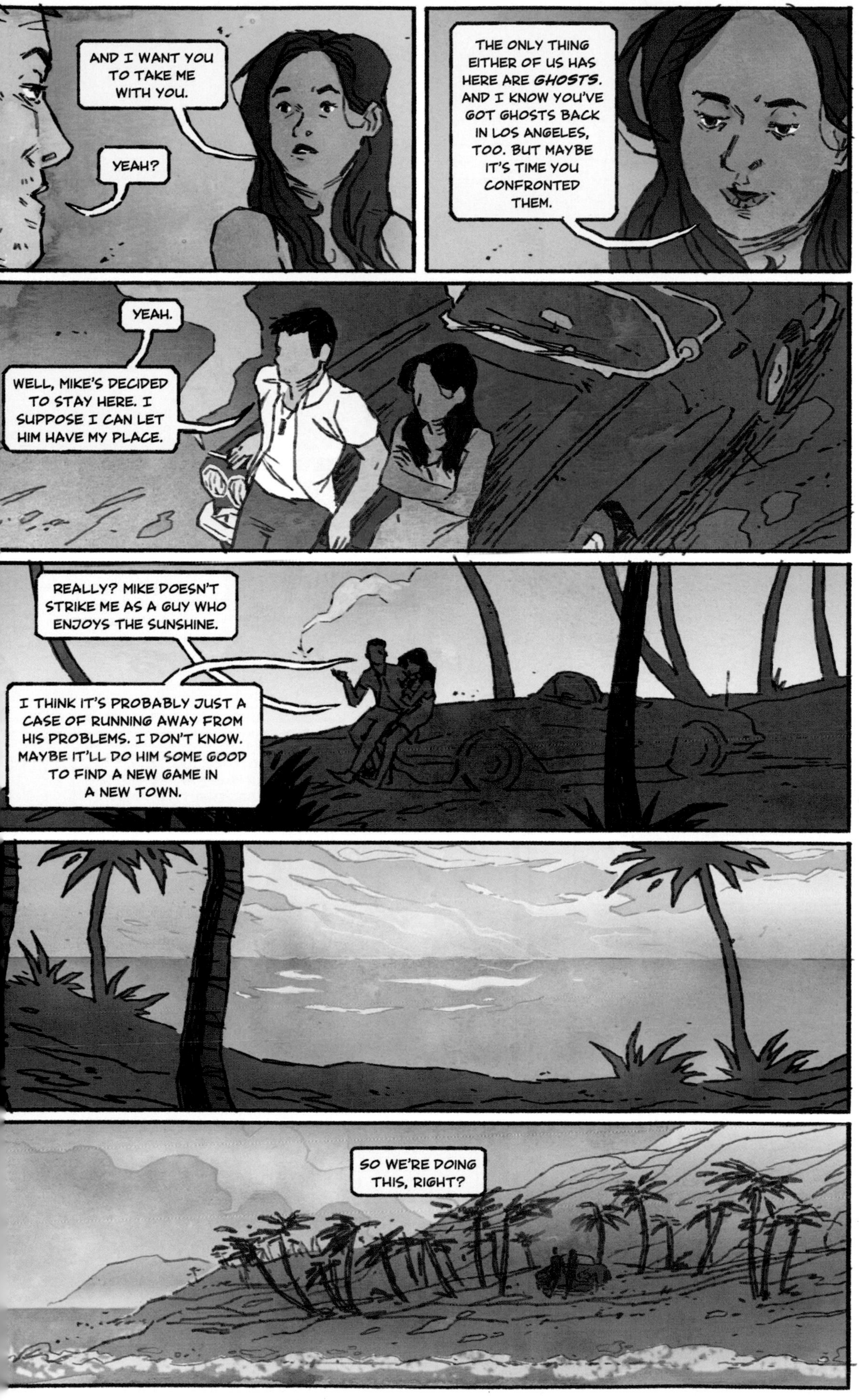
AND I WANT YOU TO TAKE ME WITH YOU.
YEAH?
THE ONLY THING EITHER OF US HAS HERE ARE *GHOSTS*. AND I KNOW YOU'VE GOT GHOSTS BACK IN LOS ANGELES, TOO. BUT MAYBE IT'S TIME YOU CONFRONTED THEM.
YEAH.
WELL, MIKE'S DECIDED TO STAY HERE. I SUPPOSE I CAN LET HIM HAVE MY PLACE.
REALLY? MIKE DOESN'T STRIKE ME AS A GUY WHO ENJOYS THE SUNSHINE.
I THINK IT'S PROBABLY JUST A CASE OF RUNNING AWAY FROM HIS PROBLEMS. I DON'T KNOW. MAYBE IT'LL DO HIM SOME GOOD TO FIND A NEW GAME IN A NEW TOWN.
SO WE'RE DOING THIS, RIGHT?

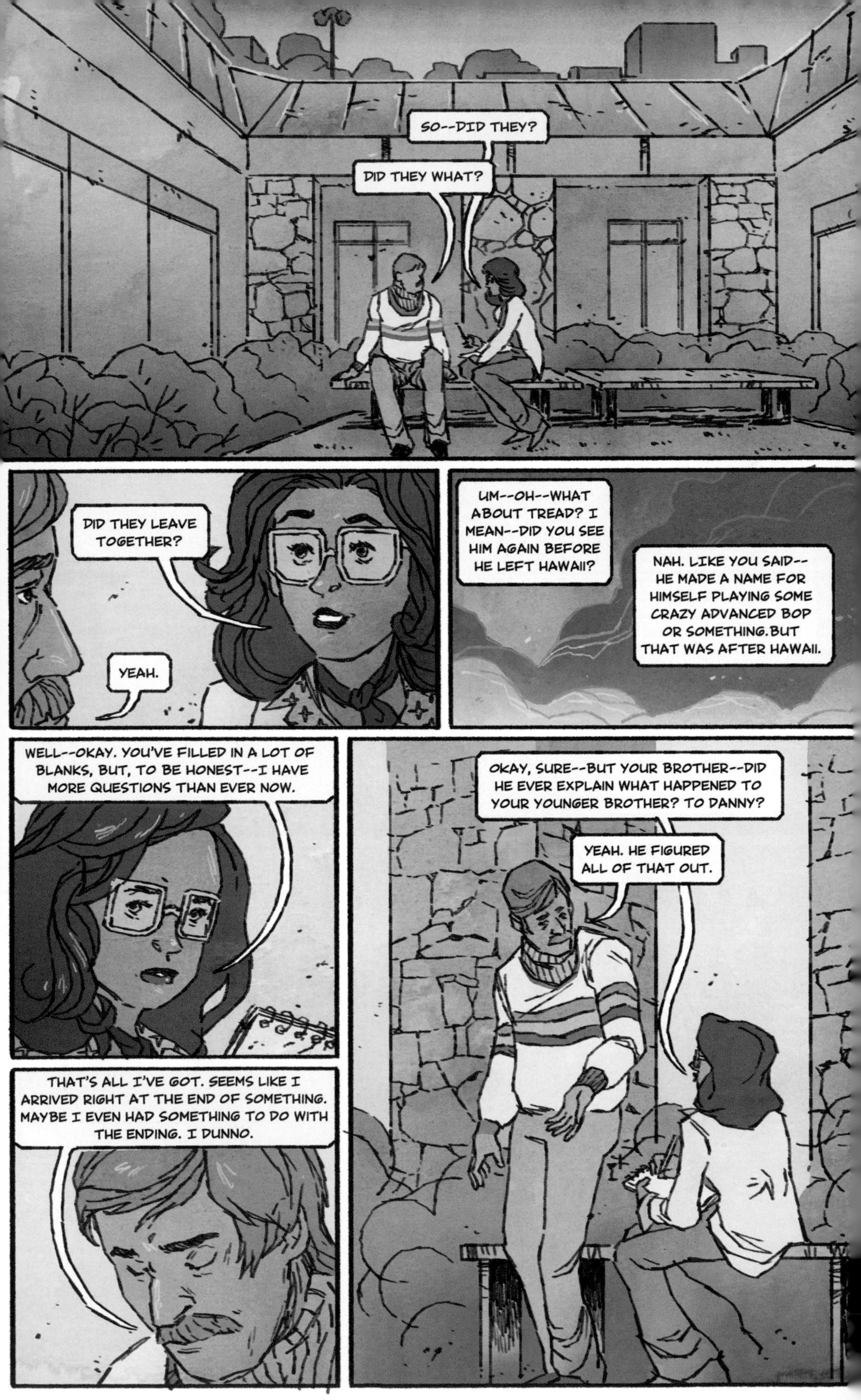
SO--DID THEY?
DID THEY WHAT?
DID THEY LEAVE TOGETHER?
YEAH.
UM--OH--WHAT ABOUT TREAD? I MEAN--DID YOU SEE HIM AGAIN BEFORE HE LEFT HAWAII?
NAH. LIKE YOU SAID--HE MADE A NAME FOR HIMSELF PLAYING SOME CRAZY ADVANCED BOP OR SOMETHING. BUT THAT WAS AFTER HAWAII.
WELL--OKAY. YOU'VE FILLED IN A LOT OF BLANKS, BUT, TO BE HONEST--I HAVE MORE QUESTIONS THAN EVER NOW.
THAT'S ALL I'VE GOT. SEEMS LIKE I ARRIVED RIGHT AT THE END OF SOMETHING. MAYBE I EVEN HAD SOMETHING TO DO WITH THE ENDING. I DUNNO.
OKAY, SURE--BUT YOUR BROTHER--DID HE EVER EXPLAIN WHAT HAPPENED TO YOUR YOUNGER BROTHER? TO DANNY?
YEAH. HE FIGURED ALL OF THAT OUT.

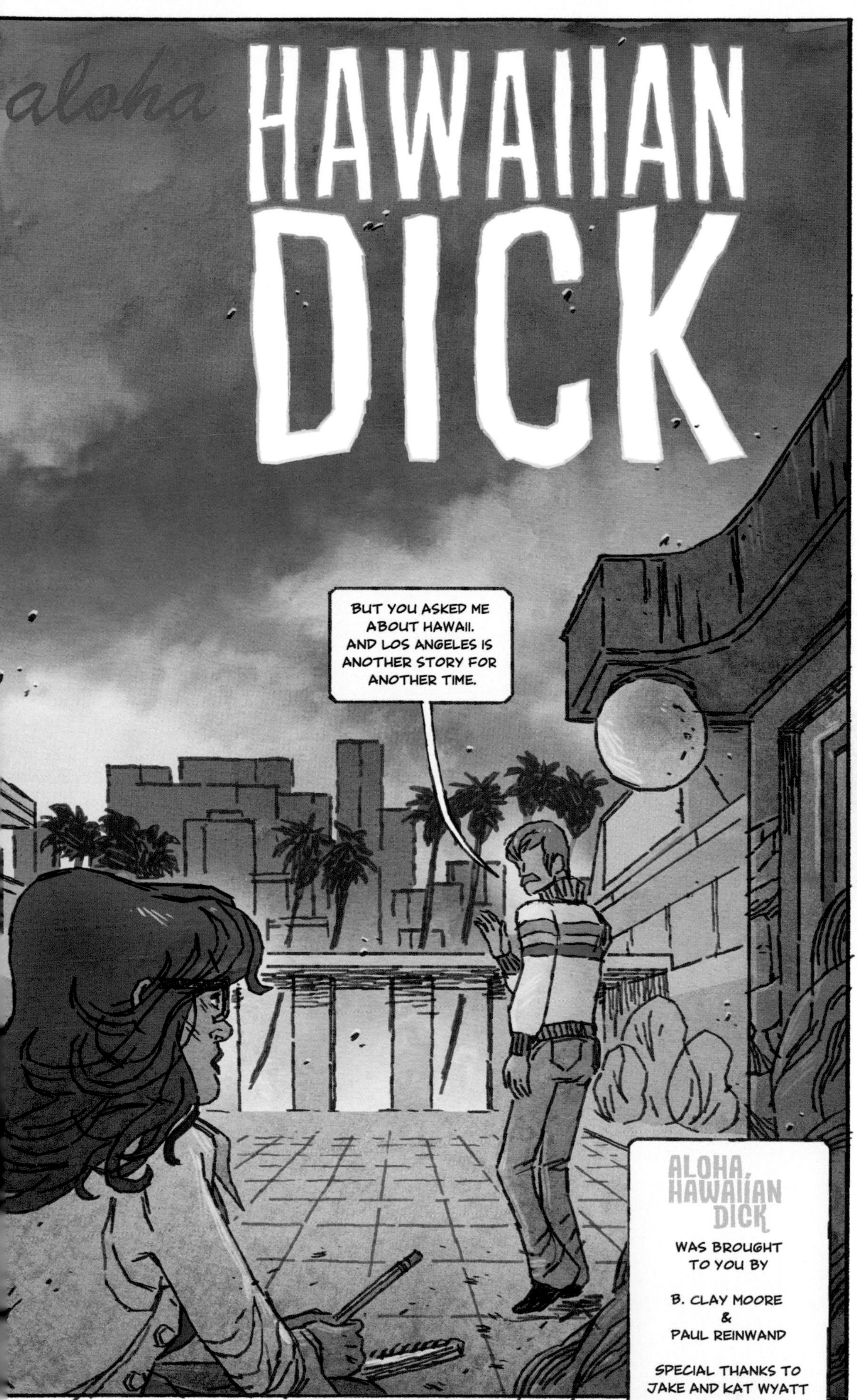
aloha
HAWAIIAN DICK
BUT YOU ASKED ME ABOUT HAWAII. AND LOS ANGELES IS ANOTHER STORY FOR ANOTHER TIME.
ALOHA, HAWAIIAN DICK
WAS BROUGHT TO YOU BY
B. CLAY MOORE & PAUL REINWAND
SPECIAL THANKS TO JAKE AND KAT WYATT

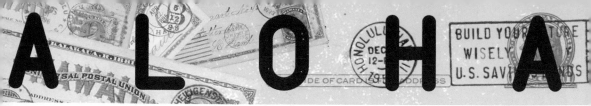

"JAZZ INTERLUDE"
3Y B. CLAY MOORE & JASON ARMSTRONG

HIS STORY WAS ORIGINALLY INTENDED AS *HAWAIIAN DICK #6*, WHICH 'OULD HAVE FOLLOWED *HAWAIIAN DICK SCREAMING BLACK THUNDER 5*. IN FACT, IT WAS SOLICITED SEVERAL YEARS AGO AS *HAWAIIAN DICK 6*. (THAT SERIES WAS ORIGINALLY INTENDED TO BE AN ONGOING BOOK.)

UE TO SOME UNFORESEEN CIRCUMSTANCES, WE CUT THE BOOK SHORT FTER THE FIFTH ISSUE, AND SHELVED THIS STORY.

NITIALLY, JAKE WYATT CAME ON BOARD TO DRAW *HAWAIIAN DICK #7*, HICH APPEARS AS THE SECOND ISSUE OF *ALOHA, HAWAIIAN DICK*. AFTER TARTING THAT STORY, WE BEGAN TALKING ABOUT WORKING TOGETHER ON OMETHING ELSE, AND DECIDED TO JUST EXPAND THAT STORY INTO WHAT ECAME *ALOHA, HAWAIIAN DICK*.

, JAKE ACTUALLY DREW THE SECOND ISSUE OF *ALOHA* BEFORE THE FIRST. E ADDED MIKE BYRD TO THE STORY AND DECIDED TO OPEN IN SUBURBAN KC TH A CHARACTER NO ONE HAD EVER SEEN BEFORE.

HAT COMMERCIAL INSTINCTS!

ISSUE SIX
hawaiian dick

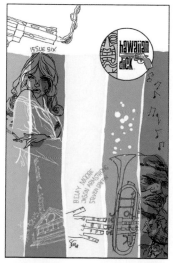

ORIGINAL SOLICITED COVER BY STEVEN GRIFFIN

Oh God, my new book only did WHAT?!
Shhh...there there. cheer up, I have a flat white on my head.

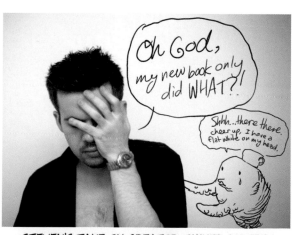

STEVEN'S TAKE ON CREATOR-OWNED ANXIETY

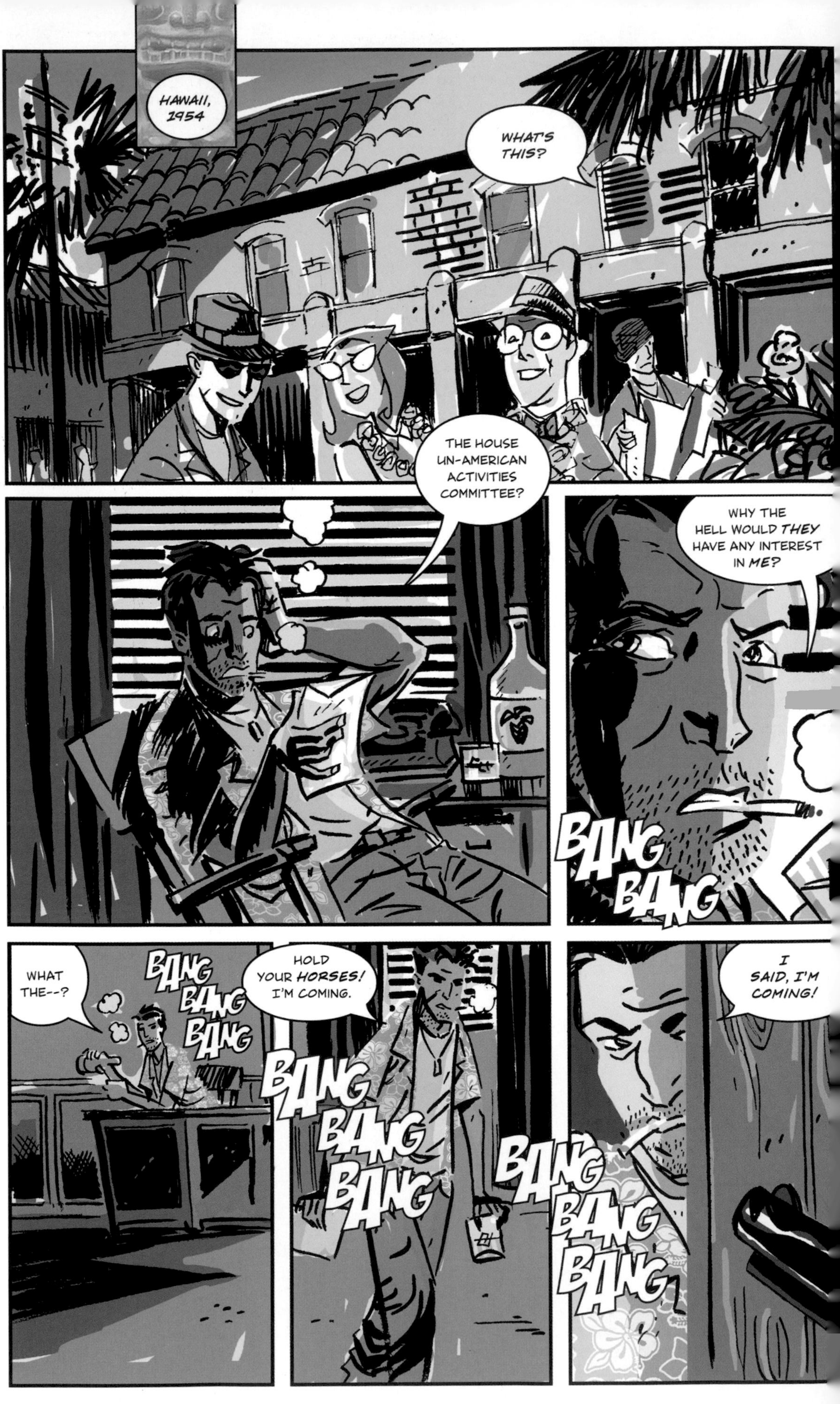
HAWAII, 1954
WHAT'S THIS?
THE HOUSE UN-AMERICAN ACTIVITIES COMMITTEE?
WHY THE HELL WOULD THEY HAVE ANY INTEREST IN ME?
BANG BANG
WHAT THE--?
BANG BANG BANG
HOLD YOUR HORSES! I'M COMING.
BANG BANG BANG
BANG BANG BANG
I SAID, I'M COMING!

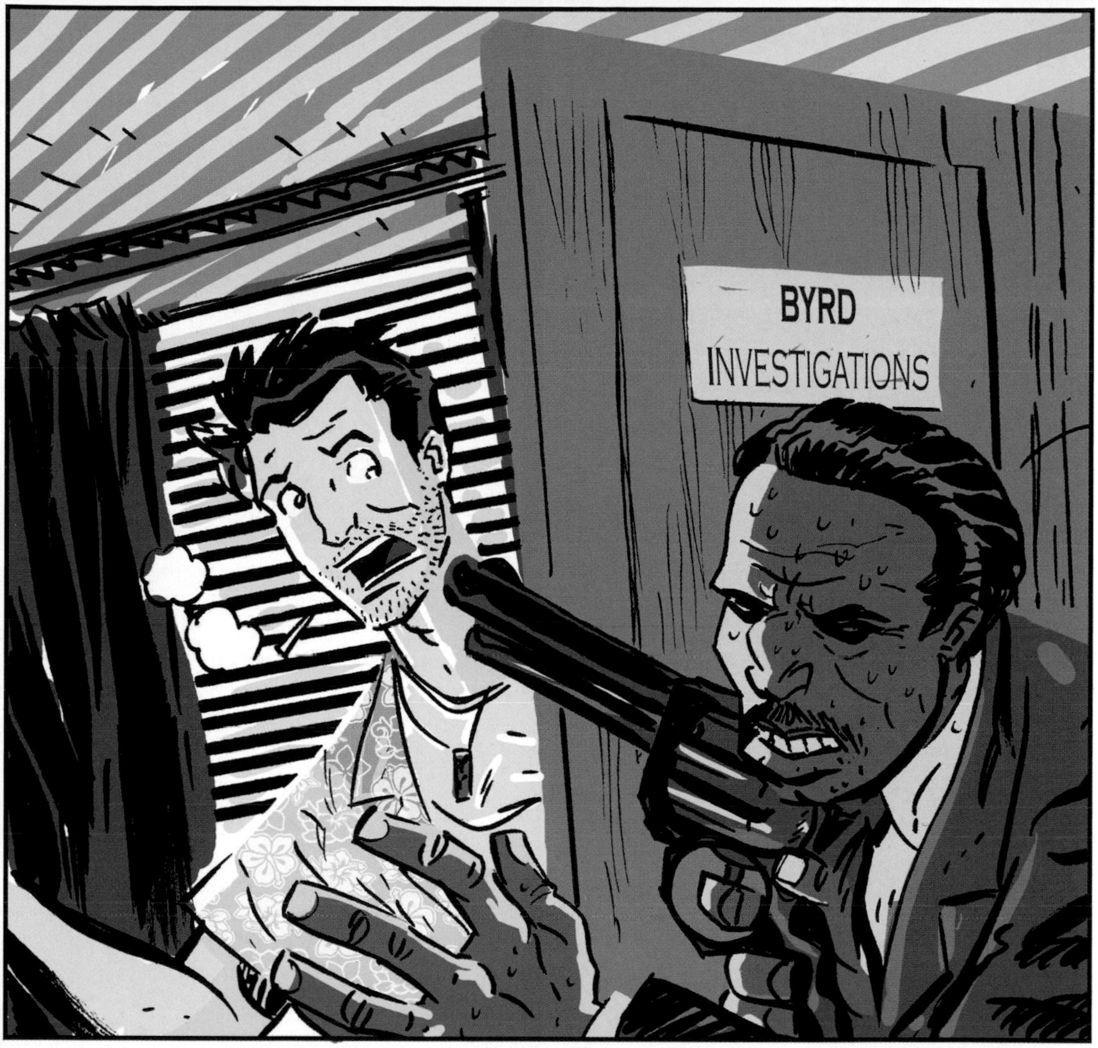
BYRD
INVESTIGATIONS

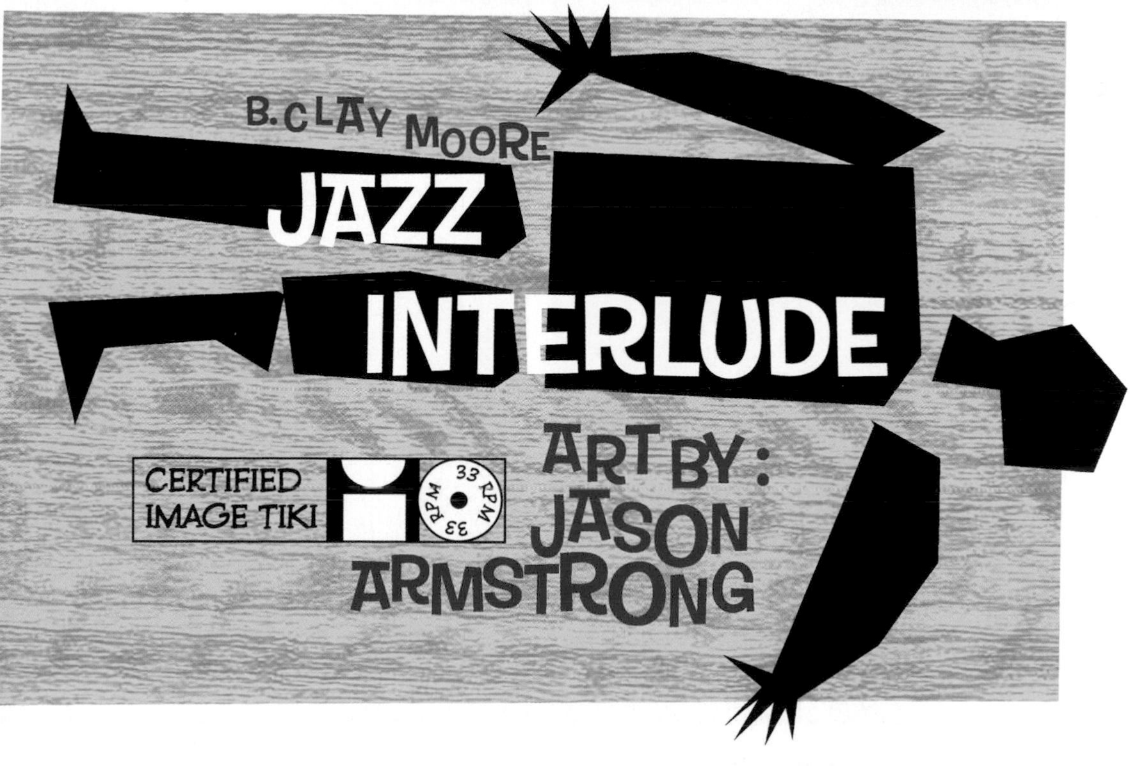
B. CLAY MOORE
JAZZ
INTERLUDE
CERTIFIED
IMAGE TIKI
33 RPM
33 RPM
ART BY:
JASON
ARMSTRONG

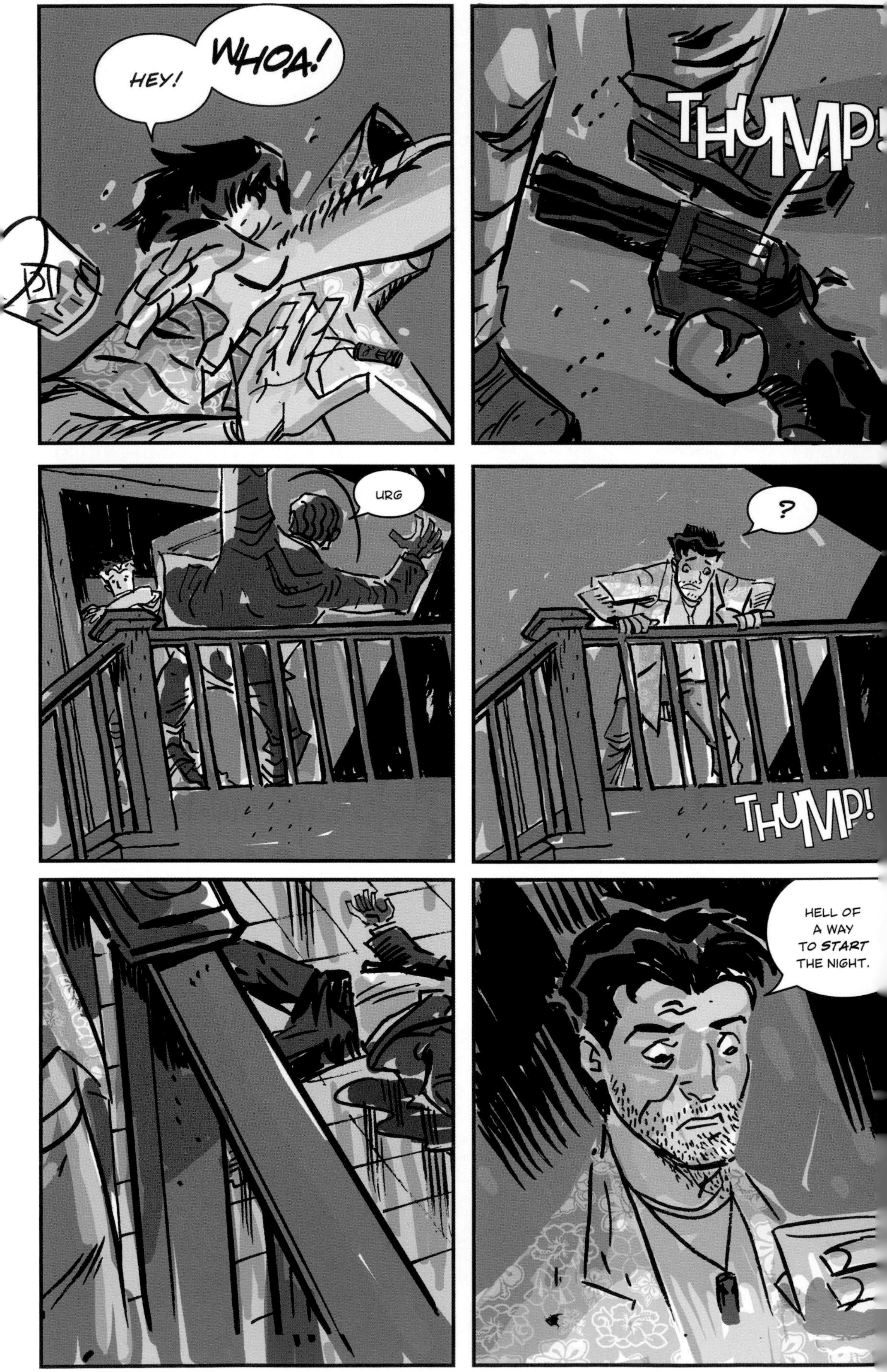
HEY!
WHOA!
THUMP!
URG
?
THUMP!
HELL OF A WAY TO START THE NIGHT.

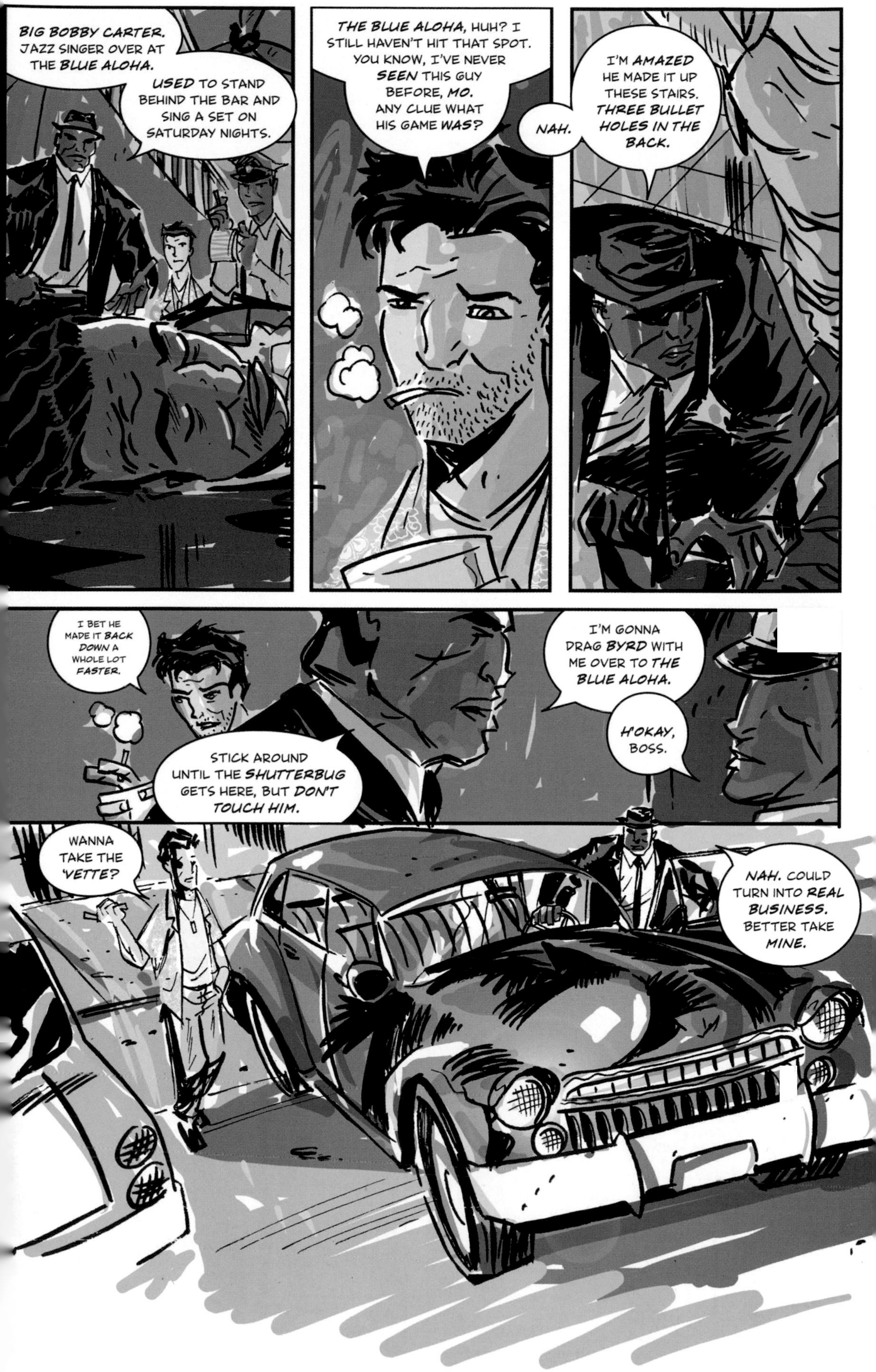
BIG BOBBY CARTER. JAZZ SINGER OVER AT THE BLUE ALOHA.
USED TO STAND BEHIND THE BAR AND SING A SET ON SATURDAY NIGHTS.
THE BLUE ALOHA, HUH? I STILL HAVEN'T HIT THAT SPOT. YOU KNOW, I'VE NEVER SEEN THIS GUY BEFORE, MO. ANY CLUE WHAT HIS GAME WAS?
NAH.
I'M AMAZED HE MADE IT UP THESE STAIRS. THREE BULLET HOLES IN THE BACK.
I BET HE MADE IT BACK DOWN A WHOLE LOT FASTER.
STICK AROUND UNTIL THE SHUTTERBUG GETS HERE, BUT DON'T TOUCH HIM.
I'M GONNA DRAG BYRD WITH ME OVER TO THE BLUE ALOHA.
H'OKAY, BOSS.
WANNA TAKE THE 'VETTE?
NAH. COULD TURN INTO REAL BUSINESS. BETTER TAKE MINE.

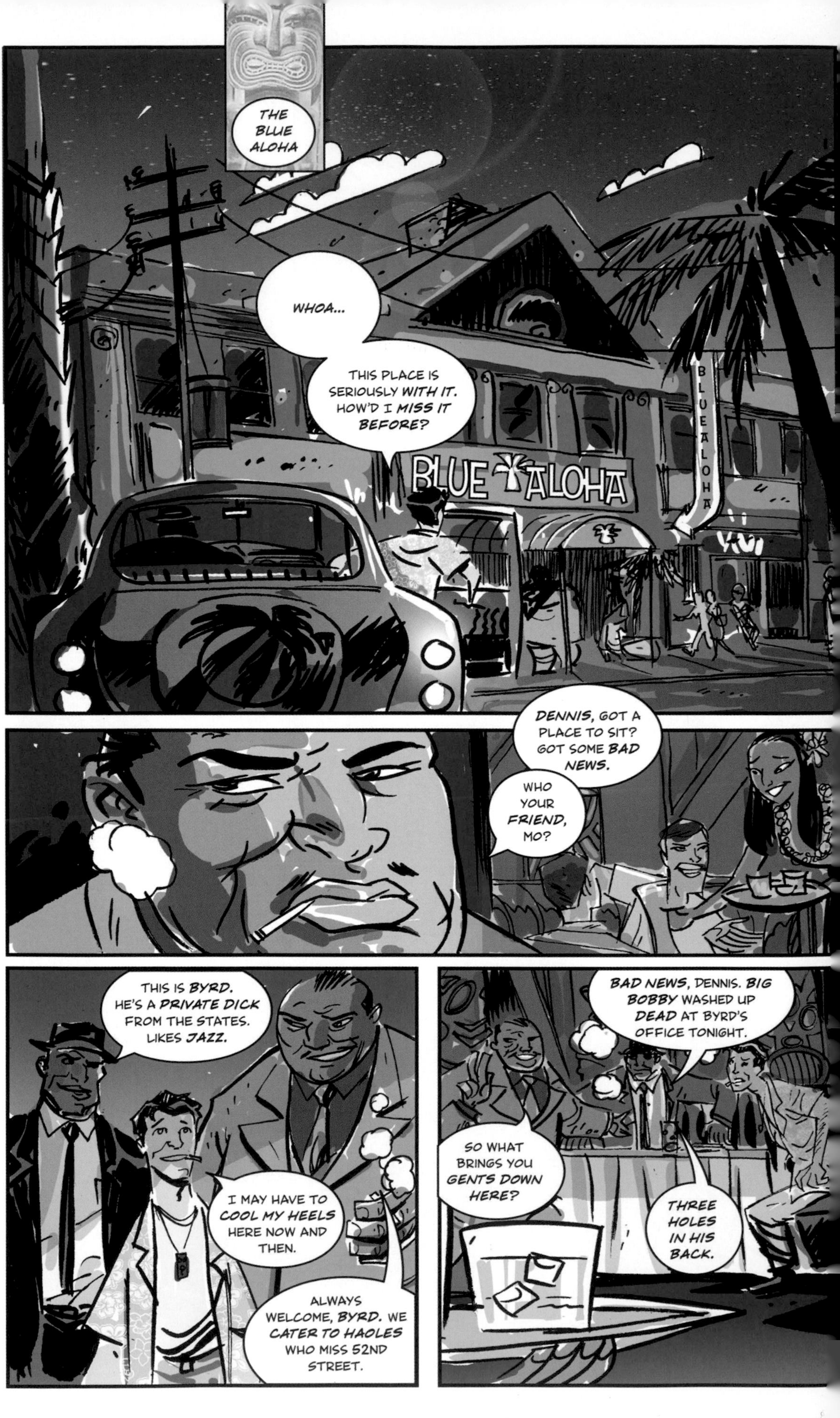
THE BLUE ALOHA
WHOA...
THIS PLACE IS SERIOUSLY WITH IT. HOW'D I MISS IT BEFORE?
BLUE ALOHA
BLUE ALOHA
DENNIS, GOT A PLACE TO SIT? GOT SOME BAD NEWS.
WHO YOUR FRIEND, MO?
THIS IS BYRD. HE'S A PRIVATE DICK FROM THE STATES. LIKES JAZZ.
I MAY HAVE TO COOL MY HEELS HERE NOW AND THEN.
ALWAYS WELCOME, BYRD. WE CATER TO HAOLES WHO MISS 52ND STREET.
BAD NEWS, DENNIS. BIG BOBBY WASHED UP DEAD AT BYRD'S OFFICE TONIGHT.
SO WHAT BRINGS YOU GENTS DOWN HERE?
THREE HOLES IN HIS BACK.

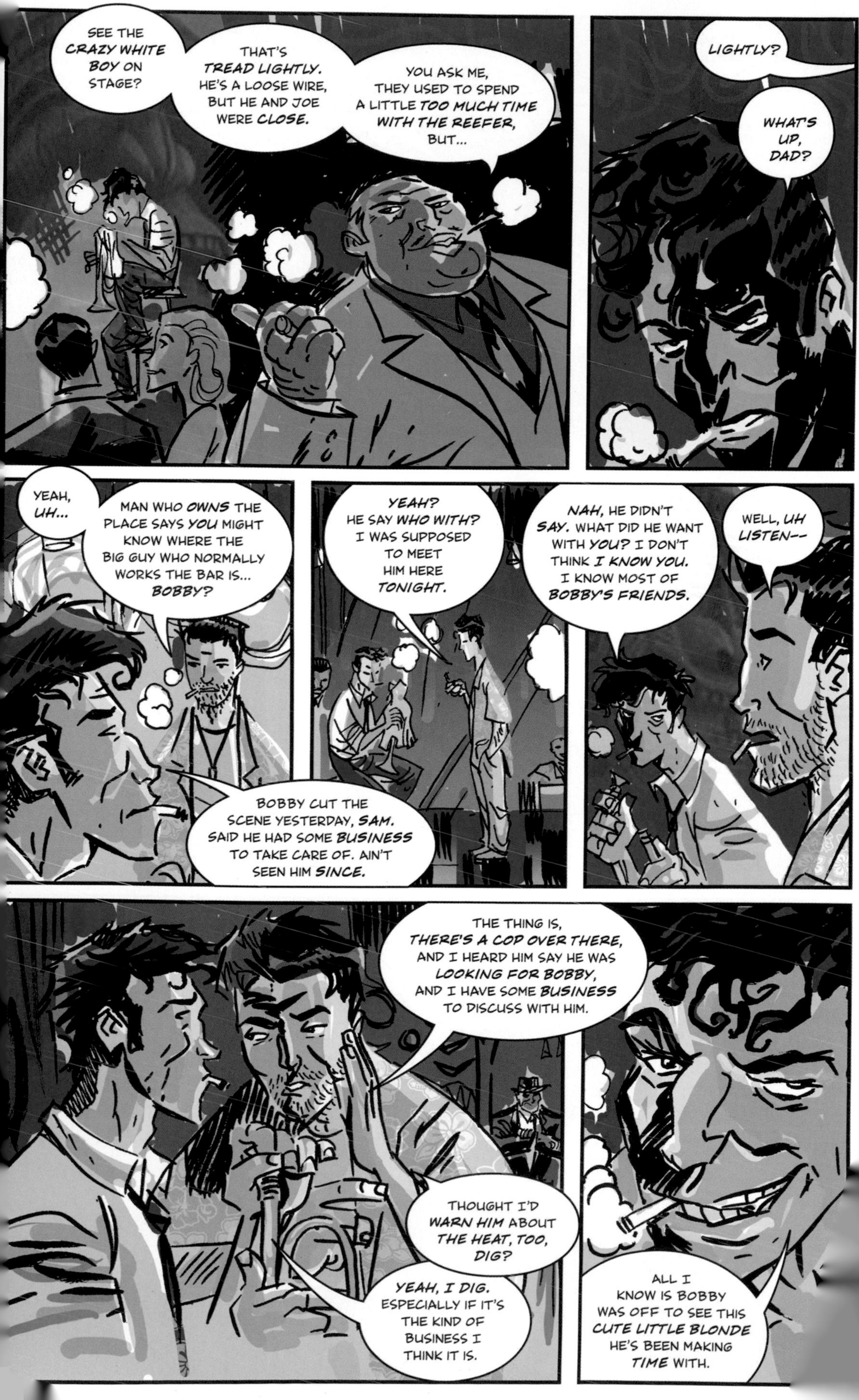
SEE THE CRAZY WHITE BOY ON STAGE?
THAT'S TREAD LIGHTLY. HE'S A LOOSE WIRE, BUT HE AND JOE WERE CLOSE.
YOU ASK ME, THEY USED TO SPEND A LITTLE TOO MUCH TIME WITH THE REEFER, BUT...
LIGHTLY?
WHAT'S UP, DAD?
YEAH, UH...
MAN WHO OWNS THE PLACE SAYS YOU MIGHT KNOW WHERE THE BIG GUY WHO NORMALLY WORKS THE BAR IS... BOBBY?
BOBBY CUT THE SCENE YESTERDAY, SAM. SAID HE HAD SOME BUSINESS TO TAKE CARE OF. AIN'T SEEN HIM SINCE.
YEAH? HE SAY WHO WITH? I WAS SUPPOSED TO MEET HIM HERE TONIGHT.
NAH, HE DIDN'T SAY. WHAT DID HE WANT WITH YOU? I DON'T THINK I KNOW YOU. I KNOW MOST OF BOBBY'S FRIENDS.
WELL, UH LISTEN--
THE THING IS, THERE'S A COP OVER THERE, AND I HEARD HIM SAY HE WAS LOOKING FOR BOBBY, AND I HAVE SOME BUSINESS TO DISCUSS WITH HIM.
THOUGHT I'D WARN HIM ABOUT THE HEAT, TOO, DIG?
YEAH, I DIG. ESPECIALLY IF IT'S THE KIND OF BUSINESS I THINK IT IS.
ALL I KNOW IS BOBBY WAS OFF TO SEE THIS CUTE LITTLE BLONDE HE'S BEEN MAKING TIME WITH.

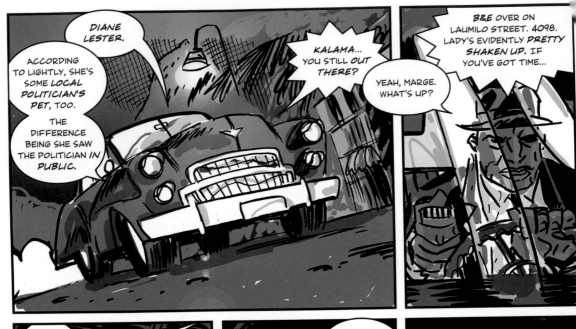

DIANE LESTER.

ACCORDING TO LIGHTLY, SHE'S SOME *LOCAL POLITICIAN'S PET*, TOO.

THE DIFFERENCE BEING SHE SAW THE POLITICIAN *IN PUBLIC*.

KALAMA... YOU STILL *OUT* THERE?

YEAH, MARGE. WHAT'S UP?

B&E OVER ON LAUMILO STREET. 4098. LADY'S EVIDENTLY *PRETTY SHAKEN UP*. IF YOU'VE GOT TIME...

...NOT REALLY, DISP

MO

THAT'S WHERE *WE* WERE HEADED.

BE THERE IN FIVE, DISPATCH.

SCCRRREEEEECCHH

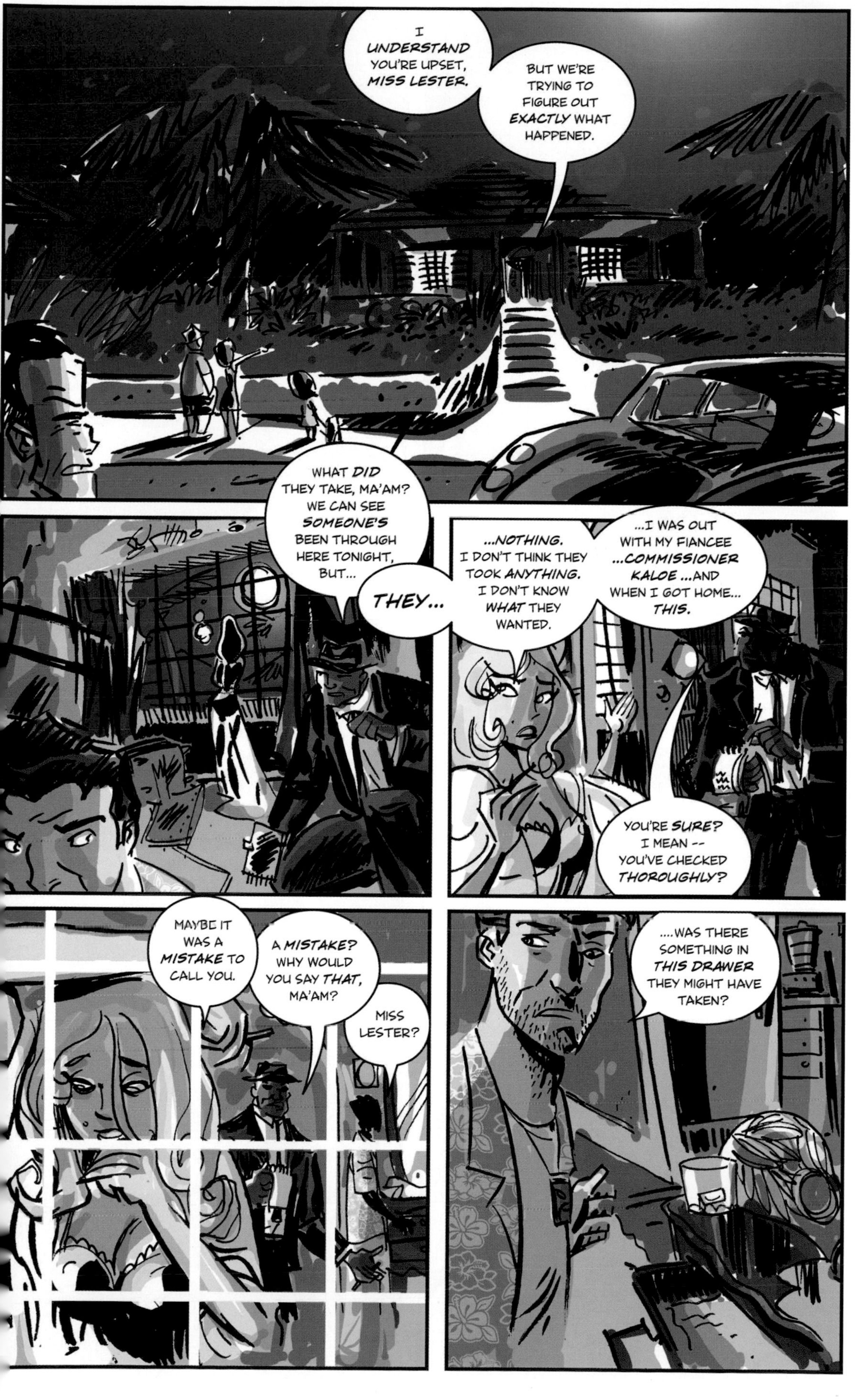
I UNDERSTAND YOU'RE UPSET, MISS LESTER.
BUT WE'RE TRYING TO FIGURE OUT EXACTLY WHAT HAPPENED.
WHAT DID THEY TAKE, MA'AM? WE CAN SEE SOMEONE'S BEEN THROUGH HERE TONIGHT, BUT...
THEY...
...NOTHING. I DON'T THINK THEY TOOK ANYTHING. I DON'T KNOW WHAT THEY WANTED.
...I WAS OUT WITH MY FIANCEE ...COMMISSIONER KALOE ...AND WHEN I GOT HOME... THIS.
YOU'RE SURE? I MEAN -- YOU'VE CHECKED THOROUGHLY?
MAYBE IT WAS A MISTAKE TO CALL YOU.
A MISTAKE? WHY WOULD YOU SAY THAT, MA'AM?
MISS LESTER?
....WAS THERE SOMETHING IN THIS DRAWER THEY MIGHT HAVE TAKEN?

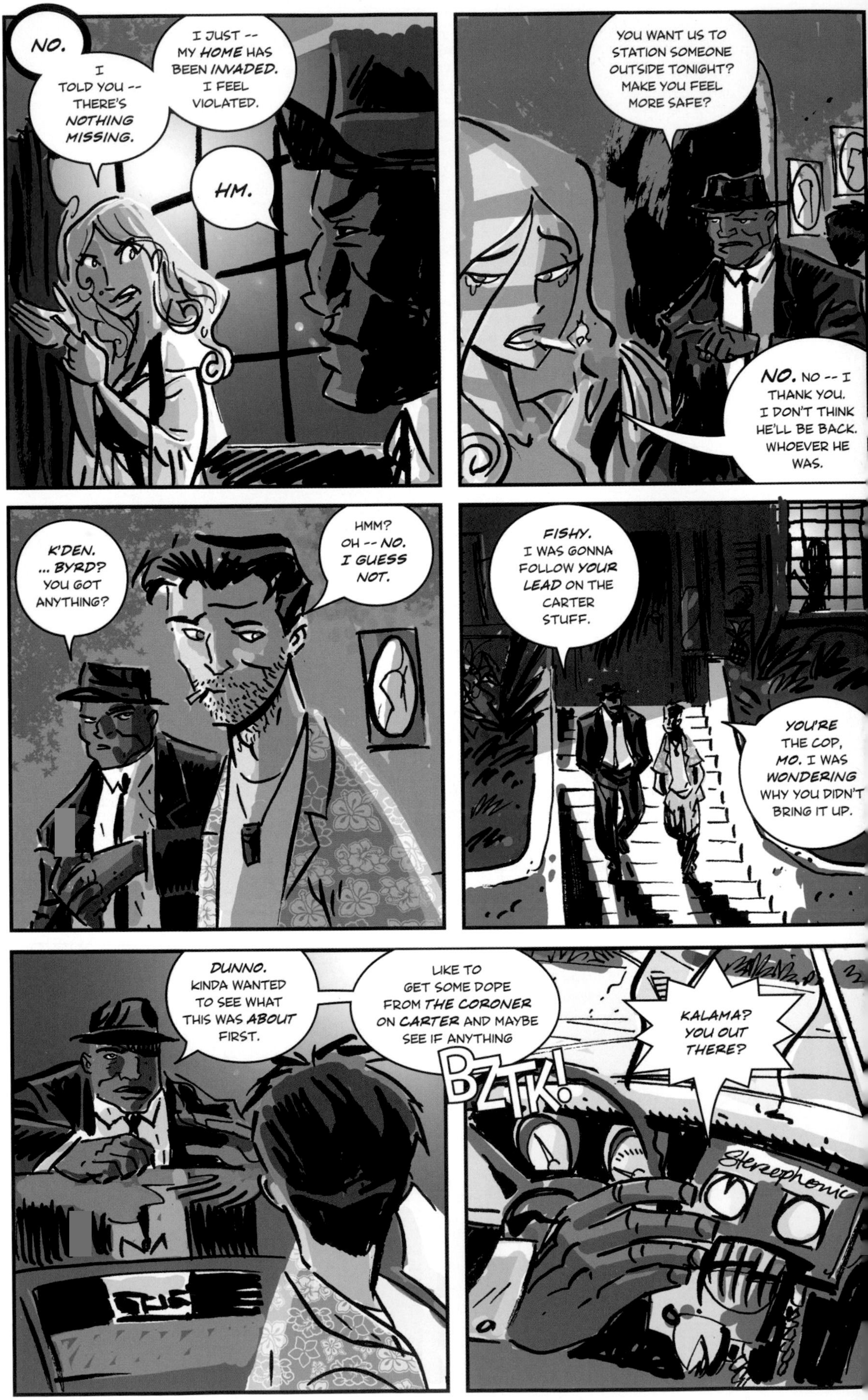
NO.
I TOLD YOU -- THERE'S NOTHING MISSING.
I JUST -- MY HOME HAS BEEN INVADED. I FEEL VIOLATED.
HM.
YOU WANT US TO STATION SOMEONE OUTSIDE TONIGHT? MAKE YOU FEEL MORE SAFE?
NO. NO -- I THANK YOU. I DON'T THINK HE'LL BE BACK. WHOEVER HE WAS.
K'DEN. ...BYRD? YOU GOT ANYTHING?
HMM? OH -- NO. I GUESS NOT.
FISHY. I WAS GONNA FOLLOW YOUR LEAD ON THE CARTER STUFF.
YOU'RE THE COP, MO. I WAS WONDERING WHY YOU DIDN'T BRING IT UP.
DUNNO. KINDA WANTED TO SEE WHAT THIS WAS ABOUT FIRST.
LIKE TO GET SOME DOPE FROM THE CORONER ON CARTER AND MAYBE SEE IF ANYTHING
BZTK!
KALAMA? YOU OUT THERE?
Stereophonic

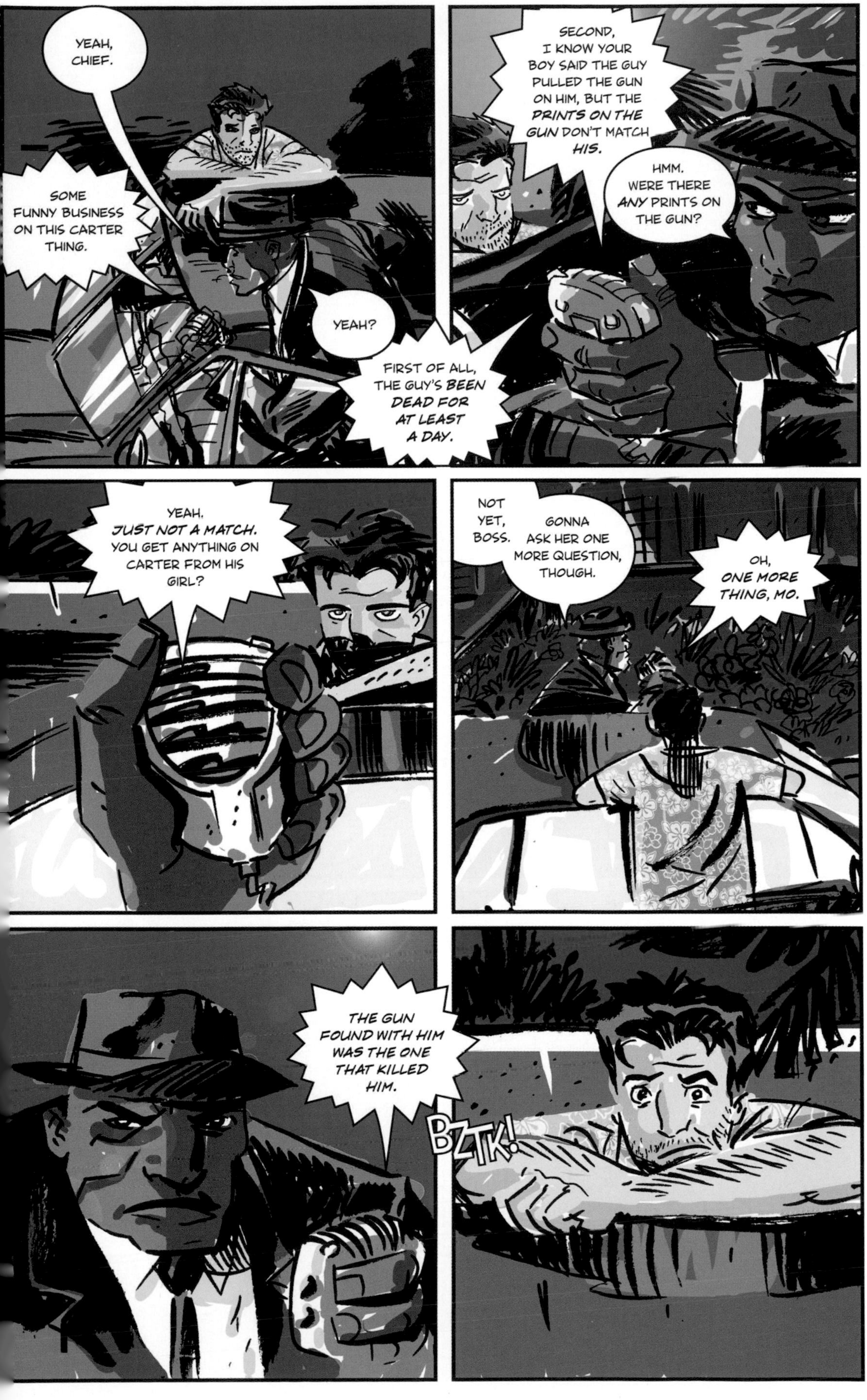
YEAH, CHIEF.
SOME FUNNY BUSINESS ON THIS CARTER THING.
YEAH?
FIRST OF ALL, THE GUY'S BEEN DEAD FOR AT LEAST A DAY.
SECOND, I KNOW YOUR BOY SAID THE GUY PULLED THE GUN ON HIM, BUT THE PRINTS ON THE GUN DON'T MATCH HIS.
HMM. WERE THERE ANY PRINTS ON THE GUN?
YEAH. JUST NOT A MATCH. YOU GET ANYTHING ON CARTER FROM HIS GIRL?
NOT YET, BOSS.
GONNA ASK HER ONE MORE QUESTION, THOUGH.
OH, ONE MORE THING, MO.
THE GUN FOUND WITH HIM WAS THE ONE THAT KILLED HIM.
BZTK!

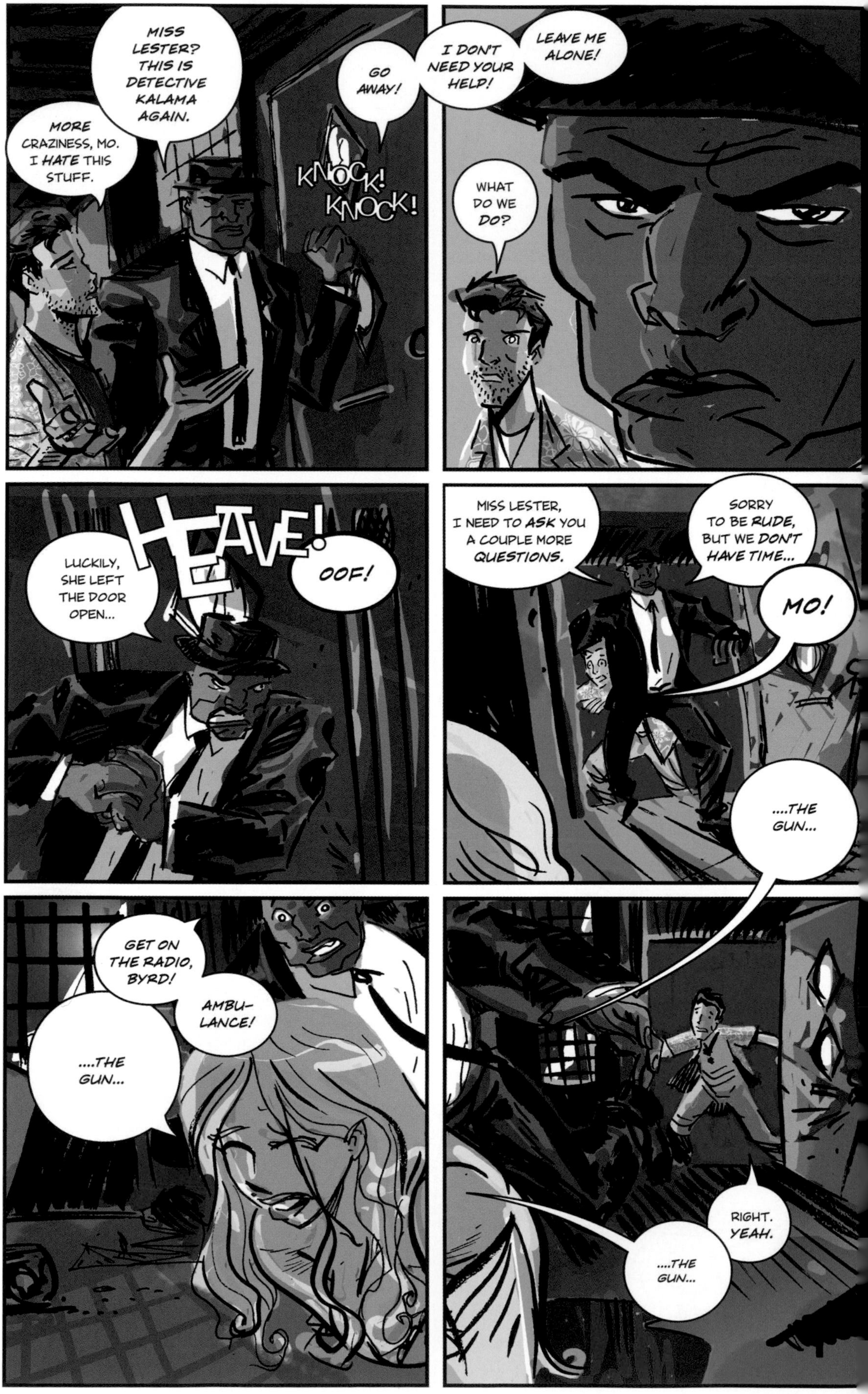
MISS LESTER? THIS IS DETECTIVE KALAMA AGAIN.
MORE CRAZINESS, MO. I HATE THIS STUFF.
KNOCK! KNOCK!
GO AWAY!
I DON'T NEED YOUR HELP!
LEAVE ME ALONE!
WHAT DO WE DO?
HEAVE!
LUCKILY, SHE LEFT THE DOOR OPEN...
OOF!
MISS LESTER, I NEED TO ASK YOU A COUPLE MORE QUESTIONS.
SORRY TO BE RUDE, BUT WE DON'T HAVE TIME...
MO!
....THE GUN...
GET ON THE RADIO, BYRD!
AMBU-LANCE!
....THE GUN...
RIGHT. YEAH.
....THE GUN...

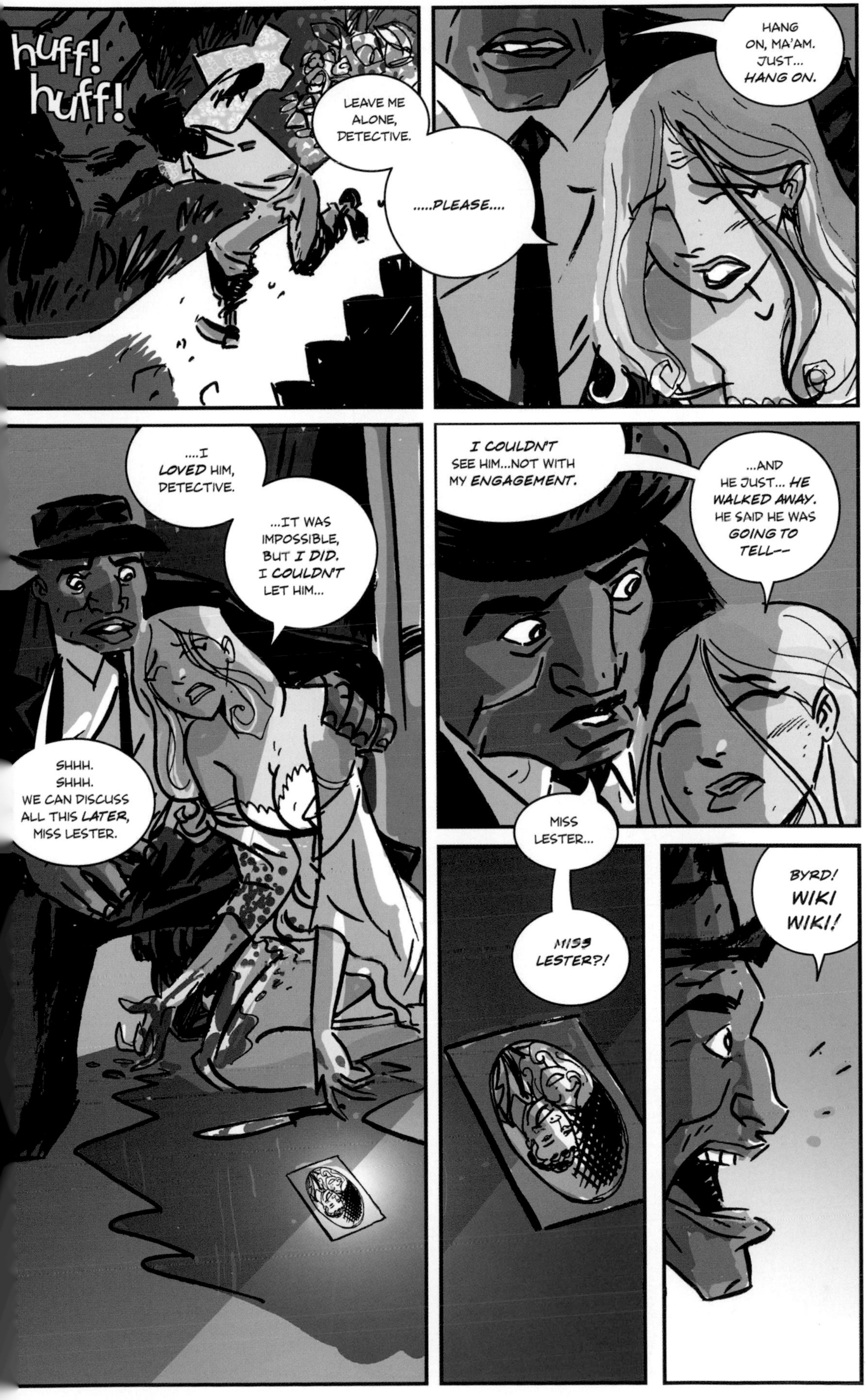
huff! huff!
LEAVE ME ALONE, DETECTIVE.
.....PLEASE....
HANG ON, MA'AM. JUST... HANG ON.
....I LOVED HIM, DETECTIVE.
...IT WAS IMPOSSIBLE, BUT I DID. I COULDN'T LET HIM...
SHHH. SHHH. WE CAN DISCUSS ALL THIS LATER, MISS LESTER.
I COULDN'T SEE HIM...NOT WITH MY ENGAGEMENT.
...AND HE JUST... HE WALKED AWAY. HE SAID HE WAS GOING TO TELL--
MISS LESTER...
MISS LESTER?!
BYRD! WIKI WIKI!

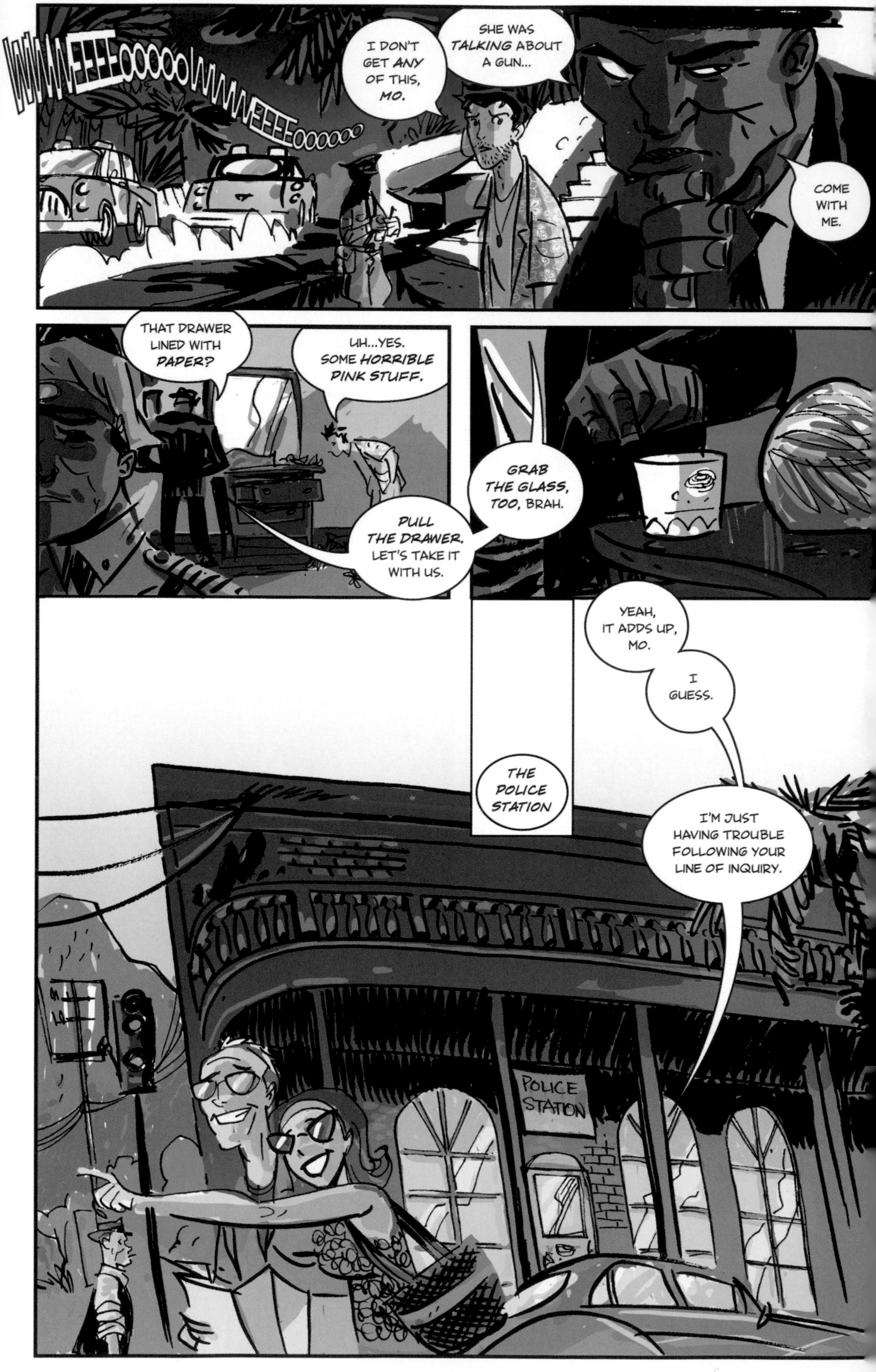
WWWEEEEOOOOOWWWWEEEEOOOOOO
I DON'T GET ANY OF THIS, MO.
SHE WAS TALKING ABOUT A GUN...
COME WITH ME.
THAT DRAWER LINED WITH PAPER?
UH...YES. SOME HORRIBLE PINK STUFF.
PULL THE DRAWER. LET'S TAKE IT WITH US.
GRAB THE GLASS, TOO, BRAH.
THE POLICE STATION
YEAH, IT ADDS UP, MO.
I GUESS.
I'M JUST HAVING TROUBLE FOLLOWING YOUR LINE OF INQUIRY.
POLICE STATION

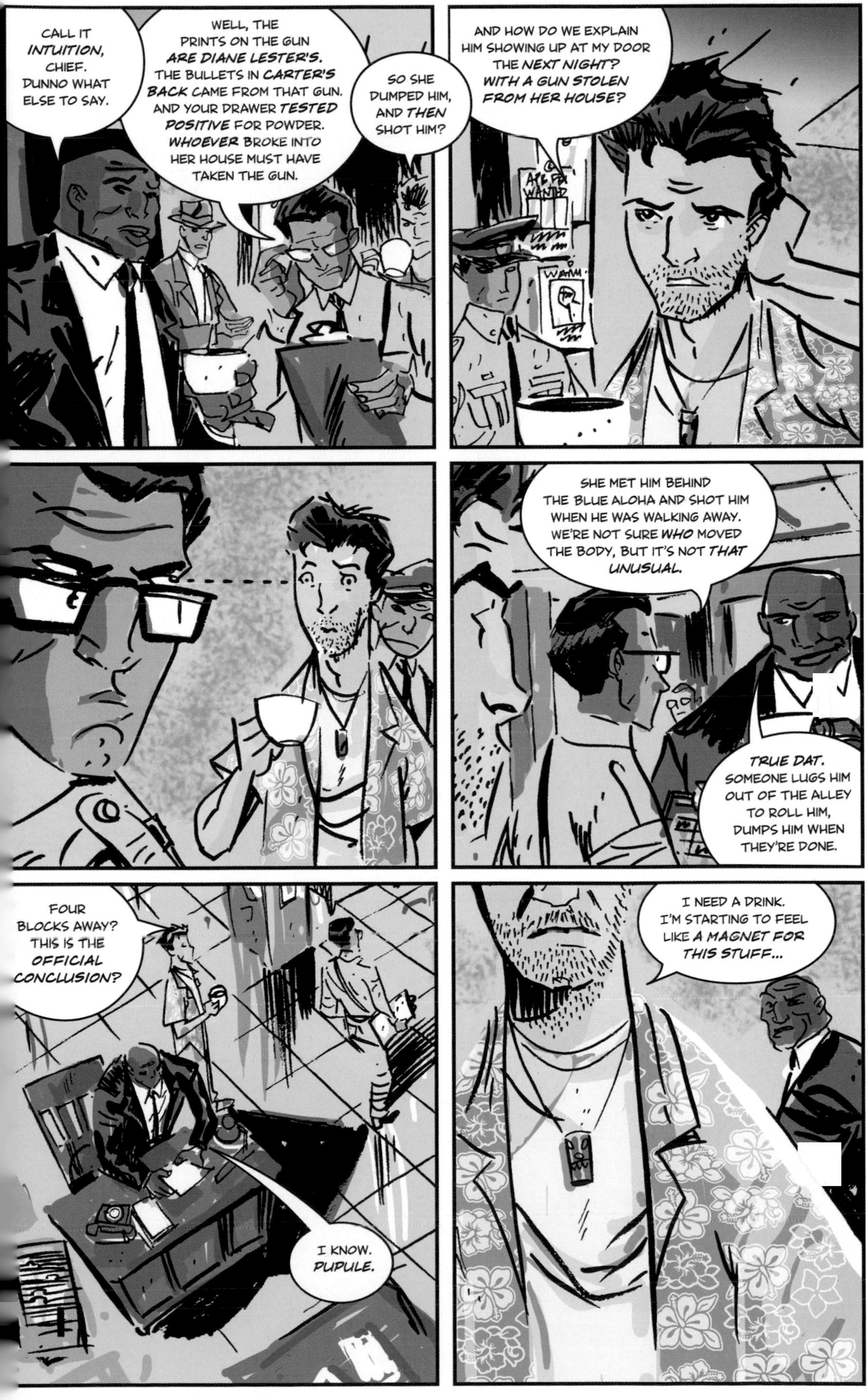
CALL IT INTUITION, CHIEF. DUNNO WHAT ELSE TO SAY.
WELL, THE PRINTS ON THE GUN ARE DIANE LESTER'S. THE BULLETS IN CARTER'S BACK CAME FROM THAT GUN. AND YOUR DRAWER TESTED POSITIVE FOR POWDER. WHOEVER BROKE INTO HER HOUSE MUST HAVE TAKEN THE GUN.
SO SHE DUMPED HIM, AND THEN SHOT HIM?
AND HOW DO WE EXPLAIN HIM SHOWING UP AT MY DOOR THE NEXT NIGHT? WITH A GUN STOLEN FROM HER HOUSE?
SHE MET HIM BEHIND THE BLUE ALOHA AND SHOT HIM WHEN HE WAS WALKING AWAY. WE'RE NOT SURE WHO MOVED THE BODY, BUT IT'S NOT THAT UNUSUAL.
TRUE DAT. SOMEONE LUGS HIM OUT OF THE ALLEY TO ROLL HIM, DUMPS HIM WHEN THEY'RE DONE.
FOUR BLOCKS AWAY? THIS IS THE OFFICIAL CONCLUSION?
I KNOW. PUPULE.
I NEED A DRINK. I'M STARTING TO FEEL LIKE A MAGNET FOR THIS STUFF...

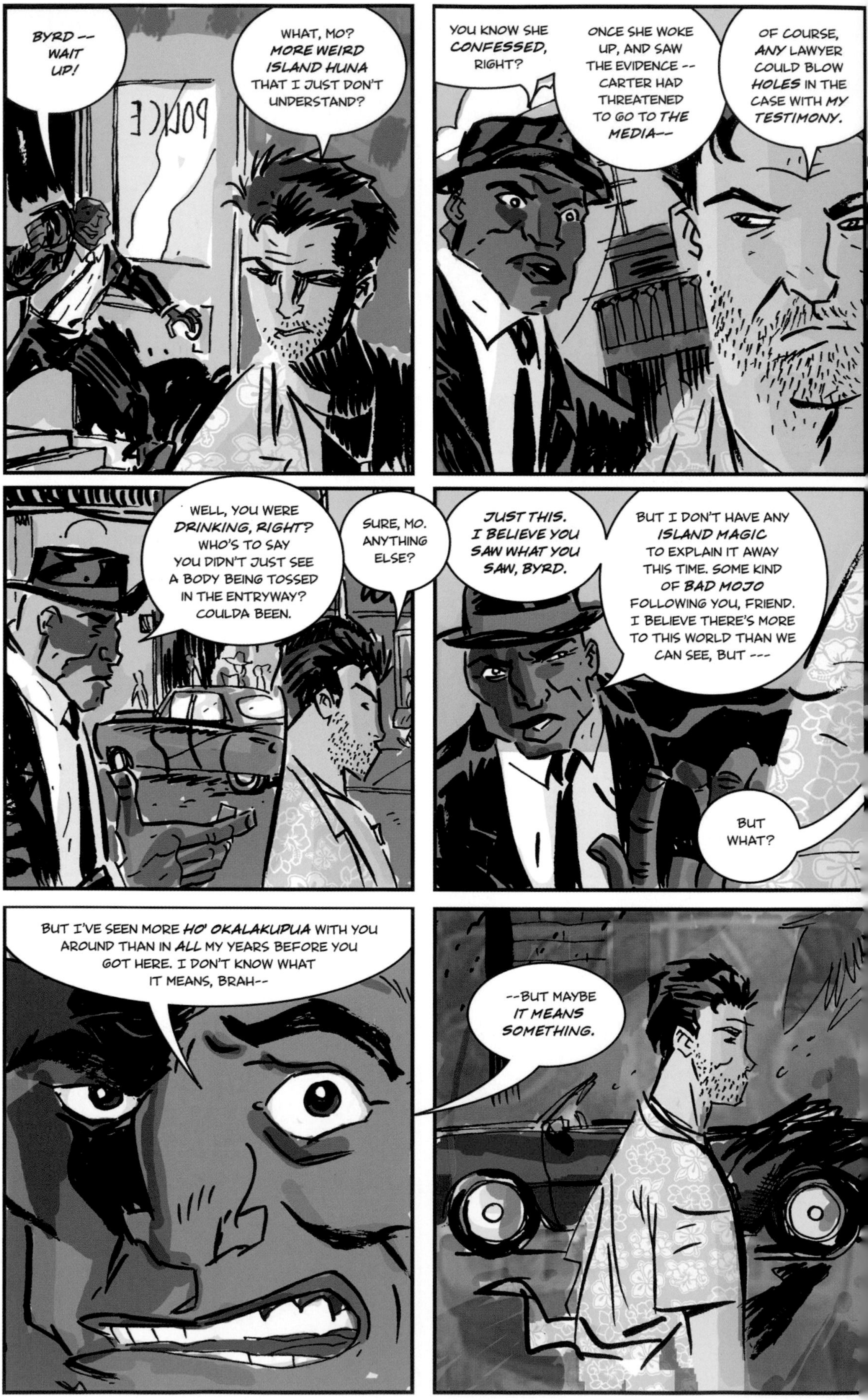
BYRD -- WAIT UP!
WHAT, MO? MORE WEIRD ISLAND HUNA THAT I JUST DON'T UNDERSTAND?
POLICE
YOU KNOW SHE CONFESSED, RIGHT?
ONCE SHE WOKE UP, AND SAW THE EVIDENCE -- CARTER HAD THREATENED TO GO TO THE MEDIA--
OF COURSE, ANY LAWYER COULD BLOW HOLES IN THE CASE WITH MY TESTIMONY.
WELL, YOU WERE DRINKING, RIGHT? WHO'S TO SAY YOU DIDN'T JUST SEE A BODY BEING TOSSED IN THE ENTRYWAY? COULDA BEEN.
SURE, MO. ANYTHING ELSE?
JUST THIS. I BELIEVE YOU SAW WHAT YOU SAW, BYRD.
BUT I DON'T HAVE ANY ISLAND MAGIC TO EXPLAIN IT AWAY THIS TIME. SOME KIND OF BAD MOJO FOLLOWING YOU, FRIEND. I BELIEVE THERE'S MORE TO THIS WORLD THAN WE CAN SEE, BUT ---
BUT WHAT?
BUT I'VE SEEN MORE HO' OKALAKUPUA WITH YOU AROUND THAN IN ALL MY YEARS BEFORE YOU GOT HERE. I DON'T KNOW WHAT IT MEANS, BRAH--
--BUT MAYBE IT MEANS SOMETHING.

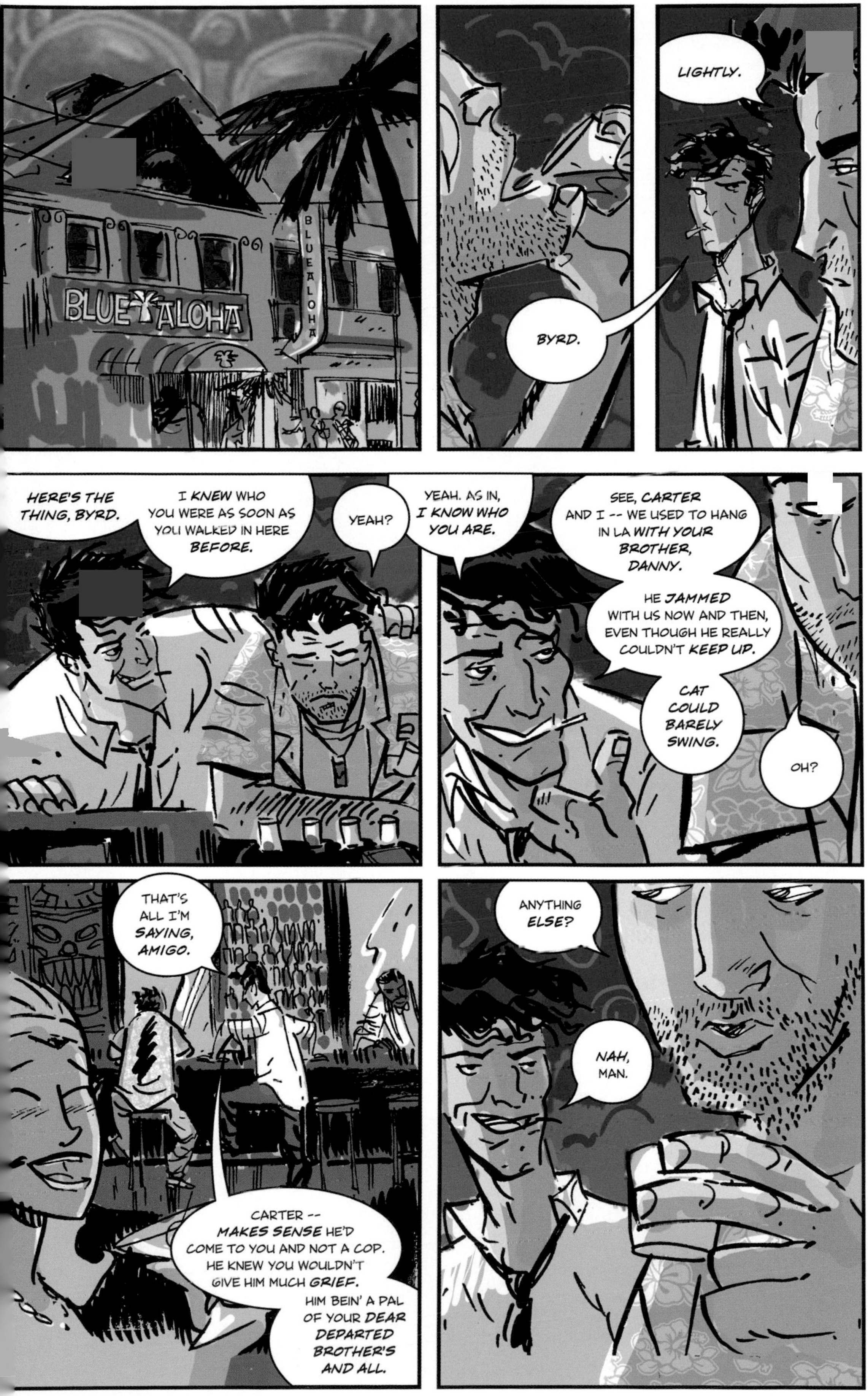

BLUE ALOHA
BLUE ALOHA
BYRD.
LIGHTLY.
HERE'S THE THING, BYRD.
I KNEW WHO YOU WERE AS SOON AS YOU WALKED IN HERE BEFORE.
YEAH?
YEAH. AS IN, I KNOW WHO YOU ARE.
SEE, CARTER AND I -- WE USED TO HANG IN LA WITH YOUR BROTHER, DANNY.
HE JAMMED WITH US NOW AND THEN, EVEN THOUGH HE REALLY COULDN'T KEEP UP.
CAT COULD BARELY SWING.
OH?
THAT'S ALL I'M SAYING, AMIGO.
CARTER -- MAKES SENSE HE'D COME TO YOU AND NOT A COP. HE KNEW YOU WOULDN'T GIVE HIM MUCH GRIEF.
HIM BEIN' A PAL OF YOUR DEAR DEPARTED BROTHER'S AND ALL.
ANYTHING ELSE?
NAH, MAN.

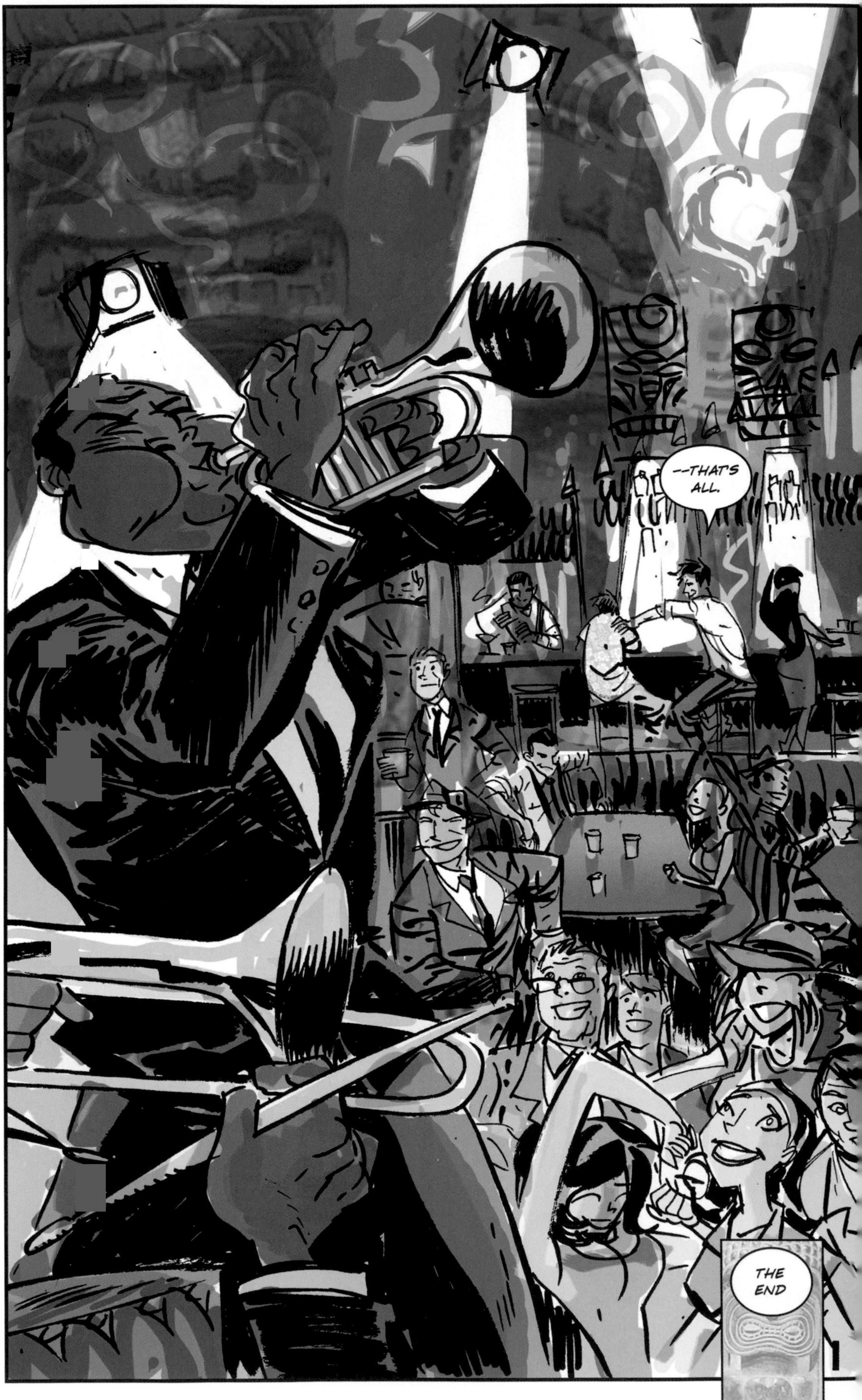
--THAT'S ALL.
THE END

OTES FROM THE AUTHOR

HE COVER FOR THE *ALOHA, HAWAIIAN DICK* TRADE WAS CREATED BY
HE AMAZING RON SALAS. ORIGINALLY INTENDED AS A PIN-UP PIECE FOR THE
PCOMING *GREAT BIG HAWAIIAN DICK*, IT SEEMED THE PERFECT OPTION TO
RACE THIS TRADE. RON REALLY CAPTURED MID-CENTURY GRAPHIC DESIGN
THOUT MAKING THE COVER LOOK SLAVISHLY RETRO.

L COVERS FOR *ALOHA, HAWAIIAN DICK* (AS WELL AS THE INTERIOR
CAP PAGES, AND THE "ALOHA" HEADING ABOVE) WERE CREATED BY CHICAGO
SIGNER/WRITER/ARTIST SEAN DOVE. FROM THE BEGINNING, WE'VE DONE
ERYTHING WE COULD TO DISTINGUISH *HAWAIIAN DICK* COVERS FROM ANY-
IING ELSE ON THE STANDS, AND SEAN'S RAZOR SHARP DESIGN SENSE LENT
OHA A NEW DYNAMIC.

IE FIFTH ISSUE OF *ALOHA* WAS DRAWN AND COLORED BY PAUL REINWAND,
ING JACOB WYATT'S ROUGHS AS A GUIDE. PAUL STEPPED IN AND DID A
NTASTIC JOB ON THE KEY ISSUE IN THE ENTIRE SERIES.

E ROB GUILLORY PIN-UP WAS ORIGINALLY INTENDED AS A VARIANT COVER
PR *ALOHA, HAWAIIAN DICK*, BUT WAS NEVER PUBLISHED. ROB, WELL KNOWN
THE CO-CREATOR OF IMAGE'S *CHEW* (WITH JOHN LAYMAN), EXPRESSED TO
THAT *HAWAIIAN DICK* WAS ONE OF THE COMICS THAT DRAGGED HIM INTO
E BUSINESS MANY YEARS AGO, AND OFFERED TO CONTRIBUTE A PIECE OUT
APPRECIATION. I'M GLAD WE'RE FINALLY ABLE TO PRESENT IT HERE.

E DARWYN COOKE "MOVIE POSTER" CAME ABOUT AFTER I'D ASKED HIM TO
ITE THE FOREWORD TO THE *BAD KARMA* HARDCOVER THAT I KICKSTARTED
TH JEREMY HAUN, ALEX GRECIAN AND SETH PECK. PERSONAL OBLIGATIONS
EVENTED HIM FROM DOING SO, AND HE TOLD ME HE "OWED ME A FAVOR" (AS IF).
IEN I APPROACHED HIM ABOUT DOING A PIECE FOR THE (STILL FORTHCOMING)
REAT BIG HAWAIIAN DICK HARDCOVER, HE ASKED ME WHO I SAW AS THE
AD IN *ALOHA, HAWAIIAN DICK*, HAD IT BEEN A MOVIE MADE IN 1972. STEVE
QUEEN SEEMED THE ONLY ANSWER.

RWYN WAS THERE AT THE VERY BEGINNING, WHEN I FIRST STARTED DISCUS-
G THE IDEA FOR THE BOOK WITH J. BONE. WE ALL MISS HIM TERRIBLY.

RE DICK EPHEMERA FOLLOWS, INCLUDING ANOTHER UNUSED VARIANT COVER
THE AMAZING (AND REMARKABLY GRACIOUS) GREG SMALLWOOD.

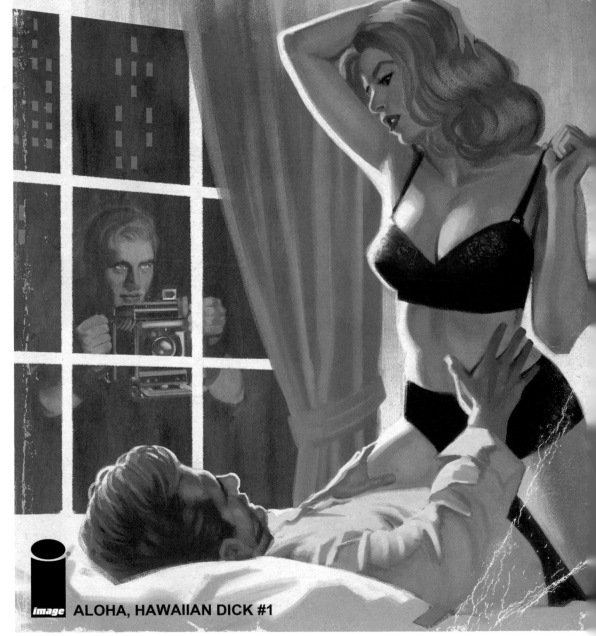

FIRST EDITION 42

25¢

ALOHA, HAWAIIAN DICK

A cheating blonde and
her gangster boyfriend
spell trouble in paradise
for Mike Byrd

B.CLAY MOORE
JACOB WYATT

ALOHA, HAWAIIAN DICK #1

Tragically unused variant cover by Greg Smallwood

PAST CASES

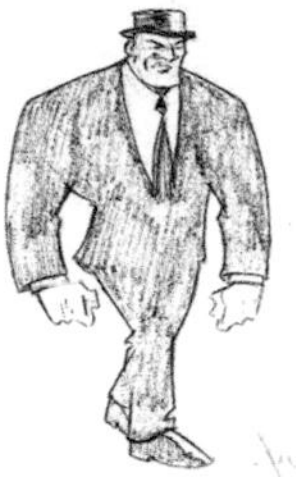

Scott Chantler Mo sketch

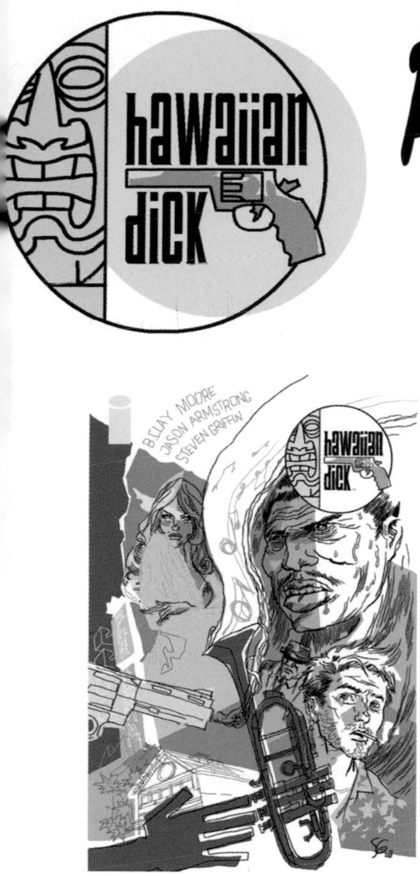
B.CLAY MOORE
JASON ARMSTRONG
STEVEN GRIFFIN
hawaiian dick

nused cover comp for the aborted **HAWAIIAN DICK #6**. he story, by B. Clay Moore & Jason Armstrong, ran in this eries, and will be included, complete, in the upcoming **REAT BIG HAWAIIAN DICK**. Steven Griffin art.

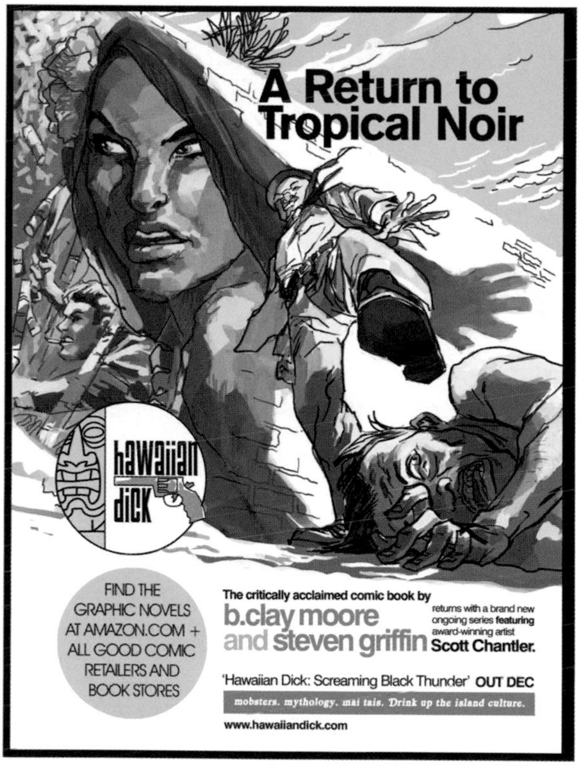
A Return to Tropical Noir
hawaiian dick
FIND THE GRAPHIC NOVELS AT AMAZON.COM + ALL GOOD COMIC RETAILERS AND BOOK STORES
The critically acclaimed comic book by
b.clay moore and steven griffin
returns with a brand new ongoing series featuring award-winning artist
Scott Chantler.
'Hawaiian Dick: Screaming Black Thunder' OUT DEC
mobsters. mythology. mai tais. Drink up the island culture.
www.hawaiiandick.com

SCREAMING BLACK THUNDER ad created for **TIKI MAGAZINE** by Steven Griffin.

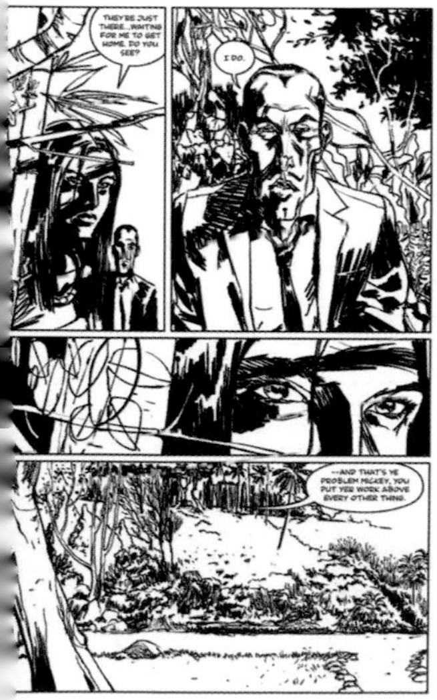
THEY'RE JUST THERE... WAITING FOR ME TO GET HOME. DO YOU SEE?
I DO.
--AND THAT'S YE PROBLEM MICKEY. YOU PUT YER WORK ABOVE EVERY OTHER THING.

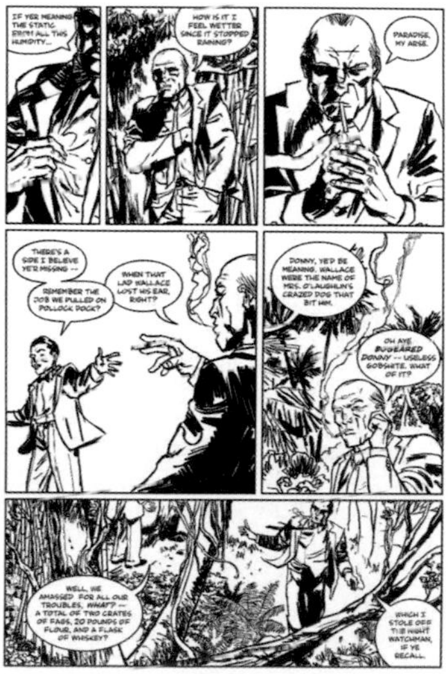
IF YER MEANING THE STATIC FROM ALL THIS HUMIDITY...
HOW IS IT I FEEL WETTER SINCE IT STOPPED RAINING?
PARADISE. MY ARSE.
THERE'S A SIDE I BELIEVE YE'R MISSING --
REMEMBER THE JOB WE PULLED ON POLLOCK DOCK?
WHEN THAT LAD WALLACE LOST HIS EAR, RIGHT?
DONNY, YE'D BE MEANING. WALLACE WERE THE NAME OF MRS. O'LAUGHLIN'S CRAZED DOG THAT BIT HIM.
OH AYE. BUGEARED DONNY -- USELESS GOBSHITE. WHAT OF IT?
WELL, WE AMASSED FOR ALL OUR TROUBLES, WHAT? -- A TOTAL OF TWO CRATES OF FAGS, 20 POUNDS OF FLOUR, AND A FLASK OF WHISKEY?
WHICH I STOLE OFF THE NIGHT WATCHMAN, IF YE RECALL.

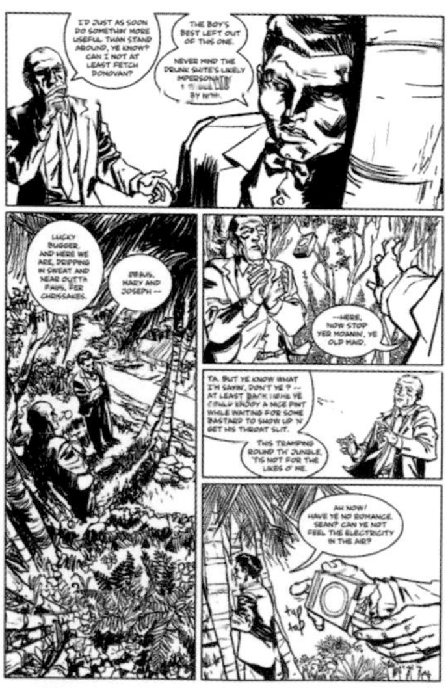
I'D JUST AS SOON DO SOMETHIN' MORE USEFUL THAN STAND AROUND, YE KNOW? CAN I NOT AT LEAST FETCH DONOVAN?
THE BOY'S BEST LEFT OUT OF THIS ONE.
LUCKY BUGGER. AND HERE WE ARE, DRIPPING IN SWEAT AND NEAR OUTTA FAGS, FER CHRISSAKES.
MARY AND JOSEPH --
--HERE. NOW STOP YER MOANIN', YE OLD MAID.
THIS TRAMPING ROUND TH' JUNGLE, 'TIS NOT FOR THE LIKES O' ME.
AH NOW! HAVE YE NO ROMANCE, SEAN? CAN YE NOT FEEL THE ELECTRICITY IN THE AIR?

ee inked and lettered pages for the final chapter of Steven Griffin's back-up story, "The Shift," starring Kahami and Anthony onio ("The Thinker"). The first three chapters ran in **SCREAMING BLACK THUNDER**, but the concluding chapter was never shed. I firmly believe Steven was doing the best work of his career here, and look forward to more Griffin Dick down the road. those curious as to why the Thinker's death affected Kahami so much, their shared adventure in this story holds the answer.

"PAULO'S GIRL"
BY AZAD INJEJIKIAN

THIS IS A STORY THAT AZAD DID QUITE SOME TIME AGO, ORIGINALLY INTENDED AS A BACKUP IN THE ONGOING *HAWAIIAN DICK* BOOK. THE EXISTENCE OF THIS STORY IS WHAT INSPIRED ME TO COLLECT NUMEROUS ODDS AND ENDS IN THE *GREAT BIG HAWAIIAN DICK* HARDCOVER THAT WAS KICKSTARTED.

IT WILL BE INCLUDED IN THAT VOLUME, BUT I PRESENT IT HERE SINCE ITS INCEPTION OCCURED AROUND THE SAME TIME AS THE ORIGINAL *HAWAIIAN DICK #6*.

AZAD WAS ONE OF THE FIRST IMAGE CREATORS THAT STEVEN GRIFFIN AND I GOT TO KNOW BACK WHEN *HAWAIIAN DICK* INITIALLY LAUNCHED. HIS BOOK *SAMMY* WAS RELEASED AT AROUND THE SAME TIME. HE ALSO CONTRIBUTED ONE OF THE VERY FIRST PIN-UPS TO *HAWAIIAN DICK*.

THIS WAS THE FIRST *HAWAIIAN DICK* STORY NOT WRITTEN BY MYSELF OR STEVEN. AZAD CHOSE AN INCIDENTAL CHARACTER FROM THE VERY FIRST ISSUE OF THE VERY FIRST *HAWAIIAN DICK* SERIES AND DEVELOPED A FUN STORY AROUND HIS ONLY APPEARANCE.

SLOW...
WHAT'S IN THE SACK, PAULO?
KA!--MO! THE--UH--SACK?
WOULDN'T BE SOMETHING YOU'RE NOT ALLOWED TO PLAY WITH, WOULD IT?
UH...NO...IT...
WALK WITH ME, PAULO. SHARE WITH ME AND I WON'T PRY.
ANYTHING, MO! YOU KNOW ME!

PAULO'S DEBUT IN HAWAIIAN DICK #1

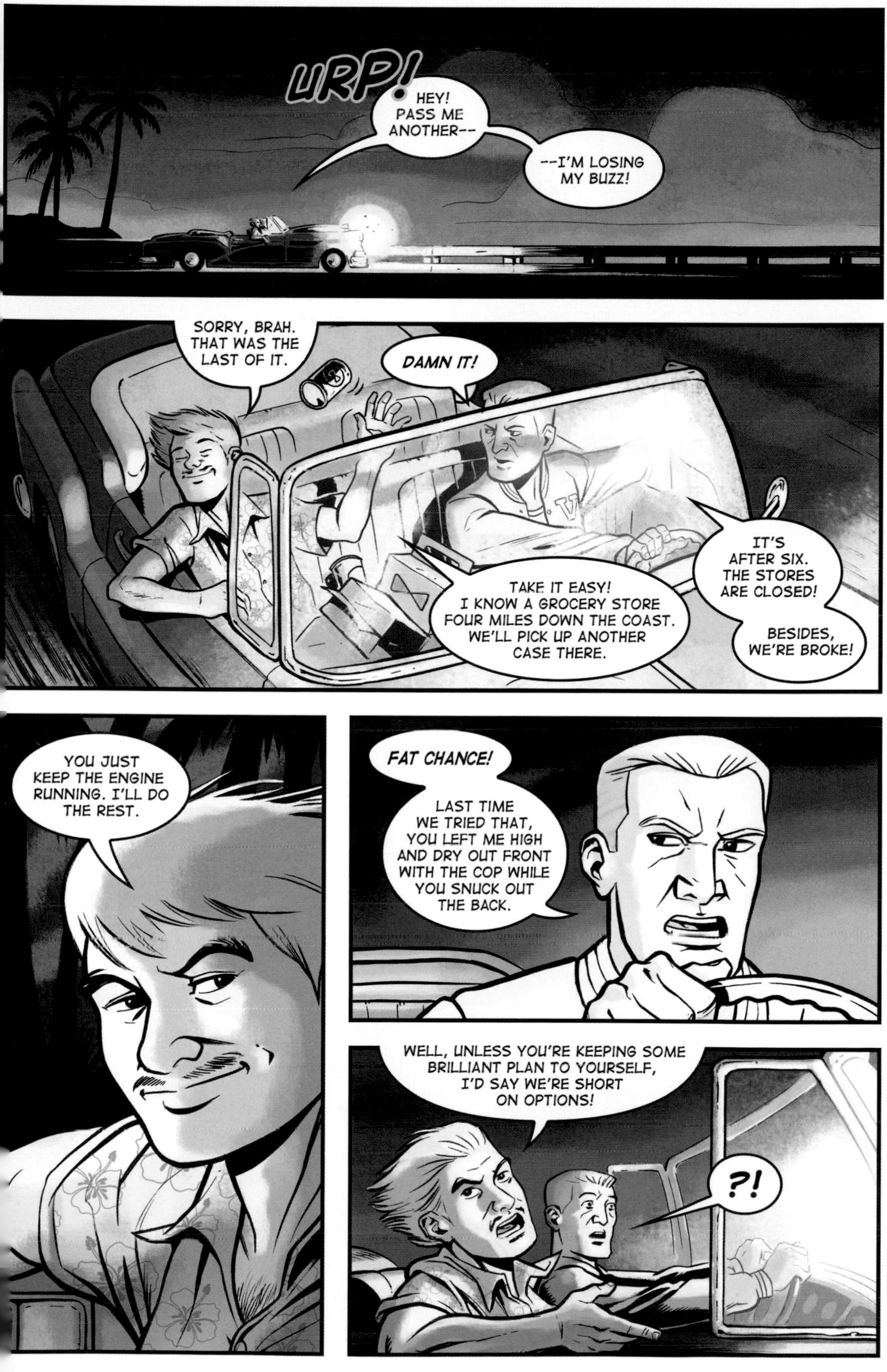
URP!
HEY! PASS ME ANOTHER--
--I'M LOSING MY BUZZ!
SORRY, BRAH. THAT WAS THE LAST OF IT.
DAMN IT!
TAKE IT EASY! I KNOW A GROCERY STORE FOUR MILES DOWN THE COAST. WE'LL PICK UP ANOTHER CASE THERE.
IT'S AFTER SIX. THE STORES ARE CLOSED!
BESIDES, WE'RE BROKE!
YOU JUST KEEP THE ENGINE RUNNING. I'LL DO THE REST.
FAT CHANCE!
LAST TIME WE TRIED THAT, YOU LEFT ME HIGH AND DRY OUT FRONT WITH THE COP WHILE YOU SNUCK OUT THE BACK.
WELL, UNLESS YOU'RE KEEPING SOME BRILLIANT PLAN TO YOURSELF, I'D SAY WE'RE SHORT ON OPTIONS!
?!

JESUS-!
OF ALL THE LOUSY TIMES TO HAVE BLOWOUT!
WHY ME?
YOU SEEING THIS, BRAH? PULL OVER!
WHAT ON EARTH FOR?
TRUST ME.
PAULO'S GIRL
Written and Drawn by Azad Injejikian

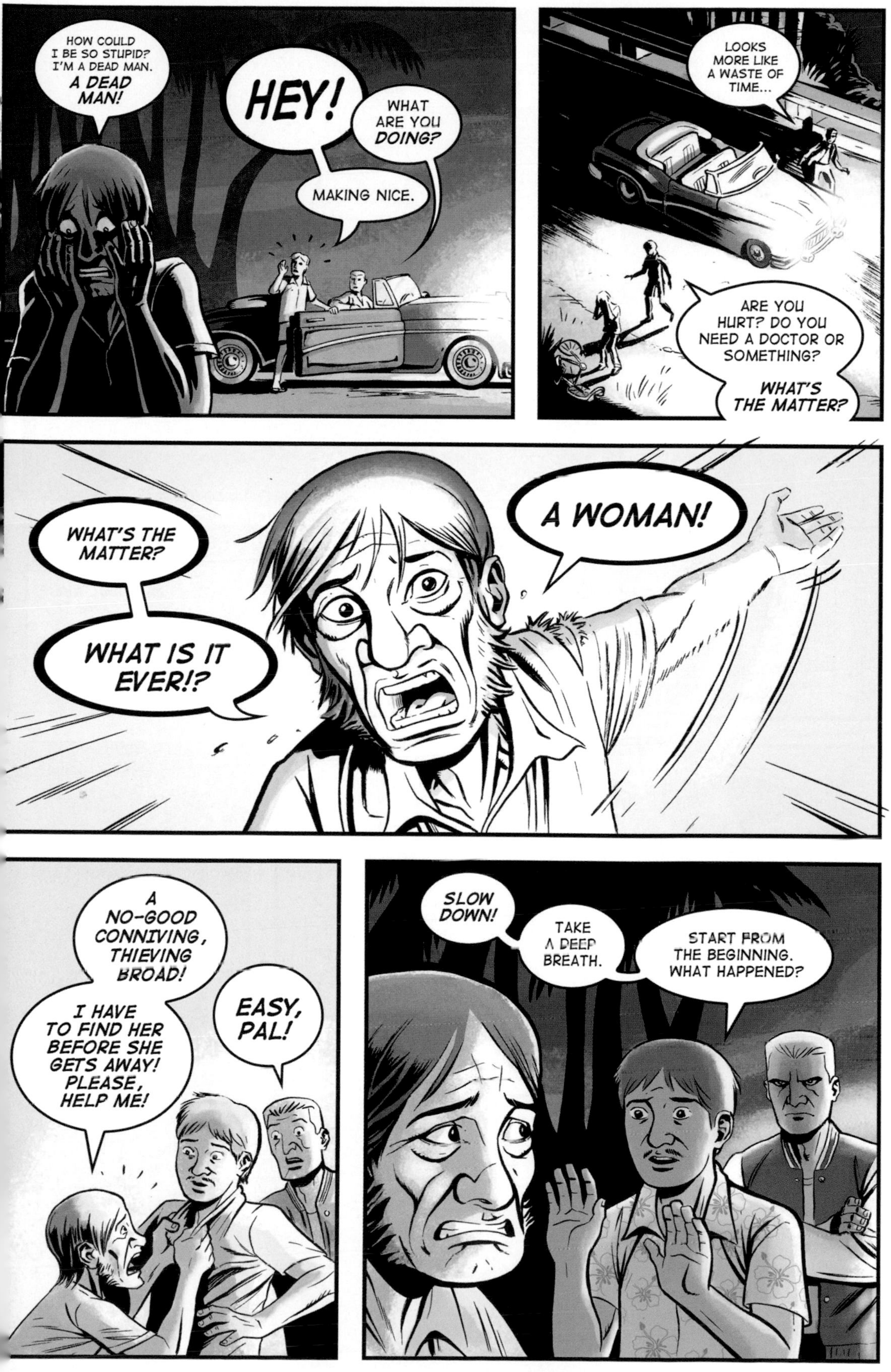
HOW COULD I BE SO STUPID? I'M A DEAD MAN. A DEAD MAN!
HEY!
WHAT ARE YOU DOING?
MAKING NICE.
LOOKS MORE LIKE A WASTE OF TIME...
ARE YOU HURT? DO YOU NEED A DOCTOR OR SOMETHING?
WHAT'S THE MATTER?
WHAT'S THE MATTER?
WHAT IS IT EVER!?
A WOMAN!
A NO-GOOD CONNIVING, THIEVING BROAD!
I HAVE TO FIND HER BEFORE SHE GETS AWAY! PLEASE, HELP ME!
EASY, PAL!
SLOW DOWN!
TAKE A DEEP BREATH.
START FROM THE BEGINNING. WHAT HAPPENED?

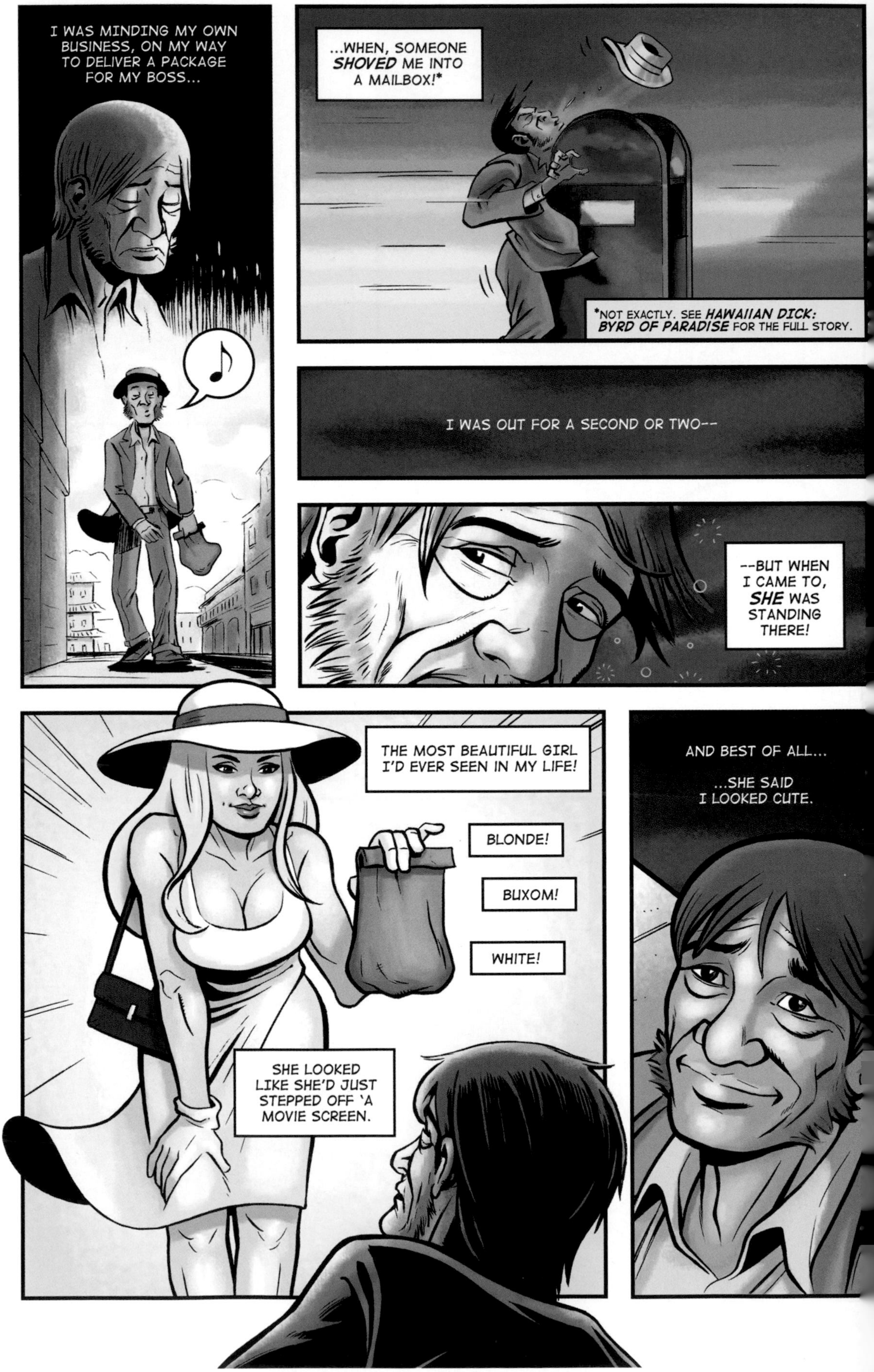
I WAS MINDING MY OWN BUSINESS, ON MY WAY TO DELIVER A PACKAGE FOR MY BOSS...
♪
...WHEN, SOMEONE SHOVED ME INTO A MAILBOX!*
*NOT EXACTLY. SEE HAWAIIAN DICK: BYRD OF PARADISE FOR THE FULL STORY.
I WAS OUT FOR A SECOND OR TWO--
--BUT WHEN I CAME TO, SHE WAS STANDING THERE!
THE MOST BEAUTIFUL GIRL I'D EVER SEEN IN MY LIFE!
BLONDE!
BUXOM!
WHITE!
SHE LOOKED LIKE SHE'D JUST STEPPED OFF 'A MOVIE SCREEN.
AND BEST OF ALL...
...SHE SAID I LOOKED CUTE.

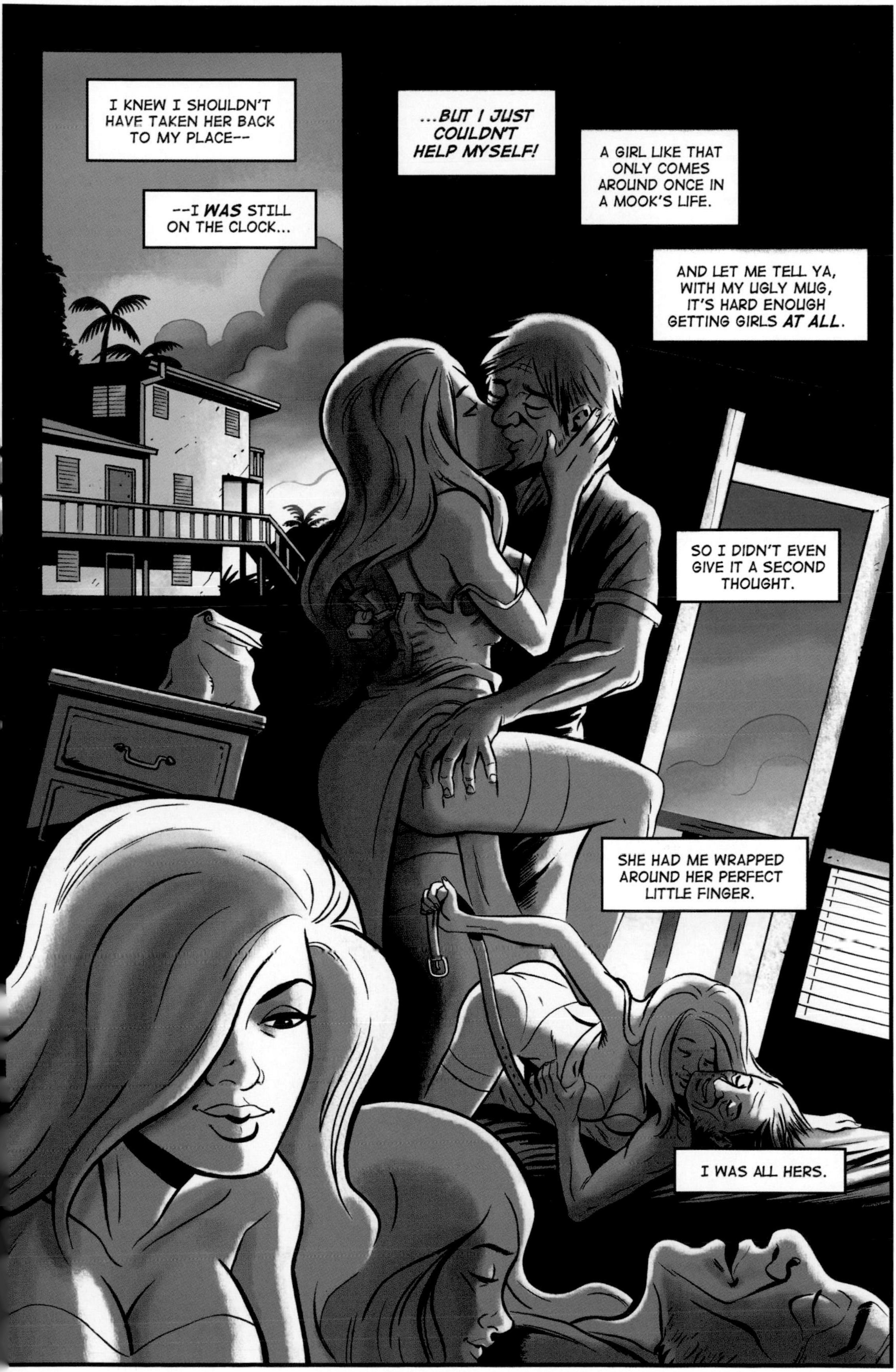
I KNEW I SHOULDN'T HAVE TAKEN HER BACK TO MY PLACE--
--I *WAS* STILL ON THE CLOCK...
...*BUT I JUST COULDN'T HELP MYSELF!*
A GIRL LIKE THAT ONLY COMES AROUND ONCE IN A MOOK'S LIFE.
AND LET ME TELL YA, WITH MY UGLY MUG, IT'S HARD ENOUGH GETTING GIRLS *AT ALL*.
SO I DIDN'T EVEN GIVE IT A SECOND THOUGHT.
SHE HAD ME WRAPPED AROUND HER PERFECT LITTLE FINGER.
I WAS ALL HERS.

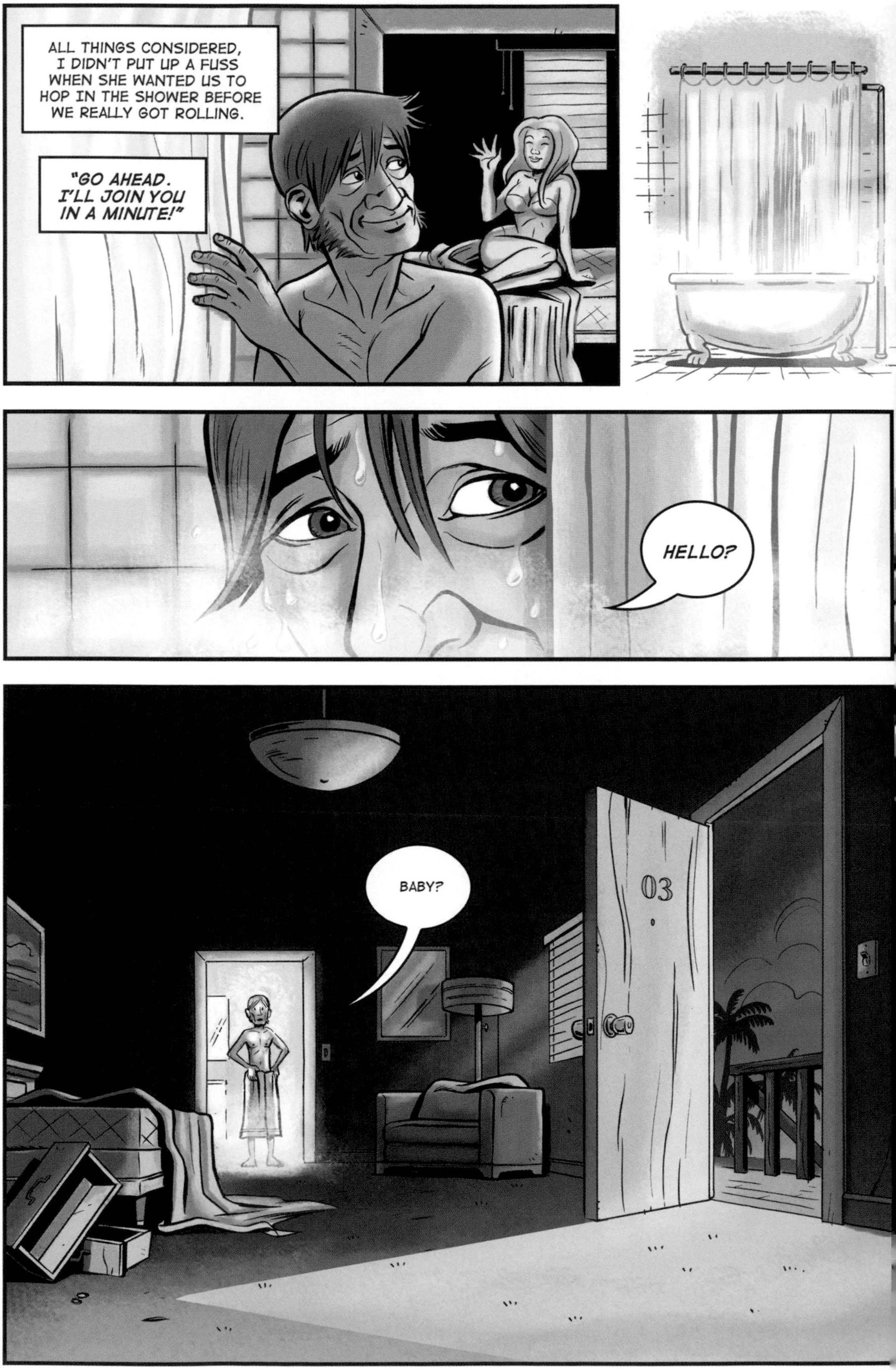
ALL THINGS CONSIDERED, I DIDN'T PUT UP A FUSS WHEN SHE WANTED US TO HOP IN THE SHOWER BEFORE WE REALLY GOT ROLLING.
"GO AHEAD. I'LL JOIN YOU IN A MINUTE!"
HELLO?
BABY?
03

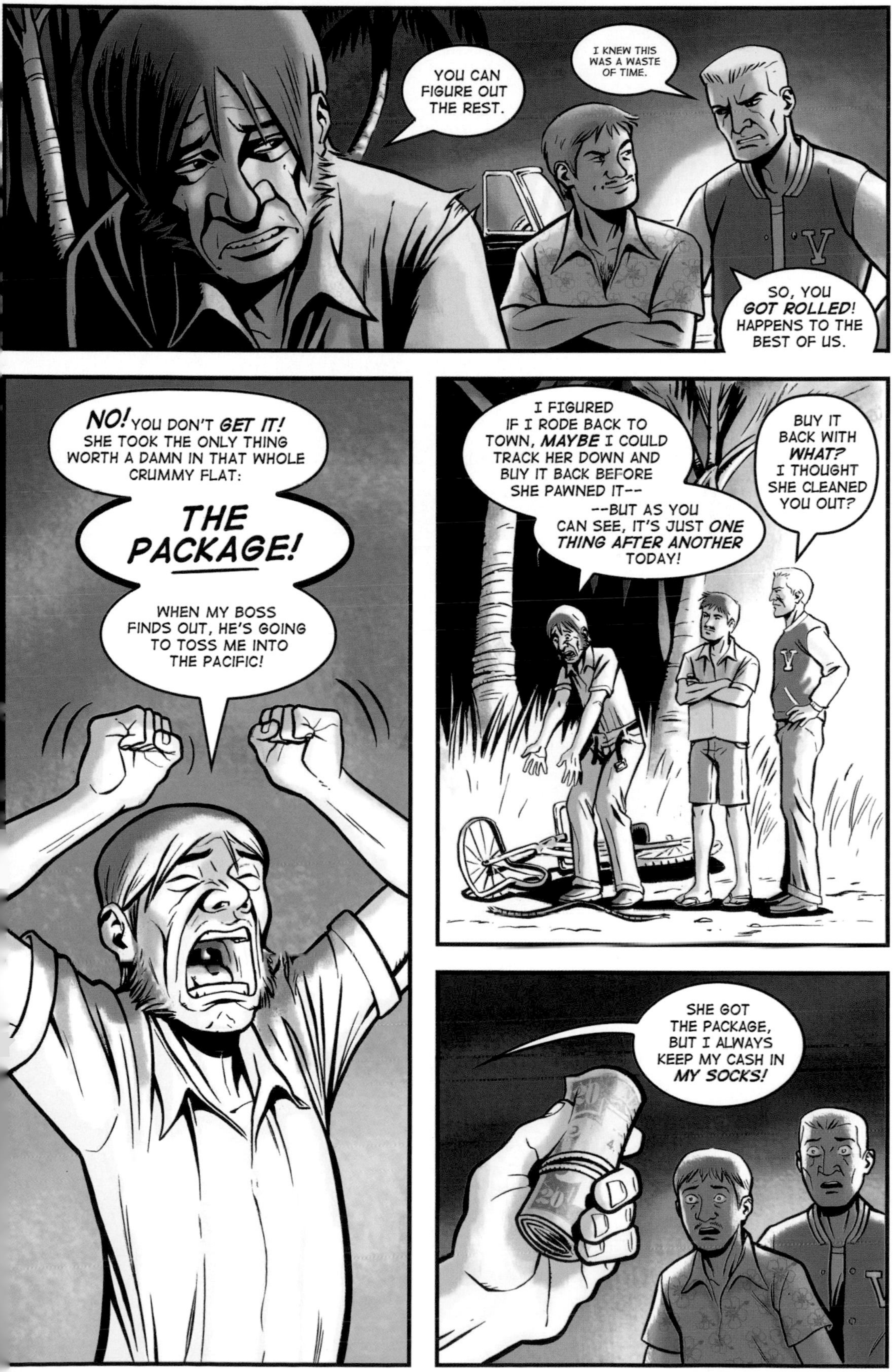
YOU CAN FIGURE OUT THE REST.
I KNEW THIS WAS A WASTE OF TIME.
SO, YOU GOT ROLLED! HAPPENS TO THE BEST OF US.
NO! YOU DON'T GET IT! SHE TOOK THE ONLY THING WORTH A DAMN IN THAT WHOLE CRUMMY FLAT:
THE PACKAGE!
WHEN MY BOSS FINDS OUT, HE'S GOING TO TOSS ME INTO THE PACIFIC!
I FIGURED IF I RODE BACK TO TOWN, MAYBE I COULD TRACK HER DOWN AND BUY IT BACK BEFORE SHE PAWNED IT--
--BUT AS YOU CAN SEE, IT'S JUST ONE THING AFTER ANOTHER TODAY!
BUY IT BACK WITH WHAT? I THOUGHT SHE CLEANED YOU OUT?
SHE GOT THE PACKAGE, BUT I ALWAYS KEEP MY CASH IN MY SOCKS!

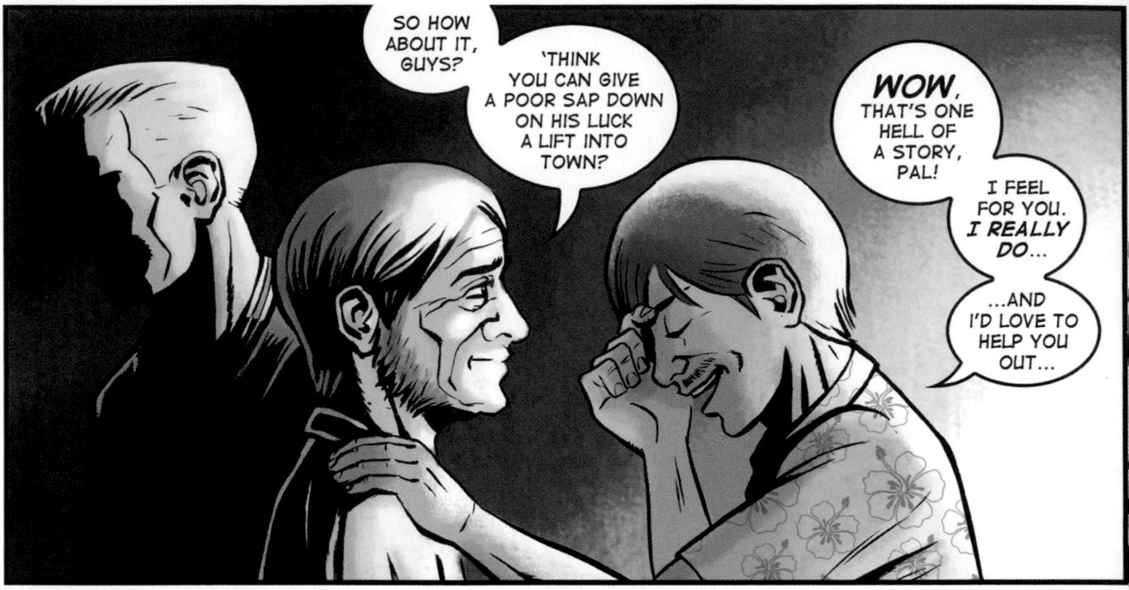
SO HOW ABOUT IT, GUYS?
'THINK YOU CAN GIVE A POOR SAP DOWN ON HIS LUCK A LIFT INTO TOWN?
WOW, THAT'S ONE HELL OF A STORY, PAL!
I FEEL FOR YOU. I REALLY DO...
...AND I'D LOVE TO HELP YOU OUT...

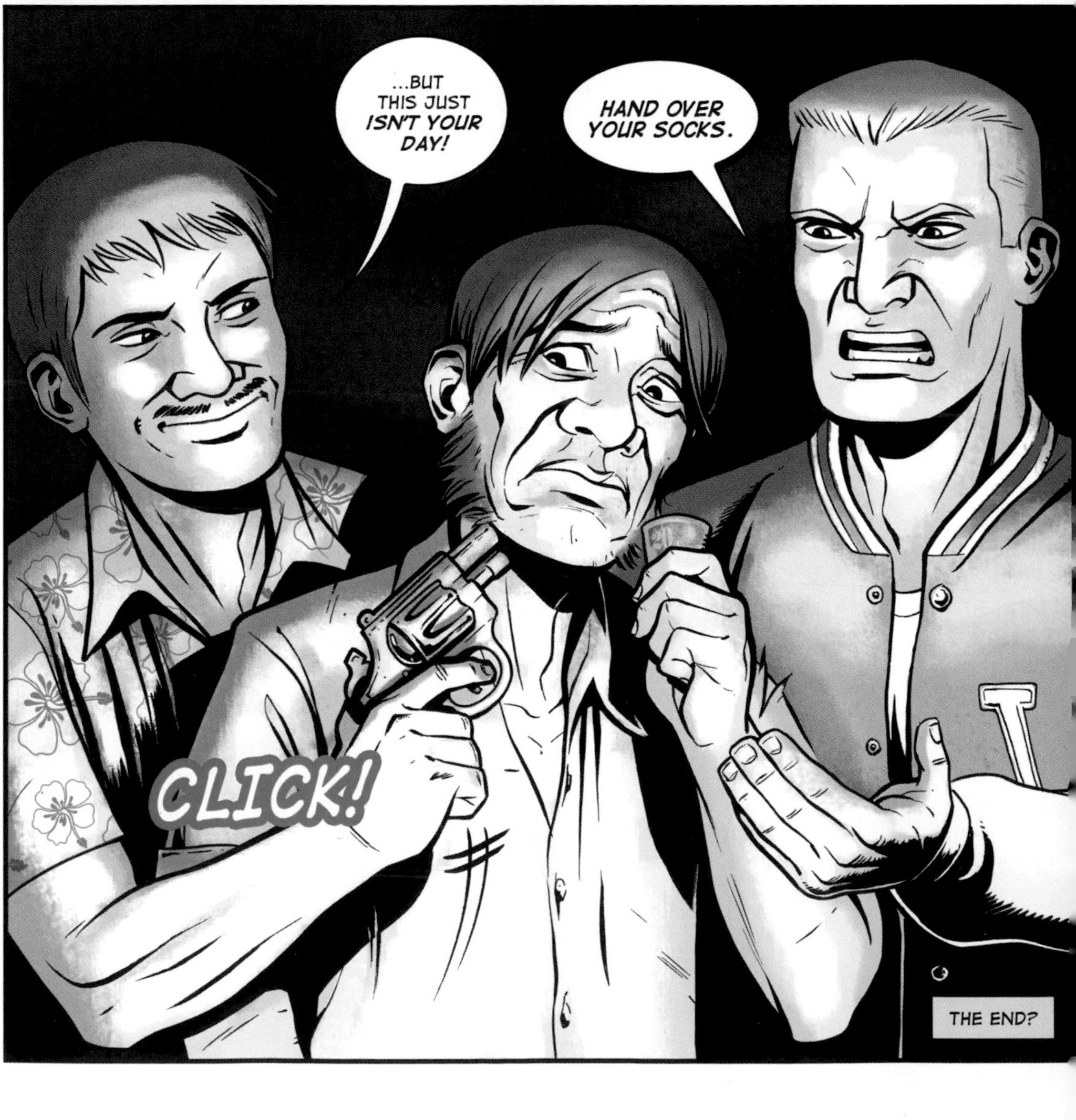
...BUT THIS JUST ISN'T YOUR DAY!
HAND OVER YOUR SOCKS.
CLICK!
THE END?

ALOHA

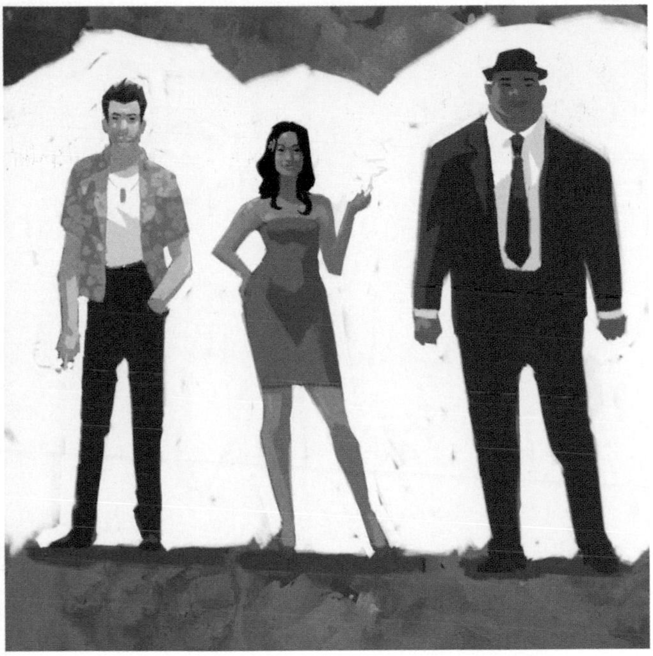

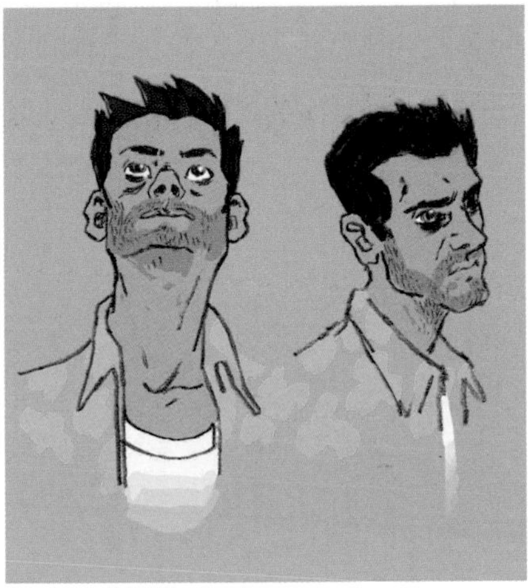

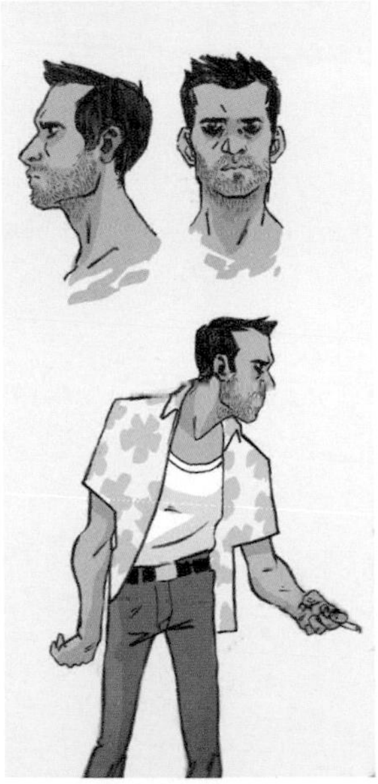

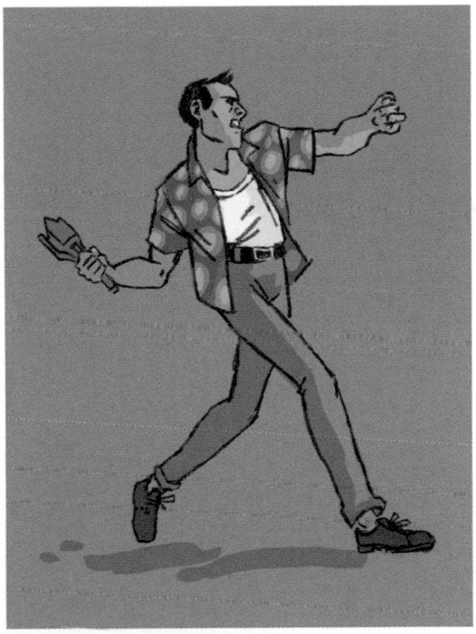

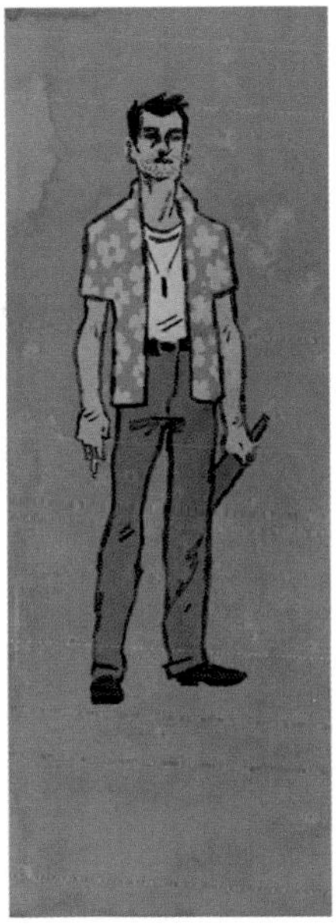

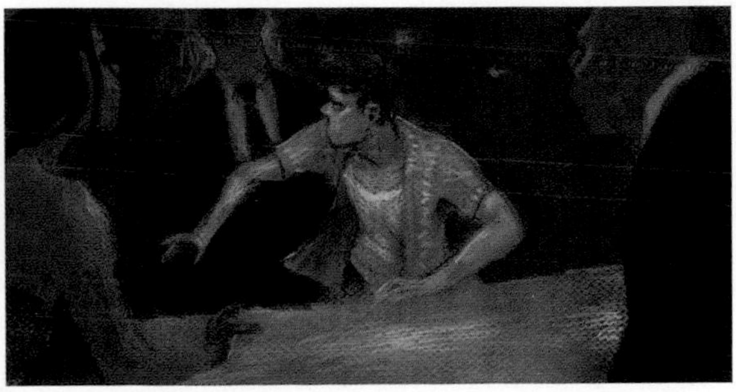

EARLY JACOB WYATT CONCEPT SKETCHES AS HE WORKED TO FIGURE OUT THE LOOK HE WANTED TO APPLY TO *ALOHA, HAWAIIAN DICK*

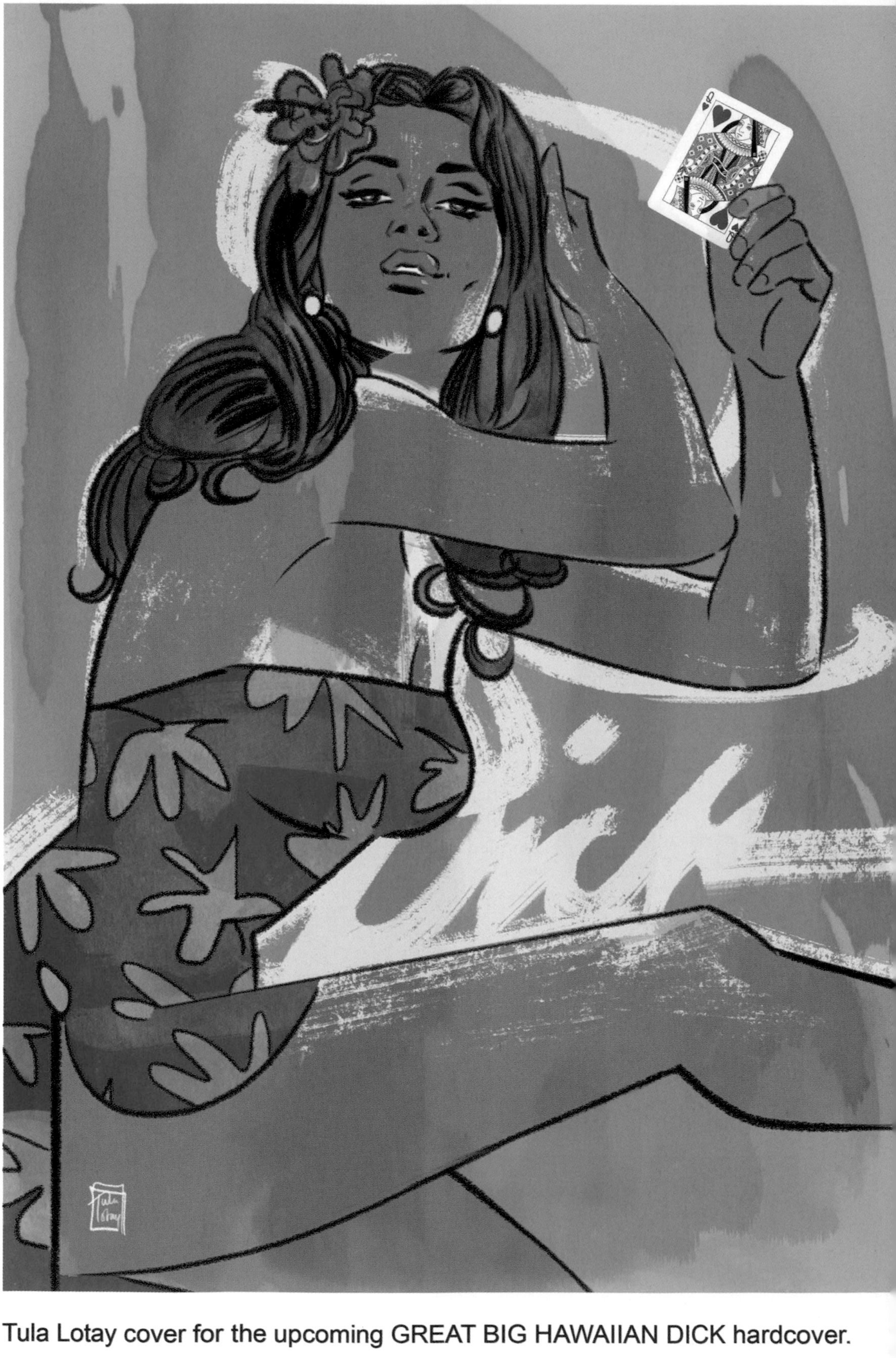

Tula Lotay cover for the upcoming GREAT BIG HAWAIIAN DICK hardcover.